THE BELIEVER

The Guard Trilogy Book 3

N. L. Westaway

Original Cover Photo by Peter Oswald
Cover designed by Beach House Press

N. L. Westaway
Visit my website at www.NLWestaway.com

Printed in the United States of America
ISBN: 978-1-7339442-5-0
Beach House Press

December 2018 Limited Edition Print Copies – Not for Resale.
First Publication: May 2019 Beach House Press

The Guard Trilogy

The Guard – Book 1

The Unseen – Book 2

The Believer – Book 3

The story continues…
The Guard Trilogy Extended Series - The Guards of Haven

The Haven – Book 4

This book is dedicated to all my beta readers, line editors, and story continuity soldiers. Thank you, Joanna, Kim, Isis, Alyssa, Dave, Cathy, and especially Peter for reading, reading, and rereading, and for providing your support and encouragement through this writing journey.

"Perhaps the butterfly is proof that you can go through a great deal of darkness yet become something beautiful."

~ Unknown

Anagram - An anagram is a type of word play, the result of rearranging the letters of a word or phrase to produce a new word or phrase, using all the original letters exactly once. *www.en.wikipedia.org*

The Guard = Daughter
Glean = Angel
A trained hug = The Guardian
Trade Four Hugs = Four Daughters

Chapter 1

"Well now, Gabriel—have you come to explain things?" Michael had asked.

The others had redirected their attention at the sound of Michael's words.

"Yes," Gabriel had said when he came to stand with his brethren. He'd spoken again, proceeding at length, making clear what had happened with his Chosen, and sharing that the answers were not in his entry. It had been the task of his Chosen to discover the *where* of the gathering, and not he who would do so. It was part of her gift. He had explained further how his Chosen had traveled to Miami days before her death. How she'd hidden the information she'd been guided to write down, the information about her pregnancy, her role in this and where the place for the gathering would be. He'd continued, giving them more, detailing why Lynn was in Miami, and how it was needed. *"But Will is not The Believer,"* Gabriel had told them. He'd assumed—hoped, this water-bearer to be a helper—believer, the one born under the sign of Aquarius. But he wasn't. *"The true Believer is still out there,"* he'd added. But where?

"What do you mean, the Believer," Michael had questioned when Gabriel finished.

Leading with a sigh Gabriel had said, *"It's all part of the change I made—my request. The Cipher, The Theologian, The Guardian, and The Believer are there, in my entry."*

"We know about the Cipher—he's present," Raphael had said, *"Luc has been functioning as a Theologian. Our Charges know about his help with all the religious items, but I presume they don't know he is needed."*

"Now they have to wait for both The Believer and The Guardian to show themselves," Gabriel had added.

"But how would the others—let alone this child she gave up for adoption, ever find this information? Why did she hide everything—and why Miami?" Uriel had asked. *"That makes no sense to keep things so far out of reach."*

Gabriel had bowed his head covering his face with both hands. Through muffled hands he'd said, *"Armaros."*

The home of Alison's mother - Thursday, August 31, 1967, Victoria, B.C. Canada

Though Gabriel knew the context of the request that his fellow Archangels had made and why they'd made the request, he reread the entry Michael had made on the olive wood over 5000 years ago.

Once the request had been accepted, the book had been created and Michael had made the first entry. It had been only after 200 of their brethren, now known as the Fallen, had betrayed the commands they'd been given, that this request had been needed.

The 200 had interfered in the lives of humans. The result of that interference had created offspring, half-man half-angel, and it was considered the highest level of disloyalty. Watch and observe, the 200 had been instructed in the beginning, but with their betrayal, came retaliation. The floods came, killing off most of their offspring, these Nephilim. In further punishment and as a warning to others, they were stripped of their powers to interact with humans. Their ability to assist and serve, had been taken from not only them, but *all* angels. And as a result, the beloved earthly creations were left to fend for themselves. Live or die, there would be no aid for them. All heavenly creations were now left with only the ability to watch, to observe for the next 70 generation, as whatever came to pass, unfolded.

It had been the four, Michael, Raphael, Uriel and Vretil, who had asked permission of Him, they, who had sacrificed their own existence in heaven to prove to Him that humanity was worth saving. As consults and companions for a millennium, He favored his Archangels the most, and as a result they were granted this favor. As instructed, the four were to choose four women to whom they would teach the proper skills *and* with whom they were to create offspring.

In turn, it would be the responsibility of these women to pass on this training, these gifts and the secret of their existence to their daughters, and their daughter's daughters and so on. It was in this sacrifice, how they would show Him they believed in humanity. But there were other conditions imposed.

As part of the agreement, four others were chosen, four picked from the 20 leaders of the disloyal 200. They, should the women fail in their task, were to be dispatched to wipe out the humans, causing the end of their world. They'd all been told it was a balance of sorts, a way to eradicate the remaining humans should the archangel's endeavor fail.

They were given 70 generations to show Him, but at such point, when the punishment of the 200 was over and they again had influence over their descendants, that all angels would able to act just as freely. But they'd also been told to keep in mind that the less they influenced their descendants and more they allowed them free will, the greater impact it would have with Him. And hopefully more motivation not to get involved in the affairs of humans as they had in the beginning. Neither side could have the upper hand in creating either a hell or heaven on earth. Heaven on earth could diminish the true Heaven's appeal. Hell on earth could influence the good towards evil as though they had nothing to lose, creating the opposite of balance.

This balance had seemed doable until the Earth's population and industrial evolution explosion had made it more difficult. With each generation that passed, the ability to sustain faith in these earthly creations, faith in the capability of these women and their lineage had begun to waver.

The horsemen had been chomping at the bit to be dispatched—so to speak, but because Gabriel believed in what his brothers had done long ago, he'd chosen to express his undying support by making his own offer and sacrifice. Gabriel had stated that the original request had weakened due to human evolution and growth. Gabriel had stated that it had been the 20 leaders and 200 angels, *His* angels—His Heavenly creations, who had impacted the balance to begin with. And that the request for only these four humans—only four each generation, to keep the balance, could not compare to the multiplying descendants of the legion the 200 had set in motion. Despite the uneven sides, Gabriel had been told that the design of this request and its flaws, were the faults of his brethren, the four Archangels, and that they'd not requested to have multiples, *only* four, and so were granted four. Gabriel had also been told that, admittedly, *He* had not predicted these four women and their lines would make it through the first 10 generations, let alone 70.

It was this that Gabriel used as part of his argument in hopes of having his request granted. 200 against four had not been a fair deal, but in spite of the exponential growth of their opposition, these four women had kept the balance. Gabriel had also noted that with the 70 generations coming to an end, the balance would shift significantly. These facts aided his plea that their maintaining of the balance thus far should gain them something, and Gabriel had requested adding more humans to their side. Unfortunately, he'd been told he could not change the agreement and that they must let things play out. *"Do your humans hold such little value?"* Gabriel had asked then. *"Are you willing to let them all perish? What would you do then, start over?"*

That must have stirred something in Gabriel's favor because then he'd been told, *"I will hear your request but do not question me again—you risk your own immortal soul."*

Originally, Gabriel had asked for an equal number of humans, 200, but knowing he had pushed the boundaries by even making this request, had been granted only *one*. Gabriel had been permitted to choose his Charge along with the form of *gifts* that would be granted to her. He was also allowed one *additional* visit with one other human, and at the time of his choosing. One Charge, one night, and one additional visitation before the 70 generations were up, and Gabriel had agreed.

Gabriel had chosen his Charge, had instructed her on how to 'see', and had gifted her with insight to things seen and unseen. He had told her how to protect her child as well as what knowledge to pass on to her.

In the quiet of the night, while Vretil's future Charge slept, Gabriel turned page after page in the codex until the look and feel of the paper revealed groupings of more modern pages sewn into the leather spine.

Here he read the entry made by the current Scribe, this one written in French and dated in May of 1940. The entry mentions the Scribe giving birth to a baby girl she named Claudette and how prior, when the Scribe had found the codex among her mother's treasured things, she'd gone seeking answers from her mother. The entry mentions this was the passing of the secret, the sacrifice, and the description of one other, and how it was now her secret to keep, and how it would further be *her* daughter's responsibility someday. She'd known the rules, known the potential sacrifice, and now she knew the love of her own child, the same love and protection she'd been given from her mother.

Gabriel had watched over the years as the information was passed down from mother to daughter, to each new Charge. Vretil's Charge had asked her now grown daughter, Claudette, to store some of her favorite things for her, namely a laptop writing desk. Gabriel knew the codex had been kept safe because it had been in this writing desk that he'd only just retrieved from the attic. The small desk had been a Christmas gift given to Claudette's mother by her grandmother, and the same place she and her mother had used to conceal the codex. It was her mother's hope that Claudette would do the same once she knew of the secret and her role in it. And had decided that it was best kept with her daughter, the next Scribe, should something happen to her in the meantime. It would at least be within reach, yet still hidden.

Gabriel flipped a page again, finding a new clean one. Using the divine script, the written language taught by Vretil and used in this Book of Balance at the beginning by Michael, Gabriel began his own entry. He fashioned the new information utilizing the same methods for outlining and concealing. He wrote of the favor he had requested, the rules, and of the sacrifice to be made by him should this endeavor not prevail, and he wrote it such for the next Scribe to find.

He'd done all this hoping to aid his brethren, their Charges, *and* the survival of both angel and humankind. He had set things in motion, now all that was left to do, was seek out the four, his brethren, let them know all was not lost, that he had ensured the balance would be upheld, and that the four would now become... *five.*

Chapter 2

Connection and a sense of belonging.

I've lost two of the most precious people in my life, my Mother and my Aunt, to cancer. I've witnessed how cancer continues to take people and for no other reason than it's a disease defined by an uncontrolled division of abnormal cells in the body. I've looked up the definition for the word and found it defined as *'a practice or phenomenon perceived to be evil or destructive and hard to contain or eradicate'* a definition that suited it better. I've also witnessed strange unexplainable things. My friends and family are aware I have this little ability to sense or know things, but they put little stock in it, other than it being entertaining. I have no control over it. Well, not until lately it seemed.

I'm adopted, and that's no secret, but whatever my birthmother had been involved in, apparently was. My adoptive mother too kept secrets, things I'd only later found out after her death through reading her journal. It contained writings from her last days before she'd passed away, of a bizarre story that unfolded and further led me and four of my closest friends to an even greater mystery.

As it turned out, the journal was only the starting point to this mystery, but to my dismay, it was also the end of my involvement in it. I've tried to move forward with my life, but more and more strange happenings keep drawing me back into this mystery, this mystery that my girlfriends keep reminding me belongs to them. Or so they believe.

Vizcaya Party - Sunday, November 1st, 2010, 1:35 a.m., Current Day, Miami, FL.

I'd been right, getting home from the party would not be as simple as I had expected. And Darius had been no help. He'd come by to check on me before leaving and had found I was in good hands with my new friend Redmond. *"Have you got a ride home?"* Darius had asked me, but he hadn't waited for an answer. I'd hoped to catch a ride with him, but he'd been swallowed up by the harem of nurses and had been dragged off before I could give my reply.

"Lost your ride?" Redmond asked. "Where do you live?"

"Hum…." Did I want to give out my address to a perfect stranger, no matter how charming he'd been? "I can catch a cab," I told him.

"Good luck with that—it's past 1 a.m. on one of the biggest party nights of the year." He waved a hand over his head, drawing the attention of a nearby stagehand. "I'd take you myself, but I have to supervise getting all this equipment out of here—there's a wedding here tomorrow."

"I'm in Palmetto Bay—not far," I let out. "I don't mind waiting for a cab."

The young stage hand with an earpiece and mic came over to show Redmond a list. They seemed to be checking things off as they organized and dismantled the event. "Make sure the band gets their gear first," Redmond told him. "Then pack up our stuff to go back to the shop. The rest is being handled by the event coordinator." The stage guy nodded, said something into the mic, and gave his boss the thumbs-up. "Where's Shade?" Redmond asked, panning the remaining crowd.

The stage guy spoke into the mic again, and then said, "Just finished packing up all the promo materials."

"Good," Redmond said.

The stage guy nodded again and spoke into the mic once more, then he strode off.

"There—problem solved," Redmond said, addressing me this time.

"What problem?" Had there been an issue with the coordination of the equipment teardown?

"Shade lives 10 minutes south of you—can drop you off on the way home," he said.

"Oh no—really, I'm fine," I deflected, but apparently, he'd arranged a ride for me with one of his staff. I'd enjoyed chatting with him and he'd been a gentleman the whole time, but I still wasn't sure if I liked the idea of having one of his people *'drop me off'*. I wasn't thrilled at the prospect of waiting out front of this place for a cab either, but making another person I hadn't even met, drive me home—it didn't sit well, especially some guy named *Shade*.

"How did you like the party," he asked, his turn to deflect.

"Waaaas... interesting," I said, "Band was great."

"Ya these parties can be wild—brings the crazies out too." He laughed.

You have no idea, I mused. I smiled. Considering earlier events, I might be one of the crazies.

"Shade," he said looking over past my shoulder.

I spun to see a small female approach then stand next to Redmond. Smaller than me, she maxed at 5-foot-tall, and had hair the colour of pink cotton candy with flashes of grey wisps through it. Her costume was that of an elf—ears and all. But unlike those slutty fairy elves I'd seen earlier in the evening, hers was straight out of a fantasy novel and more like a warrior elf than some sissy pixie.

"Hey," she said, giving me a big smile. To say she wasn't the potential staff member I'd expected was a blatant understatement. I'd wholly expected to turn and see some giant stagehand, someone who could potentially carry all the heavy equipment without a moving cart.

"Shade is the creative director for my studio, she handles all the marketing and advertising, and she makes a mean cup of coffee—so I keep her around." He laughed again, and she punched him in the arm.

I liked her instantly.

"Sounds like a big job—especially the coffee part," I said. We both laughed. She was super cute, but I got the impression she was the one who kept him and all things studio-related organized.

"Hear you need a ride?" She asked turning to Redmond for confirmation and then back to me.

"Uhmm… ya I guess—I don't want to be any trouble." I really didn't, but I was opening to the friendly ride home, now that I knew it wouldn't be with some general laborer guy, he'd pawned me off to.

"No trouble. I'm done with all the hard stuff," she said. "I leave the heavy lifting to the grunts." She punched him in the arm again.

"Ouch," he said, on this punch. She must have gotten him good this time.

"I'm Lily Shade—but everyone calls me Shade." She put out a hand.

"Lynn," I said, taking her hand and shaking it. "Lynn Westlake."

"Please to meet you, Lynn." She gave my hand another shake, then let go. "Great costume by the way."

"Thanks. Yours too—love the hair."

"I'm ready to get out of here, you?" she asked, extending an arm as if leading the way.

"Ready," I said to her, as that stage guy returned.

He and Redmond exchanged a few words and then he said, "Truck's here—gotta move."

"Okay boss—we're out of here," Lily said. "See you tomorrow."

"Not too early," he said back to her. "Was nice meeting you, Lynn. Don't believe any of the bad things Lily says about me—k?"

She threw out a punch again, but this time he dodged it. I had a feeling they played this game often. Made me laugh again, thinking about this little elf beating up her giant of a boss.

"Nice meeting you too," I said, waving back to him before following Lily in through the big glass doors.

The ride home with Lily was enjoyable. We talked about the band, the venue, and the food. She told me about the crazy things she'd seen at the party, the outrageous costumes and the drunk people, mostly, and nothing resembling what I'd seen. She didn't really mention Redmond, other than what an excellent boss he was, how great all the staff were, and it being like one big family. She loved her job but missed the cooler weather up North being that she was from New York. I told her where I was from and how I'd ended up here. She told me she had met Redmond in New York and how she had come to work for him after graduating with a degree in Advertising and a Masters in Visual Arts. She told me she did side gigs designing cover art for CDs, but her main job was the advertising for the bands and the studio, and for the occasional event like tonight's.

"Yer a lifesaver," I said, as she pulled into the drive. "Thank you soooo much for dropping me off."

"No prob—last thing you want is to get stranded out at that place at night." She gave an exaggerated shiver. "Here," she said, reaching into the armrest, "Studio business card. Drop by sometimes—say hi."

I scanned the card in the dim light. "Nice—your design?"

"Yup." She gave me a big grin. "He likes you—ya know," she added, rolling down the window as I got out of the car.

"What—who?" I asked, leaning down to the open window.

"Redmond. He likes you." She grinned again. "He never talks to women at these events—ever."

I might have blushed because I was suddenly warm, and it wasn't the humid night air. "Oh—well ahhh... thanks," I managed. I hadn't expected little Lily Shade to be a matchmaker.

"Later, Lynn," she called out, grinning again.

I waved as she rolled out the drive. Then I dragged myself inside.

Raven greeted me at the door, then followed me through the house and to my bedroom.

Costume tucked back in its garment bag, monster makeup washed off, and red contacts back in their box, I laid in bed not ready for sleep. The night's events zoomed through my mind; interesting place, great food, and loud but excellent music. That handsome redhead singing, jumping down from the stage right in front of me... it had all transformed at the onset of that horrible nauseous wave... and the pain. Stress? I think not.

Whatever, I'd seen what—I'd seen. Those four huge guys were there. I saw them, and whether part of the entertainment or not, they'd come after me. Well, maybe not *after me*, but they seemed to have been watching me. And when I'd been alone in the gardens, they'd been a little too aggressive in getting near me for my liking.

Was Darius, right? Had they been part of the event—security, maybe? They may have been concerned at my being in the gardens and outside the event's safe parameters. If that were the case, they could have easily said something, told me I needed to return to the party area. But they hadn't. They'd all rushed forward, hostility clear in their expressions, like the big blond one had done before in the hospital. Why me? What had I done? Had I imagined it? No. Or had I misjudged their intentions?

Either way, it sure felt as though I'd held them off—cast them back. Or had I misinterpreted that too? If they were security, they may have left because they'd been called to the attention of something else, a rowdy guest or drunken brawl, perhaps. I guess I wasn't sure of much. But the one thing I was sure of, was how cool the ride home and chat with Lily had been. She'd said Redmond liked me, though I wasn't sure what to make of that little morsel of information.

Letting the thoughts and images go, I turned on my side and stared out through the bedroom's patio doors. A butterfly caught in the moonlight fluttered in view near the side hedge.

"Goodnight, Mom," I whispered, and drifted off to sleep.

* * *

I woke to sunlight streaming through the patio doors, and for once I wasn't angry at the blinds being open. I had enjoyed watching the moonlight as it had streamed through the glass doors last night, and now it was the beautiful sunlight that replaced it.

As I finished brushing my teeth, Raven waited at the bedroom door for our usual morning routine. On the way through the living room I spotted a large manila envelope poking out an edge off the front entry table. I grabbed it and brought it with me the rest of the way to the kitchen.

I set it on the kitchen island and stared at it. The big envelope had the same cruise line logo as the last one. I swallowed and then tore it open. It hadn't been filled with travel vouchers, instead it contained a tight stack of papers.

Divorce papers.

The signature areas were partially filled with Will's scribbled name. The remaining had little red tabs indicating the pages and areas where I needed to sign and initial. There was no note this time either, just a formal letter from the legal representative who'd arranged the settlement.

"Nice way to start my day," I said to Raven. I snatched a pen from the kitchen junk drawer and then climbed up on the closest barstool.

When Luc arrived home early evening, I was glad he had funny stories to share with me about his Halloween visit with his sister's family in Orlando. It had been exactly what I needed, especially after staring at divorce papers in the morning and then staring at TV all afternoon. I'd been eager to tell him all about my night, but before I could gather my wits and my words, he changed directions on me.

"You know I've been corresponding with Derek. We've been discussing religious texts and such that he's found," Luc stated. "He's not the religious type as you know."

"Uhm, I see." I'd known they'd been working together to help the girls, but I hadn't asked anything about it. I didn't want to know. Initially I'd been angry he'd been in the loop instead of me, but I'd let it go because I knew how helpful Luc's religious insight would be. He could help Derek with anything he liked and if he shared with the others, it was fine too. I was over it *and* over having my help rejected. I just wish I was over these stupid bouts of nausea or whatever.

"Dunya suggested I talk to you. We've been brainstorming together on stuff," he added.

"So, she's part of the *Scooby* gang too now?"

"You could have stayed part of this if you'd wanted to—through Derek and me," he said.

"Ya, I know." But I didn't want to. And I didn't want to know what they'd all said about me either.

"They've uncovered a reference to a gathering, and they think they know where it's supposed to happen."

"I'd love to have them all here for a gathering," I said, and then handed Luc my divorce papers. My turn to redirect this time.

I'd had mixed feelings about signing the papers at first but knew there was no point in delaying the inevitable. Despite being happy that the house was mine, the sadness still lingered over how things had unraveled, and that all that remained of the marriage was this stapled gathering of papers.

Luc remained sympathetic throughout our dialog about the papers and the topic of endings. And I was thankful that any talk of his help with the girls had fallen by the wayside.

"Yer free to pursue other avenues in your life, other interests that do not require waiting around for your spouse," he said, pointing out the brighter side to things.

"Ya," I said, getting up from the couch. "I'm off—time to hit the hay." I grabbed up the papers and my cell phone from the coffee table. "Thanks, Luc."

"No worries," Luc said, pushing up from the adjacent couch. "Goodnight," he added heading off in the other direction to his room

"Night," I gave him back, heading to my own room. Raven followed me like usual.

When I entered my bedroom, my cell phone rang in my hand.

"Hello?" I answered, not recognizing the number.

"Oh Lynn—I had the worst dream about you last night," came a voice I did recognize.

I heard Louise take a breath to start again, but then another voice replaced hers. "Lynn, sorry—she's not been sleeping well these past few weeks," her husband said.

"Andre—is she okay?" I gulped. "I mean besides the obvious."

A long pause followed as if he were trying to figure out how to answer. "She's waking up in the night, every night… keeps saying she wants to call you, but I haven't let her," Andre explained. I could picture him shaking his head with the phone to his ear. "This is my son's cell phone. She must have gotten a hold of it somehow."

"Louise can call me anytime…," I tried to say, but he spoke over me.

"She's stopped her treatments—and the meds." There was another long pause.

"Andre…?"

"She didn't want me to tell you," he said.

"I can't blame her," I responded. I didn't like it—hated it. "Tell her I know now… and that I love her." I sighed. "And… that I understand."

"I will," he said, before hanging up.

My day had begun with a stab to the heart… now it had ended with it being ripped out.

Chapter 3

Between the seen and unseen - November 1st, 2010, Current Day, Somewhere in the ether

"Why have The Horsemen arrived? And where the hell is the gathering?" Michael asked, though the others sought the same answers. Dealing with Armaros was one thing, but the fact that the other four were here, not dispatched mind you, but still mingling in and around The Guardian, was a whole other level of concern.

"The Horsemen were a part of the conditions you all had agreed to," Gabriel reminded. "Four of the 20 leaders from *His* disloyal 200 would be dispatched to wipe out all humans if your four Charges failed." They all knew it was *His* way to eliminate the remaining humans, should their efforts fail. They'd had 70 generations to show Him. After that, the sentence brought on by the 200 would be over and all would have influence over their descendants. They'd also been told that less influencing and more free will, would in response have more encouraging impact with Him. *And* it would hopefully motivate all enough that neither side would have the upper hand.

"Yes—we know," Raphael shot out. "But it doesn't explain their presence now."

"What's changed," Uriel asked. "Have we done something wrong?"

"No. It's Armaros," Gabriel responded.

"Armaros—again?" Vretil questioned. "Did his interference with our Charges last night cause this?"

Gabriel took in a long breath. "It appears his influence goes back before your current Charges...," he said, letting out the breath. "... and beyond even his influence with mine."

Vretil shook his head and then let it hang forward.

"Gabriel and I have discussed and assessed at great lengths the depth of Armaros's meddling," Shamsiel injected. "Armaros has always kept a close eye on my fellow leaders, pandering to their desires, speaking of the days to come when they would rule the earth."

"Saying they would be deities on earth once again," Gabriel added.

"Don't tell me that all the leaders follow him now," Michael said.

"Obviously not," Shamsiel said. "I've never entertained the idea despite his attempts to sway me." Shamsiel panned the faces of the others. "Some like the idea—yes, but most want to be free to come and go from Earth again. They've learned their lesson about interfering."

"Is this about your Charge, Gabriel? About Armaros's influence on her hiding things in Miami?" Uriel asked. "Do you now know where?"

"It's about how Armaros found her," Shamsiel said, answering for him.

Exhausted, Gabriel said nothing, only waved a hand for his brother to go on. He'd told Shamsiel everything, all the facts and his suspicions.

Shamsiel took the lead. "On this occasion in the past, Gabriel had watched as his Charge spoke with her doctor friend. Armaros had been there too, but he couldn't have known *who* Gabriel had been there to see, it could have been her or her doctor. Unlike the knowledge of your original chosen, Armaros was not privy to who Gabriel had chosen—none of us were." He paused, shooting Gabriel a quick glance, but when Gabriel said nothing, he continued for him. "After Gabriel had left his charge in the hands of the good doctor, Armaros it seemed had remained, listening to what the women discussed."

"My Charge told her friend about the child," Gabriel said, speaking up, "... how no one else knew about it, that she'd prepared the information about the father, and how it would be available for when needed."

Adding to that, Shamsiel said, "Armaros had further questioned a fellow leader, asking, '*Why do they care who the father is?*'. He couldn't care less about these women, but because of Gabriel's interest in this woman and her offspring, Armaros must have decided to mess with things. As a result, he had Gabriel's Charge hide this information out of reach."

"He didn't care if it was important. He liked the idea of messing with an Archangel," Gabriel said. "And since he couldn't come to her in his regular form, he'd veiled himself as me—the messenger."

"But then things changed," Shamsiel cut in. "When he had appeared to her, he'd understood then that she recognized him—as Gabriel.

"And that I'd visited her before," Gabriel added. "She'd told him she's done what he'd asked—what I'd asked, and that she had all the info written down as instructed." Gabriel shook his head. "He didn't understand how I had done this, since we all remained still under the 70-generation hold. Perhaps he assumed it had been a divine task I'd been given, but still he hadn't known the why."

"Pissed him off," Shamsiel said, "that Gabriel had gotten special access to a human, when he and his fellow angels had been cut off."

"Like he wasn't already furious for being punished," Michael tossed out. "And now it seems he knows the *why* of Gabriel's actions."

Changing course, Uriel asked, "What about this whole *guarding the fifth* you wrote in the entry. Guard the fifth what?"

Chapter 4 

The apartment of Vicki Quinn - Sunday November 1st, 2010, Current Day, Ottawa, ON

Vicki had her laptop set up on the dining room table, with Alison on Skype chat. Piles of notes and papers with translations were scattered around the table. She and Alison had been going over everything regarding their adventure from the night before.

"It resembles the *Dominion Arboretum* near Dow's Lake across from the Canal," Vicki said. "He'd described a massive garden, and this place has trees and shrubs that included 1700 different varieties and species. It has an Ornamental Garden that sounds a lot like this touristy—*frequently visited area* he'd focused on in his description."

"He'd said it was also *internationally acclaimed for agricultural research*, which the Arboretum is as well," Alison said. "I'd made a special note on that person he mentioned who started it all. He'd said they were some kind of plant expert or botanist, that they had something to do with the department of agriculture."

"I checked that too," Vicki said, "The website for the place says *James Fletcher*, who was part of planting the first 200 trees in 1889, was a botanist, and it says the garden is part of the department of agriculture. So, this must be the place," she concluded.

"Now what?" Alison tossed out.

"I think we have all we need, though I'm still trudging through that second entry," Vicki said.

"We've got the *where* now, but not the *why* for this gathering," Alison noted. "Nor what we're supposed to do once we gather there."

"Let me work on the rest of this second Enochian entry. Hopefully I can flesh out the translation," Vicky suggested. "The why and/or what we do at the gathering, might be in it."

"You got it." Alison smiled hopeful. "Check in with me later if you need a break or someone to bounce ideas off," she said. "I've got a few smashed pumpkins to tend to outside, anyway." She laughed.

"Teenagers," Vicki added, laughing along with Alison as they both signed off.

Trying to organize her thoughts and paper, Vicki flipped through the notes she'd made on the first translation. Then she checked the photocopies of the second entry. "Let's see," she said out loud.

Michael stood facing his Charge as she flipped franticly through her notes and papers. He'd returned after talking with the others, after Gabriel's explanation of events and the early arrival of the Horsemen. Michael had also watched her last night as she'd panicked about the pieces the Cipher still needed to provide her. He knew she'd been frazzled after the conjuring, but she hadn't let on to her friends. He understood her angst now, they all wanted clarity about this gathering. The location for it was anyone's guess, but it was unlikely the place that his traitorous brethren Armaros had described. Why had he bothered to describe it at all—and with such detail, Michael pondered? The answer may well be in those *details,* and not at the location their Charges had decided on.

Michael moved to stand behind his Charge at the dining table where she worked. Then he leaned in.

"Conquest—in white—holds a bow," she said, aloud to his surprise.

He leaned in closer to read over her shoulder.

"War—in red—holds a sword," she continued. "Famine—in black—holds the scales. Death—pale—followed by Hell."

"Yes, the horseman," Michael said, speaking the words from behind his veil.

"Hell? What the hell, another riddle?" she questioned.

"Keep going… there's more. You've got this," Michael said, into the silence.

"Okay, it's internet search time," she huffed out. Typically, she would have given this kind of thing to Derek to solve, but he hadn't gotten back to her yet on the other items. She'd have to find the solution to the riddle on her own. She typed the words *conquest, war, famine* and *death* into the search area.

Michael knelt on one knee next to her chair, watching as the laptop displayed its results.

"What do we got…. Hmmm, it says this equates to… *the Four Horsemen.* What?" she said. There'd been no reference to them before, it must be something else she speculated. Frustrated, she searched for another link or reference with answers.

"No—that's it," Michael implored, still unheard.

"Here," Vicki said. The reference she found made a note of how The Horsemen and Revelations could apply to contemporary events and modern times. The colour white for conquest, representing *Catholicism*. Red for war, representing *communism*. Black—famine, is for *capitalism*. Death, that was self-explanatory. "Sounds like a typical day in the world to me, but how does that play into the codex's reference and the balance not being kept?" She checked a few more links, but found what she considered only nonsense, like how the horseman were associated with angels and the four winds. "Whatever," she let out, shutting down that particular search result, returning to the modern reference find.

Despite the translation still being incomplete, she felt confident with what she'd accomplished so far with the entry. She'd also solved that spell they'd used to conjure the spirit to help, as well. Though she still wasn't sure what she believed about all the magic. She did however feel assured that what she had just translated had *nothing* to do with angels and had everything to do with how out of balance the world was currently. It could represent the end of the balance she supposed, even the end of the world if she wanted to go that direction; souls dying and crying out, earthquakes, black sun—red moon, stars falling to earth, then nothing but silence. It rendered images a lot like the devastating clips from the international news coverage of late.

Still she'd found no other details in the entry about the gathering, other than the *when*, not a date, but it being when a *fifth* something was revealed. She let out a "Grrrrrrrr" of frustration.

"Bing," went the notice on Vicki's laptop as an email from Derek popped into the inbox. In the subject line it read, *Birthfather,* followed by one line in the message,

Call me—ASAP.

"Birthfather?" Vicki read aloud, before grabbing her cell.

"Oh—here we go," Michael said, into the quiet once again.

Derek picked up after the first ring. "Hey—hi. Sorry for not getting back to you sooner," he said.

"No—I'm the one who should be sorry," Vicki said, interrupting. "You've been a great help—I'm grateful—we're all grateful. I'm just confused and annoyed with this, is all."

"I have something for you… but it's more just a theory," he cut in.

"I'll take anything at this point."

"You sent me those two pieces—from the sentences, *Solacer* and *bar the fifth,* along with your translation from the second entry—remember?

"How could I forget? I've been wracking my brain over that stupid entry all morning?" she said, "What's this about a *birthfather* you wrote."

"That's the thing, it's not *bar the fifth*—it's birthfather."

"Wow—let me grab my copy of the entry," she said. "Putting you on speaker."

Derek could hear the rustling of papers through the phone.

"Got it," Vicki said. "It's just before the fifth being revealed. This gathering will keep the balance, and all shall know the… bar the fifth."

"All shall know the *birthfather,*" Derek restated.

"It's always been about daughters and mothers. Fathers have never been mentioned before in any of the codex entries. Why this one?"

"Other than the guys from the letters, I'm the only *male*—and I'm not a father. I'm just the Cipher."

"The same entry mentions the Cipher, the Theologian, the Guardian and the Believer. Could all of them be men?" Vicki questioned. "It says the Theologian is a source of great insight to all things divine. What about this *Solacer* the entry mentions, male or female?"

"I don't have solutions to all the missing pieces yet," Derek said, "but I've been entertaining the idea that Luc could be this *Theologian*, because of all his help with the religious content. You know that's not my purview."

"You could be right… the others may be men as well. And I'm willing to take a few leaps at this juncture—I'm all out of reason."

"Let's go with plausibility for now—that they're all men," Derek suggested. "Considering the mention of birthfather."

"Lynn thinks her friend Darius could be this Guardian," Vicki said. "But how could he be? He hasn't helped… or needed to guard them or whatever this person is supposed to do. Based on the codex entry, he should be revealed to us—we're the four."

"Ya, it might be a leap for me too," Derek agreed.

"Speaking of leaps," Vicki said, "The four of us are taking one. We know where the gathering place is."

Chapter 5

From across the room, I watched as a large male figure dressed in black loomed up over Louise's bed. He aided her to sit up and then he lifted her up off the bed. Carrying her, he strode towards the bedroom door.

What the hell was going on? What am I doing here? And why am I in my hospital scrubs?

The large man turned then and walked back in my direction.

I recognized him.

It was the same massive man from the hospital, the one who had come after me. The tallest of the four I'd seen on Halloween. But this time, there was no aggression, only peace shown in his expression.

And I felt no fear.

Standing before me now, he leant down and with a gentleness placed Louise in my arms.

I was shocked at how weightless she was, but she had been gravely ill, had gone through so much, and had lost so much weight due to the cancer. Much like with my mother, Louise was now a tiny weakened version of her original self.

I cradled her in my arms as though she were a baby. Her eyes were closed, a subtle smile turned the corners of her mouth. Her face was peaceful in her slumber as if dreaming of a place without pain.

Despite the knowing sense it would be the last time… the last time I would embrace her… the last time I would see her… I knew I had to hand her back to the lone horseman.

Louise once again in his arms, he turned away from me, this time continuing on through the brightly lit doorway.

Gasping awake, I turned my head towards the digital clock on my nightstand. It read 3:33 a.m.. "Just a dream," I whispered to the night. That call from Louise and Andre earlier must have done a number on me, was my last thought as I dropped back to sleep.

* * *

I'd managed to get a few more hours of sleep, but it was Monday now and back into work, and regardless of my grogginess, I was elated to find out that my charges, the twins, were now in the final stretch of recovery. And all the paperwork was completed for their adoption. They would get to go home soon with their new parents and I was excited for them, but to my dismay, my focus and the gratitude for their new direction remained shadowed throughout the rest of the morning.

I couldn't seem to shake off the images from my dream. It hadn't been a scary one, and though it had felt good to hold my friend close like that, I wasn't comfortable with the imagery of it all. I needed something else to focus on, something to help push past the shadows. I hadn't gotten any new charges of yet and since the rest of the babies were already attended to, I opted for strolling to the *other* nursery, the one for babies with only the most minor of issues and the short stays.

Unlike the NICU, I could hear the crying babies from *outside* the doors. But when I pushed through the door, the cries lessened and all but stopped. The nurse on duty stared at me stunned, and then said, "Keep an eye for me while I run to the ladies' room? My relief hasn't shown up yet?"

"Uhm sure—I guess," I told her, as she darted past me out the door and off to the bathroom. It was only me now, and a room full of sleeping babies.

The hairs on my arms suddenly bristled, followed up by a lightness of mood that flooded over me. I'd take it, but I chalked it up to being surrounded by the sweetness of all the babies. Then I sensed something… *someone.*

With only a moment to spare before the nurse was back, I closed my eyes and concentrated, bringing into my thoughts the images of the one I'd seen, or hypothetically the *unseen*. A baby cooed… and I opened my eyes.

"I see you," I gasped out, speaking to the beautiful presence in front of me. I smiled, but his expression was one of sorrow.

Gabriel made no attempt to respond. Though surprised she had easily drawn him from behind his veil, in this very moment he carried mainly sadness for her. *She does not know yet,* he reminded himself.

"I did it!"

At the sound of the door opening I turned to see the nurse as she rushed back through. "Did what?" she asked me.

I turned back.

Gone. "Uhm—nothing," I said, scanning the nursery. Had I done it… used my seer ability, or had my mind been playing tricks on me? If it *was* real, what was with the vanishing act all the time?

"You work in the NICU," the nurse said, pulling me back. "We could use someone like you here to help out. Could you find time?"

"Maybe. I'll have to check with my supervisor first," I said. I smiled and gave her a quick wave, then left on my way back to the NICU.

The rest of my shift whizzed by full of calm happy babies and nurses. I'd told myself that when I got home and was away from the distractions of the hospital, I'd give that *trying* thing another go, see if I could sense anything or anyone around me.

But when I sauntered through my front door with my mind fixed on the *trying*, my cell phone went off.

I seized the ringing thing from the side pocket of my tote and checked the caller ID. I didn't recognize the number. For a second, I hesitated to answer, but under the circumstances of Louise and her sneaking phones, I didn't want to risk missing a call from her.

"Hello?" I said answering.

"Lynn," came Will's voice. "I just got a call from my Dad."

"Hey," I responded, shock and confusion flooding my mind as I shut the front door behind me.

"It's Louise," he said next.

At the mention of her name I sunk to the floor.

"Dad told me... she passed away this morning."

"No," was all I could get out. Images of last night's dream scrambled across my brain.

"Was early this morning—sometime after 3 a.m. Andre told Dad. Andre had been checking on her every hour." Will paused when someone in the background called his name, then he said, "Lynn? You still there? I'm on my office phone—can you hear me?"

"Oh," I managed, trying to push away the images. "Ya... sorry... just... trying... to digest it all."

"Dad said Andre and the boys are taking her out East to Nova Scotia, for the service and burial. It was pre-arranged," Will explained.

"I see...." I knew that had been what she wanted, to be near their vacation home.

"Andre told Dad they are having a small gathering tomorrow afternoon for extended family. Then they're getting on a flight—taking her out East, like I said. You know they consider us family... but Dad said Andre understood if neither of us could be there."

"Tomorrow?"

"Obviously—I can't get back in time," Will said, "but I wanted you to know what happened. Dad also told me they're not taking calls at the house—but told Andre he would make sure you and I knew."

"Thank you...," I tried to get out before bursting into tears.

"I'm really sorry, Lynn... and I'm sorry about this too—but I have to go," he said, cutting off my sobs. "If I hear anything else from Dad—I'll let you know."

"Oooh... okay," I said, through a choke of tears.

"Sorry," he said again, before hanging up the call.

I leaned back against the door staring across at the drawers to my mother's antique dresser table—now entry table. Tears streamed down my cheeks as wave after wave of the reality attacked my mind, and my soul.

A soft *"Sigh"* came from the other room, and I glanced up to see Raven peeking his head out the kitchen's opening.

"Hey," I said.

Raven slowly padded over, head hanging as if sharing the heft of my grief. He slumped down next to me on the floor and touched my hand with his cold nose. I sucked in a breath. His head came up then, and he touched his nose to my cheek this time.

"Doggies know," I said, patting his big head.

He set a paw on my other hand in response.

"Bet yer hungry," I said, shifting to push myself up.

Hunger was the last thing I was feeling, but I dragged myself to the kitchen to feed my friend. It was the least I could do for the one who had tried to rescue me from my sorrow pit on the floor.

As Raven munched away on his dinner, I started up my laptop. Sitting now at one of the kitchen barstools, I sat staring at the screen as the computer flickered to life. A flood of memories scrambled through my brain. I'd witnessed Mom as she had gotten sicker and sicker, and I'd seen Louise go through the same. I knew after hearing she'd stopped treatment, that time for her would be short, but I hadn't allowed myself to contemplate how little time she actually had. At the sense of feeling sorry for myself, I caught the emotion before it grabbed hold. We all lost her, but it was Andre and his family who would suffer the most. I also knew there'd be feelings of relief that Louise was no longer in pain, but with it would also come the heaviness of guilt.

Losing someone you loved brings a whole bag of emotions, most of which you don't expect or even understand. And right now, my grief mingled with a sense of helplessness as I search the internet for a flight home. I knew making it to Ottawa for tomorrow's gathering would be slim to none, unfortunately. Plus, I couldn't even call the house, Will had said. What else could I do?

"Maybe I could write," I said to Raven, when I saw he'd finished his dinner. "Send Andre an email perhaps.... but what the hell would I say?" What could you say to someone who just lost the love of their life—their wife, best friend and mother to his children?

Frustrated, I click my *photos* folder to scan for the last images I had of Louise. I clicked the thumbnail of one of my favorite, the one of us sitting at the backyard table with all Andre's flowers in bloom behind us. Then, like a light went off, I suddenly knew what it was I could do.

I'd saved links about grief when searching for some kind of wisdom after Mom and Aunt Kay had passed. I had found a few beautiful quotes by brilliant people who seemed to understand the healing of grief. This was the *something* I could do.

I clicked the link I wanted and read through the quotes on the page. Reading them during my time of grief then had helped, and it helped now to read them again.

Having found the two quotes I'd liked from before, I opened a new email window, entered Andre's email address, and then I retype them into the body of the email;

> *"Enlightenment is the moment we realize that we are made of love. For grace comes to the heart when it realizes what it is made of and what it has risen from. In that moment, grace comforts us, that no matter the joy or pain along the way, we are already a part of where we are going. Enlightenment for a heart on Earth is the moment we accept that it is the loving that makes waves of us all, again and again and again." ~ Mark Nepo*

> *"Enlightenment for a wave is the moment the wave realizes that it is water. At that moment, all fear of death disappears." ~ Thich Nhat Hanh*

I added nothing else other than ending the email with, *I love you*. I didn't need to write anything else. Andre knew my feelings about Louise, and how I felt about them both. I hit send and let a new wave of tears come.

With a sense of purpose, I pushed through the tears and the ache in my chest, to open another email window. I began a message to the girls, writing them about Louise's passing, and how I'd dreamt about her last night. None of them really knew Louise. Olivia had met her that one time at my wedding rehearsal dinner, but they'd all known about her. I'd talked about her many times, *and* it had been her story she'd shared with me about Will's mother, that I'd subsequently shared with them. At the end of the email I added that I was sorry for, and sickened by, having to share more bad news and death with them.

I hit send, and speculated once again if Louise's illness had been because she'd told me. She'd told Andre too. I'd wanted to protect her from more of the story in hopes it could make her better or at the very least not shorten her life. Now she was gone. I wished I had told her about what we'd found, what had really been going on with my girlfriends, and that there may have been some merit to Joan's story.

A flash of memory of that big man from my dream of Louise had me thinking about the other times I'd seen him. And based on my findings on The Horsemen, I recalled pairing him with the leader named *Zaqiel*. I'd considered telling my friends all about it—about them, and about what had happened at the party too. But the last thing I needed now was more of their rejection to my insights or input. Losing Louise was more than enough pain for me to bear—thank you very much.

I was about to shut down my email when an auto message arrived via *Facebook*. It stated I'd received a 'friend request'.

"Redmond Credente," I said, reading aloud the name of the requestor. I paused for a moment, but then I continued with shutting down my email.

Chapter 6

Oblivion kept me company while I functioned on autopilot for the rest of the week. I'd hidden out in the pods with the babies, avoiding everyone, including Luc.

He'd been busy and preoccupied with his new relationship and had been over at Dunya's place, but I was thrilled to have the house to myself. And frankly, I was sick to death of, well—death and bad news, *and* having to share it. I'd periodically checked my email during the week, for what—I hadn't been sure.

I had seen the email responses from my girlfriends come in during the week, but now, Sunday night, I still had read none of them. I'd also received an email back from Andre, that one I'd opened.

He'd written telling me how beautiful Louise's service had been, about the supportive family and friends who had been there for he and his boys, and how much love and support was still around them. He'd added at the end of the email, *Please don't worry about not being able to get home. We'll hug lots at Christmas when you're here.*

"Christmas... home," I said aloud to Raven, who'd park himself at his usual spot by my feet near the couch. I sighed.

He gave me a heavy "*Sigh*" back, like he understood.

"I hadn't thought about Christmas," I added. Guess I would need to figure out where I'd be staying too. It wouldn't be at my now ex-father-in-law's place, nor would it be at my mother's. Other than out in the middle of nowhere at my brother James's place, what other options did I have? But it was still only the end of the first week of November, so what I did have was *time,* time to figure it all out.

The only other email that remained in my inbox other than the unread ones from the girls, was that one I'd received at the start of the week via Facebook.

"New normal," I said to Raven, and hit the *Accept* option on the friend request.

* * *

Monday again, and after work I was back in my usual spot on the couch, checking email.

A new Facebook message had come in, and it was from Redmond. It read;

> *Hey, Lynn. Not my preferred method of communication, but I wasn't sure how else to get in touch with you. I'm guessing you are okay with it since you accepted my friend request. Nice profile photo by the way. How are things?*

How are things?

A pang of guilt pinched my chest as I reread the message. I'd signed the divorce papers, it wasn't as if this was cheating. Besides, other than the call about Louise, I'd not heard a peep from Will since he'd left. He was after all with his true love, his job. And I had no doubt he was off on all sorts of adventures seeing the world. He was happy I was sure, and surprisingly, I was happy for him. I also knew he'd want the same level of happiness for me.

Thus, in the practice of happiness, I let any smidge of guilt that tried to linger find the exit door, then I clicked the Facebook icon to go check out Redmond's profile page.

I noticed he had lots of photos, but he had less than fifty friend connections and found it interesting for someone in his industry. But I liked it. It meant the people he connected with were a select few, and he'd selected to reach out to me. And with that comfort on the brain, I began a message back to my new friend;

Hey back!

Not a huge fan of communicating through FB either, but it helps with keeping me connected to some of my friends far away. You've got quite the short 'friend list' for someone in the music scene. Thanks—on the photo, took it the day I moved into my new house—happy day.

The photo was a selfie of me under the big live oak. The sun streaming down had made my skin appear luminescent, and I had been happy in that moment. It was surprising Redmond had found me. He'd known my name, though I hadn't appeared quite like myself on Halloween night, and I'd only recently changed out my profile picture from one of those cartoon-generated characters you can make of yourself online. He may not have even found me, had I still had that cartoon version up of myself. *Timing*.

I hit enter to send my message and then shut down the social media web page.

I still wasn't up to reading, let alone responding to the knowingly sweet and supportive words of my girlfriends' emails. Instead I cleaned up the usual suspects from my email's inbox and then shut down my computer for the night. I'd used up all my energy at work, so the idea of making dinner was not an energy-filled one. Still needing nourishment, I went for the emergency food I'd stashed at the back of the shelf with the regular dried pasta. Reaching in, I retrieved a trusty box of *microwavable* macaroni and cheese.

The food having served its purpose, Raven and I retired to my bedroom to watch TV. I'd moved the spare TV from the office into my bedroom after Luc had moved in. The original purpose had been in case he and Dunya wanted to watch the big TV in the living room just the two of them, but I'd found it convenient for my own TV viewing, *and* for time to myself.

* * *

My alarm went off, and I woke to find myself still in my scrubs and on top of the covers with Raven at my side. The TV displayed one of those morning news shows with the reporter talking about the weather. *Sunny with partial clouds and a chance of rain.* Welcome to South Florida.

Today the adoptive parents would come in for their second visit, but the twins were still not ready to go home just yet. The parents had needed special training to be ready, should the boys have any issues once in their new home, and for administering the medications the boys would need for the next few years of their tiny lives. We were pleased that these extra challenges didn't seem to faze the new parents, and that they'd wanted any time they could get with the babies.

Of late, I'd been given the opportunity to spend some of my shift helping in the low-risk patient nursery. I'd loved caring for the twins, but it was a blessing to not have any new delicate lives to watch over for the moment. Cuddling healthy babies was easier on the heart. You also had less time to get attached to these babies as they spent much less time at the hospital than those in the NICU.

The nurses were grateful for any help I could give, because '*women were still having babies, apparently*' they'd joked. One nurse was pregnant herself, and she was overjoyed for the breaks to either sit or go to the bathroom when I showed up during her shifts. I was grateful time at the hospital moved along as it always did. And before I knew it, it was time to clock out.

At home, I found a note from Luc attached to a delicious smelling Columbian one-pot-dish masterpiece he'd cooked and set out for me.

The note read;

Taking dinner over to Dunya and Mitra, but the rest is yours.

Speaking of grateful, I was seriously grateful I wouldn't have to eat more instant food today. I'd eaten out of the vending machine at work for the past two shifts, and I had no interest in another emergency ration of crappy pasta and powdered cheese.

Elated, I prepared a plate of deliciousness for a quick reheat in the microwave. Pressing on another power button, I let my laptop come to life on the kitchen island. While my meal heated, I watched as the latest emails loaded.

Among the usual bank payment confirmation emails and the local restaurant discount emails, sat another sent via Facebook.

It was from my new friend Redmond, and it read;

> *Hi again.*
>
> *Ya, short friend list, just my closest friends and family are on my personal page. I have a business page where anyone can connect with us through it, but Lily manages that for me. I spend little time hanging on Facebook unless Lily needs help with something for work. If you are comfortable with it, I'd rather use my regular email than the FB messenger. You can respond to me at RHC@CredenteStudios.com.*
>
> *Hope to hear from you soon.*

I preferred regular email over messenger too anyway, so it worked for me. And I'd gotten a good vibe off him Halloween night. He'd also had a trusted and loyal staff member drive me home. He wasn't exactly just a *stranger* I'd met at a party, either. In fact, he was a well-known studio owner and music industry person, Darius had told me, not some social media stalker. I was feeling safe with the whole communicating thing, and he had mentioned only his closest friends and family had access to this personal page, so that made me feel kind of special.

With that in mind, I sent a quick message back via FB stating I was, *comfortable with it,* and then I sent a second message to his personal email stating the same thing. He hadn't asked me anything in particular, other than about using regular email, so there hadn't been much else to say in response.

The microwave "*Dinged*" then. As did my computer, indicating notification of a new email message. Pulling my dinner from the microwave, I then set myself up on the island to eat and read the email.

The email shown the *sender* to be one, *Redmond H. Credente*. His message was your typical Q&A, with; *Where ya from, what do you do for a living, do you have any brothers or sisters,* and such of someone wanting to get to know you. And I took the time to write him back between enjoying mouthfuls of the wonderful meal Luc had prepared. But after hitting send, I didn't sit waiting for a response. The interaction was fun, though I felt a *tad* too eager for a reply.

Instead of waiting by my laptop, I shut it down and put it to the side, choosing then to clean up and package up the remaining dinner to take with me for lunch tomorrow. I hid the container of leftovers in the fridge inside my trusty lunch bag to take with me to work in the morning. I hoped Luc hadn't planned on taking it with him because he'd be out of luck.

After a run-around and fetch with Raven out back before the sun set, I closed out all the interior lights and headed to bed.

* * *

All day I'd been unusually eager for my shift to be over. Most days I didn't mind the longish hours, but today when my shift ended, that tiny girlish part of me wanted to see what—if anything, my new friend had written me back.

Despite being eager to check my emails though, I made a conscious effort to throw together a healthy dinner for myself first. No more crap meals. As I designed the perfect salad, and my email loaded, I was reminded I still hadn't read any of the messages from the girls. I hadn't wanted to revisit things, not just yet. Instead I went to the newest message in my inbox, one from Luc.

He'd written that he'd be doing something with his church's band tonight, so once again I'd be on my own. I had gotten used to being alone even when Will lived here, so I didn't mind, and I didn't mind not having to talk about Louise or explain my new friend either. What I did want, was to enjoy the little lightness that this new friendship had sparked in me. The revisiting of sorrow could wait.

And to my pleasure, other than the latest *DEAL* emails for my favorite taco place near work, the only other email I was interested in reading, was the one from Redmond.

This time he'd written a lot more;

> *So, you're the only girl with 3 older brothers and mostly male cousins. That must have been a challenge growing up. I noticed on FB your hometown is Ottawa, but I'm guessing you've only been away a few years now based on what you told me. Do you miss it, friends and family?*
>
> *That's quite the change in career going from IT to working in the NICU at the hospital, but I completely agree you have to love what you do, and it sounds like you are loving it there. Good for you, Lynn.*

I feel lucky that I found something I love and I'm grateful for the fantastic people I get to share it with.

Okay, it's my turn now.

I'm Irish and Italian, Mom is Irish, Dad is Italian. Both are retired doctors in oncology. I'm an only-child. My dad is an only-child too, but my Mom is a twin—to a brother. They're the oldest, followed by my two uncles, each a year apart, and then my two aunts, who are also twins.

My parents met in medical school, mom was in nursing, dad in pre-med. Later, after I was born, Mom went back to school to be a doctor. They live in NYC. They own a big apartment in Manhattan. They still keep my room for me, but it's more a room for visiting friends or family.

Me, I have a bachelor's degree in music from Manhattan Music School. It was a rigorous program that's supposed to prepare you to be a leader in the arts. I liked the program because it wasn't just about the traditional conservatory subjects like music history and theory, but you also got an intensive humanities focus, emphasizing on literature, history, and expository writing. It allows you to become a complete artist with a deeper knowledge of both the world and yourself. Anyway, I loved it, and feel fortunate I had the chance to go, really. My parents weren't too happy when I took the direction of a more modern take on music and moved to Miami, but that's another story.

Do you play any musical instruments?

~R

He'd been keen on telling me about his life, and since he'd shared so much, I went with writing back a little more as well;

Six kids, two sets of twins, eh? Wow, your poor grandmother. LOL Do you get to see your mom's side of the family much? You must have lots of cousins.

Sounds like quite the music program. And no, I don't play any instruments. I love music, just not musically inclined, and couldn't sing to save my life.

I miss my friends and family a lot. Miss my mom the most, she and my aunt both passed away last year, and that took a toll. My brothers and my cousins are a bit lost without them. My mom and aunt did all the planning of gatherings, so those are few and far between now. I recently lost a dear friend of mine too, Louise.

Cancer took all of them, but your parents would know all about that nasty stuff. Lots of advances now though, and it's great to hear that kind of news over the negative.

I'm recently divorced, no kids, and my ex lives overseas now. I have my buddy, Luc living with me right now. His girlfriend lives next door. She has her grandmother living with her, and they are great neighbors. I love my house and my job, but I miss my friends and wish they could come visit even more now that I have the space. Maybe soon possibly, I hope.

I'm a dog lover. I have Luc's dog Raven living here too as a second roommate. Makes for nice company when I'm here on my own.

Do you have any pets?

I ended the message with, *not sure what else to tell you,* then hit send.

For the next hour, Redmond and I exchanged emails and details about our lives.

My last email had outlined a typical day and week in the NICU. I'd gotten another email back right away from him, but this one didn't have more information. It did however have the suggestion we *Skype* instead of email, and he'd asked if I was free to do so tonight.

Tonight?

I stared at the message and then reread it two more times. *Was I ready for that?* I'd had a cool and kind of sexy facade going the night I'd met him, but right now I was all mussed hair, scrubs, and no-makeup-Lynn, and not the first—second impression, I'd wanted to make.

With a rush of panic, I shut down my computer without responding. Then I coaxed Raven to come with me to my bedroom where we could both watch TV and hide out.

Chapter 7

Coward.

I'd been a bit of a mess all day. Not a visible mess mind you, but I'd agonized some over my not responding to Redmond last night. It was just two people getting to know each other after all, but then why had I panicked? What was there to get all worked up about, anyway? It wasn't like me to be such a coward, but it had been a long time since I'd interacted with a guy in this way. Not cool of me for dropping off so abruptly and without a response of some kind to answer his request. I knew I had made too much of it, and I also knew I'd have to send him an apology email when I got home.

Sitting comfortably on my cozy couch now, I loaded my email only to find I'd received another from Redmond. The time on it showed he'd sent it about 20 minutes after the Skype request. In the message, he'd expressed that he understood if I wasn't okay with the idea *and* that he hoped he hadn't been too forward or scared me off with requesting it.

He hadn't. I'm an idiot. It had been a big scardy-cat moment for me and it had nothing to do with his request. Embarrassed that he'd felt the need to send the second email, I put my *big-girl* pants on and wrote him back.

I expressed how sorry I was for not responding right away, *but* I still gave him the BS excuse I hadn't seen the message about skyping until now, and that I'd received a long-distance call that had pulled me away. I added that, *yes,* I would like to video chat and provided him my profile name for the video chat. And in trying for another opportunity, I ended my response with stating that I'd be free after I got food into me and suggested a time of 8 p.m. tonight.

Send.

Luc and Dunya were out at the movies, so over leftovers provided by him again, *and* feeling unsure if I would hear from Redmond, I took the time to read the responses from the girls.

The emails from them had been thoughtful and kind, but I still needed to clean my brain of it all—of the hurt. Part of me had wanted to write them back, telling them all about my new friend, but then again, it felt like I was the only one of us who was still reaching out with updates on our lives.

There'd been no calls or other emails from them, not even Vicki who'd habitually emailed with me on a daily basis in the past. Vicki was divorced and currently single, it would have been nice to exchange emails with her on this whole *chatting* or potential dating thing. Olivia was busy with her life and family as was Mac. Alison was busy with baby stuff I'd assumed. I'd hoped that the pregnancy and baby topic would have been a regular discussion point for us, but it too had faded off with the four and their new focus, the one I wasn't a part of anymore. Sometimes I wish I'd never found those writings of Mom's, and that I could have just mourned like a normal person. Instead I had this mystery in my hands, one it seemed I was destined to share with my closest friends. But now it was *their* mystery and my friendship with them had taken a backseat.

I'd closed the last of their emails when a new one popped in from Redmond. He'd stated that 8 p.m. was good for him and that he'd already sent me a profile request via Skype.

This was just what I needed, an aid in clearing my brain. I liked Skype better than a phone call too because you get to see the person and their reactions. As comfortable as email was, I knew we could talk more openly about our lives this way. Also, the last time—the only time, he'd seen me, I'd been dressed as something from *Hell*. If he'd been interested in me in that getup, I could only hope he'd be pleasantly surprised to see the real me.

In time for the video call and in contrast to the all-black I'd worn on Halloween, I'd changed out of my scrubs into cutoff shorts and a light blue t-shirt with a *Superman* crest on the front. Again, in contrast I wore only a light hint of eyeliner and mascara. I'd also taken my ponytail out to have my hair down. It grew like a weed and was near down to my waist. Guys like long hair I've been told. *Whatever.*

At 7:50 p.m. I set myself up on the couch with my computer on the coffee table and then logged on.

The first thing I saw was his request to chat. His profile name displayed the name of the studio and it had a company logo rather than a profile picture. I hit *accept* on Redmond's waiting request, changed my status to show 'online' and then waited.

My contacts list showed none of the girls online, or it could be they'd blocked me for their private chats, but I didn't care at this point. Redmond must have been sitting waiting online because his video chat call request came through right then, playing its connecting tune.

I drew in a deep breath, clicked the video icon to accept, and watched as the video display swirled into action. I did a quick check of myself in the tiny video display window in the corner, to make sure I was close enough and that the view hadn't cut my head off.

Then his face appeared on the screen.

He was more handsome than I remembered, and that was saying a lot considering the quality of video chat was pretty basic. "Hi there," he said, making a big goofy grin.

"Hi," I said, grinning back at him.

"Long time no see," he added, followed by a laugh. I'd heard him laugh on Halloween, but with the music and the crowds I hadn't gotten the full depth of it. It was a great laugh.

"Ya, and no blood and guts this time," I reminded. "Guess I look a little different too, eh?" I laughed, hoping it was a good kind of different.

"Nice to see your eyes now… past all the dark eye makeup and red contacts—I mean," he said, waving a finger near his eyes. "Cool costume—but nicer to see the real you."

"I guess—ya, thanks." I hoped the quality of the video display was such that it hid the blush I felt now. Quick to redirect, I said, "What brought you from New York to Miami?"

I don't think he expected me to jump into the questions because he shifted in his seat. But I'd needed to get the focus off me. I wasn't great with all-eyes-on-me, even if it was only one pair. He had great eyes mind you, all dark coffee colour and smoldering, but still.

He cleared his throat then, dragging a hand through his dark red hair. "Well," he started. He paused and ran a hand through his hair again. Then he said, "Came down here during my last year of college on a break, met a girl and then I moved here after graduation. Cuban girl, family owned a local business. She had a degree in business and was going for her MBA. It was a one-year program—so I signed up to do it too. But, by Christmas that same year the relationship part had fizzled out. It was a civil split, and we both moved on. *And* I decided to stay after getting the MBA. I love New York, but I don't miss the cold," he ended.

"Oh, I hear ya on the cold thing—same goes for me. I love my hometown—don't mind the cold, but I don't miss driving in winter," I told him. I didn't much care for driving in Miami either with all the crazy drivers, but I was thankful it wasn't in snow storms. "Tell me about your job you love so much." This time my redirect was to get off the sad idea of missing our hometowns. I smiled again.

He smiled. "My job, my recording studio—Credente Studios, it's in the Grove. Do you know the area?" he asked

"Definitely—used to live near there," I said. "Think I've seen the sign for the studio, but I figured it was a photography studio." I recalled it being at the end of the strip in Coconut Grove near the Italian restaurant I used to go to. "Haven't been there since before I moved to the new house."

"Yer off tomorrow—Friday's off, right?" he asked, flipping through papers in front of him on the desk.

"I like my job, but ya I love having Fridays off too. And not having to work again until Saturday evenings—the short shift." I'd mentioned in one of my emails I had odd hours, with Fridays and Sunday's off.

"You should come by the studio," he said. "It's Friday the 13th tomorrow." He'd added that last bit of information like he'd just informed me it was *happy hour.*

"Are you superstitious?" I asked him, not sure where he was going with the info.

"In a way, I guess—but not like I'm afraid. More that I find it interesting." He grinned.

"So, you like creepy stuff?" I said, perhaps a tad too hopeful.

"Do you?" he said countering, his grin changing to one of mischief.

"Ya. But… do you believe in any of it?" I countered back.

"Some. But I like when fact and fiction overlap—ya know?"

"Do I." I rolled my eyes.

"Like with Friday the 13th—do you know why people consider it unlucky?" he tossed at me.

Come to think of it I didn't. "No, actually—I don't." Not sure how I would, but I was all ears to hear why.

"There's even a scientific name for the fear of the number 13—*triskaidekophobia,* and one for the fear of Friday the 13 specifically too, *paraskevidekatriaphobia,*" he rambled out, having no trouble with the big words. "It's a combo of Greek words *Paraskeví*—meaning Friday and *dekatreís*—meaning thirteen.

"Wow—it's a real thing—a real phobia." Cool.

"Oh, it goes way back," he said, "back as far as *The Last Supper.*"

"Theeeeeee last supper?" I said, jokingly.

"Ya, they think the superstition surrounding Friday the 13th may have originated from that day."

"Why?" I asked. *Luc would love that,* I mused.

"It was Christ's last supper—the night before his crucifixion. There were 13 people present—it was the *13th of Nasan Maundy*—preparation for Passover, and the night before Good Friday," he detailed.

"I don't know much about that stuff—religious stuff, but I know superstitions often seem to stem from religious events." I made a mental note to ask Luc about it. "My roommate does the church thing. He's told me a few stories about things like that," I added.

"Hey, I'm only *half* Italian, but I've heard many Italians regard Friday as an unlucky day—along with the number thirteen. One of the earliest English references is from 1869—found in this Italian guy's biography, *Gioachino Rossini,* who died on the unlucky day. There's also a publication from 1907 by *Thomas W. Lawson* who wrote a novel about a corrupt broker who uses the superstition to create a panic on Wall Street on Friday the 13th.

"Geez, you seem to know a lot about this topic," I pointed out.

"I guess, ya," he said, "but my favorite origin story is one from 1307, the arrest of *Philip IV of France*—by the Knights Templar. It's mentioned in quite a few historical novels like *Maurice Druon's* novel from 1955—the Iron King. Did you read Dan Brown's novel—The Da Vinci Code?"

"I saw the movie," I said, once again reminded of how *not* well read I was.

"It's mentioned in that story," he clarified.

"That's cool. I like that kind of mystery—plausible fiction." It's true I did, but I felt stupid not having any clue of these references he was making. How was I supposed to know this shit? I just sense the weird stuff, I don't study it.

"It's estimated that over 20 million people in the United States alone are impacted by a fear of Friday the 13th—makes it the most feared date in history," he said, raising his eyebrows and nodding. "Some are so paralyzed by it they change their regular routines in work, avoid taking planes—some don't even get out of bed." He laughed. "The money lost in one business day is estimated to be around eight or nine million." He raised his eyebrows again. And so did I.

Who knew there was that much focus on it—I didn't. The movie Friday the 13th had scared the crap out of me, but I hadn't known there was more to it.

"I got more—wanna hear it? I'm not weirding you out, am I?" he asked.

"Ha—nope." Poor guy had no idea about my weird world. "Go on."

He grinned a boyish grin and continued. "In Finland, National Accident Day, always falls on a Friday the 13th. There's a British study from 1993, that stated a significant level of traffic-related incidences occurred on Friday the 13th as opposed any other Friday, *but* a Dutch insurance statistic from 2008 stated that fewer accidents, fires, and thefts occur on that date—mainly because people are either more careful or they just stay home."

"Fear can do a number on you," I said. Boy did I know that. "I don't pay much attention to Friday the 13th—other than it's kind of entertaining how serious people can take it," I said with a hint of sarcasm. I grinned.

"Okay that's enough of that," he laughed out. Then he said, "You mentioned you were adopted—is Lynn your birth name?"

Talk about switching gears *and* to the point. "Uhm, no, the Westlakes gave me Lynn. But my birth records have me down as *Yasmin*. I know it suits me well doesn't it?" I laughed.

"Oh wow—that is quite the contrast. Though it does conjure childhood memories of Barbara Eden from *I Dream of Jeannie*." He raised his eyebrows up and down a few times.

"Right—that's me," I said, with another laugh.

"Every guy my age, secretly had the hots for Jeannie—but never admitted to watching the TV show. *Gilligan's Island* maybe—definitely *Get Smart*, but never the other."

"I loved all those as a kid."

"Shhhhh—me too," he said, making us both laugh.

"Redmond...," I started.

"Lynn," he interrupted, making me laugh again.

"... I'm assuming your name, Redmond is the Irish part, and Credente is the Italian?" I asked, completing my thought and switching the focus.

"Yup—you got it," he said. "In fact...." He paused as if considering more entertaining facts.

"In fact?" I prompted. He reminded me of Derek with all his facts, but unlike Derek he was more open to the possibility of the spooky side of things.

"... I was named after Redmond O'Hanlon," he said.

I blinked fast a couple times. "Never heard of him," I said, feeling stupid again.

"The name Redmond means *protector*, it's more popular in Northern Ireland where O'Hanlon was from."

"And he waaas?" I asked. I was done with feeling stupid, just lay it on me.

"A charismatic outlaw—Ireland's version of Robin Hood," he said, giving me a boastful grin.

I smiled, couldn't help it, he had such a wonderful way about him. "Do you have a middle name?" I countered.

"Hugh," he said, not followed by any facts.

"And is that from someone famous too?" I teased.

"Well, ya—Red Hugh O'Donnell," he said with another big grin. "He and another fella led a rebellion and won a bunch of battles in the late 1500s. It's an ancient name that means *fire*."

"Protector Fire, interesting," I responded. The whole *Red* and *Fire* thing suited him with that amazing dark red hair of his. I imagined he must have had a red halo of hair at birth and why his mom had named him as such.

"What about you—any middle name?" he redirected at me.

"Nope, just boring old Lynn Westlake—no middle name." I guess if you included Yasmin, not so boring, but that discussion could wait for another time.

"It means *lake*," he said.

"Aaah, pardon?"

"Lynn—your name. It's English, Irish, *and* Gaelic in origin, I believe. I like it," he said. "So, about tomorrow?"

I smiled again. I *liked* him.

Chapter 8

Friday, November 13th and though it might be *National Accident Day* somewhere on the other side of the world, I wasn't going to let that faze me as I drove my car to the Grove. Hell, any day in Miami was accident day. *Yeesh.*

I'd agreed to stop by around 2ish, but at the moment I was standing in my walk-in closet panicking over what to wear. I could have used some girlfriend advice right about now, but with no girlfriends handy, I decided it was best to go with my normal attire of jeans and a t-shirt. I did however choose a pink t-shirt and kept my hair down to amp up the girly quota. I'd even transferred my wallet, lip balm, and phone to a small purse instead of using my usual tote. And since I'd be wearing my flipflops, I'd made the effort to paint my toenails a light pink to match my t-shirt. *Olivia would have been proud,* I mused as I exited the room.

Before leaving, I gave Raven a good belly scratch, telling him that Luc would be home soon to play with him. Then I grabbed my keys and headed out the door.

Redmond had mentioned there would be a band visiting the studio, someone I'd never heard of, but who were apparently the latest 'new thing' in the music world. He'd said they were a cross between *U2, Led Zeppelin,* and *Green Day* with the attitude of the *Rolling Stones,* and that Lily was all psyched over doing the artwork for their marketing and CDs, etc. He'd also told me that if I wanted, I could come meet them. I didn't care about the band, but I'd welcomed the excuse to see him again.

Arriving, I pulled into a visitor parking space. I got out of my car and took a quick glance over to the outdoor patio of the Italian restaurant up the way. My stomach growled. I'd eaten before I left, but with that *hollow-leg* and all, I could always use a little more. I rubbed my stomach and continued to the studio's main doors.

Right away through the entrance it was obvious how totally cool the place was. There was a big lounge area when you entered, and off to the side instead of a reception desk, it had a self-serve kitchen/bar area with an industrial style coffee machine and a cappuccino maker.

"Fridge is stocked with water, sports drinks, energy drinks and other assortments of soda and non-alcoholic drinks," I heard a familiar voice say.

I turned to see Redmond's assistant, Lily Shade—*Shade* for short, and the one who'd driven me home Halloween night. She still had the pink hair and full-arm sleeves of tattoos. I'd assumed her hair had been a wig or a temporary dye job considering it was Halloween, but obviously I'd been wrong.

"Heeey," I said back. She'd been super nice that night, and it was great to see her again.

"The cupboards are full of snacks," she added, opening a bag of white cheddar popcorn and grinning. "I bring in bagels and muffins too when we're meeting new clients, but when they're recording, the food is specific to the artists' request." She followed up with an eyeroll and an even bigger grin.

"Lucky them," I said. My stomach growled again.

"Great to see you again. Redmond will be out in a sec," she said. Before I could say anything in response, she turned and passed back through the swinging-door she'd entered through. I continued with checking out the rest of the space.

Art depicting music of different genres filled the walls. There was a big print on the nearest wall of *The Beatles* crossing Abby Road. No recording studio would be complete without it I'm sure. At the sound of the flapping door, I turned back around to see a redhaired giant of a man... and he was coming right for me.

"Lyyynn," Redmond said, arms out for a welcome hug. He wore black jeans and a white dress shirt untucked, and he was even taller than I remembered.

"Hiii," I said as his big arms wrapped around me, pulling me in for a squeeze. My cheek pressed against the lower part of his chest. He smelled good—great, actually. Something like vanilla and spices. My arms were pinned at my side, so I couldn't hug back, but I took in a long enjoyable sniff. When he loosened his grip, I said, "Hi," again, and pushed my long mess of hair back from my face.

He smiled again, stretching out a long arm towards the swinging-door he had passed through. "Come on back to my office. Lily's got the band going over marketing options and graphics—so we can have a nice visit now."

"She's in heaven I bet," I said following him.

"Exactly," he responded, holding the door and pointing the way to his office.

"Good for her," I said, walking ahead and then entering his office.

"Good for the studio," he said, shutting the door behind us. "She's amazing at all that."

"Cool," I added, both on the subject, and at noticing the view through the now closed door. His office had an oversized door with a one-way window that exposed the hall and the areas across to the studios. It was kind of like those mirrors they have in interrogation rooms on the cop TV shows, but with no mirror.

"I can get work done and still keep a close eye on things without being disturbed," he responded, when he saw me checking out the view. "Have a seat."

I turned back and smiled, then maneuvered to sit down in the middle of a well-worn leather couch. He sat down in one of two big matching leather club chairs. All the pieces had that look of furniture you'd have found in an old western. Not cowboy'ish, but the kind of beat-up that still looked amazing, and had all sorts of stories to tell. Leather furniture over time had a way of aging well and getting more comfortable too. "Nice place," I said glancing around at the walls.

"I think the place has ghosts—crazy stuff happens here all the time that no one can explain. But I like it. I tell people it's dead musicians come back to listen in—play along."

"Ghosts," I responded. "Musicians you say."

"Yup. But there are a lot of old ghosts in the Grove," he added. "Hi, Monroe."

I shot a glance behind me over the back of the couch, then stared back at him when I saw nothing there.

"Our ghost, Monroe—*Ralph Middleton Munroe*. His home still stands on the historical state park grounds across the way from here.

"Great," I said, giving a nervous laugh, scanning the rest of the room.

The office walls had various photos of him with different artists, some I recognized, most I knew but not their names, and others I'd never seen before. On the wall over the club chairs was a case with a fancy guitar with a scribbled signature on it. Next to the case was a photo of him with *Stevie Ray Vaughn*. Stevie was holding the same guitar. *Nice*. But better than that, was the item that hung above the chair behind his desk.

It was an old acoustic guitar in a similar display case, but even from afar I recognized the signature. *"Elvis,"* I acknowledged. "Where… did you… get that?" I loved Elvis from a very young age. It had always baffled my mother, but what didn't baffle my mother when it came to me. I guess it was only fair, she'd been baffling me plenty of late. "My first love," I added, with a grin.

He laughed in a deep burst. "I could say the same, but it's more admiration from a music standpoint," he said. "My mom was a fan—she got it for me when I opened the studio. First thing I put up in the office—kind of dual importance."

"Mothers—I get it, trust me," I said, and grinned wider.

"The band will be awhile—did you want to see where I live?" he asked getting up from the chair.

"Uhm," I gave him. It was an odd request and not because I'd only just gotten to the studio.

"It's not far—we can walk," he said, at my hesitation. "I'll let Lily know."

"Okay," I said with a little less reluctance. I wasn't scared—not really, but it helped that someone would know where we were.

In the hall, Redmond informed Lily that we would be back in a few minutes, that he wanted to show me his place.

"That won't take long," Lily joked, laughing as she turned back to the meeting room.

I didn't need to be privy to the joke, because once outside, when we walked pass the studio's two-car garage, he said, "Here we are."

"We are?" I asked, confused, staring at a set of stairs on the right side of the building.

"It's up there," he said, pointing to the area built above the garage. "I built it here, so I could walk to work and to the Grove."

"Nice—wish I could say that," I responded, "but that would mean I'd have to live at the hospital." I shook my head. He laughed and made an *eeww* face, shaking his head. Then we climbed the outside staircase to his place.

"Took me awhile—but I did most of the renovations and decorating myself," he informed me, unlocking and opening the door.

Stepping inside, I saw that it was one big open room, except for the bathroom I presumed, and about the same size as the oversized garage space below. The ceilings were high, and it had a kitchen area extension on the right, built out over the back patio. I'd seen part of the patio when we'd hit the top of the stairs. All the walls were a creamy off-white. The kitchen had a huge window over the sink with a view out back. Below the window was a pale green and light blue sea-glass backsplash. He had pots in varying sizes dangling from a hanging metal frame. There was a French press for coffee on the counter, next to lemons in a blue ceramic bowl. The look was modern but still unique and personal.

"I like to cook," he said, moving past me. He picked up a lemon and gave it a sniff. "Maybe you'll let me cook you a meal sometime," he added, putting the lemon back.

He liked to cook, talk about bullseye to my heart. "Well, I like to eat," I tossed at him, "so that would work out well."

He laughed. I liked his laugh.

"Bathroom is over here," he said, pointing to a decorative antique door on the opposite side of the kitchen.

"Thanks," I said. "Wouldn't want to get lost trying to find it—if I needed it."

"Heeeey—don't knock my little place. It's cozy but functional," he said, and gave me a friendly shove towards the rest of the space.

"Kidding—I like it a lot," I said, looking back over my shoulder at him. "It's very inviting and has everything a bachelor would need."

He gave me another little shove and chuckled. I moved forward, but I could have seen everything from the doorway.

The bed was against the far wall. It was bigger than my regular king-size bed, and it had its mattress resting on a low platform of what appeared to be reclaimed wood. It was huge, but then again, he was huge, he'd need a big bed. It had grey and white linens, not made but not messy, just the one side flipped over with the rest still made. It also had lots of pillows. I liked that. Bookshelves full of all manner of books surrounded the bed like a headboard. I liked that too.

"You like to read too I see—not just cooking, I mean." I rounded the bed to look at the books on the other side. There was a small night stand on the same side as the flipped covers, and it had an antique lamp on it with a digital clock next to it. Interesting contrast.

"Music, cooking, reading—I'm a well-rounded kind of guy," he said, still standing near the kitchen.

"That you are—my friend, that you are," I said, eyeing a stack of books on the floor next the bed. There was both hardcover and soft, old and new.

"I like mysteries," he said, pulling my observations back to him.

"Really?" I said. Did I have a mystery for him.

On that same side of the bed nearer to the window, was a big old tan leather chair and ottoman. Next to it, under the window was an old wine barrel with a modern lamp on it. Again, with the contrast. And next to it was another stack of books. I leaned in to see the name of the book on the top of the stack. *And Then There Were None*–By Agatha Christie.

"I like sci-fi too—and urban fantasy, some paranormal," he said, crossing the distance to stand near me. "I have a mix of biographies on musicians as well, from Beethoven to Bob Marley," he added. "Come—have a seat." He gestured towards the section of the room that represented the living room.

On the adjacent wall opposite from the bed hung a huge TV. There was an extra-long dark grey couch between it and the bed, with just enough walk through for two people to pass side by side.

I moved around one side of it and sat. "This must be great for movies," I said, staring at the massive TV.

He followed suit and joined me. "It's the main reason I got it and the surround system. And if I'm lazy, I can watch it from my bed too," he said. "You like movies I hope."

"Elvis, food, and movies—I love them all," I laughed out.

"Yer my kind of people," he said, following up with his own laugh. "I like the solitude this place gives me... and the convenience to my work. I can come up here anytime I need a break—ya know?"

I understood needing a break even if it was from things you loved. I nodded and panned the rest of the space.

Next to the TV on the left was a beautiful well-used acoustic guitar in a stand. On the right of the TV was a floor to ceiling multi-cupboard wardrobe the same light coloured wood as the bed, with exposed shelves for shoes and multiple drawers. It stretched the rest of the wall to the corner and along another 4 feet of the front wall. Adding to the contrast, stood an old-fashioned coat rack. A lone baseball cap hung from one of its arms. The rack was at the edge of a huge window that stretched most of the rest of the wall back towards the bedroom area. "I like the plantation shutters with the flip louvers," I told him.

"Ya me too. I like the modern way they folded back to reveal the full window or closed up tight to block out the outside world," he said. "I made them only ¾ of the way up—that way there's always light coming in through the top—sun *or* moon light."

"Private, but still lots of light," I added, taking it all in.

It felt good here, safe. It even smelled good, like him, vanilla and a hint of fresh laundry. I loved my home but there was something to be said about small cozy spaces like this one. Though, I knew it was his presence that made it feel this way too. Perhaps there was something to that saying, *Home is not a place, it's a feeling.*

"Wanna see the back patio?" he asked, like a little kid wanting to show off a new toy.

"Sure," I said, getting up from my new happy place on his couch.

Locking the door behind us, Redmond let me lead the way back down the stairs and around to the rear space.

The yard was small, but had enough room for a covered patio, a two-parking spot size strip of grass, and of course a big shiny BBQ. There were a few nice lounge chairs with arms thick enough to rest a drink on, and a modern picnic table.

"What do you think?" Redmond asked, circling around to face me.

"Great place—great feel to it," I said. "You've got yourself a great setup here and the location can't be better. Close to the restaurants and action of the Grove."

"I'd like to have a house someday, but this works for me for now," he said.

"It's perfect."

"Hey, I need to run back and check on things at the studio—make sure Lily hasn't taken my job," he laughed out.

"She might take over your office if you're not watching," I noted, following him back to the studio.

"True statement," he said, opening one of the studio doors for me.

When we walked in, it appeared things were wrapping up. Lots of handshakes and *thank-yous* were being exchanged. "We'll see you Friday night," Lily said, as the band members exited past us through the front lobby area and out to the parking lot.

"See you then," Redmond said, before letting the door close. He gave Lily a high-five, then turned to me. "I'm gonna close up shop in a few—are you hungry?" he asked. "Was thinking pizza."

Am I hungry? "Silly question my friend," I said with a big grin. "Lily—you want to do pizza with us?"

"Would love to—Redmond makes the best pizza, but I have a date," she said, giving me a little girl-to-girl knowing eyebrow raise and a wink. She smiled and patted the back of her pink updo hair.

I smiled back and chuckled. "Ah—well, I'll need to hear all about it next time," I said. I liked this place, it's vibe, and she was like the cherry on top.

She giggled. "We'll talk over coffee. I like that you said *next time*—by the way," she said, giving my arm a squeeze. Then she and her pink hair and matching pink knapsack were out the door.

"She's a keeper," I said, standing near the doors as Redmond shut off the main lights.

"Lifesaver—most days," he said, opening the main door once again for me. "Later, Monroe," he added addressing the supposed ghost before locking up.

Back again at the cozy hideaway, while Redmond changed out of the white dress shirt and into an old faded grey t-shirt, I meandered around the apartment.

I stole a glance over my shoulder just as he pulled the t-shirt down over his chest, catching a sneak peek at the corded muscles of his stomach. He may not have been shy, but I was, and I spun back around pretending to examine the books on the shelf. The guy was built, likes mystical stuff, cooks, and he makes homemade pizza. Someone pinch me. Embarrassment avoided, I moved to the piles of books near the window and picked up the top one from the stack nearest the wine barrel. "*And Then There Were None*," I read out loud to my new pizza chef. "What's this one about?"

Redmond had moved to the kitchen to commence to pizza making. Chopping something, he said, "*Ten little soldier boys went out to dine—One choked his little self and then there were nine. Nine little soldier boys sat up very late—One overslept himself and then there were eight.*" He stopped chopping, then spread out what he'd just prepped on the dough laid out next to the cutting board. "Do you know that one? That rhyme?"

I shook my head. "No—don't think so." I made a face in reflect of the not-so-happy words he'd just spouted.

"It's the origin for the novel," he added, laughing at my grimaced expression.

"Tell me," I said. I liked interesting stories, as long as they weren't about me.

"Well, you're familiar with Agatha Christie, yes?"

"Yup," I said, crossing the room to the kitchen. That name I knew. I pulled out one of the two stools set up under the big kitchen island. It was like the one in my kitchen only smaller. Then I sat and waited for more.

"Okay," he said, moving the pizza to the oven. He set the timer for 15 minutes, then began again. "It's a best-seller, first printed in 1939. The book details a sequence of murders on an island. Each one of the death coincides with a line from that rhyme—it's an old nursery rhyme."

"Oh, I love a good mystery," I said. Well, most mysteries, some could be a pain in your ass.

"This one is a classic," he said with enthusiasm. He continued to tidy up as he told me about the novel. It was about how a group of people who get lured to the island under various pretexts like a job offer, summer holiday, or to meet up with old friends. All these people had been previously involved in the deaths of other people but had also escaped further legal ramifications. "After dinner the first night, a gramophone recording is played, and the guests and both servants are informed why they've been brought to the island—to pay for their actions," he further explained. "No one else is on the island, but they can't escape because of the distance to the mainland and the bad weather."

"Wowsers—I'd be freaked," I said. "Then what happens?"

He laughed amused by my eagerness. The buzzer on the stove sounded, informing us the pizza was ready. Grabbing oven mitts, he turned away and opened the oven.

I just about died. The smell that wafted out added to the comfortable feeling of the place. My stomach made a series of food-love grumbles.

Setting the pizza pan on the big cutting board, he said, "Gradually, all ten get killed, each in a manner that matches the deaths in that nursery rhyme. But, it seems that nobody else is left alive on the island by the time the last person is killed." He stopped to use a cutter to divide up the pizza. "There's a postscript confession in the novel, revealing how the killings were done and who did it," he added.

"That sounds familiar—was it a movie ever?" I asked, refocusing on the pizza.

"Ya—it was an oldie, called *Ten Little Indians*. There may have been a few remakes too," he said. "But the premise is used a lot in movies. Did you ever watch the *Saw* movies?"

"A few. They have the same payback theme for sure," I said. "Gotta love a good twist." As for the mystery that had been circling around me, it seemed to have stopped with its twists lately, but still there had been no straight paths to follow either.

"Wine?" Redmond asked, interrupting my musing, moving the food into the living room.

"Sure—can I help?" I asked, selecting two of the wine glasses that hung below the wine rack.

"Those are perfect," he said, dashing back, seizing and placing a bottle of red wine from the rack under his arm. He grabbed a fancy opener from the drawer, scooped up the plates he'd set out, and followed me to the couch. He dashed back a second time, returning with two napkins and two placemats, setting them up on the long narrow coffee table in front of the couch where I now sat.

"This looks amazing," I said. The anticipation was killing me.

"Dig in—help yourself," he said, handing me a paper napkin.

"Don't mind if I do." Without hesitation, and while he popped the cork on the wine, I plated two pieces of the fresh pizza on my plate, then repeated the plating doing the same for him.

A third piece and a second glass of wine later, I was comfortably sprawled out on the big couch. We'd chatted about movies, food and books. I'd admitted to loving the first two, but was a late bloomer to reading.

Still, I was enjoying reading, despite the late start and was gaining a love for books. "My mom and brothers liked to read. I used to love being read to when I was a kid," I shared.

"I'm sorry about your mom," he said off subject. Then he added a few sweet comments about my aunt, and how the recent loss of my friend Louise must be still weighing on me. We further talked about loss and how he'd yet to experience anything like the death of a loved one. As dialog continued, he asked me kind questions about Louise and her family, responding to my words with encouraging and heartfelt sentiments.

"I'm not sure what was worse—losing them or watching them in pain," I told him. "It's nothing you can prepare yourself for."

"Were your mom and aunt close," he asked.

I nodded. "Like two peas in a pod—my mother would say."

"How about I read you a story?" he said, shifting gears. He glanced back over the couch towards that stack of books near the window. "How about the Agatha Christie one?" he suggested.

Was this guy for real? He seemed real enough. *Go with it, Lynn,* my mind said. So, I did. "Sure—I'm game," I told him.

He got up and grabbed the book off the stack. Returning he made himself comfy at the other end of the lengthy couch, stretching out his long legs against mine. He cracked open the book, gave me a little grin, and then he began to read.

Chapter 9

My eyes burst open, and I had the abrupt realization I was not in my bed. Seemingly, the good food, good wine, good company, and the good story, had all satiated me into blissful comfort *and* sleep, because I was still on Redmond's couch, under a soft blue blanket.

I lifted my head to check the clock when jean-clad legs appeared blocking my view. A tray of steaming fresh coffee and muffins were set on the coffee table in front of me. Mortified, I said, "Oh my gawd—I'm so sorry, the wine must have done a number on me last night." I shifted and sat up, noting the digital clock next to the TV said 9:15 a.m..

"It was late when you drifted off—but I hope it wasn't the company," he said, resting down beside me on the couch. He was wearing another faded t-shirt, this time a pale green one. "Lemon muffin?" he asked, pointing to the tray. "Coffee?"

"I'm really sorry—I shouldn't have stayed so late," I said, leaning forward and taking in a whiff of the coffee. "Why didn't you wake me?" My stomach growled. "I should really get going."

"Oh gosh—don't worry about it. It's fine. Was nice having someone here," he said. "Did you sleep okay?"

"I did, actually. Not bad for a night on the couch." I looked around the room as if searching for an escape route. Not that I wanted to be away from him, more I wanted to escape my embarrassment.

"I'd have moved you to the bed and slept on the couch myself but thought it might startle you when you woke up in a strange bed." He gave me a boyish grin. "Stay—have something to eat."

My stomach growled again. "Okay," I said, smiling. I had to appreciate his happy-go-lucky whatever-goes kind of attitude. I took a paper napkin off the tray, followed by one of the big muffins. I'd slept in my clothes and hadn't brushed my teeth, but how could I resist the fresh coffee and those delicious looking muffins. I couldn't, *and* I couldn't seem to resist him either. "Coffee and a muffin… but then I have to go," I conceded. "I've been missing in action at home, need to circle back with my roomie today."

"I'd like to meet Luc. Maybe the two of you could come see the band play next weekend?" he tossed out. "One of my clients—the guys you saw yesterday, are playing at a local place."

"He'd like that I'm sure," I said. "I'll check in with him today—tell him about it."

"I didn't freak you out with all the spooky talk last night, did I?" he asked, picking up the book he'd been reading to me last night.

"Pfffff," I let out. Good thing I had my napkin to my mouth or I would have spit out my coffee. "No. I enjoy the *spooky* stuff. And it makes it more fun when you have someone else who likes it too, seriously." Once he had a taste of my spooky side, we'd see who freaks whom out. I laughed.

"Phew—good. I didn't want you to think I was over the top or obsessed with the macabre or anything," he tossed back.

After the morning snack, and a quick dash to the bathroom, Redmond walked me to my car still parked out front at the studio. The place didn't open until noon on Saturdays, so there'd be no onlookers to see me leave. Not that I had anything to be ashamed of, nothing had happened, but I *was* still in my same clothes from the day before. After a quick hug and a, *"Text me when you get home later,"* from Redmond, I was pulling out of the parking area and on my way home.

It was close to 10:30 a.m. when I pulled into my driveway. Before getting out of the car, I sent Redmond a text.

I'm home. Thanks for a great evening and wonderful morning. You'll have to tell me where you got those muffins, they were amazing.

As I walked through the front door of the house, my phone chimed a text message notification. *Redmond.*

Thank you for coming over. I had a great time too. Hope we can do it again soon. I'll send you the details about the gig later. Have a great rest of day!
I made those muffins btw LOL

He made them? The guy makes homemade pizza, I should have known. *Talk about sending me an angel,* I mused, heading for the kitchen.

"Hey," I said, strolling in. Luc was making scrambled eggs on the stove.

As I'd hoped, he was home alone. Well, almost alone. Raven was there too, chewing his morning meal and his head came up from his bowl as I entered.

"Hey back, stranger," Luc said. "Hungry?"

I laughed.

"What?" he asked, holding the spatula out like a sword.

"Just ate, actually," I said, climbing up on a stool at the island. "Sorry I haven't shown my face much... but hey, thanks for the leftovers. Food was great, a godsend."

"No prob," he said, and went back to his scrambling.

"Been a difficult few weeks," I added. "Eating—let alone cooking, hadn't been a priority for me. So it helped." Then I explained to him the *why*, about Louise and how I hadn't wanted to talk to anyone about it or talk about much of anything for that matter.

"I know," Luc said. "The girls told Derek, and he mentioned it. Said to keep an eye on you, but you were never around. Saw you were eating though, and doing laundry, etc. Figured like you said—that you didn't want to talk about it." He gave me a sympathetic grin. "You want to talk now?" He set his breakfast on the island, then sat down across from me.

"No—not really, but I'm doing okay. I've had someone I could chat with about it already," I reassured him. I put my elbows on the counter, resting my chin in my palms. "I met someone."

"Oh reeeeally," he said, giving the back of my hand a little poke with his fork.

"His name's Redmond. Met him at the Halloween party," I said. "He was the event host. Owns a music studio in the Grove."

"Music studio—that's cool. Darius said he had a great time at Halloween—lots of attention from the girls," Luc said, with a chuckle. "Guess you did well too—new man and all." He poked me again.

"Stooop it," I said, swatting away his fork. "He's a good guy, Luc. We're just doing the friend-thing." I grinned. "But he's very cute, I have to say."

"Oh yuck—I don't wanna hear it," he said, countering and making a face like he'd ate something sour.

"Best part is he likes weird stuff—mysterious stuff," I tossed out. "Told me there're all sorts of mysterious stuff around where he lives. Like how the studio has ghosts he thinks."

"Good thing he likes *weird*—if he's gonna hang out with you," he shot back.

"Shut up." I swatted his arm causing him to spill his fork full of eggs.

He scooped up the fallen eggs, shoved it in his mouth, and grinned. Then he went on to tell me about his plans for the upcoming holidays, and how he would do Thanksgiving *again,* this time with Dunya and Mitra, but they would be going up to see Dunya's daughter for it.

"Gosh—I still haven't even met Aleah yet. Tell her *thanks* for the Halloween costume from me—would ya?"

"Ya, sure—will do," he said, moving to do his breakfast cleanup. "Looks like she'll be staying up there once she graduates—already has an internship set up. And she's got a new boyfriend Dunya said. He's from the same city as the university she goes to. They'll be staying there with his family for Christmas. It's the reason they we're going up to see her for Thanksgiving."

"Makes sense. It'll be a good time for you guys, I'm sure," I said.

"Speaking of good times—Derek is coming down next weekend," he announced.

Chapter 10

It was the end of the slowest week ever, especially since Dr. Melanie had told me I'd have the whole weekend off.

Apparently, the ward was doing training all weekend with the new mobile NICU. She'd said I was free to watch, but the potential was that I'd just be in the way. Part of me wanted to be there to see the new program implemented, but the other part of me wanted to have my whole weekend open since Derek was coming, *and* just in case a certain someone wanted to hang out.

Redmond had called midweek confirming the new band was playing Friday night at *The Warehouse,* a bar in an old industrial now trendy hipster area. He had suggested my roomie and I should come check them out. Luc had said he was in for sure when I told him about it. I'd also suggested he bring Darius too, that it would be a great outing while Derek was here, since neither of us had seen Derek in forever, and I hadn't seen Darius since Halloween. Luc had offered to pick up Derek from the airport since I had to head into work. Plans were set.

Today was the big day, the twins were going home with their adoptive parents. I didn't have to be there, but the boys held a special place in my heart, and after so much time with them I wanted to be present for the hand off, *and* to say goodbye to my now healthy Charges.

"I'll meet you and the guys at the bar," I told Luc over the phone.

"Okay—cool. See you there," he said.

"Won't be long—see you soon." I hung up, tucked my cell in my pocket and then pushed open the door to the hospital's family greeting room. I waved to the excited parents.

"Lynn is here now. I'll go watch over the other boys," Shamsiel said, then he vanished. Gabriel stood alone now next to the waiting parents, shielded by his veil.

Glancing up from chatting with the parents, I spotted two nurses in swaddling robes enter the room. Each nurse carried one twin in their arms. No more feeding tubes needed for these guys.

Gabriel continued his observations as the nurses approached.

"Here they come," I said, giving the nervous new mom a soft rub on her back.

"Rylie and Finn," the anxious father whispered.

The twins were wrapped in soft flannel blankets with little elephants, hippos, tigers, and giraffes on them, similar in feel to the fabric of the swaddling robes. I'd picked these blankets out especially for them. No more repetitively used hospital baby blanket for these two now. One twin donned a light blue toque on his head, the other wore a light green one. They no longer resembled the sick babies they had been these past months, and now they were going home with their new parents. "Boys, meet your new mommy and daddy," I said to the babies, swaddled in the arms of the nurses. "Mom, Dad… here are your new sons.

"You're in good hands," Gabriel said into the ether, as he vanished.

He arrived to find Shamsiel on the street out in front of the bar. A dozen of the notorious 20 leaders were also there, standing at precise intervals encircling the front of the building. Not that he'd expected to see any of the leaders, but he noted there were no Horsemen, no Armaros, and two of the leaders, Araquel and Ramiel, were also not in attendance. "What's going on? Gabriel asked. He shifted his gaze from the leaders to the inner bar and then back again.

"They want to see for themselves," Shamsiel said. "Armaros has been busy whispering in their ears and now they want to see if it's true."

"If what's true?" Gabriel tossed back, watching as the dozen leaders took one collective pace forward.

"Here she comes," Shamsiel said, moving to stand near Gabriel at an entrance to the bar.

On the drive up the road, I'd noticed how the old industrial area had now become an artsy district with bars, galleries, and small independent breweries. Amazing graffiti art covered a lot of the warehouse's exteriors, giving the old grey warehouse buildings a cool colourful vibe. Redmond had reserved me a parking space in the rear of the club. As he'd instructed, I pulled in around the back side of the building and took one of the spots marked *Credente Studios*. Out of my car, I ventured around to the front.

The Warehouse bar itself had three rollup doors kept open during the *open* hours. Stepping in through one of the open rollup doors, I glanced up to see hinged ceiling skylight windows and massive ceiling fans. It was a comfortable temperature inside, but it hadn't been an overly warm night either. Redmond had told me about the place, what to expect, and that back before AC, these large ceiling fans and windows were all that was there to help keep the place cool.

Even from outside I'd heard the music booming, the band rocking, and now inside I saw that the patrons were dancing. Pushing through a group of people dancing, I spotted Derek and Luc at a big table, their heads facing towards two large men across the way from them, Darius and Redmond. They were at the bar chatting. I continued towards the table and noticed Redmond lean over the bar to say something to the bartender, just as Darius turned back around.

Darius had four pitchers of beer, two in each of his massive hands as he began walking towards the table where our friends sat. Then he stopped.

Without warning, the four pitchers dropped from Darius's grip. In one swift movement he spun back towards the bar. Reaching out he picked up a long industrial metal table. Turning back again, his face revealed an expression I'd never seen on him before—*RAGE,* burning across his face. He raised the table over his head, stalking towards my other two friends. Luc and Derek had their hands up as if in protection from what was coming.

"I thought he chose the light!" Gabriel roared, seeing Darius's expression.

Above, the ceiling fans and glass skylight windows shook. Jagged zig-zags splintered through the high windows, and one of the ceiling fan faltered tilting at a dangerous angle.

Outside, the 12 leaders stole two paces forward.

At the sound of crashing glass, Shamsiel was at Darius's side.

"Oh my gawd," I screamed, pushing forward in their direction, but there was… nothing to worry about.

Darius had covered our friends with the table, shielding them from the falling fan and glass. They weren't hurt, no one was. Well, almost no one. The remnants lay all around, but Darius was covered in tiny nicks from the shattered glass. Blood streamed down the back and sides of his head and neck, and across his bare forearms.

"Darius," I said, touching the front of his t-shirt. He said nothing, only appeared stunned once again at what had happened, just as he had with both the tree incident in my yard and my nearly getting killed by that truck outside work.

"Lynn," Redmond's voice came from behind me.

I turned. "What the hell happened?" I asked.

Several bouncers and bar staff shuffled around us now pushing back debris with big brooms. The band had stopped playing but there were loud murmurs from the patrons coming from all sides. Derek and Luc were up now and over with us checking out Darius for injuries.

"I have no idea," Redmond said. "Let me take him to the back—get him cleaned up and some first aid.

"Ya—okay—good," I said, and followed him as he guided Darius to the back. Luc and Derek followed behind me.

"He did it!" Shamsiel confirmed, appearing once again outside with Gabriel. "He saved the Cipher and the Theologian."

Together Gabriel and Shamsiel observed as the dozen leaders stepped back and then moved off. One of the leaders nodded his understanding of what had transpired, what they had *witnessed*.

"We need to find The Horsemen," Gabriel said, and the two disappeared.

Gabriel and Shamsiel arrived at the edge of the Rickenbacker Causeway. They found The Horsemen, *Conquest, War, Famine,* and

Death lingering on the coastline across from Biscayne Bay near the connection of Miami to the barrier islands.

"Something we can help you with," Kokabiel asked, questioning the new arrivals, his long white hair blowing in the evening ocean breeze. The others only turned and stared at their fellow Angels. Their expressions gave hint to annoyance as if to say you've interrupted us from enjoying the view.

"We need to discuss Armaros," Gabriel said, stepping closer.

"And all the rules he has broken," Shamsiel added.

"What has he done now," Zaqiel asked.

He indeed resembled that 80s punk singer Billy-what's his name, but it was really just the hair, Gabriel considered, then said, "He has directly misled the chosen four, using magic and deception."

"We are all free to do what we want now, Gabriel," Baraqel said, his jet-black hair gleaming hints of blue against the night's moonlit sky.

"No, you are free to aid or influence your own Charges—not the Charges of others," Shamsiel reminded.

Baraqel glared back at him. They were all fallen, they all knew the rules, but Armaros had seemingly made his own.

"Explain your concerns, Gabriel," Zaqiel demanded.

"There have been many occasions," Gabriel said. "Too many."

"Pick one," Zaqiel demanded again, though he was in no position to demand anything from an Archangel such as Gabriel. He knew he treaded on delicate ground, but he was annoyed with the interruption.

"One incident in particular, occurred when Armaros had been chatting with another leader. This leader had been watching over a descendant, a pregnant unwed-soon-to-be mother," Gabriel said.

"And?" Zaqiel said.

"And he saw me… hovering nearby," Gabriel added.

"So?" Azazel queried, taking his turn.

"Well, I hadn't known he saw me, and not that it should matter to him, but a few months later he saw me again around two other descendants from the same leader, sisters."

"Why the concern for these descendants?" Kokabiel added in question.

Shamsiel took a deep breath. "We both realize now he'd also spotted the baby, and that these sisters spoke of her adoption," Shamsiel informed them. "They were the perfect family to place the baby that was on its way. All sons—no daughters."

"Armaros knew I was *not* part of the original agreement the others had made," Gabriel said, "but he must have found it odd I'd been watching. Michael, Raphael, Uriel and Vretil were the only ones who had known about my *request.* And I'd believed there was no threat, considering this family was strong with boys."

"He's a curious bastard," Azazel said, his fury matching the red of his hair. "But I'm not sure why he would care if you were watching this family."

"My understanding is he must have returned to the other woman—the pregnant one, and found no baby," Shamsiel said.

"At first, he must have assumed I'd been tasked with something to do with this child, but his curiosity may have sparked after having seen me hovering around one of *his* descendants—a doctor."

"He didn't care about this woman doctor—only kept an eye on her because she worked with cancer patients," Shamsiel told them. "I'd overheard from one leader say Armaros did this hoping to find the Charges, cancer being so prevalent."

"Still, how could he find them?" Kokabiel asked.

"He—like all of us, knows how the secret changes hands. And on the rare occasion the mother is forced to pass the secret if struck by illness. He was waiting and watching—to see if one of the mothers sought treatment, perhaps hoping one of the Charges would be present, inadvertently revealing themselves," Shamsiel explained. "It would have been a long shot, but he was desperate.

"He's spent most of his existence since the fall, trying to find the Charges through each generation. Twice now he's upset the lines. But these women got things back on track as you know," Gabriel directed at Shamsiel.

"Whose—when did he interfere in the lines?" Kokabiel questioned.

"Vretil's," Gabriel responded. "1592. Esther, the wife of the Jewish merchant. She took care of things for the royal harem and was friends with the Sultan's favorite wife, Safeyeh. There was disruption among the other employees due to their friendship."

"Armaros was the reason for that disruption," Shamsiel interjected, before Gabriel continued.

"The Sultan had Esther and her son executed because of this, but not before she shared the story and secrets with Safeyeh," Gabriel continued.

"Who later passed the story on to a lesser wife," Shamsiel interrupted again.

Gabriel glowered at his friend for the interruption. "Yes," Gabriel agreed. "This wife was dismissed of her duties due to *an illness*—a hidden pregnancy. She left with the codex, a growing belly, and the secret."

Kokabiel nodded his new understanding of the events. "Who else?" he asked.

"Michael's," Shamsiel said, cutting a glance Baraqel's way.

"I know," Baraqel said. "It's clear now. It was Melissa—*Priestess of Demeter* and Cynisca, the Greek princess of Sparta and the first woman to win in the Olympic Games. The other priestesses attacked Melissa when she wouldn't tell them about her meeting with the princess."

"The secret was safe with Cynisca, but the women tore Melissa to pieces because she wouldn't tell them," Gabriel finished.

Baraqel bowed his head.

Shamsiel stepped up to his fellow leaders. "But it's his more recent influences that we're most concerned about, and I don't mean him showing his face either," Shamsiel said.

"What more has he done?" Zaqiel asked, with more empathy and less demand this time.

"He appeared to the four Charges claiming to be Uriel," Gabriel stated. "He gave them false information that has halted their progress."

Kokabiel crossed his arms over his massive chest. "If the fifth makes a stand—we will stand with them," Kokabiel said, turning to face the other Horsemen. The other three nodded in agreement. "But should the fifth fail… we will carry out our duty of the seven seals." He turned away and continued to gaze back out over the water.

Chapter 11

Like the generous guy he was, Redmond stayed to aid the club owner and the band. We'd only had time for a quick goodbye before I'd headed off back home to wait for Derek and Luc.

"How is he?" I asked, from my spot in the living room when the two of them came through the door. They'd taken Darius home to make sure he got there okay, and to clarify if he knew what had happened.

Luc set his keys on the front table and the two of them stepped into the living room.

"What happened to you?" I directed at Derek.

"He's fine," Derek said, glancing down at his shirt. He had on one of my favorite t-shirts of his. Derek wasn't your stereotypical computer geek with the dorky dark-rimmed glasses, or the pocket pen protector. In fact, he wouldn't be caught dead with one. His style was more hipster/surfer, and this particular t-shirt was light grey, with a replica of a poster that hung in the office of one *Fox Mulder*, of the X-files, with the spaceship and the phrase *I want to believe* on it. Sadly, the t-shirt was spattered with red flecks. He must have gotten Darius's blood on it trying to help the big guy out of the car and into his house. "We got him something to eat on the way—seemed to help," Derek added. "Other than a few nicks, he was practically unscathed. Little fuzzy in the memory department—but fine just the same."

"He was a little stunned when we'd left him. But we told the big guy we'd check on him in the morning," Luc said, as Derek strode off down the hall.

"That's good. And I think you need to talk to him about *things*—really talk," I stated.

"Ya he needs to understand what he may be a part of. Not everyone believes in things otherworldly," Luc said, settling down on the adjacent couch.

"So, you believe Darius is involved too then," I asked.

"Derek told me that your girlfriends still think these guys referenced in the codex are men—a patriarchal line much like theirs. They can't find proof of it but it's what makes sense to them." Luc shrugged. "They figure stuff gets passed down to these men like it had with the women, but I believe it's divine," he said. "Almost got Derek convinced too, but he's still leaning towards ghosts because he's not a religious person—no disrespect to me he says." Luc grinned. "They're still waiting for the Guardian and the Believer, Derek told me too.

"I'm a believer, but I can't be the one they are looking for," I said.

"Nor me," he says, "since I'm the Theologian. Remember, you called me that back before all of this." He grinned again. "Derek believes I have a part in this—through helping him."

"Derek, you, and like I told you before, I believe Darius is this Guardian," I said.

"I think you're right."

"Tonight, was another good show of why," I added, but I didn't need any more proof.

"No shit," Luc confirmed.

"Have they figured out what the Guardian is supposed to do?" I asked.

"No—other than guard something or someone, obviously," he said. "But if it is Darius, why would he be here, and not with the girls?"

"Could be he's here to guard you—The Theologian." I shrugged.

"Don't forget he protected Derek too—The Cipher."

"Someone call for a Cipher?" Derek tossed out, as he returned to the living room. He sat down next to Luc. He'd returned wearing a new clean t-shirt. "What are you two talking about?"

"Same thing you and I had been talking about—before we picked up Darius to go out. The Guardian," Luc said

"Ya about that. There's more to why I think it's Darius," I stated. I continued to describe the different references I'd found about the fall of The Watchers, how it mentioned that these angels had fathered something call *Nephilim*. "There are actual references to them found in both Jewish and Christian texts," I explained. "The Watchers and the Nephilim were often portrayed as evil creatures or monsters while others describe them as gentle giants and beings of free will."

"The Fallen Angels, or Watchers, were assumed sent down by God," Derek added, "A legion of 200 angels to watch over humans." He'd also done loads of research on this topic despite his scientism. "Archangels are considered *good* Watchers, but they are not part of *The Fallen*."

"Dunya told me the story of Shamsiel—how he was once a Guardian of Eden," I said.

"She told me he's referred in Jubilees as one of the Grigori," Luc added. "That's another term used for Watchers or The Fallen."

I'd known that part too, and clearly Dunya had shared the same with him. "Then you know he was the 16th leader of the 20 leaders of the 200 Watchers who fell," I said, perhaps a little too smug.

"And Mitra had alleged he'd been at your door," Luc reminded.

"A leader of watchers at my door," I repeated. "You believe that?" I paused but didn't wait for his answer. "Darius is this Guardian—I know it."

Luc nodded. "Like I said—yer right, especially after tonight," Luc conceded.

"I gave the girls information about the mountain, and we'd discussed how it must have appeared to the primitive people, like an army coming over the mountain." Derek shared.

"Mountain?" I questioned.

"The *Mountain of the Chief*," Derek reminded.

I'd packed a lot of info into my head about this mystery, but I must have misplaced that gem. "Tell me again," I said, looking back and forth at the two of them.

Luc shrugged.

"I found two references in my research that stuck out," Derek started. "*Mount Hermon,* a mountain in the Anti-Lebanon mountain range. The summit spans the border between Lebanon and Syria—near Sumer, translated it means *land of the civilized lords*. The civilization had agricultural practices starting around 5000 BC. The other reference was *Mountains of Media,* mentioned in the Book of Enoch. The Watchers were said to have come down from this mountain in 5000 BC as well, and why I'd figured, they must have resembled an army. The first four women were from Sumer as mentioned in the codex.

"And the first Scribe's entry is in Sumerian," I recalled.

"Vicki has most of the codex translated, but she's struggling with the second Enochian entry—the one found between the entries of Alison's grandmother and mother."

"Derek, you had translated the first entry for them," I said. "It was about how the four guys had taught the four women and their offspring how to do stuff."

"Correct—the offspring from the women and these men," Derek said. "But what about it?"

"Well," I said. "The assumption is that they must have been great men and knowledgeable, and the reasoning behind how they were portrayed in the entry. But I still think these men weren't ordinary men—or men at all."

Ignoring my last comment, Derek said, "But the translation stated that these men—what was the anagram? *Harbored four guest*—bore four daughters."

"Yes—and didn't you say you found mention in the first entry of the Archangels vowing it would take the strength and faith of only four women and their offspring to show the full worth of the human race?" I reminded again. "You found reference to the favor they'd requested, and the conditions placed on them, and how there must always be one daughter to whom they could pass the secret and responsibilities too." These were *not* men referenced in the codex and I knew it.

"You and Luc and your angel theories," Derek said, but his expression gave me the idea he might be doing complex calculations in his head.

"It's time we bring Darius up to speed," Luc said. "And you—young lady, you may want to bring *Mr. Redmond* in on things, considering what he witnessed tonight."

"You want me... to tell him?" I questioned, glancing back and forth to each of them.

"Okay, well maybe not everything," Luc said. "Maybe just start with your *gift*—the seer stuff."

"Right, because I want the nice handsome man to think I'm crazy—right." I stood up, took a big breath and went off to my room.

"Or not," I heard Luc say, before I shut my door.

* * *

Saturday morning, the three of us sat around the kitchen island eating our breakfasts and mulling over last night's events.

Derek and I continued with sipping our coffees while Luc opted to make *the call* to Darius.

"Darius man—we need to talk," Luc said, leaving the big guy a message.

The poor guy must still have been asleep since he didn't pick up, I figured.

"Derek—we should go check on him, explain things. Tell him what's going on, what we think is going on with him," Luc suggested.

"Agreed," Derek said, finishing up his last bite of toast.

I knew the *we* meant them, but that was cool with me. I was done trying to convince anyone of what I believed. Luc *believed* what I'd said about Darius. This time he could be the one to convince both Derek *and* our big buddy of things, but without me. I wasn't angry anymore about not being included. I didn't have much of anything more to offer, the information was all there for them.

I'd agonized long enough over stuff I couldn't explain. They could figure it all out now themselves. And despite all the changes *and* the rawness that remained over losing Louise, I'd been mostly content with how my simple little life had been going of late.

"Okay, Lynn—we're heading out over to see Darius," Luc said, as he left the kitchen.

"Back in a few," Derek said, grabbing his computer tablet off the counter. "Meet up with you later?" Derek paused at the kitchen opening.

"Sure," I said, hiding my disappointment behind a sip of my coffee. He smiled and continued after Luc. A few seconds later I heard the front door shut. I was alone again. Not quite the visit I had expected having with Derek. "Looks like it's just you and me, Raven," I said to my companion lying next to my barstool.

He, "*Chuffed,*" and tickled my bare foot with his nose.

At Darius's house, Luc rang the doorbell. But no one answered. He banged on the door, but still no answer. "His car is in the drive," Luc said, stating the obvious. Then they both banged on the door together.

Mid pound, the door flung open revealing a disheveled Darius still in his blood-spattered clothes from the night before. "Hey," Darius said, weaving back and forth in the doorway.

"Darius, you okay?" Luc asked.

The two of them pushed their way in, directing Darius to the living room and the couch he'd been sleeping on. A pillow smashed up in the far corner of the couch displayed the remnants of blood flecks from Darius's now healing minor head wounds. Two open bags of chips plus five empty beer cans lay on the coffee table.

"Here, big-man," Derek said, settling their big friend back on the couch.

Luc turned and headed to the kitchen. Returning, he handed Darius a tall water-filled plastic cup. "Here—hydrate-up" Luc said. "We've got some things you need to hear."

Darius took the cup and nodded.

"Seriously, Darius, are you okay?" Derek asked, sitting down beside him.

Luc took the chair opposite.

"I'm okay, now… just tired is all," Darius said, shaking one of the empty chip bags. "And hungry."

"We'll get you some breakfast—promise, but we need to talk first," Luc said, motioning for Darius to drink more water.

Shifting to face Darius, Derek sparked up his tablet. "Internet password?" Derek asked.

Darius grabbed his phone off the coffee table and then enlarged a photo from the phone's gallery of the lengthy password.

Password entered, Derek brought up an internet search window. "Tell us about your background—family background I mean, ancestry," Derek indicated.

Darius tipped his head side to side. "I don't know much about it. My father died before I was born, and my mother doesn't talk much about the past. She did say my father was Scandinavian though, and I have his last name. Mom said she named me Darius because she'd read the name somewhere in reference to a warrior. She wanted me to be strong despite not having my father around." He paused. "I don't see my mom's side of the family and my father was an only-child, I was told. I guess it's just me and my mother."

"Right—okay," Derek said. "Let me do a couple searches on your name."

"Start with his first name," Luc suggested. "Warrior—good place to start."

"Easy enough," Derek said, typing away on his tablet. "Let's see what we get."

Darius leaned in, then leaned back again as if realizing he couldn't read upside-down. "What does my name have to do with what happened last night?" Darius questioned, his head clearing.

"Do you remember what happened?" Luc asked.

"It was that same thing—same feeling, I had when I covered Lynn from the tree branches." Darius rubbed a big palm over his strawberry-blond brush-cut head.

"There's more to that," Luc said, "but we'll get to it."

"Okay," Darius said, rubbing his head again.

"I have something," Derek said, before he read out what he'd found. "*Darius* is a Persian baby name—meaning *upholder of good*." He paused.

Luc nodded. "Fits," he said.

Going on, Derek read, "The Greek form of the name means *to possess goodness.*"

Luc nodded again.

"Says that three ancient kings of Persia had this name, including *Darius the Great,* he invaded Greece... based on historical data, he ruled over roughly 50 million people, about 44% of the world's population at the time... but he was defeated in this Battle of Marathon."

"Okay, so mostly good," Luc said. "Try the last name now."

"*Stori*—with an i," Darius aided, with a little more interest.

Derek typed it into a new search window. "Here we go," Derek said. "The surname Story, with a y originates from the Old Norse nickname Stori—with an i, which means *large* or *big.*"

"That suits," Luc said, nodding again.

"Is there more," Darius asked. "Kind of curious now myself."

Derek scrolled the page. "Yup... saaaays... The earliest Norse settlement was in the 9th century in the northwestern part of England, along the Scottish border. The English, among whom the Norse settled, spoke a similar language, but many words were spoken differently." Summarizing, Derek said, "Your surname would have been pronounced as Styr in English. It mentions Norse blood again and other Scandinavian versions of the name. It can be traced in Northern English countries like Yorkshire. It talks about all the variations in spelling with dates and places where they are found or referenced. Between the years 1272-1307 when England and Scotland were at war, it says for the next 300 years, the Story family were caught in the middle of border wars between the two kingdoms." Derek paused. "Not sure if that's helpful though."

"Wasn't there more Norse stuff you sent Lynn—way back?" Luc asked. "Something to do with the Viking Age and Norse mythology or something?"

"What does all that have to do with last night," Darius cut in.

Derek glanced at Luc. "Right," he said, then dropped his glance to search for those references he'd sent to Lynn.

"Darius... how much do you know about secret societies.... or the supernatural?" Luc inquired.

"Secret societies—not much, but the supernatural—tons. My mom is very superstitious—believes in all of it," Darius said, nodding this time. "I have to admit, I'm a believer in some of it too. Weird shit happens around me I can't explain—like last night."

"Well, we've got some more of that weird shit to tell you about," Luc began. Then he explained everything to Darius, starting with the journal Lynn found.

For the next four hours between Luc's recollection of the list of weird and Derek's relaying of the facts, everything was laid out for The Guardian. Derek told him about ancient Sumer, the year 5000AD, while Luc matched it with its connection to The Fallen and Enoch. They talked about Norse mythology, the *tales of worthy men,* myths, legends, and the beliefs in supernatural beings like Giants and Odin, and the Valkyries who Luc explained were comparable to angels.

Darius hadn't said much through the discussion, but he took in a lot of deep breaths, letting them out with the occasional head nod. But then he said, "Tell me about the angels—the Valkyries."

"They were originally known as evil spirits of massacre, dark angels of death," Luc said. "They soared over the battlefields like vultures, killing warriors in honor of Odin. Choosing the heroes from battle and taking them to *Valhalla.*"

"Valhalla?" Darius questioned.

"It's considered a heavenly place of honor for Odin's spirit army."

"There's another reference about them where they are said to be Odin's Shield-Maidens who soared over the battlefields as swan-like maidens or beautiful horse-mounted Amazons who serve those heroes in Valhalla. It's from a 13th century Icelandic story where the heroine was a beautiful fallen Valkyrie.

"That sounds better," Darius said. "I'll take beautiful Amazons over vultures."

"Me too," Derek laughed out.

"Read him the description of the Norse descendant," Luc suggested. "History and ancestry aside, this validates why we believe you're a part of this.

"Definitely," Derek said, bringing up the original and translated words on screen. "The translation goes as such, *He will be strong of arm and heart. Towering over the average man, pale complexion, and fair hair. Though large in stature, he hides his strength and his speed. He will be…"*

"A trained hug," Luc cut in with a laugh. "Sorry—that was the original translation before Derek solved the anagram."

Derek grinned and shook his head, then he restarted. *"He will be… The Guardian,"* Derek emphasized, *"… and must choose his path, good or evil."*

"You're The Guardian, Darius," Luc stated. "You are part of this like Derek and I am."

"Cipher, Theologian, and *Guardian,*" Darius said.

"Remember you saved Lynn—from that truck outside work?" Luc reminded.

"And in her backyard… the hospital too—well, I didn't save her, but I felt compelled to—that she needed me," Darius recalled.

"And last night—you saved Luc and me," Derek added.

"I believe it—all of it," Darius said, before they could continue.

"You do?" Luc questioned, cutting a glance from Darius to Derek.

"I can't explain it—but I feel… it's real… and seriously, man, I'm tired of trying to figure out what the hell was happening to me. Now I don't have to do it alone.

"We figured you'd be thinking we were all nuts," Derek tossed out.

"Been feeling pretty nuts myself," Darius gave him. He stood then and strode off towards the kitchen rubbing his stomach. "Nice to know I'm not losing my mind," he called out to them.

"There's more," Luc called back. They still had to tell him about the Halloween conjuring and the gathering.

Chapter 12

Last night had taken a bad turn. It hadn't been the evening I or any of us, including Redmond, had expected, I was sure. And this had been the third—no, fourth time, Darius had gone into beast-mode to protect a friend.

I knew what I believed about Darius and about his role in all this. It seemed everyone had a role but me, but it also meant it wasn't my problem either. Right now it would be Luc and Derek who would be preoccupied with it all. Me on the other hand, I had the whole weekend off.

On that happy thought, I sent Redmond off a quick text to say,

Good morning.

To my delight, Redmond wrote back,

Good morning to you
Would you be interested in coming to hang out at my place?

That was an easy question. I wrote back,

Sure. I'll be over in a few after I get cleaned up.

He sent another quick response,

I have fresh cranberry lemon muffins in the oven

Food motivated, I did my fastest shower and get ready routine. Short of an hour, my hair still barely dry, I locked the front door and was off.

On the drive over, I rehashed what Luc had said about telling Redmond everything, or rather, to at least start with my seer thing. My new friend had shared an interest in the paranormal, the odd—the weird—the unusual, *and* since he'd been witness to Darius's *unusual* behavior last night, maybe I could tell him about some of the weird things from my world. Especially since he said he believed in things like it. Perhaps he wouldn't think I was crazy.

Redmond was out on the landing at the top of the stairs with the door open when I pulled up. The minute I hit the top of the steps, I could already smell the fresh baked muffins.

"Welcome," he said, extending an arm to the wonderfully fragrant way in. He was wearing old faded blue-jeans and a white t-shirt. The shirt had a retro cartoon image of *The Archies* on it with the words *Sugar, Sugar* under it.

"Favorite band?" I teased, tapping the image on his shirt. "What is that terrible smell?" I crinkled my nose.

"Get in there," he joked, pushing me along through the doorway with his other hand. I pretended to stumble and gave him a suspicious look over my shoulder. "*Veronica's* hot by the way," he added.

"Ya, but Archie preferred *Betty*," I tossed back, adjusting my ponytail.

"Coffee?" he asked, shifting to the kitchen and holding up a big blue mug.

"I could manage a cup—sure." At the kitchen island, I pulled out a barstool and sat. "Those... smell... aaaamaaazzziiiing," I drew out.

"Yer just here for the food, aren't you?" he questioned, yet amused.

I grinned. "Why else would I be here?" I said as a rhetorical question. "Not like yer good company or anything." I added an eye roll.

"I'll remember that the next time I hear your stomach growl," he shot back, plating two big muffins, and taking his turn to grin.

"Think you can control me with food—do ya?" I tossed back.

"Yup," he said, sliding a plate my way.

I ogled the big pale-yellow muffin with its deep-red cranberries poking free of the baked dough. "Dammit," I said defeated, picking up the beautiful muffin. I took a big bite, and Redmond laughed. He knew he had me. I'm weak and I had that hollow-leg thing to contend with. I grinned, muffin pushing out the corner of my mouth.

"You'll have to tell me what your favorite foods are," he said. "That way I can bribe you to come over more often." He grabbed a large cookbook off the back counter.

I recognized the famous title on the book. *The Joy of Cooking*.

"I should write a book called, *the joy of eating*," I laughed out.

"We could be a team for that one," he said back.

I grinned at him again savoring another bite. I was grateful for the invite over and I was also grateful for the food banter as I hadn't figured out where to start with explaining all the weird stuff there was to tell him. I decided it could wait until at least after we'd enjoyed the muffins. Better to freak someone out once they had a happy stomach rather than an empty one, I supposed.

"You like vanilla creamer—right?" he confirmed, reaching into the fridge to pull out a creamer bottle. Shaking it first, he then flipped the lid and poured a dose into the mug. Then he filled the mug with the brewed coffee he'd made. He filled a second mug for himself, then slid out the other bar stool and sat down next to me to enjoy his own muffin.

We sipped and savored in silence, throwing each other the occasional subtle grin. It was nice relaxing together like this, nice not having to force conversation. Aaaaand, I wasn't ready to dish on the weird just yet.

At noticing that I'd finished the last of my muffin, he said, "Let's go for a little walk—to the park across the way."

"Sure," I said. I was game for a walk if it meant more weirdness talk avoidance. I got up from my seat at the island.

As we left the apartment, Redmond said, "Have you ever been to *The Barnacle* before?" He pointed to the entry opening across the way.

"Nope," I said, as I hit the last step of the outside staircase. I'd always figured the entrance was to a private community, hadn't known a park was there. The park was across from his place, and it meant we would have to cross the busy road that made up the main passage through The Grove.

We stood at the edge of the road waiting for a decent opening in the slow but steady moving cars for a Saturday morning. When our chance came, Redmond reached back and grabbed my hand, and the two of us ran across.

Past the initial overhanging tree branches and deeper into the entrance, there was a tiny park ranger booth. Redmond walked up and paid the woman in the booth the entry fee, then together we strolled off along the pathway through to the historical park.

Once through the opening to the main area, Redmond pointed out a beautiful house that was naturally dated from a simpler time. "It was built in 1891," he said. It was the home of Ralph Middleton *Munroe* as the historical information plaque indicated. "He was one of Coconut Grove's most influential pioneers," Redmond added. "Munroe preserved the forest on the land, cutting out only a trail through the tree hammock—barely wide enough for a vehicle."

"Hidden gem," I said, as we walked towards the far part of the landscape and waters of Biscayne Bay.

"They say the park looks much as it did in Munroe's day, there's even replicas of two of his sailboats. It's a place to enjoy simple pleasures," Redmond shared. "A walk with an old or *new* friend, perhaps a picnic on the lawn. They allow you to bring dogs for a walk here too."

It offered a glimpse of frontier life, a time when everyone traveled to and from Miami by boat during *The Era of the Bay*, Redmond had called it.

We walked the length of the property and around the home, then back along near the water.

"It's a shame I hadn't known this place existed when I lived near here," I said.

"They do an old-time dance here sometimes," Redmond added.

"That sounds fun," I said, turning away from the water to take in the expanse of the grounds. There was a side hedge next to the water that stretched along the property all the way to an open-air pavilion. "Lots of room for it."

"Like you said, *a hidden* gem," Redmond echoed.

At the end of the hedge near us, there were smatterings of tiny butterflies, some light blue and others with pale yellow wings like those I'd seen around my home. They fluttered in small groups traveling from bush to bush as if on a mission. A lone butterfly, much larger than the rest, a monarch style coloured one, rested on an outstretch branch containing a single flower. The orange and black wings opened and closed like the rhythm of relaxed breath.

"Hi Mom," I whispered to my little guardian.

"I bet yer getting hungry again?" Redmond said, from behind me.

"How did ya know?" I asked. The butterfly took off then, riding the breeze towards the park's entrance.

"I think I've got you figured out, Westlake," he said, with a little chin tilt of confidence.

I laughed. "Feed me," I said with a groan, doing my best Frankenstein walk, arms outstretched in front.

At the road past the exit from the park we waited again for an opening. When a poky driver gave us an opportunity, Redmond once again grabbed my hand, and we ran.

This time when we got to the other side, he kept hold of my hand. I liked handholding. I especially liked how it was with him, how small my hand seemed in his, and how *safe* I felt.

Back in the apartment I checked my phone and saw that Luc had sent a text.

He'd written a long one,

> *Just checking in. Derek is on board with Darius as guardian, but I still need to convince him of the divine part. Darius believes everything we told him, it's great. Gonna hang out and go over the other things Derek found. We'll continue working together on things for the girls. Derek is going to try to convince them of Darius's involvement. But until the girls know more, they'll probably keep that spot open—Derek told me. I'm frustrated, and I sympathize with what you must have felt when no one believed you. Sorry about that.*

Good, I'd thought. At least I wasn't alone in that.

"Everything okay," Redmond asked, pulling food items from the fridge.

"Ya-ya—just Luc giving me the update on Darius," I told him.

"He good?" he asked, as he continued rummaging through the cupboard next to the stove, the one filled with a variety of spices and tins. "Do you like Indian food? I make a mean *Chicken Korma*."

"Yes... and yes," I said in response to both inquiries. "Mmmmm I haven't had Indian food since I lived in Ottawa. Used to frequent a place called *Rangoli*, near where I used to work. They had the best lunch specials," I said, remembering it with fondness.

"Late lunch—errr early dinner, okay with you?" he asked.

"Sure. Can I help? We can make enough so that if we get hungry later—we'll have something to snack on."

He smiled shaking his head and pulled more food from the fridge.

"Redmond...," I started. He stopped his food prep-organizing and stared at me, holding spice bottles out in each hand. "... you know how you said you liked weird creepy stuff," I finished.

"Uhm, ya," he said, still holding the spice bottles out, a worried expression spreading across his face.

"Ready to hear some of myyyyyy weird-creepy stuff?" I gave him an innocent grin hoping to clear the worry from his face.

With relief he smiled back at me. "Ready," he laughed out and continued with this food prep.

I wasn't sure of where to begin, now that I had the bag of cats open. Letting the first cat out of the bag, I led off by describing the dream I'd had about Louise before she'd died. From there the cats jumped out on their own and I shared all things related to my spidy-sense.

Redmond seemed eager to hear what I had to say, even gave me a, *"Cool, tell me more"* when I'd paused. There was no sense trying to herd the cats back into the bag, so I pulled in more courage and added the stuff I've seen, from the past and the present, then I continued on with the photos of me with wings, and the guy—*angel* from the other photo. I further explained how Darius had saved me a few times in the past bringing the talk full circle to the most recent of events.

Over dinner and tidying up, I told him about Dunya and her grandmother, about the mysterious guy at the door and the whole *seer* thing, and about Derek trying to find answers to my weird happenings.

But I stopped at telling him about the journal etc., plus the guys I'd seen on Halloween and all that came with it.

"I'm captivated—really," he said, when I'd stopped.

What I'd told Redmond made for a patchy story, but he hadn't seemed phased or put off, *and* he'd seemed to believe me. Either that or he'd just been merely entertained, I wasn't sure.

"What do you sense about me?" he asked.

"You… this place," I said, waving a hand out towards the rest of the apartment. "Feels fantastic—comfortable, safe."

"Good to know," he said, smiling big.

"My ex showed no interest in this kind of stuff. But Luc believes most of it, though it's hard not being able to talk to anyone else who gets it," I said, concluding the string of weird.

"Is there more?" he prompted.

"Ya, lots," I said, following with a nervous laugh, settling the last plate in the dishwasher.

I wasn't ready right then to share the 'more', still needed to feel him out, to see if he could handle the big stuff—the stuff about my four friends, about the four angels, *and* the secret. He'd figured out my food needs for sure, figured out I had more to tell, but could I share the rest of my weird world with him? Some maybe, but the rest—the big stuff, might be too much, and may just blow that beautiful mind of his.

"Let me show you the protection items I have around the apartment, and my book collection on different supernatural topics," he said, tossing the dishtowel on the counter. Then he crossed the distance to the bookshelf. "Perchance, I'm someone who *gets it,*" he said, pulling a book from the top shelf.

For the next half an hour, he presented his spooky book collection to me. Then I followed him around the apartment in blissful silent response to the descriptions of all his various mystical items. He was into the paranormal, the magical, and he had a fascination with the spiritual, but I still wasn't convinced it was the right time or *safe* to tell him the other stuff, about the girls and the codex, etc.

I knew now that my telling Derek, Luc, and the girls, hadn't made me sick, but I wasn't confident that Louise's illness and subsequent death hadn't had something to do with her sharing Joan's story. Mom had gotten sick from telling, so had my Aunt Kay. Vicki's mom believed she had impaired her arm from writing that message. Alison's mother had admitted in her entry that when she'd been hopped up from the cancer meds and had let part of the story slip to Alison, that she'd become ill. It may have further sealed her fate by going to see Vicki's mom and with hiding the book, but we can't know for sure.

The girls and I had discussed things freely, and no one had gotten sick. There'd been many discussions with Derek and with Luc, and still no one had fallen ill. I could only hope for the same with Luc and Derek sharing with Darius. Luc had told Dunya all he'd known, and he had not gotten sick. Could I conclude there was safety in the telling now? The safety in sharing must have something to do with the fact the four women were together now, working together. This alone could impact these conditions regarding the secret. They all have the information they need, they're together, so no need for any sickness or death curse, or whatever. I was exceptionally relieved—and lucky, in the fact my telling of things hadn't made me or anyone else sick, but I wasn't ready to push my luck just yet.

My phone vibrated in my back pocket, just as Redmond was about to explain the other books he had on ghosts, spirits and angels. I took a quick check to see it was another text from Luc.

The message read;

> *Derek and I are taking Darius out for pints since last night was a bit of a cluster.*

I wrote back;

> *Enjoy your boys' night out.*

"Your roomie?" Redmond asked

"Ya—the guys are heading out for pints," I explained to my host. "Tell me." I pointed back to the bookcase in hopes of further avoiding the 'more' from my weird world.

Skipping the books, he pointed to the bottom shelf. "Right here I have some mystery films you might like," he said. "*And Then There Were None,* 1945 version, *The Name of the Rose*, 1986, and these two more comical ones, *Clue,* 1985, and *Murder By Death,* 1976."

I grinned in response. I recognized the 'Clue' name but only because I'd played the board game.

"I have a few newer ones too," he added, pointing across the room to a stack under the TV.

That's when I realized he must have gone out shopping this week because there was a big ottoman that matched his big couch in place of the coffee table. I guess I'd been suffering from food blindness because I'd completely missed the new piece of furniture in the tiny space.

"Now we can put our feet up to watch movies," he said, when he saw I'd spotted the addition. The coffee table was on casters and could easily be moved in and out of the space, but the ottoman would make for a much cozier time together.

"I think a comedy would be good," I said. Nothing dark and mysterious for now.

Redmond was fast asleep, head on my lap when the credits for the second movie scrolled the screen. When we'd gotten comfortable on the couch, I'd spread out with my head against a sofa pillow at one end and my legs stretched out at an angle, atop the ottoman. At the start of the second movie, Redmond had grabbed a pillow to place on my lap for his head. He'd maneuvered his big body against the back of the couch, extending his legs down the rest of the length. He'd separated his arms, one running around my lower back, the other across my legs. Halfway through the movie, he'd removed the pillow to have his head against my lap.

My first visit, he'd been kind to let me sleep when I'd accidently stayed the night, so I felt it only right I return the kindness. Redmond's responses to my weird world had been positive, as if I'd been telling him something normal about myself. There'd been no skepticism either, despite my hitting him with a whole box of supernatural weirdness. I felt safe here with Redmond, and he had felt comfy enough to fall asleep on my lap.

Not wanting to wake him, I reached an arm and snagged the remote. When I shut off the TV, all I could hear was the soft sounds of his breathing. With all the lights off, delicate ribbons of moonlight shown through the upper parts of the windows, protecting the apartment from complete darkness. Comfortable in being here and in my telling of things, I rested my arm across his shoulder, closed my eyes, and let myself drift off.

Chapter 13

The temperature outside for today's sleuthing at *The Central Experimental Farm,* was just slightly above freezing. There was no snow in the forecast for this late November day in Ottawa, with only a touch of fog and overcast skies.

Playing at being the leisurely Sunday driver, Vicki rounded the car through the traffic circle to the entrance of the gardens. "Can you believe it's already past the middle of November," she said, "Wasn't it just Halloween yesterday?"

They'd all been busy with other things, life, family, and work, but they couldn't put off what had to be done any longer. They needed to find answers, sooner rather than later, and they'd agreed the time had come for them to search the garden.

"How is your mom," Olivia asked, when they pulled through the entrance.

"She's fine—glad to get the secrets out," Vicki said. "And, my dad's there to cater to her every need."

"You guys don't always get along, eh?" Mac asked

Vicki parked the car, and they all got out. "I love her and all—but she's a tad too high-maintenance for my liking."

"Do you think it's old age?" Olivia suggested.

"Nope—she's always been that way. Part of our conflict," Vicki said. "I think I identify more with my aunt and my maternal grandmother, both were very independent," she explained. "My grandmother was widowed at 24 during the depression and raised two kids on her own. My aunt was a divorced single mom before I was born. She moved to Montreal and was a career woman, an unusual thing for the time. She remarried, but still worked throughout her marriage. She's been on her own successfully for the past twelve years since my uncle died in the ice storm." Vicki stopped talking and stared at the large colourful information board just inside the public entrance. Letting go of her story she said, "There are five public areas to visit here."

"Says entrance is *Free*—open dawn till dusk," Mac noted, giving a smirk and a couple eyebrow raises.

"Ya, but the grounds cover 80-plus acres," Olivia said with a groan. "Where do we even start?"

"Do you think it would be someplace obvious—one of the more populated areas, like the Ornamental Gardens? Says it's a favorite site for wedding photographers," Mac rambled off.

"Right, because all the other things we found were sooooo obvious," Vicki shot back. "But we'll stick to the main public areas, the acreages of trees don't seem logical for hiding something that needs to be found."

"Well, what about the Tropical Greenhouse? It's an indoor area," Mac said, ignoring Vicki's sarcasm. "Or the Canada Agriculture and Food Museum?" Mac knew things hadn't been obvious to them, but they *had* seemed obvious to Lynn. She'd sensed things, a kind of compass to the target. Mac wished Lynn was here now to help with the search.

"The description given to us doesn't mention *indoors,* it mentions a massive garden, remember?" Vicki reminded them.

"From the lookout points you can see the Rideau Canal, Carleton University, Dow's Lake and the surrounding city," Olivia noted, sensing the tension building. She'd been studying and trying to master Chakra energy centers, and right now all of hers were firing. After all, the seven major chakras related to one's physical, mental and emotional interactions and the four of them, particularly Alison who was pregnant, had been subject to major impact on these areas. Chakras are invisible to the human eye, but they can be perceived by someone trained in the art and Olivia had become well versed at picking up on them with others as well. But the chakra system works best when all function together and right now she and her friends were not working in concert.

Ignoring Olivia, and based on the map they'd reviewed, Vicki headed off towards what revealed to be the Ornamental Gardens. The *Ornamental* gardens normally displayed historic and new varieties of both shrubs and flowers, but at this time of year there wouldn't be any flowers. It would still be as good a place as any to start though.

Mac and Olivia following along behind her, each scanning the grounds in different directions, doing their best to sense—pick up something, anything, that might lead them in the right direction.

"They need to conjure me—to help," Uriel said as he, Raphael and Michael, followed along behind the Charges.

"How are you going to help?" Raphael questioned. "None of us know if this is the place or what they are looking for."

"What went wrong? How did they end up with Armaros instead of you Uriel?" Michael asked, adding to the list of growing questions.

Uriel shrugged. "Gabriel doesn't know where the gathering is, but Armaros does," Uriel said.

"Maybe we should watch him instead of our Charges," Raphael suggested.

"He's already done his part—having things hidden out of reach," Michael said. "Armaros won't be leading anyone—especially not us, to the hiding place."

"I feel useless… I wouldn't have known where to lead them even if they had conjured me," Uriel said.

"Why would Armaros lead them here? This can't be the place—he wouldn't have wanted to help," Michael surmised. "Why was he so detailed in the description—why bother?"

As if hopeful, Uriel said, "Maybe he only gave them enough to find the place, but not enough to find what they were looking for."

"What for—to torment them further?" Raphael cut in.

"He's gone to great lengths before to disrupt things," Michael reminded.

Two hours later, they'd walked the Heritage Rose garden, Explorer Rose garden, Preston Lilac collection, Peony and Iris collections, rock garden, perennial and annual beds, and the hedge collections.

Olivia zipped her jacket further up to below her chin. "Cold and damp—but at least it's not snowing," she said, as she tucked her hands in the jacket's pockets. She crossed her hidden fingers in hopes it didn't rain either.

"Let's try the Tropical Greenhouse," Vicki suggested. They'd been searching for *any* kind of clue, spending too much time weaving in and around the garden paths only to come up empty now. "Might be warmer."

They walked the short distance from the gardens up Maple Drive until they spotted the elegant octagonal structure of the greenhouse. Walking hadn't warmed them, but as they entered the multi-windowed building, the fog outside turned to a drizzling rain. Inside, other than a few diehard garden fans, they were the only other visitors in the place.

"I'm gonna try a locator spell," Mac said, in earshot of just her friends. "Find what's lost kind of thing." Mac produced a tiny white tealight candle and a small lighter from her large purse.

"Here, I'll light it for you," Olivia said, taking the lighter. She'd worked with Mac on a few spells, and she knew that a little chant like the one used in a locator spell, may not seem like a *real* spell, but it could bring magical results if you put your heart into it.

"How does it work?" Vicki asked.

"It's used for when you are looking for something you've misplaced," Mac explained. "This kind only takes one candle."

Olivia lit the candle. "Normally you put the candle in a holder—easier to carry that way," Olivia said.

Mac placed the tealight in her palm and walked up the rows of plant life. Speaking as she walked, she said, "We need what we seek. Give us a peek. Draw our eyes, for the prize."

"Anything, Mac?" Vicki asked, impatient.

"You have to let your eyes wander around… until you feel drawn to the spot… where the lost whatever, is hiding," Olivia told her.

After twenty minutes of walking the building and eye-wandering, Mac said, "Noth'in. Absolutely nothing."

"Should we try the other buildings?" Olivia suggested. "The rain has stopped."

"We have to," Vicki said, heading back towards the way they'd come in.

Another two hours later, they'd wandered the other indoor venues, yet had still come up empty. They'd looked under, behind and even below ground, getting their hands dirty digging near one bench at the north-east lookout. The only reason they opted to dig was because unlike the other benches, this one was tucked back away from the main area and they'd gone with 'not obvious' hoping to unearth answers. They'd crossed the *suggested* barrier chain at the public lookout and had wandered aimlessly for the last hour over the grounds.

"Maybe you need to try a bigger spell, Mac," Olivia proposed. "Stronger locator spell—maybe."

Mac glanced around at the surrounding area where they now stood. They were out of view of any passersby and nowhere near the road or path. "Maybe," Mac said, digging into her purse again. She pulled out four tealight candles this time. Glancing around again, she spotted a large stone big enough to sit on and strode in its direction. The others followed, watching as she placed the four candles at north, south, east and west. "Light the candles for me Liv," she said, as she sat down on the stone and crossed her legs.

Still having the lighter, Olivia lit each candle. "Done," she said, putting her hands near the last candle for warmth. Then she stood back.

"Which way is west?" Mac directed at Vicki.

Vicki thought for a second and then pointed out to the right. They'd wandered for such a time she'd almost lost a sense of their position on the grounds. "The exit is that way," Vicki said, pointing left, as if eager to leave now.

"Let me try this one—then we can go, okay?" Mac said, to impatient Vicki and now cold again Olivia. She shifted to face west and then reached into her purse again to produce a tiny goblet shaped cup.

"She needs to invoke the element of water," Olivia whispered to Vicki.

Mac held out the tiny goblet and closed her eyes. "Let the water show the location of that which we seek," Mac said. Then she opened her eyes and looked into the cup. "Water," she announced. The other two stepped forward to peek into the cup. "Look into the water," Mac began, "until a picture forms in your mind of a location."

"Isn't this normally for locating a missing person?" Olivia recalled.

"Ya but maybe we can get some kind of feeling for a specific location here," Mac stated. "And that location is where we should start looking for the missing item."

"I'm not sure how all this magic stuff works, but what we're looking for isn't lost or missing—it's hidden, not exactly the same thing," Vicki pointed out.

"True," Mac conceded, following with a defeated sigh.

"Was worth a try," Olivia consoled. Then she knelt and blew out the candles.

Together they traversed the grounds back towards the exit. The whole time at the gardens had felt directionless. Mac and Olivia hadn't picked up on a single vibe of anything mother-earthly, nor had Vicki's logical brain been able to rationalize any hit of something to aid them. And no one was thrilled about reporting back to Alison on what they *didn't* find on this search.

"I'm exhausted," Vicki said, and that was a lot coming from someone who did loads of hiking in her leisure time.

"Me too," Mac said, collapsing on the closest bench to the exit.

"What if this spirit-guy's message was a load of crap," Vicki the ever skeptic tossed out. "What if he's a bad spirit and or just an asshole ghost messing with us?"

"Hey, I followed the spell to summon a helper," Mac shot back. "Why would my grandmother write a spell to conjure some *asshole,* to what—add more challenge?"

"Well, I'm not sure how we're supposed to sense or locate what we need if our Chakras are all out of whack," Olivia voiced. The other two stared back at her. "What?" she said back at their questioning faces.

"Chakras?" Vicki said, "What do they have to do with finding the answers we need?"

"You've been practicing—haven't you?" Mac recognized. They'd worked through a lot together, but she'd known Olivia had been trying to work out new skills on her own.

"Yes, Chakras—doubter," Olivia gave Vicki, her ever-reluctant friend. "Energy is not a static thing—it's in continuous flux. Chakras open and close, but they also expand and retract. That's what is happening here, and why we might have issue finding whatever it is that we need to find."

"What do you mean?" Vicki questioned again, this time with a little more interest.

"When a chakra expands the boundaries can blur," Olivia explained. "Like us, chakras are typically team players. Stress one chakra, it shuts down and the others will compensate for the stressing of the entire energy system. And like with us, it's not healthy for anyone to pull more than its share of the burden for prolonged periods of time—eventually it puts a strain on the relationship."

"Then the whole team suffers," Mac surmised.

"And if chakras are not functioning jointly or optimally—weakness can occur," Vicki concluded. "We are not working as a cohesive team."

"I know it's been harder not having Alison here. You guys are like Me and Mac—a duet within our little quartet," Olivia sympathized.

"Let's circle back with Alison via Skype," Mac suggested. "Maybe a little brainstorming after our failed search is what we need to get back on track. And maybe she'll come up with an idea—something to help us for when we come back to search again."

"Again?" Olivia said, groaning.

Chapter 14

Sunday morning had been an enjoyable extension to the comfy night prior. Over coffee and preparing breakfast together this time, Redmond and I had discussed the upcoming events of *American* Thanksgiving.

He'd shared that he was having his friends/employees from work over for a gathering at the end of the week. It was for those who wouldn't be with family for the holiday, and he'd generously invited me to join them. He'd also told me he'd be going out of town starting the Friday after Thanksgiving. The trip he was taking to NYC was a family Thanksgiving-early x-mas combo gathering thing they did with his mother's side of the family.

It sounded like a wonderful family event, and I was envious of him having such a large family in which to gather with. With Canadian Thanksgiving now past and Christmas approaching, I was missing the gatherings my mother and aunt used to organize for our family even more so. I'd told him to make sure he took lots of photos to show me when he got back. I was happy for him, but I was extra happy for the invite to his work gathering since his trip meant that I wouldn't get to see him again until after the following Friday.

After a quick hug at the top of the stairs, Redmond said, "My parents like to travel out of the country for Christmas. As they put it, since they have no grandkids yet, they'll take advantage of their retirement until then."

"Ah parents," I gave him in return. "Chat with you later—and I'll see you Thursday," I added, giving his hand a little squeeze. Then I continued down the steps.

"Looking forward to it," he called out as I descended the stairs.

I turned back with a quick glance up and a wave, then proceeded around the side of the building towards my car.

Grandkids, that word held a lot of pressure for an only-child, I considered, as I pulled out of the studio parking area.

I arrived home, regrettably to find Derek already packed and ready for his departure. In fact, he and Luc were at the door when I walked in, prepared to leave for the airport.

"Not the visit I'd hoped for," I said, before giving Derek a big goodbye hug. It was my second goodbye hug of the day. But it was good he, Luc, and Darius were a team now. The girls were a team, and I was—well, I was... fine with it all, for once. "Oh, I got started on telling Redmond about things last night, but I wasn't ready to give him the big stuff—journal, etc.," I added.

Luc and Derek stepped out through the front door.

"Hard topics—but good you started," Luc said, jingling his keys as he headed to the car.

Derek gave me a thumbs-up. "You'll figure out how much this guy can handle," he said, before crossing the lawn. He waved when he got into the car, then they drove off.

* * *

For the front part of the week, Derek and Luc spent time relaying the finer details to Darius through various in-person, phone, text, and email conversations.

On Wednesday, when they'd signed off, Luc had conveyed to me that they'd pretty much covered every aspect of our list of weird. They'd also agreed that tomorrow, U.S. Thanksgiving, *and* the rest of the weekend would be mystery-free time. I was all for that, not that I'd been included in any of the conversation, but I'd had my fill of weird, and I'd been looking forward to my own normalcy with Redmond.

As it were, as the week pushed on, I hadn't seen Redmond at all. He'd been super busy wrapping things up before he had to leave for the trip. We hadn't spoken much either, other than a few quick texts while I was on shift.

His most recent text had been him asking if I could come early today, to help set up. Obviously, I'd said *yes,* and was grateful I'd be having time with him alone before his guests arrived.

When I parked out front and got out of my car, Redmond was down the steps walking towards me. "I need to grab supplies from the studio kitchen," he tossed out, before going in for a hug. Handholding and hugs, I liked them both, and I squeezed him back.

In the studio kitchen Redmond gathered up all the items he needed into two boxes. He allowed me to take one box, the light one of course with all the plastic plates, cutlery, and paper napkins, while he carried the one with all the heavy items in it. Supplies in hand, we walked the short distance back towards his place.

At the bottom of the steps to his apartment, I let out a *"Groan"*, pretending the box was too heavy. Then a cold draft prickled my neck. A cast of clouds darkened the sky as I glanced across the road towards The Barnacle. There in the shadows near the entrance stood a huge figure. *I'd seen this one before,* was my last thought as queasiness brought me to my knees. I dropped the box and shot a hand out to the pavement to steady myself.

"Lynn, you okay?" Redmond called out, reaching out a hand in my direction. "What, Lynn—what is it?"

Tilting my head up, I glimpsed Redmond searching the area across the way. "Just a little woozy," I said, dropping my head. "Been experiencing it a lot—doctor says it's stress... from everything going on these past few months—it's nothing." When I glanced up, the figure was gone. But I *had* seen him before, just not here—not in *Miami.*

"That's the same expression you had the night I met you. Halloween—when you took off," Redmond said, crossing the short distance, reaching out both hands to help me up. "Tell me the truth... is it that spidy-sense thing you told me about?"

"No—uhm, I think that was nerves too—over being out for the first time alone," I said, sidestepping, and taking his hands. I wasn't ready to explain that night yet. "Just nerves—lots of changes." But I knew better, possibly Redmond did too. Maybe he was someone who *gets it*.

"Nate, my sound engineer teaches meditation part-time at the yoga studio down the way—bet he could help you with the *nerves* thing," he suggested, as if offering another type of hand, one to get him out of his spidy-sense question.

"Sure—sounds good," I said, brushing off my palms, and gathering up the box again.

We continued, and Redmond kept a close eye on me, cutting a quick glance or two back over across the street.

The Thanksgiving gathering unfolded without incident, thank goodness. Everyone ate and drank, and laughed, telling stories about the past year at the studio. It was enjoyable to hear stories about Redmond and his world at the studio from his close friends. The guys who worked with him at the studio referred to him as Red. It was really only Lily—or Shade as the others called her, who used Redmond's full name. I liked the concept of nicknames, I'd coined a few myself, but other than *Spooky,* I hadn't been given any nicknames as an adult.

After dinner was over, only a few of the staff remained, making for a more intimate setting. Though everyone had been very nice to me as the non-staff outsider, I much preferred a smaller group, like the stragglers who remained with us now.

"I was pleased to see you here tonight," Lily said. "Your name comes up a lot these days." She winked at me.

"I'm glad yer here too," I gave her, pretending not to understand her wink.

She laughed. "A certain redhead was all a flutter about you coming tonight—but don't tell him I said that."

"Tell who—what?" Redmond cut in.

"Nothing, just that the weather for this outdoor feast was perfect, a comfortable 77 degrees," Lily said, staring up at the clear starry night's sky.

"It's high contrast to the weather back home in Ottawa," I said, adding to the quick shift in dialog.

"I don't miss the cold temps," Lily said, referring to hers and Redmond's hometown of NYC. She winked at me again.

"I agree with Shade," Redmond said, moving to stand near me.

"Snow at Christmas is nice—but I really love the year-round lushness of this area, and all the arching banyan trees," I tossed back. A cold draft pricked along my neck again.

Redmond must have seen my expression change, because he said, "Are you okay?"

"I'm fine," I said.

"You sure?" he asked, rubbing the back of my arm.

"I'm sure." I smiled.

"Alright," he said, dropping his hand from my arm to squeeze my hand. He gave me a nod before turning, then he walked over to the dessert end of the food table.

I didn't want to alarm him, but my senses had been on high alert ever since spotting that mysterious figure near the entrance to the park. And right now... I was picking up on something... *ominous,* weighing on me... threatening, reminiscent of horror movies where at any moment the bad guy might pounce on the unsuspecting teenagers.

Something played at the edge of my vision and I turned to scan the length of hedge that divided Redmond's property and that of the homeowner's behind. With the patio being the only lit area of the yard, shadows were playing tricks on my eyes, moving and shifting with the moonlight.

"The Grove is a magical place," a deep melodic voice said, from behind me.

I turned back to see a man with midnight black hair, and I let out the breath I'd been holding.

"The yoga studio is just down the way," Nate added, pointing the direction.

I took in a clean breath of air. "So I've been told," I said, noting what Redmond had informed me earlier.

Nate and I had been introduced at the start of the evening, and right away I'd picked up on the mystical edge he gave off. I'd liked him right away. His shiny black hair was pulled back in a braid long enough it reached his belt, giving the impression he had more than a hint of Native Indian in his ancestry.

"Have you been to see the Wishing tree at Fairchild Gardens?" he redirected.

"I have actually," I told him. I'd even hung a wish for my Mom when she'd been sick. "I don't know much about it—other than Yoko Ono commissioned it or something."

"Not really part of the Grove, but a wonderous place as well." He smiled and the deep lines at the corners of his dark eyes crinkled. "And you are correct, Yoko had started the first Wish Piece in 1996. Her instructions were, '*Make a wish. Write it down on a piece of paper. Fold it and tie it around a branch of a Wish Tree. Ask your friends to do the same. Keep wishing, until the branches are covered with wishes.'*," he recited from memory.

"I love the sentiment," I said, only to realize how long it had been since I visited, since I sat on the perfect bench, under the perfect tree, near the perfect spot. I loved the place, but now my heart ached at missing my mom and my aunt at that moment.

"Redmond mentioned you might be interested in a little meditation lesson," he said, pulling me back.

"Can't hurt," I said, chuckling, my nerves still on edge. Perfect timing, I thought. I took another quick scan of the rest of the yard.

The group of stragglers had thinned out even more now, leaving only Nate, Redmond, Lily and me.

"Meditation is a practice of concentration," Nate added, taking a sip of his beer.

"I told him about your *nerves* thing," Redmond explained, stepping up and handing me two of the homemade ginger cookies he'd made.

"Doctor says it's nerves," I explained. *If he only knew*. I smiled back at Nate and then bit into one of the cookies.

"I'm game," Lily said, taking a seat at one of the patio chairs.

"Stress relief—I'm game too," I said, with a little laugh, claiming the lounge chair next to her. "Lily could use it—what with Redmond being away next week, she'll be in charge at the studio." I bit into the second cookie.

"Ha—I practically run the place now," Lily said, throwing Redmond a mischievous glance his way.

"And that is the reason I don't need meditation," Redmond said, dodging a playful punch from Lily. "No stress."

We all laughed.

"Okay kids," Nate said, clapping his hands like a teacher to get our focus back.

Holding back more laughter, Lily and I straightened in our seats. I chewed the last bite of my cookie.

"To start, you simply focus on a sound or an object, even a visualization. Your breath works well too—simple. We do this to increase our awareness of the present moment," Nate clarified, sitting down on the picnic table side facing Lily and me. "Daily practice can reduce stress, and promote relaxation. Some use it to enhance personal and spiritual growth," he added.

Redmond moved to sit in the chair next to me.

"Let's try my favorite, a *Mantra Meditation*," Nate suggested. "Try... *I am open to all that releases me*."

"I'm open all right—release away," I said, wriggling and crossing my legs, getting comfortable on the cushy patio lounge.

"Gently close your eyes...," Nate began again. "Start by taking some deep breaths... in... and out. Now begin repeating the mantra silently to yourself... without moving your lips... or your tongue."

The breathing part felt much like what I'd used when pushing away those bouts of nausea, the whole bringing in the good air and thoughts, out with the bad, sort of thing. It had worked too. This mantra routine might be just the thing I needed to top that off. I recited the words in my head, *I am open to all that releases me.*

"Remember, it's not about stopping your thoughts or emptying your mind... it's about focusing and bringing the mind back to attention when it wanders."

I am open to all that releases me, my brain repeated a second time, then a third and fourth time. I was in my head, completely ignoring all around me.

Then Nate said, "Stop now, repeating the mantra, and open your eyes."

Startled slightly, I slowly opened my eyes.

The first thing I noticed was that Redmond was now sitting on the other side of the picnic table watching me. I hadn't heard him move away. He was smiling… not because he found what we were doing funny, but I think because he recognized what I was feeling… *peace*.

"Feel good?" Nate asked, standing now in front of Lily and me.

"Not bad," Lily said, "but if I don't get up and moving, I'm bound to fall asleep right where I am." She laughed.

I laughed too and gave Lily a poke in the arm. I smiled across at Redmond, and then glanced back at Nate. "Yes, good—better, *peaceful*," I said, trying to clarify. The threatening presence was gone. Around me I now felt only unity and friendship. But there *was*... something else.

"He's a bold bastard," Gabriel said. "Lingering so near to her." Gabriel moved to sit at the end of the picnic table.

"Coward," Shamsiel responded, stepping in closer. "This hiding in the shadows like a stalker."

"She sensed Armaros was near," Gabriel stated. "But *he* sensed we were too—kept back."

Shamsiel knelt in front of the lounge chair. "I think she's sensing us too," he said, examining her preoccupied expression.

"Lynn, have you ever heard of Mala beads?" Nate asked, shifting my attention back to him. He lifted a long length of small wooden beads from around his neck and held it out to me.

"I don't think so," I said shaking my head. "It's lovely—what's it for?" I asked, leaning in for a better look.

"Here—you take it," he said, moving closer to me. He placed the strand over my head, resting it around my neck.

The long strand of natural stained wooden beads hung past my chest. The ends met at a larger bead with a soft white tassel hanging off it. I clutched the tassel end and brought it up closer to examine the lone bead it hung from.

"That's the *Buddha* bead," Nate said, before going on to explain it had 108 beads. He described how each bead can relate to the stages of one's journey of the human soul, or enlightenment. "Mala beads were traditionally created to be used as a tool in meditation."

"Interesting," I said, examining the carving on the bigger bead.

"Truth is—the significance of the 108 beads on your own mala is open to *your* interpretation. Which is why I love them." Nate gave me a warm smile.

"I love the concept—and it is beautiful, but I can't keep it," I said, lifting it from around my neck.

Nate's hand stopped me. "It's cool, Lynn—I make them," he said, settling it back around my neck. "And your journey to enlightenment, Lynn… it has already begun."

Chapter 15

Last night, after Nate and Lily had said their goodbyes, I'd stayed behind. Considering what Nate had said regarding my enlightenment, I'd chosen to take the next step on that journey, by telling Redmond everything, well—almost everything.

I'd led in by explaining to him what I'd been *feeling* in the backyard. He'd known something was up. Then I fed the rest to him as if I were telling a story, adding on to what he'd already known about me, *and* explaining it all without presenting him with the journal or my list of weird.

I told him about Louise and the story she'd told me, pointing out the similarities to that of the journal. I told him about the scavenger hunts of sort, my friends and I had made, the things we'd found, and the dialogs we'd had with the mothers. I'd added how those dialogs had helped to connect all things and helped connect my friends. He'd behaved much like my girlfriends had when I'd first shared things with them; open, curious and waiting for more. Then I'd ventured into the findings from the codex.

I explained *The Cipher, The Guardian,* and *The Theologian,* pointing out that Derek, Luc and Darius, like the other men cited in the codex, must be descendants or something like it. I hadn't mentioned my thoughts on the whole *angel* thing, but I had asked if he believed in them, and he'd given me a firm, "*Of course.*" Still, I'd been reluctant to elaborate further. Instead, I'd corroborated Derek's theory about their roles in all this, and how like with other secret societies, this one manipulated events such that certain people and certain objects were protected or could be brought together. I'd explained that my role—rather my birthmother's role, had been to bring them all together.

Redmond seemed to adjust well to the information as I told it. He'd even mentioned how he'd read quite a bit on secret societies, and how he had even done a little investigating of the ghosts and mysterious happenings in the area. He, like Derek, had found it fascinating how this secret, this same story, had been passed down so accurately through so many generations, and it was beyond any timeframe he'd ever read about.

His only struggle with things seemed to come with the idea that this *secret*, despite it being written over and over by different people and within some ancient book, was how it could somehow injure, cause illness or even kill people. My friends and I couldn't prove that part, or any part for that matter. But I'd told him there'd been too many *coincidences* that had ended in illness or death, for any of our liking. I'd left out telling him of my *nausea* incidences and the coincidental presence of these mysterious men, *and* what had really happened Halloween night when I'd taken off.

In our first chat about weird stuff, I had told Redmond about Dunya and the *seer* thing, and how it had related to earlier events in my life and seemed linked to my spidy-senses. But there'd been nothing to tie these happenings to my friends and this mystery. However, I wasn't sure how to explain the sightings—visions—*nausea* whatevers, or how to explain these guys from Halloween. Or how they were the same ones I'd seen in Ottawa, and how I'd seen one of them at the hospital. I hadn't even told Luc about seeing these guys. My theory on them was my own, and I'd share it with Luc when and if, I was good'n-ready. *Or* when I had a better idea what the hell it all meant.

I'd been nervous with the telling, but by the end, Redmond, in his charming Redmond-way, had found another remedy to ease my nerves once again. He'd picked out one of his favorite books about angels and heaven, *Paradise Lost*, and had read aloud to me.

I'd fallen asleep on his couch *again*, but this time when I'd woken, there'd been no delicious smell of coffee brewing, no fresh muffins, and no Redmond. Instead, I'd found only a note for me on the bathroom door that read;

> *Lily's condo sprang a leak—building's super gone for the long weekend.*

I'd been a little sad he hadn't been here when I'd woken up, but I was proud of his dedication to his friends. In response to the note, I'd sent him a text;

> *Good luck, and say hi to Lily for me.*
> *Will I see you later?*

He'd texted me back with;

> *I have a few things to get done before I fly up to NYC, but I'll text you later.*

There had been no sense in waiting around if he had stuff to do, so I'd headed home. I'd known what time his flight was, 2 p.m., but as the day dragged on and no text came, I assumed he'd gotten stuck dealing with the airport dance. When I'd checked later that his flight had landed safe, I'd waited anxiously for a text. But still no message came from Redmond. Trying not to make anything of it, I'd again chalked it up to him being busy with his family's welcome home. Then I'd further distracted myself by getting ready for work.

I'd taken on the extra shift to cover for someone who'd asked for the day off to travel. It seemed everyone was travelling this weekend. At the party, Lily had told me it was the busiest travel day here in the US.

Sitting in my car in the driveway with the engine running, I checked my phone again before heading to work hoping to see something from Redmond, but still there was nothing. I was about to set my phone in the pouch pocket of my tote when a face popped into view of the driver's side window.

"Lynn—so glad I caught you," Dunya said, startling me. "Mitra has been frantic all day. When she saw you leave your house—she told me what was bothering her. Told me to come straight over to tell you."

"What—what did she say?" I said, a little too stern perhaps. My eyebrows were up from the sudden appearance of her face in my car window, but I'm sure they'd been raised to their highest after that little tidbit she'd delivered. "What's wrong now?" I was a bit agitated myself with not hearing from Redmond all day, considering I'd laid out all that *weirdness* to him the night before.

"Uhm," Dunya said, putting a hand to her mouth.

"Sorry," I said, when she appeared a little taken a back. "I'm on my way to work."

"Oh, no—sorry, Lynn. I'm sorry to throw another left-field thing at you," she said, countering with a broken idiom.

She was aware via Luc, that I was no longer involving myself in the dealings of the *four* anymore, but something had gotten Mitra in a tizzy.

"Go ahead, Dunya. I have a few minutes—I'm listening." I had more than a few minutes, actually. I'd been frustrated with waiting for any kind of response from Redmond and had opted with going into work early in hopes to distract my brain.

"Well...," she started. "... Mitra had a dream last night...."

Here we go, I thought. "And?" I said, eager to move this along. She took a glance over her shoulder towards her house. I leant my head out the window and spied Mitra peeking out from behind the curtains of the living room window of their home.

Beginning again, she said, "There was a... darkness—a dark figure... lingering in the shadows near a large park." She glanced over her shoulder again.

"Dunya, please—what dark figure, who was it?"

"I... I'm not sure," she said, "but Mitra called him *Armaros.*"

That was a new one, though I knew I'd heard that name before—read it, maybe. "What else?" I asked, in hopes of more clarity.

"Mitra explained further that the *key*... the key to who you are... resides within the walls of the old... where three religions mingle... and to which is protected by a vessel with mermaids and tritons encircling it." She paused. "There was something else, something about mothers and daughters—symbols that show the truth." She gave one more glance over her shoulder.

"Right," was all I had in return. I stared at her as the messy imagery swirled in my brain.

"Oh Lynn, sometimes the Arabic translations are difficult for me, but this is the gist of what she saw in her dream."

"Okay… let Mitra know—I know now… I'll…. uhm… put some thought into it, and get back to you," I told her. What was I supposed to say? She was right, it was one of those left-field things, waaaay out in the field.

She nodded at me and backed away from the car. "Drive safe, Lynn," I heard her say, as I pulled out of the drive.

In the rearview mirror I glimpsed Mitra exiting the house to meet her granddaughter on the front lawn, but I lost the image of them as I rounded the corner.

On the drive, I revisited the words Dunya had shared, and the images they conjured. I said the words, *"Walls of the old, where three religions mingle,"* out loud to myself. And took the long way to work to kill time.

But by the time I'd pulled into a parking spot at the hospital, I still hadn't come up with any ideas on this new bit of information. This was something better solved by Derek, my puzzle solver. Before getting out of the car, I sent him a text outlining the details like an actual riddle, not mentioning it had something to do with Mitra *or* me. He would probably welcome the little riddle to crack, what with all the big ones he'd been challenged with. I tucked my cell phone in my tote, got out of the car, and headed into the hospital.

At the doors to the NICU I checked my cell phone one last time before going in. Still nothing from Redmond. Stepping through the doors… *it hit me.* I knew what it meant—those words Dunya had said… because I'd seen what she'd described, I'd seen it on Halloween.

* * *

By the end of the week, sliding into December, I'd begun to lose faith things between Redmond and me would be *okay* once he returned home. He'd handled everything I told him about my world of weird well, or so I'd assumed.

Being with family would most definitely keep him busy I knew, but he had texted little, and he hadn't responded at all to my request of finding time to Skype. The texts I had sent had been my usual brief anecdotes from my day, coupled with the occasional question for him, like, *how does it feel to be back in your home town,* or *how is all the family getting on being all together,* but he'd not responded to any of them. The few texts I had received from him, had been patchy, random, and with confusing bits and pieces about the city and food. I hadn't wanted to give him the impression it upset me, so I'd done my best to send back positive responses despite not understanding most of the context of his messages.

With an attempt to brush off the unease caused by the confusing correspondence with Redmond this week, I refocused myself on the fact it was Friday, my day off, and the perfect day to investigate my hunch—*Vizcaya.* I also wanted to share my idea with Redmond since he'd said he liked mysteries and such. So, I sent him a text, making it short and sweet, telling him I was going to check out a hunch on something mysterious Dunya had told me. He was scheduled to be on the noon flight home today, and would only see the message once he landed, but I sent it anyway, then I left on my quest.

At Vizcaya, I walked from the parking lot to the booth near the start of the long driveway and paid the guy the fee. Through the gate, I strode up the long-paved road. I rounded the circle drive to the main house just as I'd done on that Halloween night, and then took the dozen steps up to the massive stately home, now a historical museum.

The white building loomed up in front of me as it had the night of the party, only this time it was daytime. Unlike that night, I didn't have to follow other people as they filed up the steps to the front entrance. This time it was quiet with only a few other people lingering on the stairs. And at the entrance I wasn't asked to wait my turn either to take a tour, instead I had free rein to wander the property, using my trusty little map I'd gotten at the entry booth.

The front hall was pretty much as I remembered, minus any Halloween decorations. Though, there had been limited decorations set up in this space that night, as they'd been reserved for the key social areas and the back patio where the main Halloween party had taken place. Moving on, I followed a similar path to what our tour guide had shown us that night and ventured through a large main doorway to one of several reception rooms, then slipped into the Library.

It was not a large room, but I'd recalled it had numerous angel references displayed in paintings, sculptures and other smaller pieces of artwork. There were cherubs with bows, an angel with a harp, a wooden box on the desk which displayed bronze feathers on the front, and it seemed as good a place as any to start. I'd assumed the room had been roped off for Halloween only, but the barrier remained even now, so I still couldn't get up close to the artwork. Then I remembered the one thing I could touch, and the best part of this room. It was the hidden doorway behind the tall bookshelf, and it was the way to the next room. I pulled back the bookcase and slipped through to the Living Room.

This room was much bigger than the Library and had a massive floor to ceiling fireplace flanked by the entrance, and another door filling up most of the wall. It too still had the rope barriers, but for only the first half of the space. On the left side of the room next to two tall glass doors, I found the item for which I'd come back to this place to examine.

Two large tapestries filled most of the wall space, but it was the larger of the two that had caught my eye. I'd considered it a religious marker because of the symbols, three symbols representing Muslim, Christian, *and* Jewish faiths. The tour guide had called it '*the Admiral Carpet*' but as described in Mitra's dream, it was where *three religions mingled*. I took a quick peek behind the wall hanging and found… nothing but wall.

Facing away from it, I scanned the large religious painting on the opposite wall, following it down to the ornate organ below it. The large equally ornate piano bench with its two red velvet cushions was also there in its customary spot. I stepped forward and ran a hand over the plush fabric as I'd done on Halloween. I'd given the hinged lid a little lift that night, but I had been interrupted at fully opening it when our tour guide had instructed us to follow him through to the next room.

This had to be it.

I took in an anxious breath and shot a glance to the door I'd come through, listening and checking for voices of anyone else who might enter the room to catch me touching the bench. I glanced forward to the doorway to the East Loggia room and listened again.

Alone.

I was alone, for how long I didn't now, but now or never this was my chance. I gripped the underside edge of the bench's lid… and drew it open.

Empty.

It was empty, except for the dust bunnies gathering in the corners. I tapped the underside of the lid hoping to find a hidden compartment, but there was nothing. I checked the underside of the bench and found nothing again. Desperate, I ran my hands over the surfaces of the partnered musical instrument, considering it could be like Olivia's grandmother's desk and perhaps had pressure spots to open hidden drawers or compartment. But still, I found nothing, and now I'd left greasy fingerprints all over the meticulously polished wood.

At the sound of a male voice I turned to see a young man and two small boys emerging through the passageway from the Library. One boy ran under the ropes sending the father off chasing him. The other little boy waved at me and giggled. I smiled and waved back despite my disappointment with my hunch. Dissatisfied, I slipped from the room out through the other door to what had been the main indoor social area the night of the party, the East Loggia room.

This room was the largest I'd seen that night, and it had elaborately painted walls and high decorative ceilings. To the left side of the room were three huge floor-to-ceiling arched glass entryways, each with double doors. Outside those doors were the surrounding courtyards, which that night, had been the main outdoor social area. I remembered the tour guide telling us this entry had originally been the front of the main house. Then I recalled something else he'd told us.

Pushing open one of the big glass doors, I stepped out to see Biscayne Bay… and *the Barge*. That night it had been too dark to make out the sculptures on the vessel, but now I could see them clear as day. There were sculpted baskets of fruits, trophies, and treasures, Egyptian obelisks, *and*…. mermaids and tritons.

I turned my gaze to the right and was presented with the full glory of the gardens. Again, it had been dark when I'd been here, and I hadn't gotten the full magnitude of the grounds. The small hairs on my arms tingled. This was the place from Mitra's dreams, I knew it. But what would I… could I… might I… may I… find here?

Was it *the key to who I am,* as Dunya had said? "Why would the key to who I am, be here of all places?" I whispered. I panned the grounds again, turning to face the mansion.

The grounds, the home, they were both massive, and would take hours to search. Longer, since I didn't know what I was looking for, other than something about *mothers and daughters* and *symbols that show the truth,* whatever that means. I needed more information. I needed to talk to Dunya and Mitra again if I was going to pinpoint the location of whatever it was, I needed to find here.

Temporarily defeated, I returned through the big doors making my way across the great hall to the far entrance where I'd come in.

When would I be back? I didn't know, but I'd be back with more information, more clarity, and if I was lucky more help. Redmond potentially, if he was up for it.

By the time I got home it was late afternoon, creeping into dinner time, and I still hadn't heard a peep from Redmond. I sent one more quick text letting him know my hunch was a bust. I then reheated the leftovers Luc had set aside for me. He'd left a note saying that he and Raven would be over at Dunya's for the evening.

I ate the food, but barely tasted it. I found myself wondering if this was all too much for Redmond, and perhaps the real reason I hadn't heard from him, and why his other text had read more like disinterest.

Could I blame him? *No.*

As night fell, and still no text response came from Redmond, I'd pretty much lost whatever confidence I had gathered for this new relationship. I also felt like a big fool for thinking I could tell him. Who does that, tells a guy they hardly know, all about their secrets?

"Apparently, you do—ya stupid idiot," I said aloud, then headed off to bed.

Chapter 16

Vicki logged on for a well-needed Saturday morning brainstorming session with the girls. Her first order of business she felt was to discuss the disastrous hunt they'd had at the Arboretum, *and* to figure out their next approach.

But before Vicki could breach the subject, Alison spoke up first. "My husband asked me again about the codex," she announced, through the video chat. "Why he couldn't look at it, and why all the secrets?"

"What did you say?" Vicki asked. She moved her cup of tea away from the piles of paper she had on the dining room table. She'd made the table research central with her laptop, notes and translations, and the photocopied pages of the codex Alison had sent her.

"I told him—I wanted to tell him, but he might not like or *believe* what I had to say," Alison responded.

"Did you tell him?" Olivia asked.

"Yup." Alison's mouth twitched.

"How did it go?" Olivia added, adjusting a pillow behind her head. She had set herself up in her bedroom on the bed like usual for their group conversations. It was the only place she could get a little privacy she'd told them prior.

"I'm sure he supposed you—we, were nuts." Vicki tossed out.

Alison squirmed in her seat. She'd chosen to sit in her kitchen for chats and out of ear shot while her husband was in his office. "At first…

but he knows I don't take things like this lightly, being the fact it involved my mother and my ancestors," Alison stated. "But he listened until I had gotten it all out—all of it."

"Mine asked about the strange things I've been cooking—creating," Mac threw into the mix. She'd needed privacy for these chats too, but more she needed space without the noise from her two sons, and like usual, she had shut herself into her small office upstairs for talking with the girls. "He asked if it was part of my 'holistic' training," Mac said. "I couldn't lie again—I had to tell him."

"You too?" Vicki asked. She leaned back in her chair away from the screen and took a sip of her tea.

"Ya, and like Alison said about her husband, he was skeptical at first, but when I showed him a few of my little *cough-cough* spells—ya know, like playing with the lights and the foliage outside, he believed me—even thought it was cool," Mac shared.

"And what about you, missy," Vicki asked the now exceptionally quiet Olivia.

"Okay—I told Mike too," Olivia blurted out. "He'd cut himself working in the garage and I'd fixed him up with one of Mac's ointments. In the morning the cut was healed, and he'd gone on about how I could make millions if I could package the stuff. I had to tell him why *that* wasn't going to happen. He'd been a bit bug-eyed when I explained, but he'd liked how confident I'd been—and *a little less scared of things that go bump in the night,* he'd said." She rolled her eyes. "He asked me if our daughters would be involved. I told him it was more than likely that the whole *four daughters needed* thing was now moot at this point. *And,* why we now worked so hard at solving the mystery—the stuff about the gathering etc." She paused. "He did however ask why Lynn wasn't involved anymore."

"Mine too," Alison said, shifting the view of her laptop such that she could reach to stir something cooking on her stovetop.

"Same here," Mac added. "He couldn't understand why she wasn't helping us—why we weren't keeping her in the loop—considering she started this all."

"I tried to explain—but questioned my own answers," Alison added. "Especially after finding that information about the gathering in that second entry.

"I told Mike that Lynn didn't want to be involved," Olivia stated. "He asked me if I was sure about that." She shook her head.

"We've sure done a good job of keeping her out," Mac said, leaning her elbows on her desk and bringing her face closer into view.

"Could use her help," Vicki admitted, flipping through a few papers next to her laptop. "Derek is good with the theory and Luc is helping him, but Lynn was always good with the things from the *weird*—you know. I've gone over everything translated, and it all seems clear... except for these few pieces—that are making me crazy." She clenched her teeth.

"Ask her for help," Alison suggested, moving to stir the something on another burner.

"Not sure how," Vicki said. "I haven't heard from her in ages. We used to write emails back and forth all the time—every day. Guess it doesn't help I haven't sent her any either," she pointed out. "I've been so focused on work and this damn codex, that I've made no time to communicate with her."

"Yer not the only one," Olivia said. "She's been working at the children's hospital, and I know what it's like to work in a place like that... it can be hard *and* amazing. And still, I haven't asked her a thing about it."

"My mom keeps asking me about her too—I keep brushing it off," Mac confessed. "Told her she's busy back in Miami with getting her life in order. I feel like an ass for not checking in for real. The girl's marriage ended—her friend died, and I haven't bothered to double back around to see if she's okay—not since sending her an email response to the news. Some friend I am."

"Ya stupid me, I asked her if she'd heard from Will, instead of asking how she was," Olivia said. "Being friends with both of them, I found it hard hearing about the split—didn't consider how she might be feeling. I guess I didn't let myself think about it," she admitted.

"I've been divorced, but all I could think then was *good riddance*. Didn't think about how she might be coping," Vicki recognized. "Not like there was any abuse or hostility that ended the marriage, but it doesn't make it any less painful."

"She seemed okay under the circumstances," Olivia said.

"I think she is okay, but you know how she doesn't like anyone to worry," Mac stated.

"Luc keeps Derek in the loop—he's keeping an eye on her," Vicki noted. "Derek would tell us if there was anything to worry about."

"It was fun Skyping with her before Halloween—we should do that again," Alison suggested, then she took a taste of whatever she'd been stirring.

"Maybe we could see if she wants to help again. I'd be interested to hear her take on this information I've translated about war, conquest, famine and death," Vicki said. "I'll send it to Derek first, but I think it's just about chaos in the world and the balance not being kept—usual theme." Vicki lifted the paper she'd written the translation on, then set it back on the pile.

"Okay, let us know how it goes with Derek," Alison said. "But we can still arrange to Skype with Lynn—just to talk and catch up though in the meantime, yes?"

Unanimously they agreed to arrange a group-time Skype with Lynn at the soonest, and then they exchanged their salutations, and signed off.

Vicki redirected her focus now on sending a message to Derek. They needed to talk about The Horsemen references she'd found, as well as work to solve these last few pieces. She was desperate to have them resolved *and* to get some damn answers. These items were better reviewed on a phone call, rather than via email, so she sent him a quick text inquiring if he had time to talk about *things*.

Luckily for her, Derek responded with a 'yes', stating he was at home working on a few projects around the house, and would call her in the next 30 minutes.

When her phone rang, Vicki picked it up before the second ring. "Hey Derek—thanks for making the time," she said, using more sugar than vinegar. She still carried the guilt from the early video call with the girls, the whole leaving Lynn out of things topic. Plus, she'd been a bit rough with the Cipher over his not getting back to her sooner the last time, and she didn't want to make that same mistake regarding his time.

"Not a problem—not a problem," Derek tossed back. "What can your friendly neighborhood Cipher-man do for you?" He laughed in a tight burst, at his own comment.

Vicki laughed too, but it was more over his liking his own remark than the bad superhero reference. Then she said, "Horsemen."

There was a long pause from Derek, before he said, "What?"

"The Four Horsemen, to be precise. But I'm confident the reference is about the disorder in the world," Vicki gave him. "There was a reference I found on how The Horsemen and Revelations could apply to contemporary events, modern times," she clarified.

"Should I assume you found these details about The Horsemen in the second entry?" Derek questioned.

"Correct. Let me tell you what I found," Vicki offered, picking up that same paper with the translation.

"Go ahead," Derek prompted.

"The reference talks about the *colours* associated to each," Vicki started. "The colour white for conquest, representing *Catholicism*. Red for war, representing *communism*, black—famine, is for *capitalism*. Death, pale—well, that's self-explanatory."

"Sounds like a typical day to me," Derek said, realism and sarcasm mixing. "But how does that play into the codex's reference or the balance?"

"I'd checked a few other links for more information, but found only nonsense," she said. Like how the horsemen were connected with angels and the four winds. But in her opinion what she'd translated had nothing to do with angels and everything to do with how out of balance the world was. "It could represent the end of the balance," she supposed. "Even the end of the world if you wanted to go that direction."

"What else did the reference mention?" Derek asked, as if not quite convinced.

"Souls dying and crying out. Earthquakes, black sun—red moon, stars falling to earth. Then nothing but silence. A lot like the devastating images from the international news coverage we see," Vicki conveyed.

"Let me circle back with Luc on this," Derek said. "He may have another view on these Horsemen."

Oh great—sure, ask the religious guy, Vicki mused. "I feel confident on this take—makes sense to me," she reiterated. "But go ahead if you think it will help." It was fine, because what she needed right now was help on this second entry. "Can you help me with this other entry in the meantime?"

"I'll do my best," Derek said, distracted as if wondering about the latest cast of characters in this saga. Then he refocused on the task at hand. "Where are you at?"

"I adjusted the part about, *This gathering will keep the balance, and all shall know the... bar the fifth*—to Birthfather. But what about this Solacer? Nothing seems to fit, and it's not clear who or what it is, other than a *fifth* something. There's been four this whole time, four mothers, four daughters, four men with archangel names...."

"Wait no, five... five archangel names—Gabriel makes five. Could it be it's about this fifth archangel?" Derek interrupted.

"The spirit we conjured helped us with that—sort of. He'd said it was the one who held the answer." He'd not said who, but only implied as if confirming it was the Cipher—Derek, as she and the girls had previously suspected.

"It has to be five archangels," Derek stated again, noting the inconsistency.

"We assumed the fifth was you—*the one with all the answers,*" she confessed. "Because of all your help."

"I'm the Cipher," Derek said. "Luc is the Theologian, and Darius—based on his lineage, is this descendant of watchers—the Guardian, and with the Believer, that makes a grouping of four again—not five."

"Can we review that part again," Vicki asked. "Break it down into pieces?"

"Sure thing," Derek said, followed by clacking sounds of a keyboard. "Okay here we go... *When the four descendants of the original four are named*—that's you girls... *and the descendant of Watchers*—Darius... *comes forth, the guard the fifth will be revealed. The fifth will aid the final four. These four...* four is emphasized here twice, *will stand with the guard the fifth... who is one of the Solacer."*

"Yes, I see the theme of fours, but I can read this a million times and *still* not see the answer," Vicki said.

"Let me work on that too—okay," Derek said.

"Okay," Vicki conceded. "Guess now would be a good time to tell you about what we found at the Arboretum."

"You found something? What—what did you find?" Derek asked.

"Nothing... absooooluuuutely nothing," Vicki said, before diving into her explanation.

After signing off with Vicki, Derek began an email addressed to Luc. He wrote with the purpose of updating his friend with the information Vicki had relayed about the latest translation regarding the Horsemen. He shared how Vicki had been adamant about her take on the modern reference, about the world's chaos *and* the balance being off, but he stated in the email that he also questioned the assumptions she had made.

He'd wanted to believe as she had, that it was linked to world disasters and such, but when he'd done a quick search of his own on the *Four Horsemen,* his findings had come back with mainly religious content. He wasn't a religious man by any stretch, but he couldn't deny the things he found, nor the other items he'd researched over the past many months. He and Luc had had lengthy conversations on facts and fiction regarding different religions and the strong beliefs associated. As much as his logical mind wanted it to be quantitative, something else hummed at the back of that rational brain of his.

For the second part of his email, he typed out the information Vicki told him regarding the search the girls had done at the Arboretum. He specified it may be the gathering place or at least where they might find more answers, but likewise added that they'd come up empty. Ending the email on a positive note, he wrote that the girls would make another attempt to search what Vicki had called *the less popular areas,* as soon as they could manage.

Derek had contemplated sharing with Luc what he'd solved from the second entry, the piece about the *birthfather,* but until Vicki had translated more to clarify things, he'd chosen to wait. It would be better when he and Luc could talk, rather than email about the missing pieces.

He hit send on the email to his compadre the Theologian, then went back to his Cipher tasks.

Well, not his true tasks as it pertained to the four new friends he'd been helping, but on a simpler task. This one was for his longtime friend, Lynn, and it was a riddle she had sent for him to tackle. She hadn't explained its source, but she had stated he might find it entertaining to work on.

She was right.

He had been itching for something puzzle-like to distract his logical brain from the recent situational acceptance he'd been faced with. The things he could only once have believed were fantasy, were now becoming a reality in his world. Like this new information on The Horsemen, his love of science and all things mystical, now overlapped in his reality.

He had just reread the text message from Lynn about mermaids and tritons a second time when his computer "*Bleeped*" a notification of an email. His attention shifted to his computer screen, noting a response from Luc sat in his inbox.

It was a short message that read;

> *She's wrong. The Four Horsemen are definitely religious in connotation. Don't say anything until I check something first. I need to speak to someone about this.*

Derek had a feeling his friend was correct, knew they needed to speak, but he was left more curious about the topic, considering Luc's swift and cryptic response. Until Luc got back to him with answers, he'd turn his focus back again to the little riddle.

Chapter 17

Luc had made no hesitation with his response to Derek. He'd been at Dunya's when he'd read the email via his cell phone, but he knew the subject of The Horsemen couldn't wait. He also knew he needed to get the information straight before presenting it to his non-religious, waning non-believer friend.

It had only been a few months ago when Luc had heard mention of The Horsemen. That first time he'd only pondered the idea of them, but with this new finding from the codex, he knew he couldn't ignore what he'd been told then.

"Lynn," Luc said, as he burst through the front door, Dunya in tow.

"That's my name—don't wear it out," I shot back, in a poor try at humor, still staring at the TV. I'd been staring at nonsense TV shows all day as a distraction from what was truly weighing on me

"Hey, I need your help," he said, taking the remote off the coffee table, and turning down the volume.

"I'm all ears," I gave him. I needed a better distraction than the TV. And he'd taken the remote, so all I really had to focus on was him and Dunya.

"Remember our discussion about the Four Horsemen?" he asked.

Okay this was not the dialog I was hoping for. "Yesss—and I remember you thought my theory was BS," I responded, grabbing the TV remote back from him, and adjusting the sound back up.

"I know—I know," he said, taking the remote from me again. Turning down the sound again, he said. "I'm sorry—you were right."

Looking back and forth between him and Dunya, I said, "And why pray-tell am I all-of-a-sudden right?"

"Vicki found something in the codex that made reference to The Horsemen," Luc said.

I blinked a few times and shook my head. "I don't want any part of this, Luc—you know that. So why are you telling me?"

Luc sat down beside me. Dunya sat adjacent to us on the other couch. She said nothing, only smiled her sweet smile as if avoiding the line of fire and waiting for Luc to speak again.

"Well, because Vicki believes it's a metaphor for the disorder of things going on around the world—and the balance being off."

"And?" I said, knowing there'd be more.

"And..," Luc started. "… Derek—who would normally agree with that direction of thinking… well, he…."

"He thinks she might be wrong," Dunya finished for him, as if too anxious to wait for the kicker.

"And I know she's wrong, because of what you told me about them—the leaders of the Watchers, remember?" Luc added.

"How could I forget—tried to," I admitted.

"There were no ties to the codex at that time—now there are," he explained.

Thinking about my response, I took in a deep breath. Then letting it out in a huff, I said, "From what I remember of the information I'd found, it said the four Watchers were waiting on a fifth, something about the fifth being revealed—could it be that fifth *seal* you'd told me about back then?" I questioned. "Is it—is that what Vicki found?"

Luc shot a glance to Dunya.

"Well…," Dunya began.

"Well what? Go ahead—tell me," I said, suffering my own impatience.

"There's mention of a *fifth* in the codex… but in its context, it feels more as though it's about a person," Dunya explained, clarity still lacking.

"And you believe it's a religious reference in the codex," I said, frowning at Luc. "You're the one who sent me all those links. Did you even read any of them?"

"No," he admitted.

"Well—I did. And I saved them." I leaned forward and shook my mouse to wake my laptop. "Here," I said, showing him the browser folder. The folder had more than just the reference links Luc had sent me. "I'd forwarded these links to Derek back then. Even he had found it interesting that similar content crossed multiple religions. Do you remember me telling you that?"

"Ya—but that was before all this other stuff unfolded," Luc said. He cleared his throat. "He and I have discussed these topics many times. He's told me about what he's found regarding *secret books of wisdom* in Gnostic and Christian sects, those similar to scriptural texts—outside of the Biblical. What had amazed both of us—was the consistency, of the same events found in so many cultures."

"Now do you get why I was pissed when you didn't believe me? You hadn't even read all the stuff—or you hadn't connected it all. I don't believe what the girls are dealing with—has to do with spirits or ghosts. But it's not my job to convince them."

"You're right—I hadn't connected it all. This is why I wanted to talk to you—why I need your help."

"Help to do what?" I frowned again.

"Convince them—convince Derek," he said.

"Use the religious stuff you sent me to convince the girls. Might even work with Derek too. Derek never—I know," I recognized, then laughed. At that, I cut and pasted all the references from the folder and placed them in an email, then clicked send, to Luc.

"I wouldn't be so sure about that—he may be coming to our side of things. The girls on the other hand, think they conjured a spirit despite the grimoire cited, *conjuring angels and spirits*."

My eyes bugged. "What spell—what conjuring—what spirit?" I was curious, but definitely not interested in helping convince anyone of my thoughts and ideas on who or what they were really dealing with regarding the codex.

"Uh, ya—forgot you weren't privy to that bit of info," he said. "Halloween—they did it on Halloween."

"Well, you better tell me," I said, "because I have some Halloween shit to share with you too. Especially now you're on board with the whole Horseman thing."

Luc communicated what had happened with the girls and their first conjuring from Halloween night. "The guy was all in white—said his name was Uriel. He told them about the gathering," Luc shared.

When the girls and I had skyped earlier that day, they'd mentioned nothing, but why would they, if they'd believed I had no role in this.

"They assumed they knew the place he described, but they could still be wrong," he added. Then he recapped the girls' venture to the garden and why it could be wrong—the place.

"I see," I responded, a bitter taste circling in my mouth over the secrecy.

"They still think they're men—descendants, not angels, and that they had conjured a ghost of one of the descendants."

"Like I said—use those links to convince them," I countered.

"Ya maybe… though I'm not sure if it matters," Luc said.

Not my problem I thought. "My turn," I said, before diving into *my* Halloween night. As my own kicker, I added the other sighting of the same four guys from the restaurant in Ottawa.

"I remember," Dunya said. "You told me about the strange feelings you'd had that day in Ottawa—at the restaurant. But you never mentioned the Horsemen."

"I figured I had told you enough freaky Lynnie-stuff that day," I said to Dunya. "I've told you both about what I believed now." I shifted my glance to Luc. "It was frustrating—you not believing me about the Horsemen. After everything I'd shared with you back then."

"I'm sorry for not believing you, Lynn," Luc said, his shoulders hunching. "And I'm sorry I didn't make you feel more comfortable with telling me all of this."

"These Horsemen… more descendants—I think not," I continued, despite the apologies. "How could they have been in Ottawa and then in Miami? That big one—he was at the hospital. Darius had seen him too, and the others on Halloween. He thought they were part of the event mind you, but he still *saw* them."

"Why would they be after you?" Luc asked.

"How am I supposed to know? To test Darius, maybe... see if he would protect me again." I suggested. My suggestion didn't explain the little—or not so little persuasion technique I'd attempted in sending those big guys on their way. I hadn't shared that tidbit with Luc and Dunya. I could tell Dunya, maybe. She might have insight on what I'd experienced, what I'd felt at the hospital with the lone giant. Maybe she was feeling something now—about what I'd just told them. If she was *feeling* anything... she didn't share it, or maybe she didn't understand what had happened to me. That would make two of us.

"At the time he didn't understand what he saw," Luc considered. "You said at the hospital he'd been confused by the compulsion to rescue you—got there as the guy took off."

"What about Mitra's dream?" Dunya ask.

"Do you know what it means?" Luc asked.

"I guess everyone knows about the dream now, yes?" Once more she'd shared things, I considered had been for my ears only.

"No—just Luc," Dunya confessed.

"And Derek," I admitted. "But he doesn't know it was from a dream or where the reference came from, only that I had a riddle for him to solve."

Dunya made a *zip-it* motion with her fingers across her mouth and gave a little smile.

"He won't hear it from me—unless you want me to tell him," Luc said.

I shook my head. "Well, I don't think that matters either—because I didn't find anything."

"What do you mean—did you figure it out?" Dunya asked.

"Thought I did. The description matched something I'd seen on Halloween night.

"What could you have possibly seen that had religions mingling, and mermaids in the same place?" Luc joked.

"A tapestry inside *and* a barge outside," I gave him. "I still think it could be the place. But like the search of the Arboretum—this place is massive too."

"I could help search," Dunya offered. "Would be nice to get out—spend some time with you." She smiled bigger.

I smiled back, giving an encouraging nod. "Speaking of mingling religions," I said. "Redmond shared some interesting facts with me. He said Islam was the second largest religion in the world after Christianity."

"True," Luc confirmed. "It's a monotheistic faith meaning *one God,* and it originated in the Middle East."

"Redmond?" Dunya questioned, followed with a little giggle.

"Ya—he's the guy I met Halloween night," I said, "I'm sure Luc told you." I gave her a weak grin. "He also told me Islam embraces many beliefs and practices in common with both Judaism and Christianity. All three are known as *Abrahamic religions*—hence the *mingling* idea I had with the tapestry. The history can be traced all the way back to a pledge God made with *Abraham*—mentioned in the Hebrew Bible," I added, quoting more facts for Luc. Then I grinned at Dunya again. "I told Redmond all about this stuff. He believes in it—well, I presumed he did. I've hardly heard from him since I provided him the full list of weird. He *was* out of town for a week… but he might think I'm nuts."

"Yer not nuts, Lynn," Luc said, patting my shoulder.

"I need to get ready for work—Saturday night shift," I redirected, getting up off the couch. So much for distraction, I was right back where I started, in my pathetic mess of thoughts again.

"Did you tell him what happened on Halloween—with The Horsemen?" Luc asked.

"No—wanted to test the other things out on him first," I clarified. Despite his believing, it was a lot to digest in one sitting.

"Good plan. Poor bastard." Luc laughed. "I think you should tell him though—no point in keeping anything from him now.

"Ya I will… if I ever hear from him that is. I wanted to give him time—ya know… between blowing his mind, again." That was my excuse to them, but I wasn't holding my breath I'd hear from him anytime soon. I also didn't want to admit how foolish I felt for telling him in the first place.

"I hear ya," Luc said.

I nodded, grabbed up my laptop and then wandered off to my room to get ready for work.

My shift had been gratefully uneventful, and I'd opted to help the other support staff distribute the scrubs and swaddling robes to all the stations, and I ended up being later than usual getting home.

Despite Luc's car being in the drive, when I came through the front door, all but the hall lights were off in the house. That was fine though, I wasn't in the mood for more horsemen discussion anyway, so I continued to my bedroom. I found Raven sprawled on my bed, sound asleep.

Changed out of my scrubs now, I sat down on the bed to find I'd left my laptop still powered up. Ever since Vicki and I had dropped off sending our daily exchanges, I'd gotten in the habit of only checking emails a couple times a week.

I woke up the laptop with a mouse shake, then clicked to open my email. Several emails loaded, but only one stood out. Its subject line had no words in it, but it was from *Redmond*. Since this week had me emotionally spent, I was more than reluctant to open it.

I'd imagined various responses from him, good and bad—some worse than others, and I had convinced myself that *if* I did get one, it wouldn't be the happy one I'd foolishly hoped for. I figured it would be a polite kiss-off telling me something like, *I've been busy with things, so I don't have time for a relationship, but it was nice meeting you. Good luck and all.*

Raven lifted his head then and stared at me.

"No sense in speculating the inevitable," I said to him, figuratively ripping off the band-aid by clicking to open the email.

The first line read;

You must think I'm a real bastard by now, but I can explain.

The rest of the email explained he'd been texting me and emailing from his phone with no response. It wasn't until Lily had gotten a message to his parents, saying that she'd been trying to reach him too, that he'd realized something was wrong with his phone. And he'd assumed I'd been the one not responding to him. He'd written that he was supposed to have his new phone by Monday. The email also mentioned that he realized that I would be at work tonight, and that he wasn't sure if I'd see this email when I got home, but he would call me Sunday from the studio—no cell phone and all. He'd ended the email with;

PS. I have something to ask you.

"Whoosh," I said, as my body and brain flooded with relief. I'd let my insecurities get the best of me, but under the circumstances I'd had valid reasons to feel uncertain. "Some seer, eh Raven?" I said, with a hint of levity. Though I was thrilled it was a good—vs a bad email, I was pissed at myself for not being able to... *what,* mystically see the truth of the matter? Right. Whatever *gift* I seemingly possessed for *seeing,* clearly didn't work for *me*. Whatever.

To further dodge dwelling on my lack of clairvoyance, I sent off a short response to him saying;

Thank goodness—I was starting to wonder, even worry. Hope the visit went well despite the phone snafu. Can't wait to hear all about it.

This would be the first night all week I wouldn't wonder why I hadn't heard from him. Though I did wonder what the *something* was that he had to ask me.

Luc already had his computer set up in the back office when he'd heard Lynn come home, but with the late hour he'd chosen not to bother her again with more discussion. Besides, right now what he was determined to do was convince Derek-the-skeptic of things, even if it took every resource he had. Armed with the additional references sent from Lynn, he hit the Skype call-button to link up with the Cipher.

When Derek's face appeared on the screen, Luc began with, "Hey man. About these Horsemen...." Then he dove into what Lynn had told him prior about them. He also shared the experiences she'd had from Halloween, the restaurant, and at the hospital. Derek only nodded as he described Lynn's findings on the connection to both these guys and the Horsemen. At the end of the explanation, Luc restated, "If the codex mentions them, they must be involved."

"Maybe what Lynn saw in Ottawa was a vision or something—you know she's got that freaky way about her—maybe it was a sign of what was to come in Miami," Derek considered. "They didn't do anything to her in Ottawa, yet on Halloween they chased her through the grounds. Darius may have been at the top of the stairs when she came up, but he didn't save her from anything. I mean, Lynn told you they just turned away and left."

"What if they were sent to test Darius?" Luc suggested, leading into more details about the one at the hospital. "The guy left when Darius was near."

"Why do you think these guys keep showing up?"

"I think it's part of how Darius reveals himself as the Guardian, protecting his friends," Luc said.

"So what, these horsemen are like those other guys who visited the moms, descendants—part of a secret sect of some sort?"

Luc knew the rational and imaginative sides of Derek's brain continued to be at odds these days. "We need to talk about angels and spirits," Luc announced to his friend, "And you need to be open."

"Dammit—not the angel thing again," Derek defected. "Yer gonna make me listen anyway, aren't you?"

"Yep—and check your inbox. I just sent you a list of links," Luc instructed. "Let's start with the misconception that angels are strictly Christian—they're not." Luc further clarified using references from his list that the angel mythology existed long before Christianity and Judaism. Derek knew about Celtic and Norse mythology, but Luc continued the theme with how they also show up in Buddhism and Hinduism, and in numerous Shamanistic legends.

"I remember Lynn sending me similar references. We'd talked about the crossovers and similarities," Derek acknowledged. "That was before…."

"I know," Luc said, cutting him off. "… before all this." Luc took a breath. "They don't all call them angels, just like not everyone uses the term *prayer,* they may say mantra or spell of protection," Luc simplified. "They're labels for what's basically the same things. Like with Buddhists, they use the label *devas* or *celestial beings* instead of angel."

"I see what you're saying on similarities," Derek agreed. "Hinduism texts mention different spiritual beings who behave similar to how angels are referenced, playing a protective role for humans. And there's mention of fallen devas who inhabited some lower astral plane of existence, like the fallen angels maybe—the trapped ones."

"The concepts of angels may not be the same, but they coincide and overlap at certain points," Luc said, leaning forward in his seat. "In Judaism, Christianity and in Islam, some act as messengers from, well… *God*. Some act as warriors or guards."

"Like a Guardian Angel?" Derek questioned, still skeptical.

"Sure—ya, whatever—maybe," Luc said. "On the link for Hinduism, they are not referred to as angels, but are spirit beings who can regulate *karma*.

"Karma, like impacting the balance," Derek stated, a little less skeptical.

"Exactly!"

"I see," Derek said again, this time with more interest.

"Check out the link about *Sons of God*. They're mentioned in the Bible, Torah, Koran, Apocrypha, the Dead Sea Scrolls, and in the legends of the Babylonians and Sumerians.

"Sumerians—*Sumer*," Derek acknowledged.

"This last reference link compares The Watchers to the *Sons of God*. How, in earlier references in *Genesis*, God seemed to be talking to *other beings* about the fate of man. In the *Book of Ezekiel*, it specifies the *Servants of God*, how they had human form and also had wings," Luc stated. "You mentioned Sumer. There was also a story about *Sumerians* that related to the *flood story*, something about mystical beings on the earth at the time, rising into the sky to avoid drowning. Genesis also mentions the flood in the *Sons of God* story."

"The *Ancient Egyptian* creation myth details a flood story too—how the *gods climbed back up into heaven…*," Derek recalled, "… to escape the flood."

"Both Norse and Hebrew stories tell of The Watchers, Derek. Everything circles back and overlaps," Luc said.

"The anagrams," Derek tossed out. "The guard—*daughter*. Glean—*Angel*."

"The Divine Language—it's what that first entry is written in... and the undated one, from just before Alison's mother's entry," Luc remembered.

"The *Angelic Alphabet* is also known as the language of Angels," Derek added.

"Descendant or Angel, Derek—You choose," Luc tossed out, leaning back in his chair.

There was a short pause, then Derek said, "Well, I guess I should tell you about this *guard the fifth* in the second entry then."

"You mentioned that before—the fifth, it being about the fifth Archangel," Luc recalled.

"Nope—not that part." Derek gave another short pause. "It's an anagram...," he stated, "... for *birthfather*."

Chapter 18

Finally, a good night's sleep.

I'd even slept in. However, Raven had tickled my arm just before 9 a.m., but regardless of my furry wakeup call, I was refreshed from such a wonderful sleep. Though it helped to know things were all fine in Redmond-land too.

Content, I strode to the kitchen to start my Sunday. I went to feed Raven, but he had half a bowl of kibble still in his dish. Luc must have fed him, I figured. That's when I saw the note stuck to the coffee maker.

It read;

> *Had a great talk with Derek last night. We may have a believer on our hands, finally.*
>
> *I'm off to chat with Darius about the latest. I'll check in later.*
>
> *I fed Raven already btw.*

"Believer," I said out loud. Let's hope they can do the same with the girls.

Raven, "*Woofed,*" and nudged my hand.

"Yer a believer—aren'tcha boy?" I said, in response, bending to give his side a good pat. That's when I heard my cell phone ringing off in the distance. "Crap." I'd left it in the bedroom to charge.

Dashing off followed by my furry-believer, I rounded into my bedroom as the last ring sounded. I stopped short at the bedside table and stared at the phone, giving a, "*Huff*." It rang again, and I grabbed it from the charger. "Hello," I said, not checking to see who it was first.

"Lynn," came a familiar voice. "Did I wake you?"

"No-no, I'm up," I responded. But *that voice could wake me anytime,* I mused. Redmond's laughter trailed my thought. *OMG, I hadn't said that out loud, had I?*

"Ah, Lynn—good to hear your voice. I'm awfully sorry about the mix up with the stupid phone," he said. "Forgive me?"

"Forgiven," I said. "It's nothing that a homecooked meal couldn't fix." My stomach growled.

"Well, I may owe you a month-full of homecooked meals after you hear what I'm about to ask you," he responded.

"How bad could it be," I tossed out.

"Bad," he tossed back. "What's your feelings on black-tie affairs?"

* * *

"Bad," Redmond had said, but *bad* hadn't covered it.

I'd had to spend my off hours from work this week, going *shopping* with Dunya. I was thankful for her help, and I enjoyed her company, but we'd had to shop for an evening dress, one suitable for a black-tie affair, namely *The Annual Vizcaya Ball,* that was now in fact *tonight,* Friday December 11th, as it was displayed on the fancy invite card Redmond had emailed me earlier in the week.

I'd looked up the event online hoping it might be more casual than the invite reflected, but based on the description on the website I found… it was not;

> *The Annual Vizcaya Ball reflects the beauty and elegance of an extraordinary South Florida cultural icon. Nowhere else in South Florida will you find a more gracious and elegant setting for one of the most celebrated formal affairs in Miami attended by people who care about the preservation of Vizcaya Museum and Gardens.*
>
> *The night begins at the red-carpet entrance into the beautiful Gilded Age estate, leading into the gardens and Courtyard for the cocktail soiree. The evening continues with entertainment and an elegant dinner overlooking Biscayne Bay.*

Attendees bid on fabulous silent auction items and dance the night away. The evening culminates with a spectacular fireworks display from above the historic stone barge.

This Ball is held to raise funds for the Vizcaya Museum and Gardens, the 1914 home of James Deering. Today, this Historic Landmark continues to celebrate and share its history, the arts and its natural environment with thousands of guests, welcoming visitors from our community and from around the world.

"Yeeesh," I said, rereading the part about *dancing the night away.* "Redmond's gonna owe me bigtime for this," I stated to Raven, as he watched me shimmy into the much-too-fancy-for-my-liking-dress.

Redmond had said he *wasn't a fan* of these kinds of events, but it wasn't something he could get out of. Even Lily had balked at the idea of going with him to represent the studio. *"Not her scene,"* she'd told him. Wasn't mine either, but here I was, stuck in another gawd-damn dress.

Standing now in front of the floor-length mirror, I spotted Raven behind me in the reflection, tilting his head to the side as if to see my reflection better. "What?" I said to my furry buddy.

He, *"Woofed,"* and rolled over on his back as if in surrender.

"Great help you are," I said, then glanced down at my newly painted crimson toenails.

Dunya had found me a nice dress, a great dress actually, *and* matching shoes. It was a floor-length fitted black finely overlaid laced dress. The 4-inch opened-toed heels she'd found had the same matching black lace overlay. I'd struggled a bit with the updo of my hair, but with the help of an online video, I had managed an elegant look to match my dress. The dress was comfy as were the shoes believe it or not, but I still felt like a little girl playing dress-up.

It certainly wasn't a little-girl dress though with its sexy lace front and low dip in the back, and as I zipped the hidden side zipper, despite the dress's coverage, it hugged my body leaving little to the imagination. But I had to admit, I looked good. *And* I was feeling calmer now about the event. It was a shame the girls couldn't see me like this. "Mac would lose her shit," I said to Raven.

He was still on his back, stretched out as if he had an imaginary friend rubbing his belly, or perhaps it was his invitation for me to do so.

"Beautiful," Gabriel said, admiring the vision in the mirror.

"Brave," Shamsiel responded, as he continued to scratch Raven's belly. "He's here you know—still in Miami."

"Armaros—yes, I know." Gabriel stepped forward. "He wouldn't dare touch her," he threatened.

"He's been close—too close," Shamsiel reminded.

"She can hold her own—you'll see." *They'll all see,* Gabriel thought, as he vanished.

At 6:15 p.m. with only minutes to spare, Redmond's car pulled into the drive, and I peeked out the living room window.

I'd known he owned two vehicles, a *band-van* as he called it, for use for transporting musicians and equipment, running errands and such, but the one he drove tonight, was a classic fully restored 1968 root-beer coloured Mustang GT. I wasn't one for cars, but this one was a beauty. He'd told me he rarely took her out unless it was a special occasion. I'm guessing this was one of those *occasions*.

I said goodbye to Raven and exited the house before Redmond was up the walk.

"Wow—Westlake, you really clean up nice," Redmond said, straightening his bowtie.

"Don't get used to it," I said, giving myself a little spin. "*Cinderella*—one night only, Raven informed me. He helped me get ready," I added.

"Okay, Master Raven. I'll have her home by midnight—no later," he said, giving a wave to Raven who had been watching from the living room window.

Opening the passenger side door, Redmond leaned down and helped me slide into the seat. "You look very handsome," I said, as I scooped the bottom of my dress into the car. He smiled and adjusted his tie again. Then he shut the car door and dashed around to the other side.

"I'd rather we were heading out in jeans and tees, someplace quiet for beers and pizza," he said, as he got into the driver's seat.

"This was your idea—remember?" I adjusted my seatbelt.

"Don't remind me," he said, giving me a wink and pulling out of the drive.

When we approached the entrance, I remembered that even though I'd messaged Redmond about my coming here to search *and* my not finding anything, he hadn't actually received those messages. Faulty phone. Now wasn't the best time to share that little adventure, but I made myself a little agreement to share it with him when a better moment presented itself.

We walked up the steps and there it was… the red-carpet entrance. I let out a "Groan."

"Not quite the same look and feel as Halloween," Redmond said, taking my hand and leading me through the entrance of the beautiful estate. A white gloved concierge pointed the way to the courtyard for the cocktail part of the event.

As it had stated on the website, the evening advanced with formal entertainment and an elegant dinner overlooking the bay.

I glanced across to the Barge, but it appeared the same as it had the night of Halloween, the sculpted figures all muted in the darkness. I turned my head back towards the lavish gardens… and a prickling sensation cut across the back of my neck.

"The silent auction is about to start," Redmond said, seizing my attention. "This year they have something worth bidding on." At the beginning of the evening, when we'd walked through the Loggia room on our way to the courtyard, he'd pointed out the item worth bidding on. It was a vintage recording studio microphone that had been used at RCA Victor recording studios in 1956 to record Elvis Presley's first album. "It'll look great in my office," he said, getting up from his seat at the table. He put out his hand to escort me to the bidding area.

The auction items had been moved from the Loggia room to the Inner Court for viewing and bidding. I stood back as Redmond, along with other interested parties, moved from item to item surveying the other tables. He smiled at me from across the room. I smiled back admiring how wonderful he looked in his tuxedo. I noticed that some of the other women in attendance were admiring him too. That made me smile bigger because he was here with *me*. Then my smile dropped.

Across the way, at the entrance to the room that contained the religious tapestry, stood that same large man I'd seen near the Barnacle; the same one I'd seen those too many times back in Ottawa. But he'd been alone all those times. This time he was flanked by two other large men similar in appearance to the ones I'd seen on Halloween, but these men I'd never seen before. And they were all watching me.

The name *Armaros,* rang in my head as a hint of nausea crept the back of my throat. Armaros, my mind replayed, recalling the name Dunya had spoken, the one Mitra had given to the dark figure in her dream. My skin grew hot, and I swayed on my high heels. I leaned a hand against the nearest wall. *Not again,* I thought, *not now.* When Redmond's back was turned, I stepped back and slipped through the crowd of guests to find my way once again to the ladies' room.

The nausea subsided as I stood staring at myself in the bathroom mirror. I appeared as I had in my mirror, only this time I was as white as a ghost. *What the hell was going on?* "Lynn get a grip," I whispered to myself. Turning towards the bathroom exit, I took in several long cleansing breaths, then I stepped forward and pulled open the door.

But instead of returning to the auction area, I had the inkling to head through the library and through the hidden passage behind the bookcase to the room that held the admiral carpet. *Had I missed something the last time I was here?* I pondered.

From the doorway I panned the room looking for something, anything that would give me a hint. Then there at the far entranceway, I spied the same three massive men. One by one they stepped through the doorway and into the room taking up an enormous amount of space. They glared at me... but I stared pass them. Behind them had appeared four equally massive figures. *The Horsemen.*

Armaros cut a glance over his shoulder to see what had caught my attention. It gave me the opening I needed to slip back through the passageway. And rather than sliding the full way through to the Library, I snuck into a small nearly undetectable door into what I'd seen on the map prior as, the *Telephone room.*

The pounding of feet sounded as shadows rushed past the seam in the door in the direction of the library, only to fade as if they moved further through the other door to the main hall. I waited and listened.

When it was silent, and no shadows passed by the door, I opened it and stole a peek. Seeing nothing, I moved from the tiny room into the Library.

I spied the wooden box on the desk, the bronze feathers gleaming under the desk lamp. *"Feathers,"* I whispered to the air, then I ducked under the barrier rope.

I snatched up the box.

At closer inspection I realized it didn't open like a regular hinged box. But I knew how to open it. Grabbing firm to the carved inlayed piece with the bronze feathers, I drew it up and turned it clockwise. The box opened with the lid sliding away from me. It was a puzzle box, like the caduceus one Olivia's mother had hidden. "Bingo," I said, when I saw what was inside.

The symbols for *mother* and *daughter* were imprinted on the outside of an envelope. They were the same symbols shown on the front of the codex. Seizing it from its confines, I tucked it into the fancy handbag Dunya had loaned me. I returned the box to its original spot and slipped back under the ropes. Without haste, I returned through the passage to the Living room, giving the admiral carpet a thumbs-up as I passed through to the Loggia room.

The big scary men were nowhere to be seen, but neither was Redmond. Many of the guests were venturing outside again, and I followed. Once through the big glass doors to the patio area, I spotted him leaning against the wall, the same place I'd found him on Halloween when I'd given my apologies about running off that first time. And again, like that night, there was a butterfly on a branch near him.

"Hi mom," I said, to the little flutterer as I approached my date.

"Do you always talk to butterflies?" He leaned into the leaves for closer inspection.

"Yes… they connect me to my mom. I consider them sent by her to watch over me."

"Did you know…," he started to say, but then paused. "Where did you go?" he asked.

"Ladies room," I said. "Did I know what?"

He smiled at my redirection. "Butterflies taste with their feet… and smell with their antennae."

"How fascinating," I said, grinning, knowing he had more for me on the subject.

He smiled again and took my hand. As we walked to the far side of the patio area, he relayed all he knew on the subject. "Butterflies don't have lungs. They breathe through openings on their bellies, called *spiracles*. Female butterflies are usually bigger and live longer than male butterflies."

"You don't say," I said, squeezing his hand a little and tilting my head up to look at him.

"The largest butterfly, the Queen Alexandra's Birdwing from New Guinea can have a wingspan of over 10 ½ inches. There's about 24,000 species, and Antarctica is the only continent without butterflies," he said, sitting down on the lower stone wall, making us now face to face.

"Well, I'm glad I don't live there," I joked.

He squeezed my hand this time. "Thanks for coming with me tonight," he said, as the two of us watched the other guests dance the night away. "Oh, I won the bid—got my little treasure." Just then the spectacular fireworks display shot off over the barge.

"So did I," I whispered, patting my purse. So… did… I.

Gabriel and Shamsiel appeared near the side of the house as the car pulled into the driveway. At Vizcaya they had stood back observing, waiting to see if Armaros risked being too close once again or if any of the others got too close. Gabriel and Shamsiel had followed Lynn to the Library and had stepped through the passage after her. Once on the other side, they'd flanked her at the entrance of the room. The Horsemen's arrival had been opportune, for they'd witnessed for themselves the truth of Armaros *and* his two followers. In fact, it had been the Horsemen who had taken off after Lynn, but for what purpose, neither of them could surmise.

"I told you she could hold her own," Gabriel said, turning to face the walkway.

"I shouldn't have been surprised Armaros showed his face tonight—but I was shocked to see the other four," Shamsiel expressed.

"The other two with Armaros, I already knew he'd swayed to his side, like dogs at their master's heels." All three had fled at the arrival of The Horsemen.

"The four must have wanted to see if Armaros would interfere again," Gabriel suggested. "They must have tracked him there, stood back and watched as we had done."

"Armaros hadn't been after Lynn, he'd been after the letter," Shamsiel considered. "Your Charge must have hidden it without Armaros's knowledge." He chuckled then.

"Yes. All this time I thought he knew—that he'd instructed her, but he'd somehow not been privy to the hiding," Gabriel said. "It explains why he's been watching Lynn so closely—taking the risk."

"And now she has the letter," Shamsiel said. "He'll be furious."

"Yes," Gabriel said, again. "But now the four have witnessed his meddling too." This brought a grin to his face as he watched the couple take the steps to the front door.

"They're charming together," Shamsiel said, changing the focus. He too grinned.

"Back before midnight as promised," Redmond said, walking me to the front door. "How about I bring you breakfast tomorrow?"

"Whose good-side are you trying to get on—mine or Raven's?"

"Both."

"Probably a wise decision," I said, glancing down to get my key out of my purse. When I glanced up again, he stepped in closer, close enough I could see the faint smattering of freckles on his cheeks.

"Thanks again for coming with me tonight," he said, leaning down. Before I could reply, he kissed my right cheek and then the left, then wrapped an arm around my lower back in a gentle embrace.

"I survived," I managed to say, when he placed his forehead against mine. Despite the cool night air, a flush of warmth ran the length my body.

"Tomorrow then," he said, releasing me, stepping backwards down the stairs.

"Tomorrow," I agreed. I gave a little wave as he backed up towards the car.

I turned away unsteady as if I'd never worn high heels before and unlocked the front door. I glanced back and waved again as he drove out the lane.

A little off balance but in a good way, I changed out of my fancy dress and into my favorite oversized t-shirt. It was the one with Calvin and Hobbes on it that my brother had sent last year as a Christmas present. Then I put away all the fancy matching clothing into my closet, but not before taking out the letter from my loaner-purse.

Raven was again sound asleep on the far side of my bed. Sitting down I propped the pillows against the headboard, then reached over and gave Raven's soft coat a few long strokes with my hand.

With only the light from the bedside lamp, I shifted to examine the envelope and its ancient symbols. Turning it over, I flipped up an unglued edge and ran a finger under it to separate the flap. Gingerly I removed the papers and set the envelope aside. The white sheets of paper had been neatly folded in thirds. I unfolded them and set them face up on the bed next to the envelope.

The envelope had the mother and daughter symbols like the codex, minus the squished star-spider symbol—the codex had all three. But like the other letters, the first page had that star symbol in the corner. Though unlike the other letters, there was no *Dear Daughter* to start the message. Instead, this letter began with, *Dear Yasmin.*

Pressing out the folds of the letter, I continued reading;

> *Dear Yasmin,*
>
> *I was only 18 when I was first visited by the messenger. He presented himself as a man, but I sensed he was otherworldly, divine. He told me he had chosen me to help keep the balance. That he'd been granted a favor from his father to help his brothers, and in turn help the human race. He told me I was a descendant of one of the fallen leaders, one who was involved from the very beginning.*

This part was similar to the information the other mothers had shared in their letters. Though theirs had not mentioned *fathers* or *brothers,* they did however name those who had visited them. But these things, about the human race, the *descendant,* and *fallen leaders,* this screamed codex *and* the story of Enoch.

I knew it, my birthmother was involved, and more than we'd all realized. She wasn't just a conduit of information, she was a descendant. When Vicki had worked on the second entry, Alison had suggested that perchance they'd find something about my birthmom and what she'd written. I still didn't know what that codex entry held, didn't matter now, I'd found it. I had what she'd written.

I read on;

> *He told me I was to carry this child, a daughter and that once she was born, I was to place her in a family where no other daughters existed, one strong with sons.*

That would be the Westlakes all right, and my Aunt Kay with her four sons, plus all my male cousins. I found it intriguing that the request had been for me to be surrounded by sons. Everything we'd discovered so far had been about mothers and daughters. *More questions*, I pondered, and read on;

> *I'd been told that my baby would be safe there until she found her way to the other four, and then she would bring them together for the gathering.*

There it was—my role, bring the four together, but it seemed that was all there was, another screeching halt to *my* involvement.

I read further, but this next part, I already knew;

> *I'd written out the details as I'd been instructed. Though I'd been told not to tell anyone, I shared what I'd done with a girlfriend from my high school days. As it was, I would see my old friend again, when I was diagnosed with Breast Cancer, she became my doctor.*
>
> *A few years passed, and I was visited again, but this time I was told to hide the information I'd written out, hide it far away from where the evil ones could find it. I was also instructed to visit the woman who had adopted my baby. Soon after, I revisited my doctor friend, and found the cancer was back.*
>
> *If you are reading this, it means I have lost my battle with this deadly disease, but please know I risked my life, made the sacrifice only to keep you safe.*

Raven had woken as I shifted on the bed, and now his head was nuzzled up next to my leg as I read. "That PI, Anthony, had told me about these visits with the friend," I whispered to him. In a rush, all the things Anthony had told me flooded back into my brain.

The friend had known about the pregnancy, but they both had kept it a secret. They'd been close in high school, though my birthmother never told her who the father was. There'd been no boyfriend but there'd been mention of a one-night thing. There'd been some crap about a fortuneteller too, but the friend hadn't believed either story. They'd gone years without seeing each other, not until my birthmother had wound up sick and in the same hospital where this friend worked. It had been the first time they'd talked about the baby since the day she'd given me up.

"There's more, Raven," I whispered to him again, remembering. Anthony had said, '*This is where the story gets a bit off,*' like as if the first part hadn't been totally off. The friend had told him about my birthmother saying that the baby—me, was still on her correct path *and* something about the balance being kept. The friend said she'd brushed off the strange comment as more than likely being cancer medication fog. But she had also said my birthmother always seemed to *know* things, and she had considered the possibility she had been keeping an eye on me or something. When she'd asked my birthmother about the father again, all she gotten from her was that she'd *written it all down* and *the information was safe*. The friend had also indirectly confirmed the same I'd found in Mom's journal, about the visit on my 27th birthday. But unfortunately, the friend had known nothing more about the visit.

This letter didn't tell me anything more about who I was, *the key to who I am,* as Dunya had put it. I'd known I was adopted, who adopted me, that my birthmom had been a single mother, *and* that she'd died of breast cancer. The girls and I had established my role in all this too. It was nothing new. But… this second piece of paper, the one folded up inside the letter, this page… it made reference to more… something about a gathering. *Did I have something more* I wondered? Luc had mentioned a gathering and how they'd been trying to figure out further the details about it. Could this be the same gathering? It must be, had to be.

"It's in English—no translation needed at least," I said to Raven. "But I'm pretty sure I had myself a few new anagrams in my hand." I was starting to hate riddles. "More secrets than a slumber party." *Stupid* anagrams.

Chapter 19

Redmond arrived at my door at 8 a.m. sharp.

This was the first time—other than the pickup and drop off, that he'd come to my home. And it was also the first time I'd seen him in shorts.

I'd thrown on a white t-shirt with the words *Made in Canada* in red on it and had also chosen shorts, a pair of old cutoffs for this casual breakfast. I'd opted for a loose bun for my hair to save fussing with it, considering my efforts with the updo of the night before. I guess we both liked silly t-shirts, because along with his dark-grey cargo shorts he wore a black tank top with the words *powered by tacos* in white on the front.

"Warm freshly baked pumpernickel bagels and honey-almond spread," he said, stepping across the threshold. He'd gone for the kill shot, straight to my heart via my stomach.

"That's it," I joked. My stomach grumbled. I had nothing else in retaliation and could only wave an arm showing the way in.

As if ready for battle, he said, "Farmers market raspberries, strawberries, and blueberries for us to share."

"Dammit," I tossed out. "You play dirty Credente—always going for my food weakness."

He laughed and continued his way to the kitchen.

"Coffee?" I asked, pointing to the already made pot of goodness. "I was thinking we could sit out back and enjoy the nice weather."

"Sounds perfect," he said. "Plates?"

I'd had the cupboard opened to get mugs out, and in response I pointed to the cupboard next to it.

Redmond plated the warm bagels, one for each of us, adding just the right amount of that delicious spread to each side. I made myself useful by rinsing off the berries and making a pick-and-eat bowl of the variety to take with us outside.

"I'll grab napkins," Redmond said, tearing a few paper towels from the roll. "Ready?"

"Ready," I responded, liking how comfortable he was with helping in my kitchen.

Out on the patio we took up residence on the outdoor couch, using the small coffee table to set up our breakfast.

Redmond sat down next to me bumping my leg. I noticed he had freckles on those lean muscular legs of his. Trying to refocus I glanced up and said, "Who did you get the red hair from?"

He was grinning. He'd caught me staring at his legs. "My mother," he said, handing me a plate.

As if providing a new focus, a butterfly floated on the breeze directly in front of the table.

"Hi Mom," I said, before taking a big bite of the bagel. I closed my eyes savoring the warmth of the bagel and the sweet creaminess of the spread.

"Butterflies can't fly if they're cold," Redmond said, stealing my attention from my breakfast.

"What?" I asked. I took another big bite, then grinned.

He gave a chuckle, then took a bite of his own bagel. He chewed and swallowed, then said, "They need a body temp of about 85 degrees Fahrenheit to fly."

"Why?" I grabbed a couple berries from the bowl and popped them into my mouth.

"They're cold-blooded and can't regulate their body temperature. The air temp has a big impact on their ability to function—if the temp drops below 55, they can be rendered immobile, at the mercy of their enemies or unable to eat."

"That's not cool, especially the not eating part." I finished off the first half of my bagel.

"Same goes for too hot a temp—they can get overheated. Newly emerged butterflies can't fly either," he added, leaning forward, stealing a few berries from the bowl.

"I guess I never thought of them as something that would be eaten," I said.

Finishing the first half of his bagel, Redmond said, "Butterflies are low on the food chain, but they use all kinds of tricks to keep from being eaten."

"Like?" I took a long savoring sip of my coffee.

He wiped the corner of his mouth with a paper towel napkin. "Well, some camouflage themselves by folding their wings in to blend in with the background. Some do the opposite—use the colours of their wings as a warning. Predators tend to leave bright coloured insects alone—they're often toxic, so the butterfly will mimic the foul-tasting ones to repel enemies."

"Why do you know so much about them?" I asked, before taking another sip of my coffee.

"Hey, I'm not some pretty-face, dumb musician ya know—I know things," he joked.

"I know that." I gave his arm a fake punch. "But why butterflies?"

Keeping me waiting, he took a long sip of coffee from his mug. "I knew a few odd facts before, always thought they were beautiful—fascinating." He grinned. "But when I found out they were special to you, I researched more about them."

Okay, that was sweet. "What else have you researched on my behalf?"

"Pizza recipes," he tossed out.

"You really know the way to my heart, music man." With approval I clinked my coffee mug against his.

I took another sip just as Mitra came from around the far corner into the backyard. "Hiii Leeenn," she said, in her thick accent, stopping in front of where we sat. It was a welcome surprise, as I had seen little of her with my work hours, the parties and my getting to know Redmond.

"Good morning, Mitra. This is my special friend, Redmond," I said, displaying my open palm next to him.

"Hello," Redmond said, extending his large hand in greeting for a handshake.

Mitra glanced down at his hand, then glanced back up to smile at me. Then she placed her tiny hand in his, but instead of shaking it, she placed her other hand on the outside of it, lifting his hand to her cheek. Closing her eyes, she whispered something that sounded much like "*Mowmin*," and more than likely Arabic.

Redmond glanced at me puzzled.

I raised my eyebrows and shook my head.

Mitra opened her eyes. She then removed Redmond's hand from against her cheek and replaced it over top of mine. She raised a hand to my face and brushed the back of it against my cheek. Her blue eyes squinted as her smile grew wider. She glanced back at Redmond with an opened-mouth smile now. Then before either of us could say anything, she turned and was off, shuffling back across the yard.

I watched as she disappeared back around the corner. "I think she likes you," I said, giving his ribcage a poke.

"Young and old—what can I say," he responded, giving my hand a squeeze. Shifting gears, Redmond said, "Yer leaving for Ottawa—your Christmas visit, a week from this Monday, right?"

"Yup," was all I had on that topic as I observed his hand on mine. I was looking forward to seeing my friends and family, but I wasn't looking forward to the reality of those who would be missing on this trip.

Redmond loosened his grasp on my hand and then leaned in to grab up the other half of his bagel. "I need to head to the studio to meet Lily and our newest client around noon. I've got a crazy busy week ahead with wrapping things up with this latest artist. And a slew of industry holiday parties." He took a bite of the bagel.

I cringed at the words *holiday parties*.

"Don't worry," he said, "I've saved you from all that—Lily is going with me. I hate them, but she loves it."

"Well, I have two of my own holiday parties to go to," I countered. "One Friday night for staff, and one on Saturday before my shift—for the kids'n parents." I shrugged. "No dressing up for me though." I smirked.

"Actually, you have *three* parties to go to."

I frowned.

"I'm having a small gathering the Sunday before you leave. I'm cooking—super casual, you in?"

"Good food and no dress-up—I'm in," I said, grabbing up my remaining bagel half.

We spent the remainder of the morning sipping coffee, nibbling on the berries and chatting. It had felt a bit strange having Redmond in my space, my home, but it was a good kind of strange, another new normal I figured.

After Redmond left, I contemplated writing to the girls, but since they hadn't felt the need to keep me in the loop, I figured there was no need for me to rush with any updates either. Though, the person I did want to contact, was Derek.

I sent off a quick email explaining what I'd found and instructing him not to say anything about it to the girls. I wrote that *I wanted just he and I to work on it* since it was evidently *my* lineage this time and didn't belong to the others. I also wanted him to help me figure out what the hell this squished star symbol was too.

I hadn't fully digested the fact the letter was from my birthmother, nor did I understand why she'd hidden it in Miami of all places, but I did realize how fortunate I was to be here now. And when Luc and Dunya came through the front door midafternoon, I felt fortunate again. They both knew now and believed me about The Horsemen, which would make my telling them who I'd seen again at Vizcaya *and* what I'd found there, even easier.

"Hey, how was your night?" Luc asked, walking through to the living room.

"How did the dress go over," Dunya prompted, before I could answer the first question.

The two of them plunked down on the adjacent couch, all smiles and eager for the *romantic* update, but that wasn't the update I was about to lay on them.

"It was nice, actually—Redmond won the item he wanted from the silent auction," I said first, relaying the normal parts of my night.

"Armaros was there—wasn't he?" Dunya asked, before I could get to the not-so-normal parts.

"How did you know?" I asked, then realized the obvious.

"Jadda," Dunya said, aiding my assumption. "She was frantic all night—kept saying his name."

"Armaros was there," I confirmed, "Plus two others I'd never seen. They're the same—like him, like The Horsemen. And they were there too." I explained what had happened, then grabbed up my notebook of weird off the coffee table. It was already out from my review of the names of The Horsemen and in hopes of identifying the other two.

"Mitra recited two other names as well," Dunya added, as I got to the page with the names.

"Here," I said, flipping open the notepad to show her the list for the 20 leaders. I pointed to the name *Armaros* in the list, then pointed to the four names that represented The Horsemen.

Dunya leaned in to review the list. "Shamsiel," she said, when she spotted the familiar name. "There—the other two, *Araquel* and *Ramiel*. Those are the other names Jadda spoke."

"That leaves 12... of the 20 leaders," Luc noted. "Where do you think they are?"

"Where was Redmond?" Dunya asked. "Did he see them, too?

"No. He was busy with the auction. I found him outside after, but I didn't see the others again," I stated. "Darius wasn't there this time, Luc," I pointed out. "And I have something else to tell you—show you, really." I handed Luc the letter. "It's from my birthmother."

Dunya's mouth fell open, as did Luc's.

"You said you came up empty when you searched last time," Luc reminded.

"It was there?" Dunya asked. "How did you find it?"

"Found it in a puzzle box—in the library, the room with all the angel décor."

Luc stared at the envelope as if too scared to read what was inside. "How did you know it was there?" he asked.

"I didn't—not really. The guys chased me, and I hid—like I said. Was hard to run in high heels. Instead of going back to the same room where they'd spotted me, I went back into the library. That's when I saw the box with the feather on it. I'd thought the feather was a leaf originally. I don't know how, but I knew it—knew this was *it*. And I knew how to open it too, based on the one I'd found with Olivia. I put it back of course—I'm no thief." I rolled my eyes. "Stashed the envelope in my purse, the one you loaned me Dunya. Thank you again—by the way."

Luc turned the envelope over and then slid the paper from its confines. Unfolding it, he said, "You cool with me reading this?"

"Of course," I said. "You've been part of this from the start. Second page is full of riddles I think though—haven't tackled them yet. I sent a copy to Derek too—asked him to help me out. But told him *not* to tell the girls—this is about me, not them."

Luc nodded and then spread open the pages to read. When he flipped to the next page, he said. "Riddles—anagrams?"

"Why do you think they were after you," Dunya asked. "For the letter?"

"The Horsemen have something to do with your friends—we know," Luc confirmed. "And your birthmother had said she'd hidden information, but it may have nothing to do with the others."

"This message is for me—not them," I said. "Neither my mother, nor my birthmother is mentioned in the codex, but this letter states I was to bring the others together—and I have." Adding to my convictions, I said, "Why these guys are around me—I have no idea. The letter may not have anything to do with them or the stuff you're helping Derek with, but it may have something to do with my birthfather."

"Why do you say that," Luc asked, his expression shifting at my mention of my *birthfather*. He took a quick glance at Dunya, then back at me.

I suspected he was holding something back, but I let it go. "Something the PI had told me… something the doctor friend had mentioned when she'd questioned my birthmother about the father," I explained. "She had implied as though she'd written that information down too."

"Did you tell Redmond what you found," Dunya asked.

"He was here this morning—brought me breakfast. But I didn't tell him about the letter or The Horsemen." I took a quick glance at Luc, then back at Dunya. They knew I had already told him about my seer gift, that the girls were searching for answers to the mystery of their descendants, and that Derek, Luc and Darius were somehow involved, and that we considered it more secret society stuff, maybe. But sharing my thoughts with him that it all had a divine premise, might push the limits of his open mind. "Even with all I've told him, something like this—me seeing these guys etc. might be too much to handle. Once I figure out the second piece of the letter, maybe I'll share it with him—once I understand it more."

"Ya, I'm in the know—and even I find it hard to handle most days," Luc said, handing the papers to Dunya. She took her turn to read.

"Luc, you can't tell the girls… not until I solve this letter," I said.

"Okay…," he said, hesitant. "Derek is working on the gathering location with Vicki. This letter mentions a gathering—but not much else we don't already know."

"I agree. There could be more in that second page. If I figure it out or get anything from Derek, I'll let you know."

"Maybe whatever Derek discovers about the gathering with Vicki, could help you solve your letter," Dunya suggested, as if eager for a solution.

"Maybe," I said, getting up from the couch. "But right now, I have to get ready for my shift."

As I got into my car, I noticed Mitra watching me from her front step. She waved, and I waved back before shutting the car door. She was still waving as I pulled out onto the street. At the stop sign at the end of the street, I realized I had forgotten to ask Dunya about the word Mitra had spoken to Redmond. "*Mowmin,*" I recited to myself, making a mental note to ask the next time I saw her.

Chapter 20

"Sorry, I couldn't Skype last night," Derek said, through the screen of their very first video chat. "Today's my only opportunity. I've got a week of rushed project deadlines due before the holidays."

"I completely understand," she said. Vicki adjusted the angle of her laptop screen to get a better look at their Cipher. He was feeling guilty for being busy, she realized. Hell, the guy was co-founder of his company and she knew he did most of the geek work, therefore any mystery solving tasks had been put on the back burner.

"Let's go over the description again," Derek suggested, referring to the details the spirit had given them Halloween night.

"Uhm, sure," she said.

"What?" he asked, when she sat there staring at him.

They'd communicated plenty over the past months via, email, text, and phone calls. This was the first time she'd ever *seen* what he looked like. He wasn't what she had imagined the infamous computer master, puzzle-solver, skeptic, would look like. Not even close. Type *computer geek* into google search and you get back guys in bad dress shirts with bowties, suspenders, dark-rimmed glasses, and hair that looks like they haven't showered in weeks. And this was not what she was seeing. She coughed and straightened in her seat. "We all feel eager to solve this," she stumbled out, still stunned over his appearance. "There is a sense we are getting closer, but if there is a deadline for it—I haven't found one."

"Give me what you have," he said, unaware of her mental confusion. "Everything okay?"

"Yes—sorry. I don't have it word for word, but I have the highlights," she explained. "We were all in shock at the time—as you can imagine." She gave a nervous snicker.

"Ghost conjuring... I'm still trying to wrap my brain around it myself," Derek admitted. "But it happened—so give me what you've got."

"Well," Vicki started, checking her notes. "He'd stated it was, *internationally acclaimed*."

"What was?" Derek questioned.

"The place—the garden. Internationally acclaimed for agricultural research," she reiterated. "He'd also said the person who started it all was a *botanist*."

"That's pretty specific, while still being vague," Derek said. "How are you supposed to identify a place based on that?"

"There's more," Vicki assured him. "The place also has something to do with the *department* of agriculture."

"Every farm across North America has something to do with the department of agriculture—what makes you so sure you have the right place?"

Their botched search attempt had already discouraged her and she was becoming even more so with Derek's digs at the information. "I checked the website, and it says *James Fletcher*, who was part of planting the first 200 trees in 1889, was a botanist. And the place is part of the department of agriculture—so this must be the location," she stated, ending with a "*Huff*."

"That's it?" Derek asked, despite her obvious annoyance.

"The description was more about the gardens—all the trees, the plants and the flowers, etc. At the time the information felt very specific, but the place he described, the one we searched, is huge. But I agree, we need more details—specific details."

"And you're sure it's there in Ottawa—this gathering?"

"We're in Ottawa," she said, crossing her arms over her chest.

"Ya, but Luc and Darius are in Miami, and I'm in South Carolina... and Alison—she's in Calgary," he pointed out.

"She's from here," Vicki said, with less conviction. "Besides, once we find whatever it is that we need, we'll know more about the gathering and its details, I'm sure."

"Well, based on the website I'm looking at for this place—the search area, it covers a lot of terrain. You better be sure you have the right location if you're going to search it again." Derek clacked away on his computer. "Are there any other places near Ottawa that sound similar to the description?"

"I hadn't checked," Vicki admitted, "but this fits so well, I can't imagine another place that would meet the criteria."

"Why didn't you guys get more details," Derek tossed at her. "You don't even know what you're looking for. It could be anything—any size, and anywhere on the grounds."

"Like I said—we were shocked the spell even worked. None of us thought to grill this spirit or whatever. None of us were thinking clearly—we mostly watched Mac and this apparition interact."

"Don't write off looking at other options so quickly. Not until you get more information—or at least try to narrow down the search area," Derek suggested.

"Mac and Olivia are here working on the conjuring spells again," she said, giving a chin nod towards her kitchen. "They—we, need help, from a helpful spirit."

"You're hoping for what—to get more from the same guy?" Derek questioned.

"Well, the location spells Mac tried at the Arboretum didn't work—neither of them," she said. "Mac says having the location spell—any location spell, may not be enough, that it can take more than a few spoken words to find something missing using magic."

"Did I hear my name," Mac's voice called. Then she made it such that her face appeared in view of the camera next to where Vicki sat. She paused when she caught Derek's image on the screen. She shot a glance at Vicki and opened her mouth to speak, but then glanced back at the computer screen at their Cipher. She too realized that their friend Derek was not what you would expect your *expert in everything* to look like. She wasn't sure what she expected, really.

"Mac... Derek," Vicki said, in introduction though none should have been needed. "Derek, this is Mac—our resident witch."

"Not that I have *any* experience with such things, but why isn't a locator spell enough to find—whatever it is you need to locate?" Derek asked them both now.

Mac pulled up a chair to sit beside Vicki. "First of all," Mac said, scooching her chair even closer. "You need to pin down what exactly you are trying to find. It can't be for selfish purposes either. Don't even bother if you are doing the spell for yourself. What we are trying to find, is for the balance—for the greater good or whatever, not specially for one of us. And either of the spells I did—should have worked." She shrugged. "And materials are key for any spell. The words have to be just right too. Any slight deviation can change the spell or cause it not to work at all. Timing is everything. But you can't just go through the motions—read off the words. That won't make for a successful spell," she concluded.

"Why aren't they working with Lynn on this?" Michael asked no one in particular. The four had grown weary watching and listening to their Charges from outside the apartment, and now they had taken up residence in Vicki's apartment. They'd all agreed that they'd stay closer, observe every move their Charges made, together or apart.

Their Charges had been left unattended too often in the past. This had resulted in the misdirection from Armaros, which had left them, and each one of their Charges at a disadvantage now. They all knew about the letter now too, the one that had been hidden so long ago by Lynn's birthmother. Gabriel had come to them right away with the news.

Michael moved to stand behind his Charge. "I thought they'd agreed to have another one of their group sessions with her," Michael questioned again.

"How do we even know if our Charges have searched in the right location?" Uriel asked, adding to the questions. He sat down in the open chair next to Mac. "With all his interference—why would Armaros give them these details, or any at all?"

"I told you before—to torment them," Raphael said, poking his head out from the kitchen. He'd been in the other room watching over

Olivia as she helped Mac revisit the conjuring spell. "There is nothing worse than *half the information*, to drive a soul mad."

"He didn't say *where* it was exactly—just described it," Michael stated. "Could it be made up, or do you think he was referring to an actual place?"

"I think he may have given them this information to keep them *off* track, or it was just enough information to have them going in circles," Raphael added, keeping with his original idea of torment. "He'd find either option entertaining, I'm sure."

As the video chat ended, Uriel watched as Mac flipped through the grimoire. Then he said, "What about the cryptic nature of the letter—that second part, I mean. Gabriel hasn't read it—only overheard Lynn complaining about more riddles. And what about this birthfather? Do you suppose Armaros had a hand in that too? Do we know who he is—does Gabriel know?"

Olivia, followed by Raphael, came to sit on the couch in the open concept living-dining room. "Armaros instructed her to keep the letter hidden," Raphael reminded, "but told her it was of utmost importance that no one find the information—that things had changed, is what Gabriel had informed us."

Michael sat down in the remaining chair at the dining table. "So, Lynn's birthmother goes to Miami—hides this letter, but then when she returns—she goes to see Lynn's Mom, and tells her about what she knows?" Michael recalled. "It doesn't seem very logical. She knew the price—the sacrifice for telling."

"Armaros wanted to truly mess with things," Raphael said. "He must have instructed her to tell. He knew doing this would make her sick—kill her even."

"Or she felt she needed to pass it on," Uriel guessed. "She also told her friend the doctor, about visiting Lynn's mom, remember? What had been the purpose of that visit?"

"She was supposed to be cancer free," Gabriel said, appearing just in front of the living room window. "Going to see Lynn's Mom and her doctor friend, sealed her fate."

"She passed away shortly after," Uriel remembered. "The secret of the birthfather and the hiding place lost with her."

"Well, it appears Armaros hadn't known where she'd hidden it," Raphael stated. "Lynn has it now—does it mention the birthfather?"

"I'd tried to find a way to get Lynn to Miami...," Gabriel began, ignoring the inquiry about the birthfather. "That's when I had chosen which human to contact—one I felt could aid me, Will's mother. She had kept the pair in contact in the past—thought she could do it again. She was unable." He stepped closer to the table. "My hope was to get Lynn to visit him in Miami. I hadn't expected they'd rekindle their little romance. But it's why I had considered he could have been The Believer."

"What did you think she'd do once she got to Miami—simply find what had been hidden?" Michael asked. "How could she?"

"She has her gifts," Gabriel stated. "It was Lynn who contacted Will after a five-year gap in their friendship. It had been her actions that had gotten her to Miami in the first place, not Joan's efforts to get them in touch. She's also the one who brought your Charges together, helped them find what they needed."

"This Charge, why had you chosen to watch over this woman—Lynn's birthmother, Gabriel?" Uriel questioned.

They hadn't known what his actions had meant, why he had chosen her. "I chose her because she was a descendant," Gabriel answered.

"Yes, we know that—but whose descendant?" Uriel questioned again.

"Death's," Gabriel said.

"*Zaqiel*... his name means *God has hidden... God has protected*," Raphael noted. "Was she your choice because she needed to stay hidden—protected?" Raphael shook his head as if confused.

"No," Gabriel replied. He'd chosen a descendant of Zaqiel, one of the fallen leaders, one of The Horsemen, hoping to find favor, finding protection, to up the balance, and to up her power. It was the better choice—best choice, rather than choosing any random descendant.

"No wonder Lynn looked so familiar," Michael said, noting her resemblance to Zaqiel.

"*Wrong*," Gabriel whispered under his breath.

"Her birthmother was a descendant of Zaqiel's, and I understand that choice, but please don't tell me *Armaros* is this birthfather—and the reason he's so interested in her," Michael beseeched, turning to face Gabriel, only to see him vanish.

Raphael tapped a questioning finger against his lower lip. "She would have been conceived during the 70 generations," Raphael stated. "And regardless of Armaros' manipulations, he couldn't be the father… or could he?"

"If he is, that would make Lynn the descendant of Death, and the child of… *Evil,*" Uriel pointed out.

"Maybe it's best she's not with our Charges. She could inadvertently tip the scales of balance in the favor of those aligned with the darkness, allied with Armaros," Raphael advised.

"But Gabriel would have known who the father was—no?" Uriel speculated.

"Is that something you believe he would keep from us?" Michael added in question.

"Why not—because he's been so forthcoming with everything else thus far?" Raphael tossed out, smugly. He went back to tapping his lip. Too many questions, not enough answers.

Chapter 21

Riddle solving was harder than I thought.

I'd spent most of Sunday trying to solve the writings from the second page of the letter. I tried Monday, and again on Tuesday after my shift, but sadly, by the time I'd gone to bed, I hadn't even made a dent. Wednesday evening I'd reviewed the page for the 101th time. I had even made notes, separating out the pieces that were causing most of my confusion;

bar the fifth
solacer
faiths fever
heart news
guard the ~~glean~~ angel
descendant of watcher

The first part of the letter was clear, but the second page had me thinking it was the rambles of a cancer-stricken woman, much like the ramblings I'd found in my mother's journal. The only saving grace I'd had so far, had been with reviewing the *few* familiar words and anagrams I'd seen prior in email exchanges between Vicki and Derek. But over and over, the same perplexing words had glared back at me, revealing nothing new.

Work on Thursday had been uneventful like each day leading up to it, though I found myself too often checking over my shoulder half expecting to catch sight of one of those giant dudes. And even though

I *had* found what my birthmother had hidden years ago, I'd still felt the need to keep reminding myself I wasn't going crazy.

Redmond and I had exchanged our usual daily texts, but like he'd mentioned during Sunday's breakfast here at my house, he'd been otherwise occupied with work and numerous holiday events.

To add to my torture, it seemed Redmond hadn't been the only one running a demanding business. Derek too had been busy with his pre-holiday projects and work rush. I'd sent him a scanned copy of the letter, but I'd had to wait out the week before I could get any assistance from him with it. He'd promised to help me on Friday late afternoon, and today was Friday.

"Can I tell the girls yet," were the first words out of Derek's mouth, when he answered the phone.

I set my phone on the kitchen island and put him on speaker. "No," I responded, facing the phone. "Not until we solve these anagrams. This is about me—not the four."

I heard him let out a big, "*Huff*" as if frustrated, then he said, "Fine. Let's review what you have." I could hear papers rustling.

My notes, which I'd written in my notepad of weird, sat open next to my cell phone. I'd tucked the *actual* letter away for safe-guard. Safe from what—I didn't know, but safe just the same, I hoped. "*Guard the glean,*" I tossed out, as I rummaged around in the cupboards in search of all the ingredients I'd need for later. "Guard the *angel*?" Glean was angel, I knew that part. I also knew Derek struggled with the ideas of angels, but that was my best attempt to solve this one.

"Maybe," was all I got back from him, that and more rustling papers and few keyboard clacking sounds.

"Maybe Darius has to guard an angel," I proposed.

"*Guard the fifth,*" Derek tossed back.

"Darius has to guard a *fifth*? Fifth what?" I asked. "And what the hell is a *Solacer*?"

"Those were mentioned in the codex too—the part about *guarding the fifth,* and this *Solacer* person," he clarified.

"It's a person?" That just added to my confusion. "Does the codex mention anything about these other pieces? *Faith fever*, or *heart news*?"

"No, I don't believe so," Derek said.

"What about *bar the fifth*?" I said, ending my short list of confusing pieces to the puzzle page. Most of it was confusing, but these were the items I'd considered could be anagrams and that once solved, the other parts would become clearer. At least I hoped they would. "The letter also mentions *descendant of watcher,* but I'm assuming that must be Darius, and has something to do with his saving me. I'm not sure how that works, but if my birthmother could predict details about a gathering, maybe she foresaw I would—we would, need a protector too—a guardian."

"The girls are talking about heading to the garden again for a second try at finding something," he redirected. "Your letter mentions a gathering, and chances are they are one and the same."

"Maybe it's the wrong place," I said, disinterested.

"Maybe, or they conjured the wrong spirit."

"The translation could be wrong." No offence to my friends, but even Vicki wasn't perfect with her English skills *all* the time.

"I checked the translation—looks good." I heard the clacking of fingers on a keyboard again. "I'll send you a copy of the spell and the translation," Derek offered. "Your birthmother wrote that you were to bring the others together—and you did that, so maybe there is more to reveal in her letter—linking you to the others."

"Perhaps," I said. Perhaps he was just as frustrated as I was with all the unanswered questions. Or he needed a new set of eyes to help him this time. Could be he was offering it as a bribe, so he could tell the others about my letter. But that wasn't going to happen, not yet anyway. "Mac could have done something wrong with the magic part," I said. Like most of whatever they'd been doing, I hadn't been there for that. And considering my friends had only been at this a short while, they may not have mastered their new skills fully.

"Ya, but they're not ready to do another one—not a conjuring spell, but Mac's working on a locator one. She said it's hard to do it if you don't know what you're looking for."

Made sense. "Whatever," I said. That wasn't my problem, I had my own mystery to solve. *And* I had a staff party to get ready for.

"Leave it with me and I'll work on it," Derek offered.

I was good with that for now. I'd already spent enough hours wracking my brain with it, he could tackle it for a while. "Okay," I said. "Later, Shortcut. Remember—mum's the word."

"Ya-ya. Tell Darius *hi* for me, and have a good time," he said, before hanging up.

I flipped my notepad closed and set it and my phone off to the side. Then I got out the last of the things I needed to complete my task.

Cookie sheets.

"It's cookie-baking-time," I said to Raven.

He "*Woofed,*" in response.

For the Christmas parties, I'd offered to bring one of the few goodies I knew how to make, M&M cookies. They were like chocolate chip cookies but with chocolate candy pieces instead. I'd chosen to use the red and green Christmas coloured ones that came out this time of year, instead of the mixed coloured ones you got in the regular bags. Having two wall ovens, I could make twice as many in the same amount of time. "None for you though—chocolate is bad for doggies," I added. To compensate, I tossed him one of the large size dog biscuits from the container next to his bag of dog food. He slumped down on the floor next to the kitchen's entrance and chewed his cookie while I went to work on making my cookies.

"Any luck with the puzzle solving," Shamsiel asked, when he appeared next to Gabriel in the kitchen. He lent down and gave Raven's head a pat.

"Lots of back and forth between her and Derek, but no solving of anything," Gabriel said. "Derek told her to leave it with him and he'd work on it."

"He's come through before," Shamsiel said. "It's better than her just staring at her notes."

"Any sign of your dark brethren?" Gabriel asked, stepping over Raven to lean against the entry wall.

"Not a glimmer." Shamsiel crossed the kitchen to the wall ovens and peered into the upper window of the two. "I like cookies," he said, followed by a deep sniff.

When the baking timer went "*Ding*," I pulled the cookies out of the ovens and transferred them to the racks I'd set out to help them cool. While they cooled, I dashed off to my bedroom to get ready.

An hour later I was showered and dressed and heading out the drive in a cab with my cookies in a disposable tinfoil container, and on my way to the party.

The cab driver dropped me off in the parking lot and I headed to the doors in the other direction to where I normally went in. The hospital had a separate wing for training of both medical and non-medical staff, and for special conferences they held here. Through the entrance to the non-patient wing, I followed the signs for the holiday party and found the main conference area set up for the gathering. They also used this space for fancy dinners and presentation galas, but tonight's party was strictly casual and held a mix of all the staff who worked there. It felt a little strange being at the hospital for reasons other than work.

Next to the bar, I spotted Darius chatting with a guy in a white dress shirt and red bowtie. The rent-a-bartender. I headed over his way, and when he saw me, he waved.

"Happy Holidays and Merry Christmas—and all that jazz," I said, leaning in to give the big bear a baby-bear hug.

"Merry Holidays to you too, Lynn," he said, releasing me from the hug. "This is our friend and bartender for the night, Jerry." Darius turned to the young guy behind the bar. "Jerry, this is Lynn—my partner in crime for the night."

"Hey Jerry," I said, to the smiling man holding out a drink for me. "Partner in crime?" I directed at Darius, then took the shooter glass with the red liquid in it.

"Ya, I told Jerry about this cool drink he could make us—one the nurses introduced me to on Halloween," he said. Then he leaned in and whispered in my ear. "Luc told me about the gala—and the letter."

I tilted my head back to look up at him. "Luc told you?"

He gave me a sheepish grin then turned back to the bartender. "I told Jerry here—that you and I could probably use a few."

The bartender put two more shooter drinks out in front of Darius and me. "Darius said to keep them coming," Jerry confirmed.

Darius smiled at the bartender and then leaned down again to add more in my ear. "Luc knows—Derek knows—and I know, but the girls don't," he said, as if assuring me.

I wasn't happy about Luc telling Darius, even if he and Derek already knew, but as long as it was kept from the Ottawa group, I was cool with it. Besides, tonight was all about having fun, and not about discussing secrets and mysteries.

"Cheers," I said, clinking Darius's shot glass, before tossing back the shot.

Chapter 22

I opened my eyes... very... slowly.

I was a bit hungover, okay a lot hungover. I hadn't drunk that much in a very long time. It had been fun to hang out with familiar faces and the great people from work, and unlike the Halloween party, Darius had been at my side most of the night, dashing out only for the occasional dance with a nurse. Drinks had been free, and Darius had introduced me to a drink called a *Broken-Down Golf-cart*. It was 1/4 amaretto, 1/4 melon liqueur, 1/4 vodka, and 1/4 cranberry juice, shaken with ice, and drank from a shot glass, Jerry—the rent-a-bartender had informed me, *and* it tasted like *Kool-Aid*.

The drink had seemed harmless enough, being in such a tiny glass, but I'd lost track halfway through the night of how many tiny glasses I'd had. Luckily, both Darius and I had cabbed it there and at the end of the night we'd opted to share the same ride home.

I recalled that Darius had dropped me off first, just to make sure I had gotten in the door. But I'm guessing I'd been on my own after that because I found myself on the couch still in my clothes from last night. On the coffee table next to me was a plate with a mostly eaten peanut butter and jelly sandwich. Glancing down, I scrutinized my shirt to see if I'd gotten any on me, but I was free and clear. I checked my watch. It was nearly 11 a.m..

Raven's head peeked then through the opening to the kitchen. Seeing I was up, he came over and sat in front of the coffee table. He eyed the partial sandwich on the plate. "Looking for breakfast," I said, before tossing the remaining piece his way.

He caught it, chewed, and, "*Woofed,*" as if for more.

"Let's find you something better," I said, easing myself off the couch. "And me too."

In the kitchen, after getting Raven his albeit late breakfast, I made myself coffee and toast. The perfect hangover food. With a water and aspirin chaser I'd be good to go. Well, good enough to go take a shower and get my shit together. I had the kids and parent party this afternoon at the hospital. In addition, I had to work tonight after the party finished.

Showered, dressed in my scrubs, headache mostly gone, and stomach settled, I set off to the hospital for the other party, with the other batch of cookies I'd prepared. The first batch had disappeared fast at last night's party and I was sure they'd do another vanishing act today with the kids. Though, there wouldn't be any alcohol at this one—not that I'd wanted anything other than water to drink.

In the main family area at the hospital, I set the tray of cookies on the food table next to the other delicious looking treats. I grabbed a bottle of water from the open cooler and strolled over to stand next to Darius. At his right, I spotted a familiar face.

Santa Claus.

Well, not the real Santa, it was a rent-a-Santa. The guy appeared no older than Darius and wore a fake beard. "Hi Santa," I said.

He grinned and proceeded to call the names from the list for each gift he had in his Santa sack. Darius as his helper, carried whichever of the children who couldn't manage on their own, up to see Santa to receive their gift.

The children and their parents all smiled and laughed while they unwrapped their presents. After, the delicious meal was devoured, and the lovely treats were all savored. When the time came to light the tree, it was Darius to the rescue.

Much like with the Abominable Snow Monster—the *Bumble,* from that classic animated children's' Christmas movie, Darius reached all the way up and place the last ornament on the very top of the tree, an *angel*. He attached the angle's cord end to the rest of the string, and then the tree lit with the colours of the season, red, green and gold.

I stood back and watched the families mingling with the hospital staff. It was nice, a little bit of joy in what was otherwise a place for sick kids, and often sad times for families. I checked my watch again. It was about time for my shift to start.

I took a step forward to head for the exit, when I overheard a little boy say, "I see angels—do you?" He was addressing a little girl next to him.

"Ya, me too," the little girl said.

I smiled. I liked the idea of angels being here with the kids, and who knows, maybe they did see them. Kids and animals tended to be pure that way, seeing things adults rarely—if ever saw.

Then, the little boy said, "The one dressed in black always follows the giant around—but I'm not afraid, the other one is always nearby too—the one in white."

I shot a glance over at Darius. When he saw me looking, he waved me to come his way. I tapped my watch and mouthed the words *I have to go*. He nodded and continued with gathering up all the loose torn pieces of wrapping paper the kids had scattered from their gifts. I watched him for a few seconds longer. *The other one is always nearby too—the one in white,* I recited in my head. Then I turned and headed off for the NICU.

I had a new charge I'd been watching over, a little girl named Jamie. She was set up at the opposite side to where the twins had been, in the Green pod area, closer to the window. She was only a few weeks old and had been diagnosed with a *Wilms* tumor. The type of tumor had a medical name too that I couldn't pronounce, but it didn't matter—it was cancer.

The nurses had told me it usually starts in one kidney, or rarely—but sometimes both kidneys. Shows up as a swelling or lump in the belly. Occasionally accompanied by fever, pain, nausea, or poor appetite, but in a newborn those symptoms were hard to detect. But for Jamie, it had been an intern who had found it the day she'd been born. He'd followed the procedures he'd learned; wait for the baby to stop crying after the birth. That's when he'd found the lump. It was rare for a newborn, but *fortunately* they'd found it in time.

Unfortunately, similar to the twins I'd cared for, the parents were not available to help. Jamie *had* been set up for adoption, but when the prospective parents found out the baby was *flawed,* as they'd deemed her, they'd terminated the proceedings. People like that don't deserve children. The young birthmother was not prepared to take the baby either, so for now she had become a ward of the state. We all knew what it took for the agency to find good parents willing to take on a sick child, but in the meantime, she would be under my care.

"Even without parents, she's one of the luckier ones," Shamsiel said, standing near the monitors.

"How so?" Gabriel asked, stepping closer.

"Statistics," he responded. "One in five, diagnosed with cancer don't survive.

"Why such a high mortality?"

"In 80% of kids with cancer, it's already spread to other areas of the body by the time it gets diagnosed. If they hadn't caught it right away, she would have been the *one* in five. There are over a dozen types of childhood cancers and hundreds of different subtypes. So few children are diagnosed with each type—makes it difficult to do the research. What's worse, as adults, because of the treatments they had as kids, by the time they reach their 30s or 40s, over 95% of them will have a chronic health problem. 80% will have severe or even life-threatening conditions."

"Tell me something good. No more statistics."

"She's in good hands—literally," Shamsiel pointed out.

Gabriel smiled and leaned in to kiss the baby's head.

"Why don't you show yourself?" Shamsiel asked.

"I can't."

"Can't—or won't?"

"The rules—my friend, I must follow the rules, or all this will be for nought."

"She's seen you already."

"Yes, but she did that, and the other times were... *accidents,*" Gabriel reminded.

"She's seen me."

"You did not make the deal with *Him*—I did."

"Come, let's go—she's safe here," Shamsiel said. "We need to circle back with the others."

"Fine," Gabriel said, and kissed the baby again.

Apart from for the *bleeping* and *clicking* of monitor noise, all was quiet on the late shift. There were only two babies needing special care at the moment, and the staff were grateful for the low occupancy. It was only Jamie and me, along with nurse Sarah who was watching over baby Sullivan, who'd originally been called baby *Tuesday*.

When he arrived, born at only 28 weeks under emergency circumstances, there'd been no ID on the mother to identify a name. Under normal circumstances, when faced with the possibility of preterm delivery, it can overwhelm the parents, especially the mothers. There can be a mix of emotions; frightened, sad, angry, even confused. Whenever such a case occurs, the medical staff let the expectant parents know they are not alone. But for the parents of baby Sullivan, there hadn't been that calm reassurance from the medical staff getting them through. The parents had been in a car crash and the father had died on scene. The mother had been brought into the emergency with life-threatening injuries, which prompted for the early delivery in hope of saving her life and the baby's. But the damage to her body had been too severe, and she'd succumbed to her injuries once the baby was out.

The neonatology team of doctors and nurses and the respiratory therapist had worked around the clock trying to save the little guy, while the social workers had tried to locate other family members. They'd eventually gotten the ID off the body of the father, but since they'd been unsuccessful at saving the mother, they'd chosen to use his last name *only*. I'd been told that the hospital human relations staff were at a loss for family to contact, as none seemed to exist for this young couple. If no one came forward, this tiny baby—if he survived, would become a ward of the state, like Jamie.

I'd watched the nurses all week as they continue to check his heart rate, breathing, oxygen levels, and movement. A breathing tube had been placed to help him breathe. He'd received a medicine called

Surfactant at delivery to help keep his lungs expanded, to aid in breathing. Today, it was only nurse Sarah who attended to him.

"What kind of issues is he dealing with now," I asked her.

"There's a long list of problems a preemie can suffer. And this little one has had them all," she said, taking in a deep breath to go on. "RDS, respiratory distress syndrome—hence the breathing tube. Yesterday we dealt with an IVH, intraventricular hemorrhage—bleeding into the brain. Now he's developed necrotizing enterocolitis—NEC, that affected his intestines. It's causing problems with feeding. See how swollen his belly is. Poor little guy has diarrhea too."

"Wow," was all I could muster. That was a horrible battle for a grown person, let alone a tiny baby. I sighed and turned back to glance Jamie's way.

"Lynn, I need to run baby Sullivan's latest blood samples over to the lab—can you keep an eye? It's just you and me here for the next couple hours."

"How about I run the blood work over—you watch the *critically* ill baby?" I said, nervous to be left alone and *untrained*. I knew how to use a stethoscope for heart and breath sounds, and how to clean feeding tubes, but that was about it.

"The test results will take more time than this little guy has. We'll be lucky if he makes it through the night," she said, lowering her gaze from me to the baby. "And the doctor needs to review everything, anyway."

"Nurse and doctor stuff, eh?"

"Ya. This poor little guy has had every preemie issue out there. Every time we thought we were gonna lose him—he'd turn a corner, but this time... we can't seem to get him past this RDS and constant infections. It may be just a waiting game at this point." She gave a weak smile.

"Okay—I'll watch him. What do I have to do?" I asked.

"Not much, sit with him so he's not alone."

"Shame we can't hold him."

"He seems to respond when you talk to him. I mean his erratic heartrate seems to level—can't breathe on his own, but it's something."

After a pat on my arm, Sarah left, and I sat down in the chair normally reserved for visiting parents. And since this little guy didn't have any, I was it.

Talk to him, okay... or I could read to him.

I checked the eBook app on my phone. "Here, perfect," I said. "*Goodnight Moon* by Margaret Wise Brown." I scooted the chair closer. "*In the great... green room...*," I began, reading the story aloud. His erratic monitor beeps seemed to steady and level, as nurse Sarah had said, so I read on. I watched as his little chest rose and fell between pausing after each line.... "*Goodnight stars... goodnight air... good night noises everywhere....*" The room suddenly went dark, the monitors going deadly silent with only a low hum filling the darkness.

I stood.

The emergency lights came on with the monitors bleeping back into action. "Oh crap," I said, aloud, dashing across to check on Jamie. But she was just as I'd left her, sleeping soundly, and in no pain. I spun back around to return to our other little occupant... and froze.

There next to the isolette stood an enormous figure... the one from my dream of Louise—from here at the hospital, from....

His expression was solemn on his perfect beautiful face as he cradled baby Sullivan in the bend of one massive arm. There were no tubes, no wires, no bandages, *and* there was no alarming need for me to run either.

"You shouldn't be in here," I said foolishly. I glanced at the monitor for baby Sullivan only to find they still bleeped away despite his not being hooked up anymore. I glanced back as the giant man placed his giant hand over the tiny form of the baby. Then he took a giant step past the monitors, towards me. The lights flickered and went out again.

With another hum, the lights came on and back to full strength, the monitors bleeping. The large man was gone, but I was across the room in front of baby Sullivan's isolette. The baby was back under the enclosure connected to all the tubes and wires though the readings on the monitor showed he was weakening. The doors to the NICU swooshed and Sarah came through the door.

"What happened with the power—the lights," I asked.

"Lights—what are you talking about?" she asked, adding a new page to baby Sullivan's medical clipboard.

"They went out—just came back on again," I said, turning and searching the room.

Sarah checked the monitor for baby Sullivan. "If the power went out the nurse at the entrance would have come in," she said, pointing to the glass doors. "She arrived early—was there when I left."

"What?" I glanced at the doors and saw the duty nurse sitting at the station. The clock on the wall registered that an hour had passed since Sarah had left.

"What are you doing?" I questioned, watching Sarah shut off most of the monitors.

"It's time," she said, opening the lid to baby Sullivan's hospital version of a bassinette.

"Time?"

"The doctor said it's time to take him off all the support. Premature babies have trouble fighting off germs because their immune systems aren't fully developed yet," she informed me. "We figured the mother hadn't been taking very good care of herself during the pregnancy—now he can't fight any of the infections. He's had one after another. Pneumonia, sepsis in the blood, now meningitis the last tests show. It impacts the fluid around his brain and spinal cord." I barely heard the stats as I stared as she removed all but one of the monitor leads. The baby's eyes had been covered in a soft gauze to protect them, and still they remained covered. "His little body can't handle anymore. And at this point, it would be cruel of us to try," she shared. "Did you want to hold him?"

I shrugged. "I guess someone should hold him… at least once," I said, settling into the chair again. She handed him to me wrapped in one of the hospital baby blankets, breathing support still attached. Then she very gently removed the breathing tube from his tiny mouth.

No breath came, and his chest no longer rose and fell. When the heart monitor no longer pulsed, Sarah shut it off.

I gazed at the weightless angel in my arms. "*Goodnight moon,*" I whispered.

Chapter 23

It was later than usual when I left the hospital. I'd stayed to help where I could and be a witness for most of the paperwork needed for baby Sullivan. I've been one of the more fortunate helpers—meaning until now, I'd never witnessed a death in the time I'd been in the NICU.

At home I readied myself for bed, only to find that even with my exhaustion, sleep was not waiting for me like usual. Surprise-surprise. Instead, I speculated about my mother's time in hospitals, how often she may have witnessed death in the years she'd spent as a nurse. *Too often*. Death of a baby had to be the worst, I could only assume, but I understood that was something I'd more than likely experience again with my role. So far, the joys had outweighed the sorrows, despite this loss. Being able to hold baby Sullivan in his last moments, I'd counted it as a great privilege, and I'd felt honored to be the one given that gift, to comfort him in his final breath. He was gone, and as much as the need to cry had pushed at the back of my throat then, I'd also realized that he was no longer in pain. And if there is a heaven, he was with his parents now.

I know my mom believed in God, heaven or whatever. I hoped that she was right, especially if it meant she and my aunt, and Louise, and so many others, were now some place peaceful and without pain.

It was times like these that I wished I could talk to my mother. Sometimes the memories come easy, but other times like tonight, I struggled to recall the sound of her voice. But I'd found the trick to hearing her voice in my head. All I had to do was to reread one of her cards or letters she'd sent to me after I'd moved to Miami. Within seconds I can hear the words being spoken by her. Often other words not found on the page, begin to weave into those I read, pulling in more memories of conversations with her. It feels like she is speaking to me from that peaceful place.

The one I chose to read tonight, she'd dated February 7th, 2007, and she'd even put the time 7:30 a.m. on it, I wasn't sure why. The letter was a short one, but her voice was clear in it;

> *Hi, I'm using the lovely note paper you gave me.*
>
> *Mick and Kay came over for coffee Monday—I should say 'tea' because we were out of coffee. This week, James and I went out shopping (a rare happening). I got a new headboard and nightstand for my room—almost matches my dresser and will be quite an improvement.*
>
> *I read your 'ideas' for my journal and will definitely consider them when I get going. The thought has prompted me to clean through my keepsakes and I came upon a box of baby clothes—not many but there was that little sun-suit that came home with you. I'll leave that story for my journal.*
>
> *Must go—I enjoy your emails, miss you, love you and so proud you followed your dreams, and you deserve it all!*
>
> *Mom*

Occasionally, she'd written her messages using dashes, and it added to the memory and pace to which she'd normally spoke. In this one, she'd underlined the word 'when' in regard to ideas for writing in her journal, but I'm sure she hadn't imagined ever writing the content she had eventually put in it.

I have those baby clothes, along with her wedding dress, put away in my closet now. I'd kept only the top part of her wedding dress, the front of the lace bodice, as I'd wanted to put it in a keepsake shadow box. I loved how the coloured confetti from that day remained caught in the space between the silk bodice and the lace overlay as if captured in time.

To my dismay, after reading a few more letters with the memory of my mom's words, sleep was still not my friend, and I continued to wake several times during the night.

By 9 a.m., I gave up on trying to sleep in. I was exhausted, but thankful I didn't have to work today, though I had Redmond's holiday party to attend. I was looking forward to seeing him, but I was even more exhausted at the idea of having to be social.

I had met several of Redman's staff at the Thanksgiving gathering, and it would help that Lily would be there, but either way, I wouldn't be staying late. I had an early flight on Monday, and that 6 a.m. departure meant that with holiday traveling, I'd need to be at the airport by 4 a.m. or sooner.

After picking out what I would wear to the party, I rolled my carryon bag out from the recesses of my closet to make ready to pack for my trip home. I hadn't wanted to use a larger suitcase, with traveling home, my luggage often found its way on a different flight, leaving me to wait a day or even two, to get it back from wherever it had traveled. A carryon would solve that issue, but it would also make for difficult packing, considering I had to pack winter clothing for this trip.

Too exhausted to pack at the moment, I sifted through my winter items and proceeded to just pile my options on the bed. I counted out several pairs of socks to bring, the kind that went above my ankles, along with thicker tank-tops for layering over bras and under long-sleeved shirts for warmth. Next to those I made a stack of bras and underwear. For shoes, I'd be wearing my Doc Martins there, and if I needed winter boots, I'd get the ones I stashed at Mac's, along with my winter jacket. It was much easier than bringing them back and forth on trips considering I only really needed them when I was there, and I usually just brought a heavy sweatshirt on the plane with me.

My other trips had been during warmer weather and it had been a few years since I'd gone home at Christmas. When I'd traveled home during the holidays in the past, normally anyone who would pick me up, brought me a jacket to wear for the car ride until I could get mine. But this time I'd be renting a car at the airport and heading straight to my brother's place in the country.

I wouldn't have my winter boots or a winter jacket, so I got my thickest sweatshirt out, plus the light down vest I had, ready for my travels. To aid my driving in the cold, I also set aside a pair of tiny black knit gloves I'd saved from the many pairs my mom had accumulated, the rest I had brought to the women's shelter with the rest of her clothes.

I stared at the piles of winter clothing. Disinterested in sorting out what else to bring with me, I opted for taking a nice shower instead, hoping it would help wake me up and wash away this lethargy.

Clean and with a little more energy now, I padded off from my bedroom in a hunt for something nourishing to eat. I'd need more than a shower to save my body from the onset of more fatigue.

In the living room I spotted Luc and Dunya cuddled up on the couch in front of the TV.

"Hey Lynn," Dunya said, as I attempted to pass by without interruption.

"Morning," I responded with a quick wave and dash into the kitchen.

"There's fresh banana bread on the counter—if yer hungry," Luc called, from his comfy spot on the couch. "Dunya made it."

"If I'm hungry. Pffffffff," I mumbled to myself. "Perfect—thanks," I called back.

Using the knife that was already next to the loaf of goodness, I sliced two pieces. I placed one on the paper towel I'd pulled from the roll and then took a big bite of the other. "Mmmmmm, Dunya, you should come over more often," I said, taking a second bite of the still warm homemade banana bread.

"There's a cranberry one and a lemon poppy-seed one, both are wrapped up and in the fridge," she announced, from the other room.

At her words, my heart swelled with both friend *and* food love. "She's a keeper, Luc."

"Don't I know it," he said back. Then I heard giggling and noises that sounded like kissing. Cute but *gah*!

While the lovebirds continued to cuddle on the couch, I set myself up to prepare my special treat for tonight's holiday party at Redmond's.

I spent the next couple hours in the kitchen attempting to make my mother's pastry dough recipe, hoping to bake two apple pies to bring with me for dessert. The pies had been a favorite in our house and had garnered loads of praise from friends and extended family. It was my first time making the dessert myself and I could only hope to do it justice.

I'd known not to handle the dough too much and made sure that the butter was cold, cold, cold, and necessary, from what my mother had told me in the past. But I'd cursed aloud when it had taken me several tries to get the top layer of dough over the apples in the pie tin. I'd wished I'd chosen to make Mom's raspberry tarts with the dough instead, but after a holiday cookie snack break, I returned to the battle and mastered the second pie.

While the pies baked, I returned to my room to get dressed. I'd chosen to wear my new black jeans along with a red Christmas themed t-shirt that had white and silver snowflakes scattered on it in different sizes. I did my eyeliner and mascara and even added a little shimmery eyeshadow to add to the festive theme. Instead of wearing my hair loose, I swept it back and wove it into a long loose French braid, tying the end with a red hair elastic.

On the way back to the kitchen, I dropped off the black strappy sandals I'd chosen to wear, at the front door.

In the kitchen, I grabbed up my oven mitts, right as the timer *"Dinged."*

"Timing," I said to myself, and opened the oven door.

I'd only just set the pies on the counter to cool, when I heard Dunya's voice call my name from the living room. "Lynn!" she called again, as I entered the room.

Both she and Luc still sat but were staring at Raven.

He was pacing back and forth in front of the living room window. Then he halted and let loose a deep guttural, *"Grrrooooowl."*

"What is it boy?" Luc directed at his faithful pet. Luc stood then and went to look out the window.

I shot a look back at Dunya, my expression asking the silent question. *Armaros*?

"Something dark, Lynn—but not him, not Armaros," she confirmed in return. Then her cell phone rang. She grabbed it off the coffee table. "Jadda," she said, answering the phone. She continued in Arabic though I sensed the urgency in her words.

"What is it—is she okay," I asked.

Her words changed then from urgent to soothing, and then she hung up. "She's fine, but she felt it too—the darkness," Dunya said. "But there are *two,* Jadda said."

"Two?" I questioned. I moved to stand next to Luc at the window. Raven shifted to stand next to me, then sat when I patted his head.

"Araquel and Ramiel were just here," Shamsiel spouted, when Gabriel arrived outside the house.

"The two from the gala. What about Armaros?" Gabriel grilled. "Where is he?"

"Hiding. Letting his henchmen do the dirty work for him," Shamsiel tossed out.

"They want the letter—rather Armaros wants it," Gabriel stated. "Do you know where she put it?"

"No," Gabriel said. He'd only caught glimpses of it since that night after the gala. He wondered if she was keeping it on her person, in that tote bag of hers. "She still hasn't solved the second page."

"That part must be about the gathering," Shamsiel assumed. "It's even more confusing than your entry in the codex."

Gabriel waved at Raven peering through the window. "I didn't tell her to do that," he said. "Must have been another of Armaros's suggestions."

"Have you read the letter—the second part I mean?" Shamsiel put his hand against the window where Raven touched it with his nose.

"I've tried, but she makes it hard. When it's out for her review, she always has it tucked under the first page and when she's not working on it, she hides it away somewhere," Gabriel stated. "I only seem to catch her once she's retrieved it from wherever she's been hiding it."

"I've only seen her notes—the ones in that notebook of *weird* as she calls it." Shamsiel turned to scan the street and the houses across the way.

"Me too," Gabriel said, turning to conduct his own survey of the area.

"What if they come back—and we're not here?" Shamsiel stepped away from the window. "What if they find it before us?"

"I'll stay, you go watch over her when she goes to the party," Gabriel said, glancing back through the window.

"Probably best. Dunya is here and Mitra is next door," Shamsiel said, pointing a thumb to the window, then in the direction of the neighbor's house. "Both will sense if I'm around. Plus, the others won't take a chance returning if you're here too."

Shamsiel moved to stand by Lynn's car, while Gabriel disappeared to move inside.

Gabriel appeared inside just as Lynn tucked a white envelope into a small grey purse. The bag wasn't big enough to hold much. Her ID, some cash and a cell phone. *What had she shoved into it? The letter? Had she been keeping it with her,* Gabriel wondered again. If she didn't have it on her, he'd do his best to find her hiding place without disturbing anything or reveal that someone had been in her room. He watched then as she slung the purse crosswise over her shoulder and then left the bedroom shutting the door.

At the kitchen counter, I covered the two still warm pies with tinfoil, and then placed them side by side in a shallow cardboard box for transport.

Carrying the box, I passed back through the living room to the front door and then slipped my feet into my waiting sandals. "Okay folks, I'm outta here," I said, to the now relaxed couple on the couch. "You guys good?" Raven was still sitting near the window. This time he was wagging his tail.

"Yes," Dunya said. "There was something dark, Lynn—but it's gone now." She smiled, but I could tell she was still nervous, and perhaps sensing something else, hopefully something *light*.

"Haven't seen him act like that since that guy came to the door—the one in white looking for Mitra," Luc recalled. "He seems okay now though."

Maybe *he* hadn't seen Raven do that since, but I had. I shifted the box to one hip and gave Raven a pat on the head. "Raven—you take care of these guys while I'm out." Raven's ears folded back, and he touched his nose to the palm of my hand. "I won't be late," I said to all, directing it mainly at Raven. With my free hand I opened the front door, then grabbed my keys off the front table. "Later," I said.

"Have fun," Dunya called.

"Later," I heard Luc say, as I shut the door.

I arrived at the studio parking area as the last hint of light disappeared behind the lush trees of the grove. The studio lights were on, and when I exited the car, the music inside could be heard, creating an easy path to the party, guiding me to the main door.

I *felt* something… something that made me stop and take a scan around the parking lot. It was always dangerously dark in this part of the grove as it was furthest from the main bar and restaurant area, and you had to be extra watchful when driving through the canopied trees. With no streetlights, all you had were your headlights to guide you.

I squinted into the night. Something played at the edge of the darkness, just outside the reach of my eyesight. Tension crossed the back of my shoulders causing my muscles to bunch. The base of my neck pained as I turned it in a sweep to search the expanse past the parking lot and across the road. Irritation swept over me, at the idea that someone might be lurking in the shadows, *and* at the fact that my hands were full, and I desperately needed to rub the back of my neck. Adjusting the box on my hip again, I took one last pan of the parking area, then yanked open the studio door.

Chapter 24

What was going on? And what was she picking up on? Shamsiel pondered, as he followed Lynn through the studio's entrance. Her sensing of him had never garnered such a horrible reaction before, yet he wasn't sure he was the only one of his kind present.

It's just exhaustion, I thought to myself when I stepped into the studio's front lounge area. I was quickly greeted by a, "You're here," from Lily, who promptly took the box out of my hands and placed it on the big coffee bar next to the entrance. She hugged me, and I flinched. Not because she hugged me, but because my neck pinched from the stiffness. "Oh sorry—too big a squeeze," she said, worry showing in her face.

"No-no." I laughed. "Just a stiff neck," I said, finally able to give it a rub.

"Come—let's get you a drink, that'll fix your neck," Lily said, picking up the box again, giving me a head tilt que to follow her.

I smiled, then trailed along behind her through several groupings of familiar and unfamiliar faces, all sharing Christmas greetings as we passed.

Down the hall we emerged into the main meeting room where all the food was being laid out buffet style. "Here," Lily said, handing me a CD cover size piece of paper and a pen. "Write down what you brought. Put it next to the dish," she instructed. "It makes it easier for everyone—you know."

It was a good idea, especially if you had allergies or food aversions. I hated plating food only to find out that what I thought was something yummy turned out to contain mushrooms. Plus, you don't want to hurt anyone's feelings by having them catch you tossing out your serving of their dish.

"There's a variety of beer and ciders in there," Lily said, pointing to the nearest cooler. "Water and soda are over there." She pointed to an open cooler near the table. She discarded the box under the table and then removed the foil from the pies. Then she moved them next to something that looked like a ten-layer chocolate cake. The card in front of it read in mostly capitals, *DEVIL'S FOOD,* with the word *cake* after it in small letters. "Fill your plate, grab a drink, and meet me out front—cool?" she said.

"Cool," I said, just as she rushed off.

I looked down at the pies, then marked the card Lily had given me with the words, *Homemade Apple Pies,* and placed it in front. I loved mom's pies, but I'd for sure be trying a piece of that chocolate creation.

I shot a glance back at the layer cake. It looked devilishly delicious based on the thick dark icing, and I was tempted to take a swipe with my finger. I took a scan around the room to see that no one was looking my way. Then I swept up a small bit of icing from near the edge of the plate and swiftly stuck my finger into my mouth.

Anticipating the taste of heaven, I "*mmmmmed,*" then grimaced, at what tasted like dirt—no worse, like ashes. I gaged then as the gritty texture of what tasted like an ashtray spread across my tongue and further down my throat. I reached for a napkin to spit into, just as I heard my name being called.

"Lyyynn," Redmond's voice came from the doorway of the meeting room.

I forced my throat to swallow, and wiped my mouth with the napkin, then tossed it into the trash can next to the table. I planted a smile on my face and turned just as Redmond crossed the room to where I stood.

"Hi pretty lady," he said as he went in for a hug.

I let out an unexpected "*Ouch,*" as my cheek pressed against his chest. I gritted my teeth and sucked in a painfilled breath.

"Oh—gawd, Lynn—did I hurt you," he asked, quick to release me. "Sometimes I don't know my own strength."

I smiled through my annoyance, and said, "No—stiff neck." I gave it a rub again. "Could I get some water—and maybe some aspirin, if you have any?" I asked. That wretched taste was still lingering along the edges of my tongue and at the back of my throat.

Redmond grabbed up a water bottle from an open cooler near the table and twisted off the cap. "Here," he said, handing me the bottle. "I've got aspirin in my desk—I'll be right back."

I took a swig of the cool water as Redmond dashed off to his office. He returned just as I swallowed another guzzle. He opened his hand to reveal two small pills in his palm. "Thank you," I said, snatching them up. With another gulp of water, I swallowed them down. The pills went down with the water, but that horrible taste was still there. I figured I'd have to eat something else to get rid of it, and I took a long survey of the food on the table. "Did you eat yet," I asked, turning back to look at him. He had two disposable plates, one in each hand out in front of him. "I take it that's a *no*." I took another swig of water, finishing the bottle off.

"Wanted to wait for you," he said, with a big grin.

Okay, this guy was seriously sweet. But that icing hadn't been, and I imaged that most of that cake would end up in the trash before the night was out. With the harsh taste still on my tongue I smiled back at him. "Shall I fill yours for you?" I asked, since both of his hands were holding plates.

"That'd be great," said, turning to face the food.

Together we negotiated the length of the table, reading each card, and selecting the items that enticed us the most. I carefully filled the plates in Redmond's hand with the dishes we chose. Then at the end of the food table, I grabbed up two of the napkin-rolled cutlery bundles.

"Let's find a spot out in the main area to listen to the band—Lily is gonna sing," Redmond said, turning towards the doorway. I snatched up another bottle of water and followed behind him.

A group of staff members, including Lily, were set up on a small riser like stage in the corner of the lounge area. I hadn't noticed it earlier with all the people mingling, but now most of them were sitting, some in the regular furniture while others had set up folding chairs.

Redmond set the plates down on one of the available folding chairs, then went off to get another from the group of them leaning against the far wall. He set the now open chair next to the first and made a gesture for me to sit. I sat, and Redmond handed me my plate. In exchange I handed him one of the napkin rolls.

One of the guys near us handed Redmond a beer in a stubby bottle. Redmond took the beer, mouthing the word, *"Thanks"*, then the two of them tapped bottles. Redmond sat then and turned to show me the bottle. He said something I guessed was the name of the beer, but I couldn't really hear him. The music was great but loud, and it made hearing anything else difficult. He took a swig and turned back to the band.

We ate from the plates on our laps as the motley band of musicians plus one Lily Shade, sang and jammed the classics; *Heart, Zeppelin, Skynyrd, Journey* and more. The overhead lights flickered, but the band kept playing.

"Ghosts," Redmond mouthed, leaning in to speak in my ear.

The lights shimmered, and as the music boomed my spidy-senses hit an all new high going into overdrive. Irritated again, I couldn't hear what Redmond was saying. It wasn't the loud music, but I knew I needed to get out of here, *now*. Leaning away from him, I pulled my phone from my purse, then tapped Redmond's arm. Pointing to my phone, I motioned like I needed to make a call. I forced a smile. What I needed was a breather to get a grip on what was happening to me. Redmond nodded and shifted to let me pass between our chairs. I headed towards his office.

I turned the knob to the office door and found it was open. I pushed through and shut it behind me.

The booming music lessoned some, but now that disgusting taste was back, coupled with a stink in the air reminiscent of sulfur mixed with something like burning compost. The muscles across my shoulders bunched, shooting spasming pain down my spine. Unable to contain it, I *"Snarled"* out a rage of pain. If this was what *Bruce Banner* felt when he changed into the Hulk, it definitely explained the facial expressions he'd made *and* why the monster part of him was always so pissed off.

Now my muscles hummed, tight, full of energy as if filling with electricity, charged with power and strength. There was no nausea at least this time, only a growing sense of frustration and discomfort.

"What is it," Shamsiel asked, from behind his veil. *What's happening. What should I do, get Gabriel or stay with her? It's not me—is it, my presence?* he questioned guiltily. "Armaros… and the other two," Shamsiel whispered, sensing them before seeing them.

"Armaros?" I said, through another wave of pain. I glanced up to catch three large figures pass by the one-way window of the office door. A *gasp* escaped my lips as one figure stopped just outside the door.

"You heard me?" Shamsiel questioned. *Had she heard me,* he wondered.

I needed to get out of here… but there was no place to run. "They can't find me here," I said, under my breath. "What are they doing here? How could they have gotten past Redmond and the others—unnoticed?"

"They want the letter," Shamsiel said, into the air.

The large figures moved passed the door in the direction of the studio's recording rooms. I stepped forward to the door and pressed the side of my cheek against the window, trying to see down the hall. My neck twinged, I took several steps back, as my brain suddenly gave way to a striking revelation. "Why am I running from these guys?" I tossed out to the universe. "What if they are here to help me—help the girls, all of us? I keep pushing them off every time I see them." Like the premonitions from my past, those I pushed away always caused me to feel sick—like a warning, a warning I was choosing wrong.

"What? No, Lynn," Shamsiel said, countering as if she could hear him.

"What if they have the answers we need, and I'm the one who's making it more difficult by running?" I'd felt repulsed by these beings, but now I was feeling drawn to them. I could sense their power. I wanted answers. "I wanted that power," I breathed. The pain in my neck lessened, and I took a step towards the door.

"Nooooooo," Shamsiel shouted, passed his veil as the door swung open.

"Lynn—everything okay?" Redmond asked, standing in the doorway.

Without replying, I pushed past him, rushing up the hall to check the meeting room and the back studios. Then I went back down to the main area where most of the people were listing to the music. But the big guys were nowhere to be found.

Redmond approached and then stood next to me. "What is it?" he asked. "Are you okay?"

"Just a… a little anxiety… I guess—I don't know… been sort of off since last night." I glanced back down the hall to the other areas of the studio, then turned back and glanced up at him. *What a handsome face he has,* I thought, my brain returning to the *now*. I smiled at him.

"Last night?" he questioned.

I dropped my smile. "Ya… something happened at the hospital," I said, trying to push my smile back up.

"Come," he said, taking my hand and leading me back down the hall to his office. He shut the door behind us, then maneuvered me to the big leather couch, and we both sat. "Tell me," he said, still holding my hand.

Thankfully the putrid smell was gone now from the office, as was the horrid twin taste on my tongue. With a heavy sigh, I said, "Baby Sullivan died…. in my arms." Redmond knew from my text that we'd only had two babies in the NICU, my charge and baby Sullivan.

"Oh Lynn, I'm so sorry," he said, soothing, rubbing his thumb over the back of my hand.

"There's more," I said, then told him about the lights flickering and the appearance of Zaqiel in the room. "I've seen this guy before at the hospital. He's the same one from the dream I had about my friend Louise."

"Why didn't you call me last night?" He squeezed my hand gently.

"It was late—I was fine, *sad* but fine," I said. "He's with his parents now."

"Hmmm," Redmond gave in response.

"What hmmm?"

"Maybe it's a seer thing," he said then. He'd never made reference to my abilities before.

"Go ahead," I said, interested in his view. No one ever really speculated about my abilities, they usually just accepted it was one of my Lynnie things.

"Maybe it's your way of seeing that the little guy was ready to go—too tired to keep going. Your dream of Louise—maybe it was like that too. Somehow you knew she was leaving, and you got to hold her one last time—a gift, sort of. Maybe what you saw that first time at the hospital, with that kid and this *Zaqiel*—as you call him, it was similar—like death hovering around the sick when it's their time to go."

"Wow—maybe," I said. "So, you think I can see death?"

"Maybe it's more that you know when it's near," he clarified. "What did you do after—last night I mean?"

"I went to the regular nursery, to hear the babies and their crying," I said, making another attempt at a smile. "But they were all sleeping."

"Sleeping babies is a good thing," Redmond said, giving me one of his boyish grins.

My smile widened then from a memory. "My mother told me a story about how the nurses back in her day used to name the babies—the ones without parents, I mean."

"I remember my dad—or was it my mom...," he said, giving a little head shake. "One of them anyway, I'd overheard referring to a patient by a fictitious name—a baby, one without parents. I guess they have to call them something."

"Well, baby Sullivan had originally been baby *Tuesday,*" I reminded him. "But me—I've got my own baby name story." I grinned again at the thought. Then I recalled the story for him about *little baby over to the left*.

Redmond let out a laugh, making me laugh with him. "I love it," he said, letting out another laugh with complete abandonment. "I wish I could have met your mom."

"Me too," I said, squeezing his hand this time.

"Up to Ottawa tomorrow," he said, shifting gears. "You said you're staying with your brother—which one?"

"James," I said. "I've never been close with the others. He and I are the only ones who gather with my cousins for holidays now."

"Ah," he said, as if understanding the unique dynamic of families. "Well, I'll be working this week—and potentially between Christmas and New Year's."

"What—why?" I asked. The studio was supposed to be closed for the holidays.

"Remember that band you and your friends came to see? We completed their studio album—but now they want to add another track, an acoustic version of the song named for the album."

"So *you* have to do it?"

"I may be the boss, but I'm not going to make my staff work during the holidays after I told them they all had it off," he said, with a shrug. "Album has to be ready in time for release on January 1st—before they go on tour."

Kind, dedicated, and a great boss. *And* he'd handled the latest weird story I'd laid on him with ease once again. He had even taken a stab at making it sound almost rational. Could he handle hearing my theory about the horsemen *and* about my seeing them? Maybe I could lead with the letter I'd found, I considered.

I reached into my purse and checked the time on my phone, then glanced back at him. He was smiling. Reaching in again to my purse I took out an envelope. I let out a sigh. "Speaking of having to go, I have to get up stupidly early for my flight. Still have to pack—winter clothes and such." I handed him the envelope.

He looked down at my hand and smiled again, then took something from his back pocket. "Don't open it until you get on the flight, okay?" he said, exchanging my Christmas card for his.

My envelope had been white and boring with just his name on it, where his was red with candy canes and Christmas trees all over it. Cute. "Okay—I'll try," I said, feeling a tad giddy and much better than I had earlier.

"Promise?" he prompted.

"I promise I'll try," I said, laughing now. He leaned in wrapping a big arm around me, then glanced skyward. I tilted my head to look up and found a sprig of mistletoe dangling from his other hand.

Even with the sleep overs, there'd been no hanky-panky and other than some handholding and hugs, we'd been mostly just friends. I'd appreciated the slow pace, but without hesitation, I leaned forward and pressed my lips to his, kissing him… for the first time.

Chapter 25

Hello, Ottawa.

I sent off a group text to Mac, Vicki and Olivia, letting them know I'd arrived safely and would be heading to James's shortly. I'd booked my flight home using one of the many vouchers Will had sent me. I wasn't sure how long I would stay, so I'd only booked a one-way ticket. I hadn't known if I would stay for New Year's or not either. What I did know, was I'd be starting my trip out at James's place in the country and for that I'd need a car.

I gave the lady at the desk the confirmation number for my rental car. She instructed me to have a seat on the left and that someone would be with me shortly to show me to my car.

Shortly after, another woman dressed in a rental car uniform, waved me over to the side entrance. Outside we did the usual body check of the car for current dings and scratches. I signed the forms, she handed me the keys, and I was good to go.

Before leaving, I sent James a text to let him know I had my rental and was on my way. Then I drove out of the airport's rental area, noting for the first time how mild it was for winter. There was hardly any snow, nothing on the roads, and on portions of the lawns, the grass was showing through. I may not need my winter coat after all.

Two hours later I pulled into the driveway at James's little country house. He was out front with his two dogs when I got out of the car.

Off their leashes, one white and the other a chocolate lab, came running over to see their *Auntie*.

"Hi Skye—Hi Radar," I said, to my four-footed niece and nephew, bending to give each a good pat. Over the years, my mom had called any of the dogs we had grand-dogs, and after I'd moved away, I'd started calling these James's *kids*.

"Just taking them for a walk up the hill—give them a quick run-around, burn some energy," James said. "Door's open—go on in."

"Good idea on the run," I said, taking my suitcase by the handle.

"Let's go," he called, causing them to run back over to him.

They headed up the hill while I headed inside and up the stairs to the guest room.

I didn't really need to unpack, it was easier to just take things out from my suitcase as I needed them. The only thing I would need today would be my toiletries, and I'd purposely placed my toiletry bag in my tote for easy access at the airport. Along with my laptop, wallet and phone, and the latest novel I was reading, the only other things I'd put in my tote had been Redmond's Christmas card.

I'd promised to wait until I'd gotten on the flight to read it, but I'd only made it as far as the waiting area at the gate.

Like I'd done with my card, he'd put my name on the envelope. Mine had been a generic red Christmas card with stylized silver snowflakes on the front, and just the words *Merry Christmas and a Happy New Year* inside, but I'd personalized it with, *Can't wait to spend time with you in the new year,* and signed it *Lynn.*

At first glance, I considered his card sweet, with the words *All I want for Christmas is you…* on the front of it, until I opened the card and read, *So, if a fat man puts you in a bag at night… don't worry. I told Santa I want you for Christmas,* followed by the words *Missing you at Christmas.* I'd laughed out loud in my seat at the gate. I adored sweet and funny over sweet and sappy any day. But the best part of his card had been his own words, *Can't wait to see what the new year brings. P.S. You can tell me anything, Lynn. I believe in you.*

Gabriel stood behind Lynn as she opened to reread Redmond's card.

Shamsiel had come to him last night after the party. He'd told Gabriel of the sighting of Armaros and the other two, *and* about the unforeseen and unnerving reaction Lynn had had, and the reaction she'd had even before they'd shown up. Something had been bothering her from the moment she'd arrived Shamsiel had told him, yet he had sensed no one around. But it wasn't that reaction of hers that had bothered Shamsiel most, it had been her words and the choice she'd been ready to make. She'd wanted to be found—more so, she wanted to find them, not just because she believed they might help, but because she liked the feel of their power. Luckily, Redmond had opened the door. Though she had questioned whether it was her previous actions of running from them, that had prevented her and her friends from finding the answers, Shamsiel had noted as well.

Gabriel knew this was not the case, but he also knew he'd taken an enormous risk choosing Lynn's birthmother, considering her links to the fallen and to The Horsemen. He speculated now if the risk had been too much. Plus he'd made no progress in finding the letter at the house. Now he came to watch over her here in Ottawa, while Shamsiel had offered to stay behind to watch over the house, should the others attempt to do their own search.

"Redmond believed in me," I whispered. Maybe I should have told him about the letter, but there was no rush since I hadn't solved it yet. I would for sure tell him about it when I got home, *and* about The Horsemen. It would all be out there for him, and he could do with it what he wanted. Believe the stories—or not, it didn't matter. All that mattered now, was that he believed *in* me.

On that note, I sent him another text;

I arrived safely at James's place, the roads were clear. Not much snow for this time of year and it's even a mild temp too, lucky for me.

It had been too early in the morning to text him before I left, but I had texted him when I landed. I let him know I'd arrived, and that I'd tried not to open his card but had failed, and I'd thanked him for the wonderful card. I'd also let him know I too was looking forward to all the great things the new year had to offer. He'd written back saying, *you're forgiven,* and *thank you for keeping me updated,* and adding *be safe on the long drive.*

My phone chimed a new text had arrived. Redmond.

It read;

> *Enjoy your time with your brother. I'll be thinking of you having fun while I'm working away in the studio. LOL*

And like the other text he'd sent after my flight, he'd added a separate line of X *and O's* to this one. I sent back my own line of hugs and kisses and then tossed my phone on the bed.

Downstairs I found James in the kitchen making grilled cheese sandwiches. Skye and Radar were both busy making chomping sounds in their food bowls.

"How's about grilled cheese and tomato soup for lunch?" he asked, pointing to the pot simmering on the stove. "You still like them, right?"

Once a big-brother, always a big-brother, I thought. "You bet," I said, putting my finger in his ear. Once a little-sister, always a little-sister.

After lunch we spent most of the day outside with the dogs playing. The weather was too good to pass up. Exhausting the dogs was always a good idea too, if you didn't want to be up at 5 a.m. with them looking for someone to play with. And by supper time, they were both passed out next to James's recliner.

Our evening meal was made easy by the ordering of pizza from the only restaurant in the little town near here. The pizza had been good, not as good as my Ottawa favorite Georgie's Pizza & Subs, but it would do for being in the middle of practically nowhere. And like we always did, James, and I stayed up to watch movie after movie until one of us dozed off. This time it had been me.

"Wake up—sleepy-head," he said, rousing me from my almost slumber. "I'm too old to carry you up to your bed—yer on your own."

I laughed and pushed myself up off the couch. "Too old? Your bedroom is on the first floor—yer just too lazy," I said, making my way to the stairs.

"Night, Lynn," he called as he turned the corner into his bedroom. Radar followed him.

"Night," I called down, halfway up the stairs. I turned to see Skye following up behind me. "Hi—you coming with me?" She took another step up the stairs. "Okay," I said, turning and continuing up to my room.

Gabriel sat in the chair across from where Lynn now slept. He reached out a hand and pet the head of her furry companion. Skye rubbed her face against his hand, then she slumped to the floor to sleep.

* * *

It was Tuesday and day 2 of my trip home. It was also *tree-cutting* time with Mac and her family.

James knew I'd be in and out during the week, in Ottawa visiting my friends. He'd said he'd be taking advantage of the warmer weather to do a few extra repairs on both the inside and outside of his house, *and* he had said it was best I wasn't around for all the banging and sawing and such. He'd also told me to keep out of the basement, saying he was working on a special project he wasn't yet ready to show me. He was ever the handyman, and if he didn't have projects to fix something, he had projects to create something in his workshop in the basement.

I pulled out of the drive, grateful for the clear road. I had a genuine fear of driving in snow, so it was a real treat to see the dry roads and no snow in the forecast. I'd told Mac I'd meet them at the tree place instead of going into Ottawa first, being it was about the same distance.

The *Thomas Tree Farm* was a sweet little farm and going there at Christmas time had become a new tradition for Mac's family. This was probably their fourth or fifth time going there to pick out a Christmas tree, but it was only my first time going with them.

Mac had texted me this morning to let me know what time to meet them. She'd also informed me that her husband had started another tradition last year, that once everyone arrived, they gathered around the back of their van for the adults to have a shot of Sambuca to warm up before heading out to pick a tree.

When I pulled in, I could see a small group gathering around the family's minivan. I shut and locked the car door and then called out to Mac as I approached. "Hey—wait for me," I said, seeing the shot glasses being passed out.

"Yer just in time," Mac's husband said, handing me a plastic shot glass filled with dark cloudy liquid.

"Welcome home, Lynnie," Mac said, tapping her tiny glass against mine. She winked at me and then downed her shot.

"Happy holidays," I responded, and tipped back mine. The black Sambuca's licorice flavor coated my throat and then warmed my entire body.

"We always take a picture of the kids on the wooden stairs while waiting for the wagon," Mac said, pointing to the meet'n greet area.

"Wagon?" I questioned. "We don't walk?"

"No, the wagon takes us back into the tree farm area," she said, as we walked over. "Wait until you see the beautiful horses." Her kids rushed ahead past us. "There's not enough snow this year, but they usually use a horse-drawn sleigh ride—instead of the wagon, that you can jump on and off as it goes around the tree farm," she added, just as our ride pulled up.

Mac's mom and dad were already at the greeting area waiting for the rest of us. There were two other couples and their kids, all friends of Mac and her husband's, organizing themselves to get on the horse-drawn transport.

Mac and I were last to get on, and we sat at the back of the wagon with the lower half of our legs hanging over the edge. "I forget—you've never done this with us before," she said. "When we get to the selection area, we spread out and find our perfect tree. The kids actually cut down the tree—with help."

When the wagon came to a stop, I followed as Mac jumped off the back.

I panned the mini forest and took in the rich enchanting scent of the spruce trees. It was the *smell* that truly captured the spirit of the holidays.

"I can feel them you know—the trees," Mac said. "This one is sick, if we cut it, it won't make it through the holidays." She patted the tree to her right.

"Do you want a healthy one?" I asked, as we walked further off the trail.

Mac took off her gloves and touched a tall tree that seemed to stand as if all alone. "I want this one," she said. "It's sick—but won't die until the new year. I like to leave the healthy ones for the forest."

"It's a beauty. Must be almost 8 feet," I said, giving one branch a closer sniff.

"It's harder now—doing this. Now that I can feel nature," Mac clarified. "Boys—your mom has found the tree."

I stood back as the boys ran over to where their mom stood next to her pick. They were followed by their dad who carried a bow saw. It was the kind of saw that anyone could use, and it was durable as heck I recalled Mac telling me on the ride in. But instead of helping, the boys attempted to make snowballs from what little snow was on the ground.

"Lyyyynn," came the sweet voice of Mac's mom. Monica and Fred had gotten on in front and we'd missed our usual greeting. "So wonderful to see you."

I opened my arms to take her in a warm embrace. "Good to see you too," I said, through a squeeze.

"Let me look at you," she said, stepping back and examining me like I was a kid who'd grown a foot. "Something about you has changed." She stared at me. "Didn't I hear a little something through the grapevine?" she questioned.

"She means you met someone," Mac simplified, stepping up next to us. "Derek said Luc told him you met someone on Halloween, but he didn't elaborate. You know how boys are." She rolled her eyes.

"So, tell us," Monica insisted, ignoring the tiny balls of snow that were being shot around us.

I looked at Mac and she gave me one of her big toothy grins.

In response, I grabbed up a small mound of snow, patted it into a ball and tossed it at Mac.

She batted it away and laughed. "Com'on, Westlake, give it up," she added in response to her mother's prompt.

I grabbed up another mound of snow, this time tossing it at the boys running by. "We're just doing the friend-thing right now," I admitted, brushing my now wet hands on my jeans "Going slow. It's nice."

"That's the best way to start," Mac's mom said. "Let it grow from there."

"I think so too," I said. "We went to a big gala together. You'd have been proud of me, Mac—I wore a fancy dress and all." I'd thought of her when I'd gotten dressed for the gala, about how proud she would have been seeing me in a dress again.

"I'd say I'm impressed, but you'll have to show me pictures to prove it though," she replied. "I want to see a picture of this new fella too."

"What fella," Mac's dad asked, from over my shoulder.

"Lynn's new guy-friend," Mac said.

"What does this fella do for a living?" her dad prodded.

"He plays music," Mac stated. "Derek told us that too." She gave me a mischievous smile.

"Not a musician," Fred said, smacking my arm jokingly.

"Dad!" Mac shot back.

I gave him a friendly smack on the arm back. "Redmond owns and runs a very successful music studio," I told him.

"What kind of name is Redmond?" he asked, this time giving my arm a squeeze coupled with a playful grin.

"Irish," I said, laughing now because it was always like him to tease me, no matter the subject.

"Well that makes up for the musician part," he countered.

"Daaad," Mac objected again. "Boys—enough with the snowballs, come over and help grandpa and your dad with the tree."

Mac redirected her attention to rounding up the boys. Her husband finished cutting down their pick, then he and the rest of the fathers got the trees on the back of the wagon. We all hopped on after and took the wagon back to the welcome area.

"You'll like this part the best," Mac said. "We get free hot chocolate and homemade cookies, and there's always a bonfire to sit around to warm up."

"It's not very cold—but I like the hot chocolate and cookie idea," I said. That's the part she knew I'd like.

After the treats by the bonfire, I went with Mac to pay for the tree. "This part *is* cool," Mac said, as we watched the tree get sent through a machine that shook the crap out of it. "It's to get rid of all the loose needles," she added, as the tree went through another process where it got wrapped in a mesh bag.

In the parking lot, Mac's husband put the tree on the top of the minivan, and then that was it.

"Time to head back to our place for the potluck dinner—Mom had left already to set up," Mac informed me. "Might as well just follow us," she said, making sure the kids were fastened in. Then she got in up front in the passenger side.

"Okay," I said, then dashed off to my car.

When they passed by, I pulled out of my parking spot and followed behind the tree decorated family van.

At Mac's house, Monica had a big spread set up on the dining room table, with both regular chili and vegetarian chili and all the fixings. There was a bunch of other appetizers as well, and as each couple or person entered the home, they added to the table with whatever they'd made for the gathering.

I stared at the food like I hadn't eaten in a week.

"My mom always makes that chocolate log for us—you know the one," Mac said when she came to stand with me. "Chocolate cookie wafers with whipped cream between each one and on the outside, all covered in whipped cream. She leaves it overnight, so the whipped cream softens the cookies." I was already salivating over the food, but now she'd just pushed my taste buds over the edge. "It's divine," she added, handing me a dinner plate.

The rest of the evening we spent hanging out, drinking and eating. I did mostly eating, as I had to drive back to James's after. I tried to do a head count and found there were about 16 adults and 18 kids in attendance this year, not including me.

I enjoyed seeing everyone interact and watching all the kids play the game Mac had said she'd constructed a few years ago. She buys a bunch of small prizes; candy, chocolate, hacky sack balls, notebooks, gift cards etc. and then she wraps them over and over and over in Christmas paper. In the game, the kid tries to open the gift while wearing oven mitts, while at the same time the kid next to them throws dice. The first kid gets to keep trying to unwrap it until the dice thrower rolls a pair, then it goes to the next person. It was simple, but it kept them entertained and allowed the adults to relax and enjoy their socializing.

"What are your plans?" Mac asked, handing me a massive slice of her mother's dessert. "For the rest of your visit—I mean." She sat down on the arm of the big sofa chair I was in.

"Heading back to James's tonight," I responded, taking the dessert plate from her. "Tomorrow is over at Vicki's while she bakes. Then dinner with Olivia and family."

"Good to know I'm not the only one feeding you," she giggled out.

I poked her thigh with the plastic fork that had come with the plate of cake. "Small burdens," I said. "Be thankful you don't have to dress me."

We both laughed.

Cooper came over then, slumping down on the floor near my feet. He rolled over on his back. "Need a reprieve from all the commotion I bet, eh?" I said to him, as I leant down and scratched his belly with my free hand. I rested back in my seat, but he stayed upside-down.

Uriel knelt and gave Cooper's belly a rub. "It's a nice gathering," Uriel said, "But it's not the gathering they should be focusing on."

Gabriel said nothing.

"With the holidays all of our Charges have been busy with their families, and they've put their solving of things off for now," Uriel added.

"Lynn is here now—what would you have me do?" Gabriel responded. "Weren't yours and the other Charges supposed to contact Lynn—have a group chat?"

Uriel stood and crossed his arms over his chest. "We were discussing the same thing the other day," he said. "But why isn't Lynn telling them about the letter? Maybe they could solve it."

"Derek has a copy," Gabriel stated. "She feels kept out of things. This is her letter and hers to solve, she feels. I'm sure she will tell them once the second page is unraveled. We all know it has to do with the gathering."

"And this birthfather—apparently," Uriel tossed out. "If we knew who he was—or how he fits in, maybe we could better prepare for the gathering."

"The gathering isn't for or about you—or Vretil, nor Raphael, or Michael. It's about them... it's for all of them," Gabriel expressed. He gave a breathy sigh.

"This was great, Mac—thanks for including me," I said, moving to get up out of the chair.

"Yer always welcome—you know that," Mac said, as we walked to the front door. "Oh Lynn—I made you something."

"More food?" I asked, going in for a hug. "Being fed is all I ever need."

"I've accepted that burden—as you called it," she laughed, releasing me. Then she reached into a big satchel-purse that hung next to the coat closet. "It's a *Safe Travel Charm*. For you know, traveling—to keep you safe."

I held up the little red flannel pouch to take a better look. "It's no homemade muffin, but I like the *safe* part," I said. Mac gave the side of my shoulder a little push. "No really—I'm traveling alone now, it's perfect."

"It's not just for safety, it'll keep you from getting lost. Of course, that doesn't mean don't use your GPS, it doesn't tell you *how* to get places," she joked.

"What's in it—or should I ask?" I laughed. We hadn't talked about magic or the mystery they were working on, but then I had shared nothing about my new little potential piece in the puzzle either.

"Dirt," Mac said. "A few large chunks of rock salt—and a silver coin." She grinned, and my mouth opened ready for another laugh. "Hey—don't laugh, I sewed the little bag myself. I filled it with the other stuff—then I sewed it shut."

"That's it?" I questioned, tucking it into my front pocket.

"Just keep it with you when you travel," she said, all serious. "That's it."

Chapter 26

Wednesday, and day 3 of my trip home, I maneuvered out of the driveway to head back into town.

Today's visits would be split between time with Vicki at her place while she did her yearly Christmas baking, then later over to Olivia's for dinner with her family. It would be a tough day ahead—*not*.

As per usual, my visit with Vicki began with us eating a healthy lunch she'd made. But soon after, *my* healthy eating slid downhill once she began with her holiday baking. Vicki had been requested to do some baking for her family's get-together that she would attend later this evening. The request had been for traditional treats and not her usual healthy snacks, *and* it had been the reason my resolve had weakened in that department.

You name it, she was making it, and nothing escaped having sugar as an ingredient. Between sampling, I struggled to distract myself away from the baking by combing her apartment for new additions to her decor. When I'd first walked into the apartment, I'd noticed her dining table was piled with papers, and unlike usual, we'd eaten lunch at the tiny kitchen table instead of taking our regular spots at the dining table.

Standing in front of the dining room table now with the latest sample in my hand, I asked "What's all this?" I'd considered it might be more work on the codex, but if it was, it would be a surprise she'd left it out, especially with me coming over.

"Work stuff," she said, poking her head out the kitchen entry.

I nodded and sifted through a small pile of printed pages. "You're taking your work home with you now?" I questioned.

"It's not my usual work," she said. "Here—try this one." She held out a cream coloured cookie. I took it, bit into it and grinned.

Between more samplings of homemade goodies; shortbread, butter tarts, and chocolate fudge, Vicki explained all about the new opportunity she'd been presented with, the translating of documents and archives. "I can read the transcripts—translate them into English, but I don't speak any of the languages. So, I can't function as an interpreter, just the translator of the written word," she clarified. "I love it, but I struggle having to clarify how I know the languages yet can't speak them. The clients are mainly happy someone can do the work, so they don't dwell on the *why* of things."

As Vicki went on further with the list of challenges facing translation, I took up residence on the sofa in the living room. I listened, watching her through the kitchen entrance as she scrambled around the small room explaining as she baked. Her latest creation, instead of it being back and forth from the counter to the stove, this one was being made in the microwave. Apparently, both the almond-roca type candy and the peanut brittle required numerous ins and outs of the microwave, adding various ingredients, all set at different intervals. Add, stir, heat, and repeat.

"How was tree trimming?" Vicki asked, changing topics, shutting the tiny door and setting the microwave for another 60 seconds.

"Good, fun." I said. "Had to be over 30 people there once we got back to Mac's place—18 of which were kids. Poor Cooper." I laughed at the memory of him surrounded by all the craziness.

"Ya—no kidding. I'm not sure I'd be okay surrounded by that many kids," she laughed out. "I'd love to get a pet," she started to say, "...but maybe not if I end up traveling a lot." She set the microwave for another 60 seconds, then moved to the far counter.

"I have Raven at the house for now, but I'm sure when Luc and Dunya move in together—you know that's inevitable, I'll have to get my own companion," I said, through a sigh. "Speaking of companions, I guess you heard I met someone." I leaned to one side trying to get a better view at what she was mixing in the latest bowl on the counter. "Mac told me, you all knew," I added.

"Yup," she said, coming back into view. "Derek said Luc told him. Halloween night, right?" She held the spatula in her hand like how you'd hold a sword.

"Yup," I said, eyeballing the chocolate clinging to the spatula. "You gonna use that—or let me lick the remnants off it?" I smiled at her.

"Here," she said, chuckling and handing it to me. She grabbed a clean spatula from the drawer and set it next to the bowl. "Okay, you met a new guy—tell me about him already."

Smiling again, I took a long lick off the spatula, then I took a quick glance out the 3rd floor window. "Well...," I began.

"Our brother Uriel informs me, that your Charges are not focusing on the task at hand, that they're otherwise occupied with the holidays," Gabriel said, addressing Michael who stood near the kitchen entrance, watching his Charge in action. "It looks like between baking for her family's gathering and her new translation work, Vicki hasn't put much energy into the details of the other gathering."

"None of us are pleased with it, Gabriel. There's no need to point it out," Michael said between gritted teeth. "Why doesn't Lynn just give Vicki the letter? I'm sure she and Derek could figure it out."

Gabriel sat down next to Lynn on the couch. "Derek has a copy of the letter," Gabriel reminded him. "But it's not Vicki's to solve." Derek had a scanned copy, though Gabriel hadn't found any printed copies, nor been able to figure out what computer folder he'd hidden it in.

"Maybe not," Michael shot back, "but it's not as though Lynn is a master puzzle solver."

Oh really? Gabriel mused. "She figured out most of the pieces that led the others to find their letters—and even led them to the codex."

"With Derek's help," Michael stated, glancing over at his brethren.

"He's not helping now—hasn't even worked on it," Gabriel pointed out. "But there is still time."

"Is there, Gabriel? Is there really?" Michael blew out a breath and turned back to watch Vicki.

Vicki ran her finger over the new chocolate covered spatula. "Mmmm," she said, then popped her coated finger into her mouth. Swallowing, she added, "I like a tall guy." She gave me a few eyebrow raises. "I'm like you—not musical at all either." She laughed. "But he sounds hot." She took a lick straight from the spatula this time.

"Handsome face aside, the rest of him didn't look so hot on Halloween—not at first anyway, blood-spattered scrubs and all. But wowsers, you should have seen him in his tux—at the gala," I expressed, savoring the last of the chocolate from my own spatula.

"Returning to the scene of the crime, eh?" Vicki tossed out. "Where you met—I mean. Talk about high contrast events."

She didn't know the half of it. "I got to do US Thanksgiving and a Christmas party with some of his friends and staff." I smiled. "We've had some nice time alone too," I shared.

Part of me wanted to tell Vicki everything, all about what had happened at both events. Perhaps even brainstorm over the letter from my birthmother too, but neither she nor Mac had mentioned a word about what they'd been doing in my absence. They had been working on the particulars for the gathering, Derek had told me. He'd also said there might be something in my letter that could help them. Even so, those wounds of rejection still ached from my past offers to help. They had disregarded my ideas and theories about their mystery despite my getting them together. I wasn't ready to open those wounds with more rejection. I'd resigned to wait until I had proof, until I'd solved that letter. With or without Derek.

"I'd like to meet someone—but like with the pet idea, I don't really have time with this new career direction," Vicki gave me.

"Well, sounds like there's lots of travel involved—like you said, so who knows," I gave her back. "Never know how or where you could meet someone—look at my meeting Redmond."

"True," she said, nodding, licking the last morsel off her spatula. "Speaking of time, I need to get these treats packaged up, then head to my brother's place asap. And you my friend, need to get yourself out to Olivia's for your nightly feeding." She tossed the mostly clean spatula in the sink and then rummaged around in the cupboard for what I assumed was plastic containers.

I got off the couch to assist with the cleanup since I was no help with the baking. "Will your son be home for the holidays?" I asked, running the water into the sink and rinsing out the mixing bowls.

"No. He's in Toronto with his girlfriend and her family," Vicki said, as she attempted to match lids to their container mates. "He's too old—too cool, for all the kid stuff that goes on at my brother's place." She made a *whatever* face. "But I miss him," she added. "Plus, I have too much work right now to spend any quality time with him, anyway." She gave me a weak smile, then went on with placing the baking into the containers.

At the apartment door Vicki handed me two rectangular clear plastic containers filled with the assortment of treats she'd made. "One's for James, the other one's for Olivia's girls." I looked longingly at the treats through the clear lids. "You can have some too, Lynn. But tell Olivia I said, *get over it,*" Vicki joked, pointing out that her readily available healthy snacks were not part of this mix.

We both laughed because we knew how strict Olivia was with *healthy this* and *healthy that*.

"I'll do my best—*bad influence* treatment with the girls," I said. "But I may end up being the only one allowed to eat them."

"Hmmm," Vicki said, as she swung open the front door. "Tell Olivia I used natural sweetener in them. Sugar is natural right?" She gave me a smart-ass grin.

"Right," I said, winking, then heading out the door. "Have fun," I called as I descended the stairs.

"Will do—drive safe," Vicki called, before I heard the door shut.

Drive safe was easy, as I'd lucked into another nice snow-scarce winter drive out to the Whites. The roads had remained clear of ice, and no new snow had fallen during my visit with Vicki.

With the streets clear, I parked alongside the patch of lawn between Olivia's house and the neighbor's driveway.

I could hear Bella, their dog, barking from inside as I walked up the front path. The front door opened then, and both Kate and Rachel came out to greet me. But before their mom could see, I passed them the container of treats Vicki had prepared. They squealed, turning and rushing past their mom back through the open door. Then I passed through the door and into the cozy warmth.

"What was that?" Olivia inquired, giving me a one-armed hug and shutting the door behind us.

"Christmas treats from Vicki," I said, "Made with natural sweetener." I gave her an innocent grin. She gave me a suspicious smirk back. "Wine," I suggested, diverting her from my sneaky ploy.

It worked, because she said, "Oh, I have a new one you have to try." Excited now, she led me to the kitchen where Mike was busily working on something wonderful involving pasta.

"Hey, Lynn," he said. "Merry Christmas."

"Same to you—that looks delicious," I said, leaning in for a sniff.

Olivia nudged me and handed me a nearly full glass of wine. "I made my famous Caesar salad to go with it," she countered.

"You guys are the best," I said, feeling the teensiest bit guilty now for sneaking in the bad-for-you treats. I gave another innocent grin. I had a feeling Olivia would need a few more glasses of wine before she'd buy my innocence, though. "Merry Christmas," I added, reaching out to clink Olivia's equally full glass.

Typical of time with the Whites, dinner was a scrumptious success, and filled with loads of laughs and banter from both the girls and the adults.

After, once the girls cleaned up the dishes, they and Mike were off out the door once again to the barn for some Christmas event. A second after the door shut behind them, Olivia and I were up the stairs to her bedroom, wine bottle and glasses in hand, on a mission to finish whatever wrapping was left to do for the girl's gifts.

"Are you going to see Will's father on this trip," Olivia asked, placing the last piece of tape on an oddly shaped package.

"No. He's away at Will's sister's place," I told her.

"Oh, that makes sense," she said. She pulled a new roll of decorative paper from the bundle.

"Andre—his neighbor, told me Will's dad would be away," I explained. "I'm actually going to stop in to see him tomorrow evening before his boys arrive." Before I'd left to come up to Ottawa, I'd emailed Andre to let him know I was coming. He'd informed me that Will's father would be away, but *he'd* be next door if I still wanted to come by. I knew it would be a tough visit without Louise there, but of course I wanted to see him. Both Olivia and I were missing people this Christmas, my missing just involved a few extra people.

"Mac told me you met a guy," Olivia said, redirecting, keeping the topic off the obvious.

"Ya we're just friends—it's nice, slow," I shared, despite the mixing of emotions and her mentioning Will's father. I was aware they all knew I'd met someone, but I was more nervous Olivia was going to ask me if I'd heard from Will again. She gave me a tiny grin. "He's really great and easy going. I don't have many friends in Miami. So it's nice to have another avenue to meet new people." I gave her a hopeful smile. "He has an assistant at work, Lily—she's fantastic. She actually drove me home from the Halloween party," I added, giving her a bigger smile.

Olivia's smile changed then to something brighter. "Heard you guys went to some fancy shindig," she tossed out, full of levity.

"Ya, fancy dress and all," I tossed back, happy for the mood change.

Olivia stopped mid-wrapping of a shoebox size gift, and said, "I'm happy you have someone nice to spend time with—I worry about you being there alone." She gave me a sweet smile this time. "And you're not driving back out to your brother's tonight either," she said, in her usual motherly way. Then unmotherly, she poured more wine into my glass.

"You worry too much," I told her. "Luc is there. Dunya is next door, and I have Raven too. I'm not really alone. And I have work," I reminded.

"Hospital job," she acknowledged, with a smirk and an eye roll.

"I'm involved with some great people, but some of the work is really sad, like losing baby Sullivan," I said. Between the wrapping of more gifts and the pouring of more wine, I shared the joys, and the trials and tribulations associated with my new job.

"I can relate to all of it," Olivia said, with a sigh. "I've seen it all running the office for a NICU, with seven doctors and their different specialties."

Compared to what Olivia juggled at work, I knew I had it much easier. I didn't envy her job in the least. "I love being there though, despite the harsh realities of some of it," I said, taping up the last of the gifts from my pile.

"No more work talk," Olivia stated, topping up her glass of wine. "What are your plans for the rest of your stay?" She took a long swig of her wine before setting it down on the nightstand, then she grabbed the next gift from her pile.

"Tomorrow I'm hanging out with James—doing the Christmas eve thing with him and the dogs," I said, before transferring my pile of wrapped gifts into the empty laundry basket. Olivia had set it out for an easy carry down to the main floor. Olivia still had three more gifts from her pile to wrap, so I leant back against the headboard of the bed and sipped at my wine and watched as she continued.

"I'm sure James is happy you're home," Olivia noted. "Nice he has the dogs too—so he's not alone."

"Ya—he needs the company," I said, reaching forward to give Bella a pat. She'd trailed along behind us up the stairs and was now lounging near the foot of the bed. "Bella," I said, as she rolled onto her back. "Ha—that funny, the other night at Mac's, Cooper did that same thing when he'd been sprawled next to my feet."

"Ah, a dog's life, eh?" Olivia said, struggling to get dog hair off a piece of tape.

Gabriel watched as Raphael passed a hand back and forth over the chest of the outstretched dog.

"This visit of Lynn's could have been made a lot easier if they'd all just gotten together in one place," Raphael declared. "Then they could talk about everything, *and* she could have told them about the letter."

"This is how she does her visits. At least it's how she used to do them—before the girls all knew each other so well," Gabriel clarified. "And Michael and Uriel as well, shared their concerns with me. I know Derek hasn't spent much time working on the letter, but they're all so close to finding the answers."

"They're close to losing their minds," Raphael stated. "With The Horsemen here—and Armaros and the other leaders, I'm about to lose my mind too."

"Just don't give up on them—don't lose faith," Gabriel pleaded.

"Christmas just isn't the same without Mom and Aunt Kay," I expressed, knowing Olivia would understand. I sighed and gave Bella's ear a rub.

"I know—I miss my Mum too," Olivia said, confirming my thoughts.

"Too much wine is making me warm," I said, but I knew it was the mix of emotions. I placed my glass on the bedside table and then unzipped my fleece vest.

"Mala beads," Olivia said, noticing the strand around my neck.

I glanced down. "A friend of Redmond's made it—showed me how to use it for meditation." I took it from around my neck and handed it to her.

"It's beautiful. This one is hand knotted between each bead," she said, examining it. "It allows you to chant your mantra—keep track of where they are. Most malas have 108 beads, but some have 216—double, or 54—half. I've read a few different references for why there are 108, but my favorite is for Chakras, of course."

"Chakras?"

"The seven energy points of the body," she pointed out, literally pointing them out on her own body, starting at her head and working downward.

"Right," I said, remembering her brief reference from way back when we'd all gathered at Mac's on my last visit home.

"They say there are 108 energy lines connecting to the heart. One of them is believed to be the path to self-realization—whatever that is," she giggled out. "But for meditation, some people recite mantras. Some even in Sanskrit. Vicki told me the Sanskrit alphabet has 54 letters. That each letter has a feminine and masculine form, making up the 108 beads. Do you have a mantra?"

"Yes," I said, all proud of myself. "*I am open to all that releases me.*"

"Oh, I like that one," Olivia said, then she leant over to pull out the little drawer from her nightstand. From the drawer she pulled out a similar strand of beads to mine and handed it to me.

This mala strand contained much darker beads with a burgundy coloured stain to them, like she'd left them to soak in a glass of wine overnight. "Nice colour." I grinned.

"Don't say it—Mike teased me already about it when I made them. So what if I like the colour of wine."

We both laughed.

"I like it—the colour, *and* your new wine," I said, grinning again.

"Have you ever heard of *Shanti Mantra*?" she asked, handing me my strand back, exchanging it for hers.

I shook my head *no*.

"It's a chant for peace… for when I've had a rough day," she explained. Then she went into, "*May there be well-being for all, may there be peace for all. May there be wholeness for all, may there be happiness for all.* If I'm short on time, I use a quick version; Om Shanti Shanti Shanti. It means *Om Peace Peace Peace.*"

"Om Shanti, Shanti, Shanti," I recited. "Because we could all use a little more peace in our lives. I know I could after a 14-hour shift." I laughed.

"Well, I have a little something else you can use," Olivia said, shifting to reach back into the drawer again.

"It's not another little bag of dirt and salt, is it?" I laughed again.

"Ha! I guess Mac already gave you her *Safe Travel* charm." She giggled. "No—mine's more along the same theme as the mala beads. I made it though."

Turning back, she handed me a multi-coloured beaded bracelet with a lineup of black beads strung running two-thirds the length.

"It's a lava rock bead bracelet—for your chakras," Olivia said, as if clarifying. "You can add essential oils to the lava rocks if you want. I made a little cloth bag to go with it. It's adjustable too," she added.

"You made this—that's cool," I said, still unclear how it worked. "What are the other beads made of?"

"Amethyst. For your crown chakra," she started, pointing at the purple bead, going from the right side of the short strand, then tapped the top of my head. "Lapis Lazuli. For your third eye chakra," She tapped lightly on the center of my forehead. "Turquoise for your throat chakra." She pointed to my throat. Then instead of going further down the line, she skipped to the left side and she said, "Red Agate. It's for your root chakra." Then she continued towards the center of the bracelet. "Amber, is for your sacral chakra, and Tiger Eye is for your solar plexus chakra." Once at the middle again, she said, "Green King Stone. This colour is for your *heart* chakra. It's considered the fourth chakra whether you go from right to left or left to right. This one is connected to *love*, relating, integration, and compassion. Its true name is *Anahata*."

Thinking she was done, I said, "Thank you—my favorite gifts have always been handmade ones." I glanced up from admiring the coloured strand.

Olivia was smiling at me. "Vicki told me that Anahata translated, means *unhurt, unstruck*, or *unbeaten*. You can use this with your mantra too—*I am open to all that releases me*. To open your heart to love again."

Chapter 27

After coffee and breakfast with Olivia in the morning, and then a slew of *I love yous, miss yous,* and Christmas hugs from her and the girls, I ventured out on my two-hour return drive back to James's place.

These visits with my friends had been as wonderful as they'd always been. Well, like they'd been before I'd stumbled upon those pages in my mother's journal, and before they'd all become such a tight unit. I was grateful for the time with them now, though I wondered if we could have found a way to get all of us together, but my doubts were high on that, especially with all the family functions going on. I'd take what I could get, I always did with visits in my hometown.

Before bed last night, I'd sent Redmond a text letting him know how things had been going with visiting my friends. I may have written *I miss you* a few too many times, but I blamed it on the few too many glasses of wine. Thankfully, I'd gotten an equal number of *I miss you too* back from him. Thankfully again, when I'd sent my good morning text to Redmond just before leaving Olivia's, I'd received a, *Be safe and text me when you get there* response back, assuring me my drunk texting hadn't annoyed him. He'd even ended his text with *XOXO.*

Arriving at the little country home again I found that James's truck was not in the drive. I'd considered he may have taken the dogs up the mountain to let them loose for a run, but I could already hear the barking when I came around to the back door.

Opening it, my furry niece and nephew greeted me, and like always they were full of energy. "Hi kids," I said, bending down on one knee to greet them properly with pats and hugs. "Where's yer dad?" I asked, not expecting a response.

When I stood, I spotted a note next to the backdoor on the leash table, addressed to me;

> *Lynn,*
> *Needed supplies. Gone to get groceries.*
> *Dogs have been fed and run.*
> *Back soon.*
> *~James*
> *p.s. there is leftover lasagna in the fridge—Mom's recipe.*

It *was* almost time for lunch, and I'd oblige him by getting rid of some of those leftovers. Especially if it was Mom's recipe and all, wouldn't want it to go to waste.

Skye and Radar watched with sharp attention as I plated and then microwaved a large piece of lasagna. "You two were fed already—so don't get any ideas."

Skye gave a "*Groan.*"

Radar tilted his head and licked his lips.

"Well, okay," I conceded, then let them lick the remnants from the big spoon I'd used to dish out the slab to my plate. "Just don't tell your dad."

An hour later, my big brother was through the door with his supplies. And as he travelled the house putting away the large non-food items like toilet paper and laundry soap, I helped by emptying the remaining grocery bags with the actual food.

James came around through the kitchen just as I pulled a block of white cheddar cheese and box onion soup mix from the last bag. "Can't have Christmas eve without our traditional French onion soup," he said, with a big grin.

"I love French onion soup," I said fondly. Mom always made it for us on Christmas eve. She'd even continued after we'd grown up and moved out. She'd always made extra soup and shredded extra cheese, just in case she had unexpected visitors, like one of my cousins or any friends of the family showed up.

"We can heat up a tourtiere pie to go with it," James suggested. It was another Christmas tradition, but was more of a *Canadian* tradition to have meat-pies than it was a tradition of ours. "There's one in the freezer."

"Sounds good to me," I said, folding up the last paper grocery bag.

"How's six o'clock for dinner?" James asked, pushing the backdoor open, letting the dogs out for a run-around in the yard.

"That's cool—as long as you let me help," I said. He liked being the big brother, but it would be fun making dinner together for once. "Oh—I forgot, Vicki made you some treats." I pulled the plastic container from my tote I'd left hanging off a hook by the door.

"That Vicki—she never disappoints," he said, popping the lid and taking one of the shortbreads from the top. Then he put the container on a high shelf out of reach before letting his kids back in.

The two happy doggies circled around us like they hadn't seen us in weeks. Dogs were funny that way, always happy to see you even if you'd only been out of sight for a minute.

"Shortbread," James said, appreciative, tossing back the last piece of cookie before giving the dogs another good pat.

I rubbed my stomach remembering all the sampling I'd done at Vicki's. "I was her baking guinea-pig yesterday—so I hope you enjoy the sacrifices I made," I said, with a hint of sarcasm.

"Such sacrifices," he laughed out. "Tell her thanks for me, eh?"

"I will," I said. "Hey, I'm just gonna check in with Alison—give her a call." I needed to touch base with her since she wasn't on my available for a visit list.

"No prob," James said, heading in the other direction. "I need to finish up something in my workshop."

"Gotcha." I nodded. Skye and Radar followed behind me as I headed for the stairs to make the call from my room.

"Don't come down," I heard him call, as he shut the door to the basement.

I wouldn't have gone down, but now that he'd told me not too, it made me want to. He used to do things like that when I was a kid. Say *don't* just to drive me crazy. But I knew he was working on my Christmas gift, so I would stay out of the basement. Like I'd said to

Olivia, homemade gifts were the best. It helped if you were one of those people who had talent to make stuff though.

I wasn't one of those people, unfortunately. I'd ordered James's Christmas gift a few weeks ago and had it delivered to his house instead of my place in Miami. It saved me having to make room for it in my carryon, and for my personal enjoyment, it added a bit of torture for him having to wait until Christmas to open it. It's what brothers and sisters do.

Pushing the pillow up against the headboard, I leaned back against it and hit *dial* on my cell phone for Alison's number. As it rang, I watched as the dogs spread out on the floor near the entrance to the room like doggie barriers.

"Ho-Ho-Ho," Alison said, when the call connected. "Merry Ho-Ho, Spook," she added with a giggle.

"Hi, Spook," I giggled back. "What's Ho-Ho-happening out there?"

"The *yuuwwjsh*—getting ready for a big gathering with Ken's family at his brother's place. You?"

"Hanging with my brother tonight—tomorrow is Christmas lunch with my cousins," I gave her.

"Ya, I've got my Dad, brother and sister coming tomorrow. My niece is coming too, but I won't see my step-kids until Boxing day. They're at their mother's for Christmas," she added. I could picture the eyeroll and annoyed face that came with her last comment. Ken's ex was a piece of work, but that's another story.

"Sounds like a lot," I said. "Hope yer not doing too much—over doing it."

"Ken won't let me," she laughed out. "I could probably take him—I'm only 6 months, but I feel like a sumo wrestler. I've got a couple pounds on him." She laughed.

"I bet you look beautiful," I said, squashing her self-deprecating comment. "Is your house all decorated?"

"Of course—plus all the gifts under the tree," she said. "Ken and I picked up lots of baby stuff already—but I still wrapped some and put them under the tree. Next year it will be mostly toys." She giggled again.

It was true, next year's Christmas will be all about the baby toys, new clothes, and pictures with Santa. "There must be lots of *blue* too," I recognized.

Originally, Alison hadn't wanted to know the sex of the baby, but due to the whole *daughter* thing, she'd changed her mind. She'd made the excuse to Ken that it would be easier to decorate the baby's room. She didn't care either way if it was a boy or girl, especially after everything they'd been through with the fertility treatments, she just wanted a healthy baby.

"And green and yellow," she said. "I'd been surprised when we learned it was a boy—but was thrilled that all was well in the *womb without a view*," she added with a burst of laughter.

"Always with the movie references—screenwriters," I tossed out, shaking my head.

"I'm off work until after New Year's. What are you doing for New Year's?" she asked. Undoubtedly, she also knew about Redmond. "Any big plans—hmmm?"

"Here in Ottawa—no," I said, purposely holding back. "And I don't know when I'll be heading back to Miami."

"What about plans iiiinnn Miami," she nudged, seeking more.

"Nope—no plans," I shared, tormenting her a little longer. I wasn't lying, I didn't have plans, but I knew the information—or lack of information as it were, was killing her.

"C'mon," she pushed, breaking from the anguish. "Tell me about the new guy."

I laughed. She laughed. Then I shared all the facts, well most of them, just about meeting Redmond on Halloween, then I further went on about us going to the gala. I joked about the sacrifice I'd made for him with wearing the fancy dress, but I left out the details on being chased in my high heels through the place. Now wasn't the time for that kind of sharing. Instead I added the fun stuff, like about the studio Redmond owned, and the holiday party he'd had. "He likes to cook, and he reads a lot too," I ended.

"You know Ken plays guitar too—kind of cool they both play," she said, suggesting commonalities with the two as if they'd be buds. It would be nice for her and Ken to meet Redmond, but with the baby coming, it wouldn't be anytime soon.

"He's got red hair, a deep fiery sherry-coloured red—not that classic stereotypical red," I told her. "More like *Bryce Dallas Howard* or *Julianne Moore*." She'd appreciate the movie star references. "His is darker, but not quite auburn," I added.

"Oh Spook, you know I've always loved a ginger—and freckles," she gushed. I did know it. Her husband had freckles, despite him not having red hair.

"We're doing the friend-thing," I said, "but we kissed under the mistletoe before I left the holiday party." The party details, like the details of the gala and Halloween, I vetted the non-Redmond related ones.

"Sounds nice Spook. Someone to do fun stuff with—someone who doesn't travel for a living," she recognized.

"He likes all things *spooky*," I said, grinning, because I knew she would be too, at hearing that.

"That's a good thing—since I'm spooky too," she laughed out.

Like with Mac, Vicki and Olivia, she hadn't mention anything to do with the others or the mystery etc., not even the letter—none of them had. I concluded that Derek must have kept it to himself like I'd asked. Or maybe they'd all considered it unimportant or unrelated to their cause, and why they'd not mentioned it. Either way it wasn't a topic I wanted to discuss.

"Hiii, Lynn," I heard Ken's voice say, in the background, pulling me from my musing.

"Tell him—Hiiii, Ken," I responded, with a laugh

"Hey, Spook—I gotta get my ass in gear," Alison said, "We should do another group Skype," she tossed out, over the background voice. "I'm coming," she called to Ken, who was rambling on in the distance.

"Sounds good," I said back. "Say *Merry Christmas* to everyone for me—okay?"

"You got it. Have a great night—love you, Spook," she raced out.

"Love you too, Spook," I added, before hanging up

After our starter meal of meat-pie at the dining table, James and I moved to set ourselves up with TV tables in the living room to eat our finisher, hot cheesy—bubbling French onion soup. Then we commenced to watching the old classic Christmas movies James had saved on DVD.

"Mom loved old movies too," I said, blowing on a hot spoonful.

My big brother smiled and nodded back at me, then blew on a spoonful of his own soup before clicking play on the first movie.

When the broth and onions were all gone from my bowl, I picked at the melted cheese along the rim. Back when James and I had gone through Mom's things before selling her house, he had asked to take the special bowls with the handles for himself, the ones Mom always used on Christmas eve for the soup. She'd given me a new set as part of her wedding gift to me, so I didn't mind him claiming hers.

Savoring the sharpness of the melted cheese, I said, "Between, you, Mac, Vicki, and Olivia, I've been well fed on this trip."

"Yer easy to please when it comes to food." He chuckled. "No mushrooms—I know," he added. He loved them, but he knew I couldn't stand them.

In response to his mushrooms comment, I made a *gagging* noise and then laughed. "Start the second movie—would ya," I added.

Nearing the middle of the third movie, James said, "I'm not going to make it to the end of this one." With a big yawn, he moved the TV table to the side and got up from his chair. Grabbing up his soup bowl, he strode off to the kitchen. "Don't stay up too late," he said, doing his big brother routine.

"See you in the morning," I called out, as he went down the hall to his bedroom. "I guess it's just you and me kids," I said, to the lazy lumps on the floor next to the couch. They'd sat up when James had gotten up to leave, but for whatever reason they stayed where they were instead of heading off to bed with him. When the bedroom door shut, they both rolled on their backs, legs stretched out. "What is it with the dogs?" I said, under my breath.

Lacking any shred of arrogance, Gabriel sat on the floor in front of the two labs. With outstretched arms, he petted *then* scratched the tummies of each. *Petting animals was therapeutic,* he mused, and after the exasperating conversation he'd had with his brethren, he'd needed some canine therapy time.

Uriel, Michael and Raphael had been staying close to their Charges, and it was no doubt Vretil was keeping a close watch over his. Gabriel had been doing the same with Lynn, but for very different reasons. He hadn't sensed any shift in her, but after Shamsiel mentioned her lack of fear in the presence of the dark ones, he'd been watching her even closer. As *Franklin D. Roosevelt* had put it, '*The only thing we have to fear is fear itself*', meaning that fear only made things worse, but in this situation with Armaros, Lynn *not* fearing… well, Gabriel knew it could mean *something*… something substantially more profound.

Chapter 28

Friday morning, steaming coffee, *and* Christmas Day.

"I enjoy this part of my day—before the dogs start to get crazy," James said, from his spot at the kitchen table, sipping his coffee.

"Me too—the quiet before your day starts," I responded, retrieving my toast from the toaster. "Though, Skye and Radar are like having kids—without the college or university expenses."

James laughed. "The toys are cheaper too," he said, tossing each of them each a new chew toy as their Christmas gifts. "I took the squeakers out of them," he added, taking another sip of his coffee, and continuing to enjoy the silence.

"Where is the gift I sent you?" I asked, before spreading a generous amount of peanut butter on the slices.

"Over there," he said, pointing across the kitchen to a tiny 6-inch potted Pinetree. Under the pot was the still unopened package I'd sent him. "I would have opened it already—if you hadn't been coming up for Christmas. Talk about torture."

"Hey yer the one who kept saying *'Don't go in the basement',*" I said, countering, crossing the room to retrieve the package.

"One day," he said, "You had to wait one day, I had to wait two weeks with that package staring back at me." He laughed again.

Stealing the package from under the potted tree, I crossed back bringing my plate of toast with me to the table. "Here—you can open it now," I said, sitting, sliding the unopened package his way. "Merry

Christmas." I bit into my toast. "Should keep you entertained through the rest of winter," I added, taking another bite.

James raised his eyebrows speculatively. "Not much to entertain a person out here," he said, turning the package over to find the taped seam. Ripping the side open, he stopped and grinned at me. "X-Files."

"All nine seasons," I said. "If you take your time—you could make them last until spring. Or you could get cable and watch some current TV—your call." I laughed. We both loved the show and would have watched the repeats even with other newer shows on.

"Oh, man—perfect," he said. "I was due for some new content—can only watch the same movies so many times." He continued unwrapping and then reviewed the box sets. James didn't have full cable out in the boonies here, but his collection of movies and now these DVDs would keep him entertained, especially during the colder days in winter. "The weirder the better," James said, flipping the last set over.

"Nothing weirder than X-Files," I laughed out. But I bet I could give him weirder.

"Hey, grab your gift," James said, pointing back towards the potted tree. "I hid it behind yours."

"Figures," I said, glancing back over to the tree to see a small cardboard box the size of a bar of soap. I missed it when I'd pulled James's gift from under the makeshift Christmas tree. Doing double duty, I got up and I set my breakfast plate in the sink and then snatched up the small box before returning to the table.

"Open it," James prompted, stacking his new DVD box sets next to his coffee cup.

I slid the lid up off the box. Inside was a carved piece of wood with a metal pointy part attached. Lifting the piece out, I realized it was in the shape of a butterfly, stylized and inlaid with different pieces of stained wood. "Wow—James, it's beautiful."

"It's a wine bottle stopper," he said, as if realizing by my confused expression that I didn't know what it was. "The metal part has a stopper with a rubber ring to seal the air out of the bottle. I got the extra metal parts from the specialty hardware store.

"That… is sooo… cool," I pushed out, excited even more now that I knew what it was. "I love it when you make me stuff." I leaned around the table and hugged him.

"Get!" he said, as if I were one of the dogs. "Glad you like it." He got up from the table, but I stood and hugged him again. I knew he didn't like the mushy stuff, so I held the hug longer to make him squirm. "Okay-okay, I got to go pack a bag. I'm gonna stay in town tonight," he redirected, breaking free from my hold. He gave the side of my head a quick kiss and then moved off down the hall to his bedroom.

Our plan was to go into town for Christmas lunch with my cousins and family at his house. My cousin had told James that the dogs were welcome as well, and that there was room at the house should we want to stay the night.

James also mentioned that they hoped that I would be bringing Aunt Sal's 5 cup ambrosia salad to add to the meal. It was one of my uncle's favorites. My uncle was without his wife this year, my Aunt Kay, and with the dual losses of both her and my mom, he, like all of us, would need as much joy as we could provide, even if it was only a favorite dish. James had also hoped I would make Mom's dish and had grabbed up the needed items on his last grocery trip. So, while he packed, I set to making the salad.

The dish required; 1 cup of sour cream, 1 cup crushed pineapple from a can, one cup canned mandarins—minus the juice, 1 cup sweetened coconut, and one cup marshmallows—with a few extra for good measure. I stirred it all together in one bowl. It was easy to make and easy to transport, I considered as I set the sealed dish into one of James's mini coolers. Then I went upstairs to pack.

As James gave the dogs one last run-around before loading them into the truck, I put my carryon, along with the mini cooler, into the backseat of my rental for the drive into town. Then I slid into the driver's seat and shut the door. Patting my vest pocket, I checked to make sure I still had the *safe travel charm* Mac had made me. It was there. Then I started the car and followed along after my brother's truck.

My cousin's house was small, but full of love and laughter like always. It was also full of people and dogs. Between, myself, James, my Uncle, his sons—my three cousins, their spouses, my cousin's two teen boys, plus three grand-dogs—James's two and my cousin's black Shepard mix, we were quite the crew, and this was very reminiscent of when I was young, and we had Christmas gatherings with my family and my Aunt's.

My mom and aunt always had everything organized, while all us kids had to do, was eat and play. As it was, with everyone being so much older than me, I was usually left watching the older kids play their games, but it was better than listening to the adults talk in the living room after dinner. Although, I usually ended up asleep on Mom's lap from either the boredom of not understanding the games of the older kids, or from the boredom of adult conversation. This year's gathering had been wonderful, but it was obvious how much everyone missed Mom and Aunt Kay. Stories of past Christmases had brought loads of laughter, but the occasional glimpse of sadness had shown through, indicating the missing of them not being there.

As the food coma set in for the others, I became restless with the sitting around *and* the reminiscing. I couldn't relate to the teens in the room and the conversation with the adults had turned to sports—hockey in particular, and other than helping my cousin's wife clean up, there wasn't much else to do. Much like Olivia, she wouldn't let you do anything even if you offered. I also found myself thinking about another person who was missed this Christmas, *Louise*.

It was strange to not be staying next door to the home she and Andre shared. But he and the boys would be dealing with a completely different Christmas this year, one without her. I'd seen everyone I'd wanted to see on this trip—had my special time with each, but I hadn't had time with Andre. He'd confirmed with me earlier in the week, asking for me to come for a visit today on Christmas before the boys would be over for dinner. I'd agreed but hadn't told James yet.

"Well," I started, pushing myself up off the couch. "I have another visit I need to make. You remember Andre and Louise," I directed at James. "I'm going to make a quick visit to see him at his place before his family arrives later for dinner."

James nodded and gave me a sad smile. "Say hi for me," he said, "and Merry Christmas."

"Sure—I will," I said, countering and feeling the need even more to escape the sitting around. It was time to skedaddle to my next destination. "I'll probably stay with one of my friends tonight, so don't worry about me," I added.

Hugs and thank-yous all around, and the several enthusiastic pats for the dogs, I was then on my way out the door.

It had snowed while I'd been inside for the family gathering and now a light dusting of snow covered my car. As I'd done at James's before leaving, I checked my pocket for Mac's charm. Then I pulled the snow brush from the backseat of the car and cleared off the snow.

The snow continued to fall as I drove the route to Andre's. I wasn't thrilled about driving in the snow, but it made it feel more like the holidays. Christmas in Miami just wasn't the same.

When I pulled up to the house, I parked alongside the yard to make sure I didn't get blocked in should his sons arrive before I took off. Andre was out front trying to clear a path free of snow from the driveway to the front door.

"I bet it's strange not going next door, eh?" he asked, when I ventured up the drive.

"Ya, a bit," I said, giving a big smile. "Would be harder if I lived in Ottawa still though."

"A lot has changed since you moved away. I miss having you over for meals... I miss...." His voice faded.

"I miss her too," I said, taking the small shovel from him, and turning him towards the front door.

Once inside, Andre said, "Will's father is celebrating with family in Toronto." It was his try at shifting the subject. "It's good he's not alone for the holidays. Will's sister and brother are there too."

"That's good," I said, stomping my Doc Martins. It was a winter habit, but there was no snow since Andre had been so efficient clearing the way in.

I unlaced my boots and set them aside. The floors were warm, as was the house due to the roaring fire that burned in the living room's fireplace. The whole house smelled of delicious treats and holiday foods cooking. The living and dining room were decorated in Christmas fare as usual, and Andre had set out the over 60 nutcrackers he and Louise had collected over the years.

"I love these, especially the 3-foot tall one," I said, moving the nutcracker's mouth up and down with the lever.

"Decorating isn't fun when you don't have your someone special to share it with," he said, straightening a tiny red and green nutcracker on the mantle.

It didn't feel like Christmas without Louise, despite all the decorations. "Ya Christmas feels off for me too—all the changes... losses... I miss my mom and Aunt Kay more at this time of year. I just came from Christmas with my brother and cousins, but it's not the same without Mom and Aunt Kay." I gave him a sympathetic smile. "They loved your back garden—brought it up often. My Aunt loved gardening, too."

"Here," he said, handing me a photo album. "It's photos of me and my sons and the extended family, from the service out East."

"It's a beautiful place," I said, flipping the pages, and taking my usual spot at the kitchen island. "I've never been out East—not yet, anyway."

"Louise mentioned having you... and Will, come for a visit—out East," Andre said, as he continued to fuss in the kitchen, readying things for their Christmas meal. "That was before she stopped treatment—when she hadn't lost hope yet."

"I never believed we would lose her, Andre." I shook my head. "Being away from Ottawa—I forget sometimes that she's gone. Like with Mom—when I accidently think to call her with the latest, then I remember... remember she's gone."

"I dream about her." He sighed. "She comes to me in my dreams—talks to me," he clarified, leaning to adjust the dial on one of the stove's burners.

"Those are good dreams," I said. I smiled, picturing her sitting in the backyard under the dreamy flowers that bloomed in Spring throughout Andre's amazing garden.

He smiled too, but then his expression changed, and he glanced down as if remembering something else. "Louise was having strange dreams a few weeks before… before she passed," he began. "About someone being in her bedroom." He paused again, stirring something in a tall pot. "We moved her to her own room across from ours, when we needed all the medical aids like the special bed and monitors."

"She mentioned something about that to me too—about someone in her room… and that she'd had a horrible dream about *me*. She told me about it on the call, when she'd snuck your son's cell phone," I recalled. Andre nodded his recollection of the call. "Told me Billy Idol was standing by her bedside," I reminded, hoping to shift the mood again.

He let out a little chuckle. "Yes, she told me something along those lines too." He laughed a little harder as he put a lid on the simmering pot.

"She came to me in my dreams too, once," I said, leading into details of the dream. I explained to him how I had felt no fear as the guardian had gently placed Louise into my arms, how I'd cradled her to me. "Her eyes were closed," I described, "and a soft smile turned the corners of her mouth. Her face was peaceful in slumber as if dreaming of a place without pain," I ended. I left out the part about recognizing the guy, and about sensing it would be the last time I would be with her. The dream was a beautiful one if you didn't think about the circumstances.

"What a gift," Andre said, his smile brighter now. "Let me feed you."

"I just had a big lunch," I reminded him, but he knew me too well.

"Dessert then," he said, turning towards the fridge and then pulling open the big door.

As Andre rustled around in the fridge for treats, I got up from my chair at the kitchen island to go stand at the large window that faced out to the backyard.

I surveyed what little I could see of the white blanketed garden. The warmth from inside the house had added in fogging the windows like those of an indoor pool, making the view appear dreamlike in its frost and obscurity. I rubbed my hand over the frost of the window, melting a spot clear. Movement from the left side caught my eye. Someone was in the backyard.

Zaqiel.

I gasped when I saw him, but without saying a word, I moved seizing hold of the doorknob to the back door and twisted. One yank and I was outside, standing on the back deck under the covered porch, in sock-feet nonetheless. But he was gone.

What is with the disappearing act with these guys? I thought. How could he be here? Had he been the one watching Louise? He'd been the one from my dream the night she'd passed. He was one of The Horsemen, and he was the one who also represented *Death*. Could he have been the sign of her death to come? Maybe it was a seer thing as Redmond had surmised. Like with Baby Sullivan, my dream of Louise, and being around the sick when it's their time to go. And like Andre had said, *a gift,* to be with her one last time.

"But no one is sick—why is he here now?" I whispered, to the cold air. I pulled the hoodie up on my sweatshirt, then stomped my foot in frustration.

"Lynn," Andre called, through the partially opened door, just as a patch of snow slid off the roof to land on my head. "We wanted snow for Christmas," he laughed, opening the door further.

I laughed too. I needed that, not the snow but the laughter. "Thought I saw something in the back yard," I said, pushing the hood back and letting the snow fall.

"Santa—or was it a reindeer?" he asked, holding the door wide to let me back into the warmth. "Why don't you stay for dinner?"

As amazing as the food simmering and basting in the kitchen smelled, and as much as I missed Andre *and* his cooking, I knew I needed to leave this gathering, let it be enjoyed by his family only.

"I would love to—but I have more people to visit on this trip," I said, faking that I had some place else to go. Really though, I was all visited out. I did however agree to hot chocolate before leaving, *and* a few fresh baked goods.

I hugged Andre several more times on my way to the door, giving him even more thank-yous for the sampling of Christmas treats he'd set out for me, and for making time to spend with me on this trip.

I was glad I'd pushed past my fear and had driven in the falling snow to see him, but what I needed most now was to be in my own home—back in Miami, and off the emotional rollercoaster. So, off to the airport I went.

Goodbye, Ottawa.

Chapter 29

"Sorry, but there are no flights available—but we can place you on standby," the nice flight agent offered me.

Why I'd assumed I could get a flight out at such short notice and on Christmas day, escaped me. But the airport did make for interesting people watching, especially today. Speaking of which, there goes one now.

A few meters away from the agent booth, a burly older gentleman stopped and sat down on the empty bench. With his stature, white hair and beard, the guy could have easily passed for *Santa Claus,* if it weren't for the lack of the traditional red coat and pants, a sack of gifts, sleigh *and* reindeers, that is.

With my curiosity piqued, and to kill time until—or *if,* I should say, I got a flight, I moseyed over to take up space at the other end of the bench to this seasonal visitor. He gave me a smile when I sat down, and I smiled back. His hair was pure white, as was his moustache and beard that reached to his chest and hid his neck.

"Hi," he said, when he caught me staring, then he put out his hand for a shake.

"Merry Christmas," I said, giving him a smile, I'm sure betrayed my bewilderment. I reached out and shook his big hand.

"Where ya going to?" he asked, as he let go of my hand.

"Miami. I'm from here—but live there now," I shared with the interesting stranger.

"Me too," he said back. "Going to Miami to see my daughter and my granddaughter. My wife is already there," he added, just as his cell phone rang. He held up a finger as if to say *one second* and answered the call. "Hi honey—don't worry Dad's on his way. Tell my sweet angel I'll be there soon—okay?" He grinned at me when he saw I was watching him. "Alright, I'll see you soon—I love you too." He ended the call and grinned at me again. His cheeks bunched up like tiny blush-coloured apples.

Feeling guilty for eavesdropping, I said, "It's nice you're going to see your family soon."

"She's in the hospital—my granddaughter," he said, his smile dipping.

"Oh gosh—I'm so sorry. That's not how a little girl should spend Christmas. Will she be okay?" I asked. It was none of my business but having worked at the children's hospital I knew how tough it could be for kids over the holidays, and how tough it was for their parents as well.

"She's in the cancer ward," he said, and not what I'd wanted to hear. "There's a big guardian watching over her—some gentle giant, my daughter tells me," he added, his grin returning.

"Think I might know the big fella you're talking about," I told him. It had to be Darius. "I work at the children's hospital too—in the NICU."

"What a coincidence." He grinned bigger like I'd solved the problem. "It's Leukemia," he exhaled in a heavy breath. "She'd been having joint pain, sleepy all the time, very weak. And for a child living in Florida, her skin had become very pale. There'd been fever and weight loss too, my daughter had told us. *Acute* leukemias can grow rapidly, so they needed to get her treatment as soon as they found out," he explained.

"It's a great hospital—the doctors are amazing. She's in excellent hands," I reassured him.

He grinned again. "What are you doing at the airport on Christmas?"

In the theme of sharing, I said, "I came home to see friends and family but… I find it hard coming home now. I lost my mom and my aunt last year, and a close friend recently." I left out the cancer part. He needed all the hope he could get at the moment. "And since it's Christmas day, my friends are busy with their families. Wasn't feeling like Christmas for me," I added.

"I'm not feeling very *Christmassy* myself," he said. "When's your flight?" It was clear he hadn't recognized the irony of his statement considering his resemblance to Mr. Christmas and all.

"No flights available until tomorrow—but I'm on standby. I need to figure out what to do with myself until then," I informed my Santa lookalike. "I was staying with my brother who lives out in the country—over 2 hours from here, but I'm not going back there. I guess it was stupid of me to think I could get a flight out today."

"Well, you're in luck—there's room on the flight I'm taking."

"How do you know?" I gave him a puzzled face.

"I know the pilot, and there's one extra seat," he informed me. "I could introduce you to him if you're interested—get you to Miami safe."

"Sure!" I said, perhaps a tad too eager. I'd only just met this person moments ago.

"Nicolaas Bakker—with two As and Ks, but my friends call me St. Nick for obvious reasons," he said, extending his hand again. "But *Nick* will do just fine."

"Yer the pilot?" Surprised, I extended my hand for another shake.

"At your service," he said. "I own and fly my own *Maverick Solo jet.*"

I'd caught the word *jet,* but as long as it had a seat for me and room for my luggage, I was good. "I'm in," I said. "Yer sure it's not a sleigh—right?" I pointed to his beard and then to his red toque. His coat was a navy-blue fleece lined bomber jacket and shifted the whole look, but still.

"My wife knit it," he said, giving me a big jolly laugh. "In case yer wondering, I've been flying all my adult life—really. Military first, then commercial, then private planes for others."

I hadn't wondered, but hearing it put me more at ease since I had just accepted a ride—flight, from a perfect stranger. "And now you own your own plane?" I reestablished.

"I did well for myself, retired a few years ago and bought this beauty from one of my wealthy past clients." He laughed again. "Got a deal because the thing never left the ground. Guy bought it for his wife, but she was afraid of flying—bought a yacht instead."

We both laughed.

"My wife is already there with our daughter—said I'd bring the plane. That way we could come back and forth when we needed. Our granddaughter is out of the woods they tell us, but I didn't want to chance not having a way to get there in a jiffy if we needed."

"Smart plan," I said, giving him a couple nods.

"We've got four dogs—I'd needed to find someone willing to watch them for us," he added. "Neighbors' son moved back in with them, said he'd take care of the place and the dogs for us. I've known the boy since they first brought him home from the hospital—when he was born. Just finished university—he's a vet. Perfect don't you think?"

I nodded again and smiled at the ease of conversation with my new friend and pilot.

"Dad's a vet too—son's taking over the business for him," he added. "I like when things work out that way. Don't you?"

"Kind of like this, eh?" Lucky coincidence. "Thank you again for the offer—yer a life saver."

"Works for me too, nice to have someone to talk with on the flight. You ready?" he asked standing as if ready to go himself.

"Ready," I said, standing and grabbing hold of my rolly-bag.

"It's just under 1200 nautical miles from here to the small airport I use in Miami. It shouldn't take us more than 3.5 hours to get there." He continued forward, and I followed along next to him.

We advanced through the usual immigration process but via the charter area instead, and only a few people in line. Nice for a change, not to have to deal with that painful part of the airport dance.

"We have to go out on the tarmac to board the plane," he informed me.

"Tarmac—outside?" I questioned, still following alongside and zipping up my down vest.

We passed through the sliding doors to the area that, based on the signage, was for *Small Planes*. He waved at one of the airport staff people, then motioned for me to go left.

And there before me, was the smallest plane I'd ever seen—real plane that is. He pulled the door latch, and the door opened like a DeLorean, but on the driver's side only.

I couldn't help it, I laughed equally nervous and amused. "Never been in a plane this size," I called out, through the surrounding airplane noise. He smiled, took my bag and exchanged it for his mittens, which were red and knit like his hat. I put them on and up to my face for warmth. They smelled like cookies.

"Climb in—across to take your seat," he said, holding out his hand, this time to help me in the plane.

"Thank you," I said, maneuvering my way to the *extra* seat. It was much like a car inside except for all the extra switches, though it did have a gearshift like a car.

Nick got in next to me, and the airport staffer guy shut the door and backed away from the plane. Then Nick showed me how to buckle the seat belt. He put on a set of heavy-duty headphones, then handed me a second set. "Lets you hear the guys in the tower when they talk to us," he shouted. "You don't need to wear them if you don't want to—but it helps with cutting the noise."

Putting them on, I overheard the guys in the tower give us our first direction out to the runway lane designated for us. We pulled away as Nick dialoged with the guys in the tower. Further down, he brought the plane to a halt at the start of the runway. Then I heard one of the tower guys say, "Santa, you are good to go," and we are off. I laughed. And we were, full speed ahead and into the wild blue yonder.

Nervous, I touched the right-side pocket of my down vest, the pocket that had the *safe travel* charm.

When the plane leveled, Nick said, "Hungry?"

My anxiety shifted. "Always," I told him, laughing again.

"Here, better you eat them than me," he said, handing me a plastic freezer bag full of decorative Christmas cookies. "My wife made them."

I took the bag and gave him a big grin.

"Wait—you better give me one. I'll make sure they taste good." He winked and grinned back. Then took a cookie from the bag.

For inflight entertainment, Nick told some amusing stories from his flying for *client* days. He shared sweet and sad, but mostly funny stories about his wife, his daughter, and his granddaughter. I smiled and listened, enjoying the distraction from the fact I was thousands of feet up from the earth, in a tiny jet plane being flown by, albeit someone who looked strikingly like Santa Claus, but someone who was merely someone I'd met at the airport and who had offered me a flight home.

As a further part of the entertainment he sang me a few classic Christmas songs, *in the theme of Sinatra and the gang,* as he'd put it. At the end of his serenade I told him that my mom would have loved his renditions, that classic style had been her favorite for this season.

What a view, and what an amazing experience to fly above the clouds. We set down just under the 3 1/2-hour mark, and Nick had been a safe, skilled, and entertaining pilot. He'd said the tailwinds had helped some with the speed of our arrival, whatever that meant. But I was happy to be back in the warmth, and safe on the ground, safe if you didn't include the Miami drivers that is.

I loathed driving in Miami, but what was even worse was trying to find parking at the airports. Thankfully I'd left my car at home, in the garage for the first time, assuming it was best out of the way of the circle drive such that Luc could come and go easier while I was away. I'd taken an early morning cab to the main airport when I'd left on my trip to avoid having to park my car. But main airport or this smaller airport, I still needed to call a cab to take me the rest of the way home.

Being the gentleman Nick was, he waited with me until my cab arrived. "Here comes your taxi," Nick said, spotting my ride as it pulled around into the passenger area.

"I'll be sure to drop by to check on your granddaughter on my next shift, *and* let Darius know he's been watching over a friend's little angel," I told him.

"Thank you," he said. Then he gave me a big unexpected hug.

"You really are a lifesaver," I told him again before I got in the cab. "Thank you."

As the cab pulled away, I glimpsed back to see him walking back towards the main entrance. There at the door was an older plump, white-haired woman. She wore a red t-shirt with a reindeer on the front, white capri-pants and sandals. *Mrs. Claus,* I presumed. They embraced, touched foreheads, and then kissed. I lost sight of them as the cab rounded past the parking exit.

Chapter 30

It figured that the cab ride felt longer than the plane ride, though once I was out of the cab and through the front door of my home, all was well in my universe again.

"Raven," I called, when he wasn't at the door to greet me. I called again, but he didn't come running. Luc's car hadn't been in the drive I'd noticed. Then I remembered he'd mentioned something about the possibility of going to see his sister in Orlando for the holiday, and I supposed he had taken Raven with him for the 4-hour drive up to see the family.

Dropping my keys in the basket on the front table, I spotted an official-looking envelope set next to the basket.

The return address had the name *Anthony Merenda,* my PI, as the sender. His *bill* I assumed, since he hadn't had much else for me of late. I shoved it into my tote.

Before even taking my shoes off, I started a text to Redmond. I'd wanted to text him from the Ottawa airport, but when it had looked as though I wouldn't be getting out until tomorrow, I'd chosen to wait until I could secure a flight home. When things had shifted in my favor with the flight with Nick, I'd opted then to make it a surprise instead that I was coming back.

I hit send on a message that read;

Guess who's home early.

A second later, he wrote back;

Wanna come celebrate Christmas with me?

"Uh—Ya!" I said, to my empty house. I wrote back asking;

Got any food?

Quick with a response, he wrote;

I think I heard your stomach growl. LOL

I had to laugh at the accuracy of that one, then wrote back again stating that;

I have to get cleaned up first, but I'll be over soon.

I didn't bother to unpack, it was mostly winter clothing, anyway. After a quick shower and blow dry of my hair, I changed into the most festive clothes I had. Okay, it was just jeans and a white t-shirt, but the shirt had a graphic of a red Christmas tree on it with the word *Joy* in silver under it, and it would have to do.

"Crap," I said, as I grabbed my tote to leave. I couldn't go over there empty handed. Then I remembered the bag of Christmas cookies Nick had given me. Checking my tote, I confirmed that the bag of Christmas bliss was still there, and then I snatched up my keys from the basket and was off.

I knocked first before walking into the apartment.

Redmond was standing in the kitchen in a pair of jeans and a red t-shirt with *'Tis the season...'* and a cartoon Santa on it, playing guitar. "Merry Christmas," he said, greeting me, arms open for a hug. He had a tin of what looked like cocoa powder in one hand and a carton of milk in the other.

"Merry Christmas to you," I gave him, welcoming the hug. "I brought Christmas cookies—homemade, well, not by me—but still homemade." He stepped back. "And they are delicious," I said, pulling the bag of deliciousness from my tote. I'd been so excited to see him, I'd almost forgot about them. *Almost.* I set them on the kitchen island along with my tote.

"From Mrs. Claus, I assume?" he said, setting the two cooking items on the counter. He grinned.

"As a matter of fact, yes," I said, remembering Nick and his wife embracing.

"I have something for you, too. But I wanted to keep it for when you got back." Redmond bent down to an open space under the kitchen island. "If you're going to keep sleeping over," he said, retrieving something from the space. "You'll need something other than the clothes you wear over to sleep in." He handed me a Christmas gift bag.

"Redmond," I said, feeling a blush. Taking the bag, I pulled back the red tissue, then spied something with red and green plaid. I drew it from the bag. "Christmas pajamas," I laughed out. He'd gotten me Christmas PJs. The top was like one of those old-fashioned men's PJs, but with boxer style bottoms instead I noticed, and they were just my size.

"I got the same, just the bottoms—full length though," he said, striding over to the bedroom area. He held up a length of matching fabric. Then he tossed them on the chair next to the bed.

"I always knew there was something I liked about Christmas," I said. "Just hadn't known it was you." I walked over and stuck the red bow from the gift bag on his chest. "Best gift ever."

"The best gifts come in small packages," he said, pulling me closer and sticking the bow on my head. Then he leant over passed me and reached into the bedside table drawer. Straitening, he said, "Meet on Halloween, shared Thanksgiving, and *now*, cozying up on Christmas." He handed me a small red box. "Can't wait to see what New Year's brings," he added, leaning in for a kiss.

Kiss number two, and as amazing as the first, were my thoughts as our lips parted and I opened my eyes to look at him.

"Open it," he prompted.

I changed my gaze from his face, down to the small box in my hand, and grinned. "The PJs were sweet, you didn't have to get me anything, really," I said, though a little giddy at the fact he had gotten me anything at all.

"Just open it silly," he prompted again.

I grinned again, and then I slid off the lid. Something silver shone back at me from inside its tiny confines.

Lifting it out, I saw that it was a delicate silver chain adorned with two small charms, one a tiny butterfly, the other displaying the letters XO.

"It's a hug and kiss," he said, "The symbol, XO, is also used to express good friendship. The butterfly—it represents your mom."

I shook my head in disbelief at how perfect it was. "I love it—thank you," I said, raising the delicate chain completely out of the box to get a better look at it.

"The custom of placing an X on notes or at the bottom of letters—most people know is used to mean kisses. I read that the custom dates back as far as the Middle Ages." He took the necklace from me, and then he maneuvered to fasten it around my neck.

It hung just past the line of my collarbone. "Thank you," I said, again, giving him a hug, then tippy-toeing it up for a kiss. "It's perfect," I said against his lips, then I kissed him once more.

"I missed you," he said, when I relaxed down my tip-toe. Then he leant in and kissed me again.

"I missed you too," I said, reaching my arms around him for another hug.

He squeezed me tight, and then let go and stepped back. "Got any plans for New Year's?" Before I could reply, he slipped out of his jeans, swiftly swapping them for his new PJ bottoms.

"I'm…." I paused. "… happy to say—I have no plans," I stumbled out, turning then, heading to the bathroom and trying to hide a grin. I probably should have turned around sooner, but I didn't, the view of him in his boxers had been too nice. Even—if he was, I wasn't comfortable changing out in the open, not yet anyway. I had gone for comfort with my jeans and t-shirt, but I wasn't too keen on sleeping in them. "How about you?" I called out before shutting the bathroom door.

"Me either—no plans," his voice muffled, through the bathroom door from the kitchen.

When I came out of the bathroom, he had his back to me, but then turned my way and smiled.

"Cute," he said, handing me a cup, of what I assumed was hot chocolate based on the mini marshmallows floating on top.

I took the mug and sniffed. It was the real-deal, rich dark chocolate. "You really do have me all figured out—dammit."

He laughed. "Tell me about your trip," he said, plating a few of the Christmas cookies from the bag. He slipped the bag of remaining cookies back into my tote. "Just in case you get hungry when you go back to work." He patted my tote.

"Smart man," I said, taking the short stroll to the couch. "My trip was good. Nothing unusual happened. The girls never mentioned anything either—was all Christmas… and no talk of angels."

"Angels?" he said, more as a question.

I cringed. *Crap*. Nice slip, Westlake.

"Lynn… did I miss something—what aren't you telling me?"

I guess it was time to give him the full deal, the big stuff, the *angel* stuff. "Ya about that," I started.

Then I took the next hour to relay my theory on these descendants, the Archangels rather. I explained the research I'd done on the Fallen angels and the 20 leaders, how I'd identified these key four as the Horseman. How, Luc hadn't believed me but now he did, and he was working to convince Derek and the girls of these things. I told him about Halloween—what really happened, and about the gala *and* where I had gone, the truth this time. I even told him about what the girls had gotten up to that night with the spell. Lastly, I shared what I'd found, the letter addressed to me from my birthmother. "I haven't figured out what the second page says—might be something more about this gathering. Could have something to do with what my friends are working on—the where and when… or not," I ended.

"It is a lot to wrap my brain around, but I'm glad you told me all this," he said. "Though I wouldn't have expected any less considering what you've already told me." He rubbed the palm of his hand against the side of his jaw. "It could all be true—I don't know. Maybe your friends *will* figure out this whole gathering thing, *and* what they need to do with all this stuff. Or maybe nothing will happen, at least nothing right now."

I couldn't have asked for a better response to the last in my list of weird. There were a lot of *maybes,* but he was open, and that was what I needed.

"I should show you my books on magic, angels and other worldly beings, that I've read," he said, adding to the ease of the dialog on all things weird.

"Sure—maybe I'll find something in there to help make me feel less crazy," I laughed out.

"Yer not crazy, Lynn," he countered. "You've just been privy to more proof of otherworldly things than most."

"I guess… just figured I'd be used to all the weird stuff by now. You know—after experiencing strange things for so long… but no."

"Hmmm," he said, before taking a long sip of his now second cup of freshly made hot chocolate.

"What—hmmmm?" I asked. "Changing your mind about the crazy part?" I laughed again.

"Ha—no," he said, "was just thinking about the volume of women involved in all this."

"I know—right," I said.

"But like you mentioned, your letter refers to a father and brothers. And we're assuming the angels are male, based on the descriptions. Luc, Derek, and Darius are involved—more males."

I took a moment to digest what he was saying, then I said, "Four angels, four women… four Horsemen…" I stopped, considering who I may have missed in the list.

"Four helpers—or whatever. Cipher, Theologian, Guardian, and Believer," he added.

"Wait—six angels," I said. "Shamsiel and Gabriel make six, and there are 20 leaders—The Horsemen also belong to the group of leaders. That makes 26 angels—if you don't count the 200 other fallen," I calculated. Then I gave my head a shake. "Oh, and we can't forget the Solacer. Derek said it's a person."

"Solacer? Doesn't that mean defender or consoler—or something like that?"

"No idea. I asked Derek about that too. He's still trying to figure that out, but it's from the codex also, he tells me."

"It appears to be matriarchal, but there are still quite a few males involved," he noted. "What about your birthfather—any idea who he was?"

"Nope, I have no record of him. Kind of came to a screeching halt with having no name on my birth records," I told him. "I had hoped the PI would have found someone who knew—but that was a dead end too. With all the focus on mothers, I haven't spent much time thinking about fathers. Well, not until recent when I found the letter. All I can really hope for is that he's not some horrible guy—and not the reason my birthmother kept his name a secret."

"You said the PI was told something—something that implied your birthmom had written down information about him—told her doctor friend, yes?"

"She didn't tell the friend about the father—just that she'd written it all down," I clarified. "It was that comment from the doctor, that made us think she might have written details about him." I shrugged. "It still could—have details I mean. I just need to figure the stupid page out," I huffed.

"From what you've told me, it's a sure bet that Derek will help figure it all out," Redmond assured me.

Later after more talk and multiple trips to the kitchen for food, we'd ended up watching TV in bed this time, in our new Christmas Pjs. We'd been kind of hit and miss with the whole intimacy thing, but the friendship to more-than-friends shift had come at a nice easy pace.

I'd be lying if I said I hadn't thought about the possibility of more on the drive over, but with both our schedules, mine with the running around visiting and flying, his with the extra *long* studio work, we were both officially exhausted. So cuddling it was, for now. I was just happy to be with him and I felt even more comfortable and safe now after finally giving him the rest of the pieces from my bizarre world.

We were right near the middle of our Christmas movie-marathon, watching *It's a Wonderful Life,* when the heaviness of my lids clouded my ability to watch....

...'Twas the night before Christmas, when all through the house.

Not a creature was stirring, not even a... it was nearly dawn as I stood on a small hill in a large open area surrounded by tall trees, mist swirled around my bare feet, underneath them was snow...

When out on the lawn there arose such a clatter... I spun around towards the noise, peering into the dense darkness of the trees...

The moon on the breast of the new-fallen snow, Gave a luster of midday to objects below, When what to my wondering eyes appeared, But a miniature... plane and St Nick—Nicolaas Bakker...

He was dressed in fur, from his head to his foot... I rubbed my eyes and looked again but he was gone... Armaros emerged from the darkness...

And his clothes were all tarnished with ashes and soot... two more large figures appeared from the darkness of the trees to flank him....

To rouse him, Shamsiel whispered past the veil into Redmond's ear. When he didn't wake, he spoke louder, "She's in the park—wake up."

Redmond jolted awake. "Lynn?" He reached out to the covers beside him. *Empty.*

"She's in the park—she needs you," came a hint of a voice, through Redmond's haze like a message in his brain. That's when he noticed the door to the apartment was open.

Redmond rushed to the open door. "Lynn," he called, leaning over the top rail to the backyard area. When no response came, he stepped back into the entry, slipped on his flipflops, then returned out the door and descended the stairs.

Frantic, he scanned the areas up and down the roadside, noting that Lynn's car was still parked at the studio. Turning back the other way, his mind replayed the words as if a memory, *She's at the park—she needs you.* No cars passed at this hour of the night and he dashed across the road to the entrance of the Barnacle.

Near the entry booth on the bench he spotted something. He ran to the bench to find Lynn barefoot and slumped over to one side.

"Lynn!" he roared, before putting his cheek to her face. "She's breathing," he said to the night. "What are you doing out here?" Redmond said, half panicked, half relieved. "I need to get you home." He picked Lynn up and ran back out and across the street.

In the dimness of the outside stairway lighting, he noticed the bottoms of her feet were scraped, and mixed with grass, dirt and blood.

"The gathering," I murmured, tilting my head up slightly. *Was I floating?* "My feet hurt," I garbled, as my vision clouded to black again.

Chapter 31

"Luc, I'm telling ya—it felt so real," Darius explained. "She was standing alone in a field somewhere. Then these massive guys showed up—five of them, no wait—seven."

Luc shook his head with the cell phone still to his ear. "Darius man, she's up visiting her friends and family in Canada." He'd never heard Darius unnerved like this before despite the weird stuff he'd been privy to. "I seriously doubt she'd be standing in a field somewhere in the middle of the night—especially not in winter," he added, trying to reassure his friend. "It was just a dream." Darius had said it himself that he'd woken from this dream, but he'd also said he couldn't be sure it was *just* a dream.

"I'm sure I've seen some of these guys before too," Darius added. "Luc, it's like those other times—where I felt that compulsion to protect her—it's like that. But this time I felt helpless."

"Okay, take a breath." Luc put his cell phone on speaker such that Dunya could listen in on what their friend was describing. "Yer on speaker—Dunya's here too. Tell me again what you saw in the dream."

Darius pushed out a heavy breath. "It was night—but looked like it was close to dawn. She stood on a small hill in a field with trees on all sides. She was in red pajamas, and she was barefoot. Out of the darkness of the trees came a huge man dressed in black. A second later two more big guys stepped from the shadows to stand with the other guy, one on each side of him. I called out to her, but she didn't hear me.

She leant down to pick up a large roll of what looked like paper off the ground in front of her feet. Her lips moved as if she was reading something from the paper, but she was too far away for me to hear her—I couldn't hear anything, actually. Was kind of like being underwater. I glanced quickly at the men, then when I looked back at her, instead of the paper, she had a baby lamb in her arms. Then I heard something… a loud voice—her voice, say, *Come and see.*"

"And?" Luc asked, followed by a long pause from Darius.

"And, well… there was a white horse next to her," Darius said, followed by another pause.

"And?" Luc said again, anxious, cutting a glance Dunya's way.

"Then the horse was gone—replaced by a guy, a big guy with long white hair."

"Did this guy have a bow?" Luc asked, sensing this might head into the theologian realm.

"Yup," was all Darius gave them, trailed by a few staggering breaths.

"Go ahead," Dunya said, encouraging him.

"Lynn said it again. Said, *come and see.*" Darius cleared his throat.

"Red horse?" Luc said sharply, more a statement than a question. "Then replaced by another big guy with a sword."

"Uhm, ya," Darius said, letting out a blow of air.

Nodding though only Dunya could see him, Luc said, "Then Lynn said it again—didn't she?"

"Am I crazy," Darius asked. "How do you know what I'm gonna say—when I don't even know what happened? All I know, is I couldn't get to her—couldn't move, could only stand and watch her."

"Yer not crazy, man… but what you're describing sounds eerily like accounts from The Horsemen of the apocalypse." Luc drew a hand over his shaved head. "Black horse next? Then a guy holding a pair of scales in his hand—am I right?"

"Ya… then the guy said something about wheat and a day's wages and wine." Darius huffed. "It felt so real, Luc, but when I say it out loud—it sounds totally nuts."

"Revelations," Luc said then, *"it's a quart of wheat for a day's wages, three quarts of barley for a day's wages, and don't damage the oil and the wine.* Or something close to that."

"Yes!" Darius shouted. "After Lynn said those words, a pale horse appeared, only this time it morphed into someone I knew—well not knew but recognized. It was that big guy from the hospital—the one that had gone after Lynn. The thing is, I recognized all of them—from Halloween—same guys Lynn had described—the ones I thought had been security or something for the event."

A sputtering of Arabic words and phrases came from behind where Luc and Dunya were seated. They both turned to see Mitra standing in the doorway of Dunya's kitchen.

"What?" came Darius's voice through the phone.

"Darius—I'll call you back. I'm gonna look into this," Luc said, his attention back to their worried Guardian. "I'm sure Lynn's fine. Let me circle back—call Derek, maybe. Cool?"

"Ya—keep me posted. Tell him I'm not crazy, okay?"

"Sure thing, man. I'll check in later." Luc ended the call and turned to Dunya. "What?" he asked, when he saw the frightened expression on her face.

"Call Lynn," Dunya said.

* * *

It was Sunday now, Saturday had been a write-off for me.

I was exhausted due to whatever the hell I had done the night before. Sore feet and feeling like I had the 24-hour flu, I spent most of the Saturday either sleeping or watching more TV next to Redmond. He'd kept me hydrated all the while keeping an eye on my healing tootsies. Not quite the romantic Christmas I'd anticipated, but then when did anything go as expected in my world. Luckily it hadn't sent my handsome nurse running for the hills, and it was nice to know I could count on him for more than just hydration.

Over a bowl of chicken soup, I tried to explain the dream again. "It was the same three guys from the night of the gala—must have been all that angel talk the other night. But how did I get over to the park?"

"You must have sleepwalked," Redmond said. "Your feet are much better—tender still but are healing now it seems."

I'd never sleepwalked before—probably all the stress of the travel. All the mixed emotions with my friends and my first Christmas without my mom. And telling him the last pieces to my story of weird, certainly added some anxiety too. "It felt so real," I said through another slurp of soup. "The dream I mean—my feet are real, obviously." I gave him a playful grin. "Thank you for taking such good care of me—sorry for being so out of it for the past day and a half." And for ruining what should have been a more normal time together. I didn't say it, but I felt guilty that our hanging out seemed to always have a taste of the weird and wacky to it and not the sweet taste of romance of a typical evolving relationship.

"I like taking care of you, but what I don't like is you getting hurt or being sick. You scared the crap out of me, lady," Redmond said from the kitchen, pouring the remaining soup from the pot into an oversized mug for himself. "Let's hope there won't be a repeat. Might need to get a second deadbolt for the door—one that needs a key on the inside." He went over to examine the front door and the locks.

"I'm sorry—I've never done that before—zone out or sleepwalk, or whatever." At least I don't recall doing anything like that with my other strange dreams. It had me wondering if I might have taken a stroll in the middle of the night other times. Maybe I needed to get better locks at my place. Speaking of checking, I hadn't bothered to check my phone since I'd gotten to Redmond's.

I hadn't wanted to see any messages from my friends, sharing their disappointment at my leaving without notice, again. I tapped my phone but thankfully there weren't any texts, but... there was a voicemail. When I checked the log, it showed the call had been from Luc. I put my phone on speaker and hit 1 to play the message.

"Hey Lynn—it's Luc. Darius called me all worried about you. He said he had a dream that really shook him up, about finding you in a big field, you

were in danger, but he couldn't get to you. There's more—call me when you get this message."

I glanced up to see Redmond's eyebrows raised almost reaching his hairline. He didn't have to say a thing, I knew I had to call Luc right back.

"No answer. Must be busy up at his sister's in Orlando," I said, before leaving my own message. I informed Luc I was back in town, over at Redmond's. I also gave him Redmond's number just in case, in case of what I didn't know, but Luc's voice had sounded a little too anxious for my comfort. Part of me wanted to know what the *more* was, but considering the details of Darius's dream—and the field in my dream, I was pretty sure the *more* was not going to be about his Christmas holiday with family.

"Interesting dream—don't you think? Uncanny—weird even," Redmond said.

"Weird? Have you met me?" I joked. "You sure you still want to be friends with me—bearing in mind all the added weirdness?"

He let out a laugh in a short burst, then slid the small plate with cheese and crackers he'd set on the coffee table, in my direction. "Eat. I have a feeling you're going to need your strength."

"I'll call work—see if they could use an extra hand this week," I said, needing the distraction, instead of dwelling on the dreams and the more whatever.

"Do you think you should—I mean do they need you to work this week?" Redmond inquired, settling in next to me on the couch again.

Before I could respond to him, the hospital administrator came on the line. I held up my forefinger and listened to what she was saying. "Yes, I can do Monday and Tuesday," I told her, nodding like she could see me. "No problem—bye." I looked to Redmond who was still waiting for a response. "She told me they were short staffed since it was the holidays and could definitely use all the help they could get. I agreed to two shifts to help with the backlog—to ready them for the upcoming craziness of New Year's Eve that's bound to follow," I said, pushing myself up off the couch and padding over to the chair next to the bed. I'd been in the same clothes for two days—pajamas.

"You do look healthier—how are you feeling," Redmond asked, leaning over the back of the couch.

"I feel good—tired but good, but I'd feel a lot better after a shower and a change of clothes." I grinned then made a goofy face.

"How about I take you to get a change of clothes—bring you back here after," he suggested, worry blanketing his handsome face.

"I'm fine—really. Plus, you still have to go finish formatting that last-minute song for your client, remember?" I said, deflecting. Gathering up my clothes, I gave him a reassuring smile, then went off to the bathroom to change.

The expression Redmond gave me as I pulled out of the parking area, told me he wasn't so sure I was fine, though he respected my need to regroup and get myself situated for the next two long shifts ahead of me at the hospital. I'd proposed to him we find something fun to do for New Years since we were both free. He'd happily agreed to more fun, but he made me promise to check in often over the next two days.

When I pulled up, I noted that Luc's car was not in the drive still, nor at Dunya's, and as I walked in, I half expected to be greeted by Raven, but then remembered he would be up in Orlando too. Then as promised, I sent Redmond a text to let him know I was home safe.

Just before bed, instead of texting, I called Redmond to thank him for a wonderful Christmas, and again for taking such good care of me.

He expressed that he enjoyed any time we got to spend together and about how happy he was that I was back in town. "Take it easy on those feet of yours," Redmond said. "Let me know how your days go."

"Will do." I smiled to myself. It was nice having someone looking out for me.

"Sweet dreams," he said, ending the call.

I leaned over to plug in my cell to charge, but it rang in my hand. It was Luc.

"Hey," I said.

"Hey, yourself—just pulled up. Saw your car in the drive."

"Just getting in from your sister's?" I asked.

"No, church—got home Saturday. Was at the church helping take down the Christmas decorations. Didn't expect you to be back so soon—at least not until after the new year."

"Ya, well… the visit was good—but felt the need to come home." I was too tired to explain my reasons. "I'm doing two 14 hour shifts Monday and Tuesday, so I won't be home much," I said changing the subject. "Where's Raven?" I heard a door opening and closing through the phone.

"He's here at Dunya's. I wasn't sure when you'd be home," Luc said, clarifying my suspicions. "You have time to talk about the whole dream thing?"

"Just getting ready for bed. I have time—but yer not going to like what I have to add to it," I told him.

"Why did I know you would say something like that?" Luc stated, then he recapped Darius's dream. He mentioned the four men, the description matching The Horsemen and how Darius said it was the same guys he recalled from Halloween. "Darius sounded pretty shaken up about the not being able to help you," Luc added. "But the kicker, Lynn…."

He paused long enough that I got out a, "What?"

"… Mitra had the same dream—not exactly, she wasn't trying to rescue you, but she did see Darius trying to, and the same seven guys. It's why I called you even though you were away—or at least I thought you were away," he scrambled out. "She'd come into the kitchen right after I got off the call with Darius—described the same thing about the leaders and a big field. Dunya had to translate obviously—said Mitra was upset too."

"Weeeeeell," I started. "… I had a dream too." Before he could say anything, I lapsed into my recall of the dream and the sleepwalking. "I don't remember seeing Darius or Mitra in the dream, but there were only three guys in my dream—that Armaros guy, and those two lackeys of his I'd seen at the gala. They'd appeared out of the darkness from the trees and flanked him."

"Poor Redmond," Luc said, regarding the part about my sleepwalking.

Poor Redmond? I'd been the one walking around unaware in my bare feet. "Probably travel stress—emotional time of year. And I did finally tell the *poor* guy the last parts to all the weirdness—there's anxiety for ya," I said, brushing it off like I'd done with Redmond. I'd almost had myself convinced it was nothing to worry about, but three people with eerily similar dreams probably wasn't something I could brush off now.

Luc didn't seem so convinced either, because he said, "There was some other odd stuff—something Mitra told Dunya. She told her something about the Valkyries, the seers—oracles, like she and Dunya, and how your birth mother may have been one too. Remember the Valkyries in the Norse mythology Derek sent?"

"Sounds more like confirmation that Darius is the Guardian," I said, calling to mind the details Derek had sent us, and redirecting the attention off myself.

"My thoughts exactly," Luc agreed. "I'm going to pass this all on to Derek—have him tell the girls, solidify Darius's involvement even more."

I was thrilled I wasn't the one having to tell the girls about the dreams. Derek would have a better go at convincing them about Darius, anyway. How much had Derek told them about my being a seer I wondered? Luc knew—he believed it, mainly because Dunya had said it, believed it. My birthmother may have been like Dunya and Mitra too I considered. Then I laughed out loud at the idea of being an *oracle*.

"What?" Luc asked.

"It's just the oracle thing," I said. "An old friend of mine used to joke about my spidy-sense. When I'd get one of my *feelings* and then something weird would happen—he'd say, 'the oracle knows'. I laughed again, this time at the memory.

"Suits," Luc laughed, relating to weirdness. "I hope you got one foot tied to your bed—just in case you sleepwalk again?"

"No," I laughed out. "I'm sure I'll be fine. I miss Raven though. Night Luc—tell Dunya *hi* for me."

"Will do. Night, Lynn."

Chapter 32

Despite the stagnancy of what to do next regarding the gathering, Vicki had set up for yet another Monday night video session hoping to spark ideas. As was usual for their video chats, it was 8 p.m. in Ottawa, 6 p.m. for Alison in Calgary, when the video chat windows jingled the sound of each of them coming online.

"Let's review the details from Halloween night and this spirit who visited Mac," Vicki began, once all the faces of her friends appeared on screen. "Mac, you said we didn't need to be in the same place to do the spell—are you sure of that still?"

"Yes," Mac said adamantly. "It's all about knowing the elements and stating the words, not about where you are."

"Okay perfect." Vicki noted the annoyed expression and the crossed arms of their witch. Timidly, she said, "Could you review it for us?"

With a huff, Mac said. "My list says, 1 black candle, 1 grey candle, 1 blue candle, 1 white candle, and 1 red candle."

"Don't forget the Lavender and the mixture with the rose petals and thorns," Olivia interjected, smiling as if trying to help.

"And, matches and a knife," Mac added, smiling back at her helpful friend.

"We all had our stones too," Alison chimed in.

"Oh yes," Olivia recalled. "Alison, you had the blue and white stone, *Sodalite*. I had the *Moss Agate*—the mossy green stone. Mac had both the *Rhodonite,* the dark pink stone with the black patches and the *Rose Quartz* for the Goddess…."

"And I had the *Smokey Quartz,*" Vicki added, cutting her off.

"Yours was supposed to be mentally beneficial and raise cooperation in a group—to *support* their efforts," Mac cut in, emphasizing the word support. Before Vicki could counter, Mac said, "I lit the black candle, the white candle, the grey, and then the blue, all with the same match." She gave a sarcastic grin. "Then I took a piece of lavender and burned it with the black and then the white candles."

"You told us to concentrate our thoughts," Olivia recalled. "You wanted us to imagine the spirit of Uriel filling us—drawing the energy—concentrating on the awareness of his arrival."

Mac nodded with pride at her magic partner in crime. They'd worked together the most on the spells and healing elements. "I'd recited the start of the incantation, then I'd lit a new match and held it near the red candle."

"Then we all held up our stones," Alison added. "Then held up both hands—and closed our eyes."

"We spoke the next words in unity," Mac reminded, directing her words at Vicki.

The red candle was lit when they'd all opened their eyes, Vicki remembered. "You said that when the match went out, we had to take in its remaining energy in order to light the red candle."

"And it worked," Mac spouted. "Then I used the knife to carve Uriel's name in the candle. Then I used the water mixture to put out both the black and white candles. The grey, blue and red ones were left to continue to burn."

"Then you called the elements," Vicki said, as though she were questioning a witness.

"But we all called for Uriel to appear," Olivia said.

"Yes," Mac said, but not as a confession, more as a statement. "Water, Fire, Wind, and Earth."

"Summoning the power to show in sun and shade," Vicki said, checking off something on the paper in front of her. She'd had the full translation on her desk next to the laptop.

Mac's shoulders bunched, appearing as though she were frightened.

"Mac?" Olivia questioned. "What is it?"

Mac gave a shudder and then relaxed her shoulders. "I remember the wind beating against the living room window, seeing debris swirling around the streetlights. I remember thinking my hair would get in the way somehow, and I'd pulled it back. The front door swung open then and the wind gale filled up the space. My hair came loose flying around my shoulders. Then the door slammed shut." She shuddered again. "Then he was here," she ended.

"I practically had my face pressed to the screen, but all I could see was the shadow of something cross your face," Alison shared. "I remember how scared you'd looked."

"White suit," Mac whispered the words, same as she'd done that night when she'd seen him.

"We could only see the lower side view of his white clothes through your laptop camera." Vicki said. "I heard him speak though. He said something about us needing *guidance*."

"We were in need," Mac reminded. "And he'd answered our questions about the gathering. And based on the description you said it resembled the Arboretum here in Ottawa." She shrugged. "But I'm not so sure that's the place." Mac crossed her arms over her chest again.

"He also implied that Derek was this *fifth* I found in the second entry. Not directly that it was Derek—just that it was about the one who held the answer. We'd suspected as much."

"The time had gone by so fast," Alison said. "We'd spent over an hour by the time it was done."

"I still can't believe we conjured a spirit," Mac said. "I just wish I believed he was the right one." Her shoulders bunched again.

"You never said what he looked like—just that he was beautiful," Alison stated. "I never thought to ask more."

"What difference does it make," Vicki chided. "It's not like we knew what Uriel was supposed to look like—like we'd recognize him or something." Vicki felt nothing in the spell had been proven incorrect, yet they hadn't gotten any further in solving the whereabouts of this gathering.

Mac rolled her eyes. "He was tall, dark and handsome. Black hair, olive skin, bright white teeth. Had a line of black facial hair down the center of his chin—that made him appear a little frightening, to be honest." Mac gave another unexpected shudder.

"Whaaaaaaaaaat?" Alison shot out, blue eyes bulging.

"What—what?" Mac asked.

When Mac still appeared puzzled, Alison said, "The guy from the airport… remember the one who kept staring at me at my gate—that time I went to Ottawa—I told you about him."

"I remember," Olivia said, sliding herself into the conversation. "You said the guy was hot—model material. You used the word beautiful then too."

"Beautiful like a panther," Alison directed at Olivia. "Does the phrase, *looks like he ate small children for breakfast,* ring a bell?"

Olivia shivered then as if remembering.

"Your guy wore black—head to toe, you said," Mac recalled.

"He had black hair, and a thin black pinch—the facial hair," Alison reminded, repeating the motion of drawing a line from her lower lip down to the tip of her chin, like she'd done when first describing him.

"How could it be the same guy?" Mac screeched.

"Girls—girls," Vicki interrupted, raising her voice. She'd been reviewing her translations while they'd all been discussing the *beauty* of the spirit. "I found an error… my error, in the translation of the spell. It's not *dark* versus light, it's *night* versus light." Oh my gawd she thought, what else had she gotten wrong? Frantic, she flipped through all her other translations, organizing papers chronologically instead of details and facts.

"Did we conjure the wrong guy?" Olivia asked, paling.

"Clearly we didn't conjure who we thought—in fact the spell shouldn't have worked, but this other guy came anyway," Mac deduced.

"How could changing such minor words—bring this guy instead," Alison questioned. "I thought we conjured a spirit—holy crap, are you saying I saw a ghost at the airport—an evil ghost?" Alison was freaking out and scaring the crap out of Olivia in the process.

"Calm down—spells don't work like that," Mac said, trying to be the reasonable one, and she knew better than to tell another woman to calm down. "Listen," she continued, "Materials, the words, the timing, putting it all together, going through the motions and reading off the words doesn't make for a successful spell. We did all the right things, focused our minds, visualizing our intentions—the energy around us. It's our thoughts that make spells work, it's not something you can be taught. And learning the spell before you begin...." She paused. "Vicki? Are we keeping you from something?" Mac asked when she noticed Vicki was not paying attention to the concerns at hand.

"Vicki!" Alison assisted.

Vicki looked up from her paper organizing. "Sorry," she said. "I didn't think it meant much when I noticed it before, but the scribe and linguist must have crossed paths in the past, or the breaks in their lineage wouldn't have been noted."

Calming at the redirection, Alison said, "In all the translating and transcribing, I hadn't thought of that. These are pretty accurate accounts under the circumstances."

"They all must have crossed paths at different points in order to keep all the records straight," Olivia suggested.

"Maybe that's why they were told of each other," Mac added. "They must have made sacrifices to do so—risked their lives."

"My mom made such a sacrifice to keep things straight, to keep things safe," Alison said, with a note of grief.

"What about those symbols on the cover of the codex?" Alison asked, lifting the big book into view. "Didn't Lynn say she was going to figure out what this star symbol means?"

"Uhmm," Vicki said, drawing them from their frustrations.

"What?" the other three said in unison.

"Well... I didn't want to say anything—you know since we figured we'd conjured a *spirit* or a ghost—or whatever."

"What, Vicki—did you figure out what the symbol means?"

"Yes... it's on the letters too, as you know," Vicki drew out.

"We know," the others said together again.

"The first two symbols on the codex are Mother and Daughter as I mentioned before...."

"And?" Alison questioned, ahead of the others.

"And, well... the third one—the star shaped one, by itself represents the Sumerian word for *sky* or *heaven,* and...," Vicki said, pausing.

"And?" they all shouted.

Vicki cleared her throat, and continued, "... and it's also used to indicate a god in general—a deity, but...."

"Don't make me say it," Mac pushed, her eyes wide in frustration.

Looking back down at her papers, Vicki said, "Together, with the other two, it's the ideogram for... *Angel.*"

After a confusing discussion about who or what they had conjured, they'd all signed off even more confused, but agreed to allow Vicki to reach out to Derek again for help.

"Guess who?" Vicki said, when Derek picked up. Her hope was to complete that damn second entry, perhaps permitting for more clarity and direction on what to do next.

"How can I help," Derek said in response.

There must have been something in her voice, because as busy as he had been of late, he didn't lead with his usual rushed response. "I found an error in my translation of the spell," she explained, giving him the details of her mistake.

"Code-switching," Derek said, without even a hint of criticism. "It's the alternating or mixed uses of two or more languages, within the same discourse."

Vicki was well aware she'd messed up on the spell's translations and didn't really care how. "I'm more concerned over what I may have messed up in my other translations, this second entry in particular, as it also has pieces—words that didn't seem to fit, *solacer* for one." She let out a sigh. "Nothing I've tried seemed to fit, or if it did, it hasn't furthered things along. The words seem clear, but the context of the entry isn't, and all I've filtered out was that it is about a *fifth* something or someone."

"Hmmm," Derek started. "I belong with the other four. Luc is the Theologian and Darius—whether you all agree or not, based on what Luc and I found in his lineage, Darius is a descendant of watchers *and* the Guardian. Only one left is the Believer."

Vicki let out an exhausted huff, surrendering. What could she say, really? She had nothing to prove them right—nor prove him wrong.

"I'll work on the other pieces from this entry," Derek offered. "The answers must be here—in this entry. I'll get back to you on it as soon as possible."

"Okay. Bye, Derek—thank you," Vicki managed through fatigue and disappointment with herself, then ended the call.

Chapter 33

Tuesday evening, Derek stared at the photocopy of the entry in question, then read it aloud for the umpteenth time. "*When the four descendants of the original four are named and the descendant of Watchers comes forth, the guard the fifth will be revealed. The fifth will aid the final four. These four will stand with the guard the fifth who is one of the Solacer.*"

Derek checked the time on his phone and then he hit the speed dial number for the Theologian.

"Hey man, what's up?" came Luc's cheery voice through his cell.

"What else," Derek countered, before going on with the detail regarding his discussion with Vicki. "They thought I might be this fifth, but I reminded her of my place in the other group of four."

"There's been five Archangels all this time—how did we not see that—the connection I mean?"

"We'd set those other two aside, Gabriel and Shamsiel—since they hadn't played a role—or weren't mentioned in the codex," Derek reminded. "Though I feel pretty confident that this *fifth* is this guy Gabriel."

"His name falls under the ones listed as Archangels," Luc confirmed. "Shamsiel is one of the fallen leaders—not an Archangel, but where does Gabriel fit into all this?"

"What kind of role does Gabriel play in theology?" Derek asked reluctant, hoping the role might translate into something more modern or relevant.

"Messenger," Luc shot out. "In many religious texts he's referred to as a messenger, mostly."

"Brings messages—knows things, or what?" Derek questioned.

"Ya—both," Luc said. "But...."

"But what?"

"He could be more like Dunya, an Oracle," Luc added.

"Try that again," Derek said with a headshake, as if he'd missed part of the conversation.

Luc let out a laugh. "Sorry. Think of it as a spiritual person who advises or has insight like a messenger."

"Ah," Derek responded. "And Dunya is one of these?"

"Both she and Mitra are. They come from a long line of them, remember?" Luc gave him. "Remember the Valkyries in the Norse mythology? Dunya said they are like seers, oracles. She thinks Lynn's birthmother may have been one too."

"I remember the seer part—and that Dunya thought Lynn was one. Didn't Lynn's birthmother mentioned the name Gabriel—it was in her mom's journal," Derek reminded back.

"I told Lynn about what Dunya had said about her birthmother—being like she and Mitra," Luc told him

"What did Lynn have to say on that?"

"She made a joke—told me about how one of her friends used to say, *'The oracle knows'*, whenever she got one of her weird Lynnie feelings." Luc laughed. "Read the phrase from the entry again for me," he redirected.

"A fifth was chosen, one who was descendant of watchers," Derek started. "I told Vicki that Darius is *a descendant* of watchers based on his lineage—and he's the guardian. They may not agree or like it—but it's a fact."

"Lynn is who kept saying Darius was the descendant of watchers... that he was the guardian—I think it fits too. Keep going."

"When the four descendants of the original four are named... well, we have that, Alison, Vicki, Mac, and Olivia... *and the descendant of Watchers comes forth*—we have that part too, Darius... *the guard the fifth will be revealed."*

"That part still doesn't sound right, but obviously a fifth something is revealed," Luc interjected.

"*... and the fifth will aid the final four,*" Derek continued.

"Like you said, maybe it's a fifth Archangel—the messenger. Possibly aiding the four others?"

"I'll have to revisit that. This is the last part," Derek said, "*... these four will stand with the guard the fifth who is one of the Solacer.*"

"Seems either these four other Archangels—or maybe the ladies, will stand with this fifth whomever, for whatever reason—but what's a Solacer?"

"I told Vicki I'd have to get back to her on that too—let me work on this for a bit."

"Well, my brain is officially mush, but keep me posted."

"I will," Derek said ending the call.

Derek took out his printed copy of the Theban alphabet once again and placed it next to the entry.

"Firstly," he said aloud, followed by a pause. "Oh, Vicki should have had this one... but she's right, she'd been at it too long." He paused again. "I already gave her the solution for *the guard*—hello—daughter, so that makes the anagram of *guard the fifth...* fifth *daughter.*"

Derek hit the speed dial number 4 on his phone, the number he'd designated for Vicki, and his main contact for the four ladies. When she didn't pick up, he left a message saying he'd call her back—that he had something big. Then he hung up and hit the speed dial, number 5 again, the one for Luc.

"That was fast." Luc said on pickup, excitement beaming through the phone. "What did you find out, man?"

"Luc...?" Derek said, pausing.

"Ya, who else?" He laughed.

Taking in a deep breath and then letting it out slow, Derek said, "Luc... after playing with all the anagram solutions... I know who—or at least *what* this... Solacer is."

The Skype startup music played through Vicki's laptop speakers, then one by one the questioning faces of the Witch, the Healer and the Scribe appeared on screen.

"I know we aren't supposed to meet for another week, but once again the Cipher has found the solutions to the riddles—or missing pieces as it were," Vicki said, via the unforeseen video chat.

"What was so urgent it couldn't wait?" Olivia asked. "The girls just got in from the barn—and they're starving they tell me." She rolled her eyes.

"Derek just called me—yer not going to believe what he told me," Vicki said, then she went on to explain the details behind the need for the call, getting them up to speed on the latest from Derek.

"It's Lynn? But you told us that *guard the fifth* was the correct translation—considering the Guardian was mentioned as well," Alison questioned.

"We all assumed Derek was the fifth because of his help, well… until he told you the fifth could be another Archangel," Olivia added.

"But like I just told you all, it's not a fifth *angel*," Vicki said. "Derek pointed out that *the guard* is daughter—as we know, so that makes *guard the fifth*, into fifth daughter—not someone guarding the fifth," Vicki clarified. "He also said, Solacer is… *Oracles*, like Mitra and Dunya. And Dunya told Luc that Lynn is one of these Oracles. She'd known Lynn was like her and her grandmother after they'd first talked, Luc had told Derek."

"I knew—ya know, think I always knew it!" Alison burst out. "Let me write this out properly," she added. "When the four descendants of the original four are named and the descendant of Watchers comes forth… the *fifth daughter* will be revealed. The fifth will aid the final four. These four will stand with the *fifth daughter* who is one of the *Oracles*. Okay—I got it."

"That sounds right," Mac said. "Sounds perfect in fact." She wiggled in her chair.

"We need to tell Lynn—but I think this kind of thing needs to be done in person," Olivia noted.

"We need to make it special—make it up to her. You know—for pushing her off when she should have been part of this," Alison said.

"She has to be part of this whole gathering thing. Now if they could only find the gathering spot," Mac said, wondering.

"Either way, Lynn needs to know she has a role in this," Vicki admitted. "This is something big—like Derek said."

Alison clapped her hands together, and said, "Let's surprise her—let's all go down for New Year's Eve."

The distraction of working had helped lessen some of the anxiety I'd been feeling. I'd offered to help with the laundry duties needed in both the NICU and regular nursery. I didn't have to wash anything—thank you very much, but I'd had a mountain of baby blankets and burping clothes to fold as part of my shift. Right now though, it was finally my dinner time—or second breaktime of the second 14-hour shift I'd taken at the hospital.

The same building that housed both nurseries, and the family area, also had a beautiful rooftop garden just for staff breaks. The family area had its own outdoor space for patients and alike, but this high up spot was reserved for hospital personnel only. It was for eating meals outside, or for simply taking a breather from that which was the reality of infant and child medical care. And like I had done last night on my dinner break, I retreated again up to this rooftop to eat and get away from the piles of laundry. Similar again to last night, not only was I alone at the picnic table, I was alone on the rooftop.

Ever since that night Nate had shown me how to destress with meditation and the use of the mala beads, I'd made a point to practice the technique. I'd tried it several times while in Ottawa. Even before spotting one of the four—Zaqiel, in the backyard at Andre's place Christmas Day, handling my emotions over the Christmas visit up north had been more than difficult. Despite the joy I'd felt spending time with my family and friends, I missed Mom, and I missed Aunt Kay and the gatherings they would have normally organized for the holidays.

Between the too-often sightings of that Armaros guy and his henchmen, not to mention those four other giants, along with the ominous whomever presence that seemed to be incessantly around me, having to manage my stress and spidy-sense or whatever, had been a constant thing. But the meditation seemed to be helping.

Tension crossed the back of my shoulders then, bunching my muscles. Now was a good time to take advantage of the solitude, I thought, pulling free my mala bead necklace from beneath my scrubs-covered long-sleeved t-shirt. I took in a cleansing breath, then on the exhale, I began reciting my mantra, "I am open to all that releases me."

Zaqiel stood to the left near the arbor of trees watching her from behind his veil.

"Why do you watch her?" Shamsiel asked, appearing at his side.

"You know why," Zaqiel responded, his gaze remaining straight ahead.

"Because she's one of yours," Shamsiel specified. "Why have you shown yourself to her?"

"For the same reason. And because she's also one of his," he added.

Shamsiel nodded and took a step forward. "She's not afraid anymore."

"Means she is also not afraid to make a choice either," Zaqiel noted.

Shamsiel turned to stare at his pale haired comrade. "Do you think he knows who her father is?"

"Yes."

"The others, they are coming here," Shamsiel stated, glancing back towards the picnic table.

"So it seems," Zaqiel said, before vanishing.

Chapter 34

The best-laid plans of mice and men often go awry.
~ Robert Burns

Last night, after considerable organizing of schedules, contacting the Cipher once again, coordinating with the Guardian, and then a little strategizing with the Theologian, they, the Scribe, the Linguist, the Healer, and the Witch, had all concocted a plan to visit the Oracle.

Derek had been scheduled to arrive today Wednesday, at 9 a.m., and would be staying at Darius's place, and the girls were set up to arrive Thursday evening. Luckily for them, Luc had remembered the travel vouchers, the ones Lynn had offered up should he and Dunya want to do some traveling. She'd said she had 50 of them but couldn't possibly use them all. He'd called customer support to find out how they worked. The customer service lady had told him that in order to use them, all that was needed was the code, the 14-digit number found on the bottom of each voucher. Luc had distributed the code-numbers right away, five, one for each of the friends who required a flight to get here. They had all coordinated their own flights, but Alison had informed the group that the booking agent who had arranged *her* flight, had mentioned that these were VIP vouchers, and that normally the dates they were choosing, would have been blacked out, *and* that she wouldn't have been able to fly direct. Lucky again.

This morning, as added support, Luc had let Redmond in on the surprise, but he'd not given him the full truth—the *why* of the surprise. They'd all felt Lynn should be the first to know the truth, despite what she had already shared with Redmond. "Could you keep Lynn busy at your place on Thursday—New Years, until everything gets set up here with the others?" Luc asked.

Redmond chuckled. "I'll do my best to keep her at my place during the day. But I'll tell her later that it will just be too noisy in the evening, being so close to the Grove—then suggest we head back to her place."

"Perfect," Luc said, grinning into the phone. "Darius already went to pick up Derek at the airport—I'm meeting them at Darius's. Keep your cell close."

"Will do—and I'll text Lynn as soon as we get off this call." Redmond chuckled again.

"Good man. I'll keep you posted," Luc said, ending the call as he pulled into the drive at Darius's house.

Inside, they promptly set up a Skype call to touch base with the girls.

"It seems that Lynn has been doing a little sleuthing on her own," Luc shared with them. "She found a letter from her birthmother—it mentions a gathering."

"But like everything else—it's full of riddles," Derek informed them. "I started working on it with her—but I finished it without her. I haven't had a chance to tell her yet.

"Why didn't you tell us," Vicki asked. Derek had known she'd been struggling with the translations and the meaning of the remaining parts.

"It was her letter," Luc cut in.

"And we've kept her out of things for a while now," Olivia added. "I don't blame her for keeping a little to herself."

"She's been a part of this from the beginning—but we only chose to exclude her because we thought her part was over," Alison admitted. "I knew it didn't feel right."

"No point in feeling guilty now," Derek said. "Let's figure this out, come together and then we can celebrate the victory." Derek straightened the papers he had next to Darius's computer. Then he clicked his pen and said, "Shall we go over the letter?" He held up his copy of the letter in view of the video chat window, allowing them to read the full translation.

"*Heart news*?" Vicky questioned

"The answer," Derek responded.

"What about *faith fever* and *guard the glean*?" Vicki questioned again. "Oh—hey, based on the new info from the letter, coupled with the details that spirit gave us—I know where the gathering is now."

"That's what you said the last time," Olivia noted, with a hint of exhaustion.

"I know—but look at the comparisons," Vicki said. "Look up Fairchild Botanical Gardens."

Using Darius's computer setup with the dual monitors, Derek brought up both websites, Fairchild and the Arboretum.

They all had the websites up now.

"The spirit said it was *internationally acclaimed for agricultural research*, which the Arboretum is," Alison said. "I'd made a note of his mentioning the person who had started it all—the plant expert—botanist, linked to the department of agriculture."

"The website for the place says *James Fletcher* who was part of planting the first 200 trees in 1889 was a botanist, and it says the place is part of the department of agriculture," Derek said, glancing back and forth from the descriptions on each site.

"Yes—but Fairchild gets its name from one of the most famous plant explorers in history, *Dr. David Fairchild*," Vicki began. "He travelled the world in search of useful plants, but he was also an educator and a renowned scientist. He created the Section of Foreign Seed and Plant Introduction of the United States—you got it—*Department of Agriculture*."

"It had sounded like it was in Ottawa, but it's really this Fairchild gardens," Olivia said. "Why had the spirit wanted us to think it's here?"

"For what reason—hell only knows," Vicki said.

"That's the same place Lynn has those memorial bricks," Mac added. "This asshole spirit had actually given us the right info."

"But left it so vague that we'd never have figured it—not without Lynn's letter," Luc tossed out.

"We still don't know where on the grounds we need to go," Darius said.

"Does the letter say what we're supposed to do at this place?" Mac asked. "I might need to pack some supplies."

Derek shook his head. "We'll figure that out once you're here and we're all together."

Considering the long shifts of the last two days, I'd slept in, *and* I'd enjoyed every minute, right up until I'd been woken by a wet kiss.

"Raven," I said sleepily, in response to the doggie alarm. I hadn't set my real one. "What time is it?" I glanced over to check my alarm clock when my cell phone vibrated on the bedside table next to it.

Redmond's smiling face appeared on screen displaying his contact picture, with his name under it. "Good morning," I said, with a smile.

"Morning? It's almost noon," he laughed out. "Don't tell me you're still in bed?" He laughed again. "Or are you spending the rest of your time off in bed?"

I pondered the idea of spending time in bed with him—but knew that hadn't been the real question he'd ask, so I just laughed back

"Lynn—don't fall back to sleep on me," he said, through another deep sexy laugh.

"I'm up—I'm up," I told him.

"I'm just heading over to help Nate decorate the yoga studio for his New Year's Eve party," he tossed out. "He asked us to come—but told him you and I were staying in this year. You're still coming over to hang with me here for New Year's—aren't you?

"Definitely," I tossed back, shifting to get up out of bed. Raven trailed behind me to the bathroom.

"Good," he said. "I'm looking forward to an evening in—spent too many years partying on New Year's."

"Luc sent me a text last night, saying he and Dunya were going to stay in for New Year's too."

"How romantic," he said, followed by a gagging noise.

"They're such copy-cats," I laughed out. "He's supposed to be out running errands with Dunya today. Wrote he'd be at her place later tonight, so it's just Raven and me here." I patted Raven on the head.

"How was your shift?" Redmond asked, changing topics.

"Uneventful," I said, looking at myself in the big mirror over the double sinks.

"Considering where you were—that's a good thing," he said. "What are you going to do for the rest of your day?"

"Chill, check email, watch some TV with Raven," I said, turning to leave the bathroom.

"Productive." He laughed.

"Actually, Derek sent me a copy of the spell the girls did on Halloween," I said. "I wanted to see if there was anything in it that rings familiar—you know, with anything else I'd come across in my spooky research." Or from the letter my birthmother wrote I thought as I padded out to the living room.

After a few more pleasantries and a sweet goodbye with Redmond, I focused back on my day ahead. I reheated leftovers and then got myself all set up in front of the TV with my trusty laptop.

Raven was already crashed, snoring away at my feet when my email loaded. Derek's email was waiting in the inbox and I clicked on the attachment.

Gabriel and Shamsiel had seated themselves on the adjacent couch. Their long legs were stretched out ankles crossed in front of them watching whatever show was playing on the TV.

"The Cipher is here now," Gabriel said. "He's with the Guardian and the Theologian. The others arrive tomorrow night." He smiled.

"Zaqiel was at the hospital last night," Shamsiel said.

Gabriel's smile dropped.

"Death, he's always there… but nothing happened," Shamsiel added.

Gabriel's smile returned. "Maybe nothing will happen. Maybe The Horsemen understand, maybe they all do."

"Did you find the letter?"

"No," Gabriel said, his smile disappearing again. "I saw her scan it for Derek, so there's a copy on her computer too. But the actual letter—I think she hid it again." He smiled again through that tidbit of frustration.

"Somewhere safe, I hope," Shamsiel said.

Gabriel's smile dropped again, and he sighed.

Chapter 35

New Year's Eve Day.

Yesterday, I'd taken the day off and relaxing to an all new level, only getting off the couch to go to the bathroom or refill my plate with food. Between TV shows and re-watching a few old classic movies, I'd spent most of the afternoon and the evening reviewing the spell Derek had sent me. The overdoing it with the TV and riddle solving had not aided in my sleep last night either, I had been up every hour tossing and turning.

First thing this morning, Redmond had texted me, writing he had some *last-minute work to finish up*, so that meant I'd be stuck at home doing more nothing again until he was done.

With nothing to do for the day, I tried watching more TV, but found it was all New Year's eve prep, and it didn't interest me. I'd made and eaten lunch after, and I had even taken a short nap on the couch, but by the time Luc came through the door at 7 p.m., I was still exhausted, thought mainly from the nothingness I'd done all day.

"Aren't you supposed to be over at Redmond's," Luc said, passing through the living room to the kitchen. Raven got up from his spot on the floor next to the couch to follow his master into the kitchen.

I had plans to go over to Redmond's soon, but I thought it very suspicious, yet funny it concerned Luc why I was still home. "Redmond had to go into the studio today—finish some tracks. Why—what—you got a romantic night planned here or something?" I asked, remembering Redmond's comment. I peeled myself off the couch to go into the kitchen.

"No—I'm hanging at Dunya's tonight—told you that," Luc said.

"Right," I said, but I wasn't buying it. I watched him go from the cupboard to the fridge, then back to the cupboards again, flustered as if he'd lost something. "You okay?"

"I'm good—fine," he said, giving me a big stupid grin.

He was up to something. Whatever. "Come on Raven," I said to my lounging compadre. "You can help me pick out something to wear tonight."

I left Luc in the kitchen to find *whatever*, while Raven and I went off to find me the right outfit for staying in on New Year's Eve with Redmond.

"Later, Lynn," I heard Luc's voice call from down the hall.

"Later," I hollered back, before hearing the front door shut.

Raven turned his head towards the sound of the door.

"Romance," I said to Raven. "Speaking of romance. I think tonight might be *the night*."

Raven turned back, tilting his head as if confused, adding to my struggle with what to wear even though we were having a cozy night in.

Several *woofs* later from my stylist, and even more dog-tired, I finally settled on wearing a pair of cropped summer weight jeans that folded up several times to hit at calf height, coupled with a light blue tie-dye t-shirt. To add to the comfy-cozy factor, I grabbed a lightweight white sweatshirt from my closet. I gave Raven a quick goodbye pat before leaving, and then I was off.

At the top of the stairs to Redmond's place I found the door to his apartment wide open. "I have a surprise for you," Redmond said, as I walked in. "But I have to run an errand first—I shouldn't be long."

"Hi—to you too," I said, grinning yet confused. He'd been busy all day and now he was running more errands?

"Hiiii cutie," he said, grabbing his wallet off the kitchen island. He stole a kiss and then was off out the open door.

He and Luc were both acting funny. "Fine," I said, to the now empty apartment. "I need a nap anyway," I called out, exhausted and glad we were staying in. But another nap couldn't hurt, I thought, especially if I was going to stay up and watch the ball drop on TV later.

"Hey, Luc," Redmond said, into his cell phone as he got into his van. "Sorry—I had some last-minute studio stuff I had to get done."

"Lynn at your place, finally?" Luc asked. He'd had asked Redmond to keep Lynn busy today—but she'd been at the house all day. He'd also asked if he could pick up a few decorations to liven up the house, help bring in the new year with friends. *And* he'd thought it would help make what he and the others had to tell Lynn a bit more celebratory and a lot less focused on them for keeping her out of things.

"Ya—she's here now—heard her say something about taking a nap. Told her I had to run errands." Redmond checked left and right before pulling out onto the road. "But I'll be right over with the supplies for the party—I had some left-overs at the studio from the staff-party."

"Oh great—thanks," Luc said, giving a sigh of relief. "Thought she'd never leave. Darius and Derek are on their way here now."

Redmond laughed. "It's all good, my friend—no worries. See you soon."

I kicked off my flipflops and then put my keys and tote on the kitchen island. I pulled my cell from the tote and then padded to the bedroom area of the apartment. Using Redmond's charger next to the bed, I plugged in my cell to get some extra battery life.

The bed was made but there was a book resting on the pillow. I tossed my sweatshirt on the bed and picked up the book. Then with one lazed movement, I sprawled out atop the covers of the bed.

Paradise Lost, by John Milton, it was the book he had started reading to me the night before he'd left for his trip to see his family.

I smiled at the memory of Redmond relaying all the details and well wishes from his trip. His visit to see his family had been a great one, but I'd only found out about it after he'd gotten back. We'd had serious miscommunication problems due to his phone acting up, but silly me, I'd assumed he had changed his mind about having a relationship with me. Thankfully, I was wrong. We'd straightened out the phone issue, and he'd told me all about the visit, *and* how he'd told his whole family about me. They'd all been thrilled to hear he had a new person in his life, his mother especially. She'd commented that it was good he had something other than work to focus on, and someone nice to have fun with.

I flipped to where the bookmark stuck out the top of the book, then moved the bookmark to a spot near the end and began to read. Less than two pages in, my eyelids grew heavy....

I stood in the opening at the edge of a vast garden. It reminded me of images I'd seen of the famous Garden of Eden. On either side of me were large groupings of flowering trees and bushes... but I wasn't alone. The figures of three women in white gowns resembling old-fashioned nighties, were crouched down behind the bushes to my left. Something about them was familiar. The woman in the middle turned her head to look up at me... It was my mother.

"Mom?" I gasped out. The women on either side of my mother turned then to look at me. The familiar faces of my Aunt Kay and... Louise, regarded me with terrified expressions. "What are you doing here?" I questioned.

"Shhhh," my mother whispered, turning back and pointing towards the open field.

Out in the center of the field of green grass was an assembled mass of men, no—angels, legions of fallen angels. The dark one, Armaros was out in front. His voice rose as if giving a speech. "I know the way to take back what is ours. We don't need to recover heaven. We can create our own world here—take our revenge for being cast out—for being imprisoned, for being weeeeak, for taking the daughters of man."

Another angel appeared then, this one had long blond shoulder-length hair. Gabriel. It was him, the one from the photo taken in the garden, the one I'd seen across the street from my house, the one I'd seen—called forth, in the nursery. "You want to tempt the humans," he called out to the masses. "Have you forgotten what happened when the jealousy against humanity led another once favored angel to wage war? If you don't recall, it was Archangel Michael who led the faithful of you into battle against that rebellious angel. Like it had been written in the old, the new prophecy also tells of a savior who will redeem humankind."

"The descendants of the four have failed," Armaros shouted, addressing the gathered. "Now is the time for us, for our descendants—the descendants

of the fallen, for them to follow the darkness over the light. It will be a child of ours—of mine perhaps, and not of the four, who will rise up and stand at my side...."

I startled awake, breathing out the words, "The second part of the letter—that's what it meant." I knew now where the gathering was supposed to be. Then I was reminded where I was, in Redmond's bed, and still *alone* in the apartment. I checked my watch. It was still New Year's Eve. I'll have to tell Derek, I thought, but it could wait until later.

Right now, my heart ached with missing my mom, over missing them all. A force pushed at my will with an overwhelming need to go to the gathering place, a compulsion of sorts to go there, *now*.

I knew what denying a compulsion like this would do, what they had done to me in the past when I rejected the push or pull. Refusal had made me uneasy, nauseous, even pained me. I knew Redmond would make me wait until tomorrow, but I couldn't. I could however leave him a note, and I got up from the bed

I placed the sticky note I'd written, on the fridge where he'd see it;

> *Gone to check something out about the gathering.*
> *Won't be long. XO*

Then I grabbed my keys and tote off the counter, and left.

Pulling up to the entrance to Fairchild Gardens, I checked the clock on my dash. It read 8:15 p.m. and I realized the place was closed for the day. I pulled into one of the empty spots and I realized I was also starving.

Christmas cookies, I thought, remembering that Redmond had put the bag back in my tote. I'd carried them with me to and from work for the past two days just in case I needed a little sugar pick me up. Taking one from the plastic bag, I bit into it only to find they were stale, but I didn't care, I was hungry.

I took a second cookie from the bag and placed the rest back in my tote. That's when I spotted the letter from Anthony. I'd forgotten all about it, forgotten I'd shoved it in there, but the last thing I wanted was to review my bill. As an alternative, I rolled down the car window, and sat listening to the evening nature noises.

I'd been brave and determined with driving here, but now I was nervous. My overactive imagination coupled with the crazy sounds of the night were not putting me at ease. It wasn't as if I could go into the park anyway, it was closed until tomorrow. Sounds of early fireworks broke through the unnerving sounds of the garden, breaking through my fear.

At the calming of my nerves, I decided that what I needed was real food, or at least real—not stale munches. Redmond had said he had a surprise for me, so figured I'd surprise him with food. Hopefully it would ease any annoyance he might have over my leaving without a word too. I'd text him now, tell him I was on my way to get food and would be back soon. But searching my tote, I soon grasped the fact I didn't have my cell *and* that I had left it charging by the side of the bed.

"Alison's flight arrives in 45 minutes and the others arrive shortly after," Derek confirmed, checking the flights statuses on his tablet.

"From here, it'll take us 30 minutes to get to the airport—so we should leave soon," Darius stated, jingling his keys as he got up off the couch. "Decorations are up—foods ready, so all we need is for Redmond to bring Lynn back over—once we're all back here again—right?"

"Decorations—check," Luc said. "Food—check, pick up the four—almost check, and ya Redmond said he'd get her back over here."

"Luc—there's someone out on the front lawn," Darius said, standing near the front window. "Uhhh Luuuuc—it's that same guy from the hospital."

"What?" was all Luc got out, before Darius yanked open the front door. Luc followed him.

On the front lawn stood a blond-haired giant of a man, even more enormous compared to Darius's own massive size.

"Zaqiel?" Darius said as a question, remembering the reference to the Four Horsemen. Before he could say another word, a second large man appeared, this one with long black hair.

"Baraqel," Luc said, uttering the name of the newly arrived horsemen. Luc went to stand next to Darius on the lawn just as a third hulk donning long white hair appeared. "Kokabiel," Luc, said. He turned a fast glance back to the open door to the house. Derek stood in the open doorway, mouth gaping. Luc turned back just as the trio of giants disappeared, vanishing into thin air.

"Those... those guys are the ones I saw on Halloween—but there's one missing," Darius sputtered, turning to look at Luc and noticing Derek in the doorway.

"Did that just really happen," Derek questioned, taking a few unsteady steps towards his friends. "It's all real—isn't it." His words were a statement not a question.

"You finally believe?" Luc asked.

Darius put a big hand on Derek's shoulder as if to steady him. "It's real, man," he said to his normally skeptical friend.

"Saw it with my own eyes—the proof doesn't lie," Derek said, glancing back and forth from Luc to Darius.

"I don't know what it means—them showing up here, but we'd better get the others from the airport," Luc stated, turning back to the house. "We need to all be together." Luc locked the front door, then turned back, running across the lawn to the driveway where the other two now stood near Darius's car. He felt his cell phone ringing in his pocket. Checking it, he saw it was Redmond. "Hey," Luc said, switching the phone to speaker so the others could hear.

"She was supposed to be napping," Redmond's panicked voice rang out.

"What?" Luc responded, looking at the other two and shaking his head.

"She's not here—she's gone," Redmond shot out.

"What do you mean she's gone?" Luc questioned again.

Redmond made the sound of taking in a breath. "After I dropped off the supplies to you, I came back here. She said she was going to take a nap—but she's gone. She slept walked the other night—so I checked the park across the street where I'd found her, but she wasn't there either."

"I know about the sleepwalking," Luc interrupted, staring back at Derek's still shocked face.

"I had a dream about her getting lost that same night," Darius said, adding to the interruption.

"Darius? She told me about your dream," Redmond said back, taking another breath. "I'm going to call the police."

"No wait," Luc said. "I know Lynn told you stuff—all about the things we have been working on—but what's happening to her might be something else."

"What the hell are you talking about?" Redmond's voice roared.

"She's involved—majorly involved," Luc said. "It's the *real* reason her friends are coming."

"What the... there's some huge guy out front...," Redmond started to say, but the call cut off.

"Call him again," Derek said. "We need to find Lynn."

Luc dialed Redmond back but got nothing, not even voicemail. "Derek—you try," Luc said, reciting Redmond's number to him.

"Nothing," Derek said, showing Luc the cell screen with no connection. "Let me try Vicki." Derek dialed Vicki and put the call on speaker. It rang three times and went to voicemail. "Crap—she can't pick up—she's already on the flight—they all are," he said, oddly stupid for once. "I don't want to make her worry," he said, calling again, this time leaving a message stating they would be there to pick them up. "Luc—give me the house key," he said in demand, hand out.

Though puzzled, Luc still handed him the key. He and Darius got in the car. Derek was off into the house and then back, shoving something in his back pocket. "Head to Redmond's," he shot out, hopping in the backseat of Darius's car.

On the drive, each of them tried calling Redmond, but there was still no answer. Then when they pulled up to the studio parking lot, they spotted Redmond out front.

"The guy just disappeared," Redmond shouted at them, as they exited the car. "Vanished—right before my eyes." Redmond's stunned expression mirrored that of Derek's when he had seen the disappearing act of the giants on the front lawn. "The guy was huge—bigger than you Darius, taller than me," Redmond said. "Had red hair like me—but brush-cut—said he was *War*. What the hell?"

"My dream," Darius said, directing his words at Luc and Derek.

"Azazel—the missing one," Luc confirmed, realizing it was the fourth Horseman. Luc's phone rang in his hand. "It's Dunya," he said, clicking the answer button.

"Luuuc," came Dunya's voice, loud enough that the others could hear even before Luc put her on speaker. "It's Jadda—she's so distraught. She's doing that thing with her arms—flapping them—calling out names, Kokabiel, Baraqel, Zaqiel, Azazel—keeps saying mowmin, mowmin, mowmin."

"That's what the guy said—*mowmin*... then he disappeared," Redmond broke in. "Literally disappeared."

"It means *believer*," Dunya's voice added.

Luc stared from Darius to Derek.

"Could he be the Believer?" Darius asked, with a shrug.

"Believer—it's my name," Redmond cut in again, then he turned in a circle as if still looking for the large man.

"Your name—what?" Luc questioned, watching the tall man turn.

"What?" Dunya said through the phone, adding to the question.

Luc redirected his attention. "Dunya—we need to find Lynn. Try to keep Mitra calm—I'll call you back. Things are about to get real here," Luc said to her.

"I'll do my best—find Lynn—call me ASAP," Dunya said, before ending the call.

"What do you mean," Luc directed back at Redmond, as he slid his cell back in his pocket.

Redmond stopped scanning the parking lot. "Credente—it's Italian, means *believer* in English," Redmond clarified.

"Yer the missing piece," Darius added.

"It's you, man," Luc said, relieved for the sign of clarity. Luc then explained that what they'd just seen—the four they'd just seen, were the Four Horsemen. "Shit's about to get real," he added.

"We were supposed to be picking up the girls," Darius reminded.

"We need to find Lynn," Redmond addressed all.

"You said you found her near a field?" Derek turned addressing Redmond. "But you checked—and she wasn't there, right?" Derek asked him as if trying to solve another puzzle. "Let's check your place again." He turned with a purpose but didn't know where to go.

"Up there," Redmond said, pointing to the stairs leading to his apartment.

In the apartment they spread out as if looking for clues. "Her tote is gone," Redmond noted.

"Has anyone tried calling her?" Darius asked.

"Can't," Redmond said, standing next to the bed. "She left her cell—charging."

"What about shoes," Luc asked. "Wasn't she barefoot when she sleepwalked?"

"Never looked," Redmond said, checking around the side of the bed. "But she usually leaves them at the door.

"Nothing—gone," Darius confirmed, from the area near the door.

"So is the sweatshirt she had with her," Redmond added.

"Looks like she left on purpose, not sleepwalking this time," Derek surmised.

"Where would she have gone—why wouldn't she have told me?" Redmond asked no one in particular. "Do you think we should call the police?"

"And tell them what?" Luc asked, panning the small space. "They'd never believe us."

"Maybe she figured out the spot like we did—and went there?" Darius suggested.

"What—where?" Redmond questioned, his worry rising. "Spot?"

"Gathering spot. We think the gathering is at Fairchild," Derek said, pulling the letter from his back pocket. "She may have figured it out herself."

"We should have told her," Luc said, his frustration matching Redmond's worry.

Redmond grabbed his keys off the kitchen island. "I'll go to the Fairchild Garden—see if she's there," he said, heading to the door.

"I'm going with you," Darius stated, following behind him. "But I'll drive."

Shutting the door behind them, Derek and Luc followed them down the stairs.

"Here, take the van—get the girls," Redmond offered, tossing Luc the keys. "And keep your phones handy."

Luc and Derek climbed into the band-van and then headed off in the direction of the airport. Redmond and Darius pulled out onto the road heading in the opposite direction, towards the garden.

Darius's car rolled to a stop at the front parking area of the garden. "Closed," Darius said, pointing to the hours of operation on the main parking sign. "We'll head back to your place—just in case she comes back."

Redmond nodded. "I'll call the others," he said, bringing up Luc's number. "I can't seem to shake this uneasy feeling." He hit dial on Luc's number.

"We'll find her," Darius said, despite the uncomfortable feeling building in his own gut. He turned the car around and headed back out to the road.

When I pulled into a parking spot at the studio, I saw that Redmond's van wasn't out front. "Those were some long-ass errands," I said to the night, as I got out of my car.

At least if he wasn't back yet he wouldn't be mad at me for leaving without telling him. Besides, I had all the fixings to make homemade guacamole and two types of tortilla chips for dipping. He'd be happy to have something to munch on while we made our real dinner. "I'm starving," I said, opening the door, though I knew he wasn't inside making me a New Year's eve meal. Not yet anyway. It was getting late, but a girl has to eat, and I wasn't going to survive on just munchies.

I set the bags of food on the island and then removed the stale cookies from my tote. The bill from Anthony came with it as I pulled the plastic bag free. I had to admit, I was curious what a PI bill would comprise. I knew he had an hourly rate but how much time could he have spent on dead ends? Taking the envelope, I slipped a finger under the corner and tore it open.

Only I didn't find a list of dollar signs and a due date, instead I found a short letter from Anthony, stating that I'd find a copy of my birthmother's poem attached, the one the friend had given him. There was also a pamphlet of some sort, with another note attached with a paperclip, this one was from the friend.

A place for wishes, her note had begun. It went on to mention she had not understood the words of the poem, but that reading it still made her miss her friend. The note referred to *wishing trees* that had been mentioned in the poem, and how she had gone to California in 2009, to the Stanford university campus where she'd seen one of the wishing trees. She'd written how she had made a wish for her friend's daughter, adding a message on the tree for her to be safe and healthy. Her message here, ended with the words, *Make a wish*.

I flipped up the note to see the pamphlet.

The label on the front read; *The Wishing Grove at Fairchild*. Below, it stated that it was the latest in the series of *Wishing Tree installations* that began in 1996 and have appeared throughout the world. It gave the location and the instructions about how to make your wish at the tree. There was more below it, about Yoko Ono and that she'd sponsored them, and how the wishes from the trees were collected, then stored to be sent to the Imagine Peace Tower on Videy Island, Reykajavik Iceland. The tower is said to be lit by 15 searchlights with prisms acting as mirrors to reflect the light skyward. It stated that she'd chosen Iceland because *100% of the electricity is provided by clean geothermal energy*.

That was cool I thought, but the part I liked the most on the write-up was how the words 'IMAGINE PEACE' were inscribed on the base of the tower in 24 languages. The tower is lit every year on October 9th, John Lennon's birthday, until December 8th, the date of his death. The last part of the pamphlet mentions that Yoko described this tower as, '*the best thing she and John had ever done*'.

I set the letter and pamphlet aside next to the bags of food. The words and instruction for the wishing trees from the pamphlet had me remembering Nate's words about the garden, how he'd said it was a *wonderous place*, then recited the same instruction; *Make a wish. Write it down on a piece of paper. Fold it and tie it around a branch of a Wish Tree. Ask your friends to do the same. Keep wishing, until the branches are covered with wishes.*

Taking just the poem with me, I went and sat down on the bed. I unfolded the paper and read through the words. A tingling sensation ran from my neck at my hairline down my arms to prickle at my fingertips. "I have to go back," I said, to the empty apartment. I grabbed my cell phone from the bedside table. Then snatching up my keys again off the island, I took off for the garden.

This time, I parked down the road at the staff parking area hoping to find a way in. Before getting out of the car, I made a call to Redmond. It went straight to voicemail, and I left a message telling him what I'd figured out, and that I had to see it for myself. I added that I hoped he wasn't mad and understood why I had to come here.

I got out of the car and then circled around to the side to where the care staff had entrance to the garden. "Bingo," I whispered, when I found the gate next to the tool shed open.

Through the small gate, I noticed there were lights still on showing off the trees and providing minimal lighting along the path. I followed the path from the side entrance along to an area I recognized. I went a little further and found the path that led to the perfect bench, near the perfect tree. I stopped and bent down to touch the perfect spot. "Hi ladies," I said, running my fingers back and forth over the three inlaid bricks. "I'm going to go make a wish now." I stood and continued on. I knew now in which direction the other tree was.

Redmond came through the apartment door and spotted the bags on the kitchen island. "Lynn," he called out as he walked further into the space, but it was clear it was only he and Darius who were in there. Turning back to the island, he inspected the bags of food and found a pamphlet with a note attached. "She's obviously been back here—but why did she leave again?" Confused, he turned back to face Darius who still stood taking up most of the room in the open door.

Darius was holding a blue sticky note outstretched in his hand. "The corner was poking out from under the fridge," Darius said. "I think it's from Lynn."

Redmond's eyebrows pinched as he leaned in to read the note. *"Gone to check something out about the gathering,"* he read aloud. Redmond cut a glance back to the island and the pamphlet. Putting two and two together, he said, "We need to go back to the garden." Then he took his cell from his back pocket and dialed Luc again.

"Did you find her?" Luc's voice burst through the phone.

"No—but I know where she is," Redmond said, turning Darius around to direct him back down the stairs. "Do you have the others with you?"

"Yes," Luc said. "They know Lynn's missing—they know we saw The Horsemen, so they know as much as we all do. We're on our way back to the house now."

"No—meet us at the garden," Redmond rushed out.

"Okay, we're 15 minutes out from the garden now," Luc informed them, before ending the call.

At the gardens again, Darius pulled into the main parking area. "I don't see her car," Darius said, maneuvering the car in a slow circle around the empty parking lot.

"There's a smaller parking area just past the main entrance—maybe she went there," Redmond suggested.

Darius pulled back out onto the road taking them the short distance to the other entrance marked for *staff only.* "There," Darius said, pulling in beside Lynn's car.

"I'll text Luc where we are," Redmond said, before getting out of the car.

When the band-van pulled in at the side parking to the garden, both Redmond and Darius watched as all the doors opened and the crew piled out.

"This way," Redmond directed, pointing to the side gate. He went through followed by Darius and then Luc on their heels.

"The Horsemen will be coming," Darius called out, taking a quick glance back over his shoulder.

"Who the hell are these Horsemen guys, anyway?" Vicki, called after them through the gate.

"ANGELS!!" Derek yelled, running past her to follow them.

Vicki took off faster to catch up to them.

Mac and Olivia weren't running, but they were walking fast. Someone needed to be by Alison considering she was 6 months pregnant, though she was still managing at a quick pace. "It's on—like a prawn at dawn, Baby!" Alison called out, pulling a quote from a favorite TV show as she hustled along.

I found the massive tree was more like a grove, having three trees intertwined together, and all were lit up. They were *Ficus* trees, based on the plaque next to the 1-foot square box containing the white cards and tiny pencils. It didn't matter to me what they were, they were beautiful, magical even. I gazed up into its branches, to see hundreds of fine white threads hung from the limbs, dangling tiny white cards with messages on them. *Wishes*.

Stomping sounds broke through the night, coming from the far side of the expanse beyond the grove, and pulling my attention away from reading the lower hanging wishes. I cut a glance to the right to see a large man erupt through the low-lit brush of trees across the expanse on the far side.

Redmond. He was followed by an even larger man. *Darius*.

Thrilled yet somewhat perplexed, I waved my arms back and forth over my head. Redmond spotted me and began at a jogging pace in my direction. Darius on the other hand, charged at full tilt towards me, passing Redmond on his way.

Behind them, bursting through the same opening came Luc—and to my surprise, *Derek*. Then one by one, smaller figures pushed through the brush to stand in the opening next to the guys. *My girlfriends*.

With my bafflement heightened, I moved forward out from under the trees onto the plush grass of the grounds to cross the large expanse then, only to find my way blocked.

Separating me from my friends about ten paces away in an area shy of light, stood a shadowy figure facing me… the one I knew now, as *Armaros*.

Darius halted his rush forward, then Redmond came to a stop at his side.

Armaros turned away to look over his shoulder at the others, then back at me again. "Do you know who I am—what I am?" he asked, his voice a deep baritone.

The field was weakly lit by the reflection of spotlights off the surrounding trees, and though his eyes were shrouded in shadow, I knew they were black. I said nothing in response to being blocked from my friends, however my brain did cue the *Imperial March* theme music from Star Wars.

"Do you know who stands with me?" he roared. The two massive figures I'd seen with him at the gala appeared at his left. "Do you understand what is about to happen? You have read all about it, but it was your *theologian* who told you what was to come—remember?" He swept a hand out addressing all my friends. "The Four Horsemen have been dispatched and are here for you—for all of you." One at a time, The Horsemen appeared next to Armaros at his right.

My other friends finally catching up, came to a halt next to Redmond and Darius. All watching now as the growing ominous presence separated us. The worried faces of my friends turned back and forth to each other as if searching each for answers.

"The Fifth seal—when opened...," Armaros began again, "... the souls of those willing to die for their beliefs cry out. They will be Martyrs—all of them." He pointed to Luc this time. I recalled the words, only because Luc had recited something similar. "Sixth is earthquakes, the sun blackens, and the moon goes red like blood, and the stars—fireballs, will plummet to earth." As the words left his mouth, the skies darkened, and the cooling winds halted. The scent on the air was now stale and dry as if filling with invisible smoke and ash. Then he began again, "Seventh, the heavens are silenced. Then seven of my brethren will sound seven trumpets, their deafening pitch releasing devastation on man and earth." Seven tall figures appeared behind Armaros, all of them holding up long trumpets.

At my count that made fourteen against one, and all I had behind me was the expanse of the open field. One on one I could manage, I had held off four at once similarly, but this host of angels.... was sending me into a nasty dose of vertigo.

I swayed... and my eyesight began darkening around the edges....

Chapter 36 

"Believe something and the Universe is on its way to being changed. Because you've changed, by believing. Once you've changed, other things start to follow. Isn't that the way it works?"
~ Diane Duane - So You Want to Be a Wizard

I was born on a Friday at 10:37 in the morning, and based on the almanac I'd read for that year, the weather for that particular day had been a cool 45 degrees Fahrenheit or just above freezing if you preferred Celsius.

Not that these facts were poignant in any way, but back when I'd read the details of my birth from the birth registration documents and then later read the weather conditions from the almanac, the details had conjured a feeling—not quite a memory, of something else, something I couldn't quite put my finger on at the time. You know how when you finish a book and then you start another, the story and characters from the previous blur or overlap, and the residue from the prior seeps into the new? I often feel that way with my life as if something from before keeps seeping into or overlaps with the present. It's not like a déjà vu, where you think you've seen it before, it's more like something you've experienced, witnessed or heard, gets replaced by small parts of what's happening in the present moment.

This was like that.

If Armaros's words hadn't been so ominous, I'd have made a joke about a choir of angels or back-up musicians the minute those seven horn toting angels appeared, but not even I was in the mood for jokes. In fact, I hated having the attention on me, and don't even get me started about standing up in front of a crowd. But unwanted attention or not, it was time—time for me to show this asshole not to underestimate little old *me*. No one—and I mean *no one,* threatens my friends and gets away with it, let alone threatening the entire human population.

I took in a deep breath. "I am open to all that releases me!" I hollered so all could hear me, raising my arms up and out to the sides, all the while glaring back at the big... *bad*… angel. I shot a hasty glance at each one of my girlfriends, then commenced to recite the words they all knew. "For ours is the Air, this Fire, this Water, this Earth, Forever and Ever. Blessed Be…," I began, then caught sight of my friends' worried faces.

I'd known by Alison's expression she had recognized Armaros first. Then Mac's expression morphed next. "Oh-my-gawd she's reciting the conjuring spell—but it's wrong," Mac cried out. The others only stared in my direction, fear plastered across their faces.

I shook my head *no,* and continued, "Uriel, we appeal to you on the words that fly, appear in my presence, *night versus light*. We are the Air that blows, the Water that swirls, the Fire light, the strong Earth, elements gather in this safe place. I call out to the energies and forces of nature, Water, Fire, Wind, and Earth…."

"Waaaait," Vicki screamed then, her hands raised as though she thought she could stop what was coming.

"I summon the power of *Sunshine and Shadow*," I finished, knowing the *correct* words to say. I had found and corrected *both* errors they'd made in the spell.

"Wait—what? That's it!" Vicki shouted, full of delight this time, realizing herself then that the other anagram hadn't been *Show in Sun and Shade,* but was Sunshine and Shadow, as I'd spoken.

I lowered my arms, and Uriel appeared next to Mac. They all turned to see the true beauty of the one they had needed to conjure. I smiled, seeing the elated yet bewildered expression on all my friends' faces, especially Vicki's, being she was usually a skeptic.

"Smile all you like—your death is coming," Armaros scoffed, redirecting my attention. "Enjoy your last breath." He smiled, the corners of his mouth curving with distain.

I said nothing again in addressing his taunts. Instead, I held up a single piece of paper, the *poem*. I'd woken from my nap, from that dream, knowing where the gathering was to be, but it hadn't been until I'd seen the note on the pamphlet that I knew *exactly* where to go. I hadn't needed to know or understand all the words my birthmother had written, all I'd needed I had found in my heart, in my soul. I knew now that the *poem*—her words, were the invocation for the gathering and the plea for the balance. And before Armaros could spew more malice, I read the words aloud,

What have you done?
An obscurer of darkness as perceptions disappear.
Once we experienced heaven, free and innocent,
but your love vanished.
A vengeful vision of hatred - emotions follow darkness,
follow hate, love condemned.
In a storm of righteousness, I see you.
The night falls with a hushed sigh, entwined are we.
The restoration for which you pine flares once,
then dies, taken by your obsession.
All faith must fail. Your soul thrives no more.
How could you neglect to believe?
Angels surround us, weeping, we are fallen. Heaven Shunned.
Slender beams of moonlight enter this darkened place as I rise,
ever hopeful, ever alone, suspended here, waiting.
Angelic forms wrought in shadow loom as ash dances in the air,
forming an image in my mind, sparing not my secret soul.
Realization dawning on an angel's face.

Armaros's smile shifted then to an expression of doubt.

"I see you," I said. Then the Four Horsemen who had been hidden from my friends, now appeared for them next to Armaros, and I smiled again.

Armaros lifted his arms up and out to the sides. "Smile *fool*—and witness all those who oppose you. Witness before you your executioners." Armaros cut a glance to The Horsemen on his right, and then to the two leaders on his left.

"I see you… I see you all!" I shouted then, raising and extending my arms out to the sides.

The Four Horsemen together took one giant step towards me.

"You are powerless against us—descendant or not," Armaros spewed. The two leaders who had been at his side stepped up to flank The Horsemen. Armaros gave me a malicious smile now as if victorious. Then, like a wall of destruction, the six gigantic beings stepped forward as one.

But instead of attacking, they continued forward, passing where I stood to stand behind me. To stand *with* me.

Shock and further disbelief spread across Armaros's beautiful wicked face. He stood alone now.

It was then I sensed the remaining leaders appear behind me, spreading out to flank the other six. Last to appear was Shamsiel, who came and stood at my side, making up the last of the leaders… well, except for one, Armaros of course.

As if comprehending, Armaros stole a glance back behind himself. Even the seven angels and their trumpets were gone now. He was alone, one lone fallen leader.

"I got this," I said, addressing the leaders, then I completed the invocation,

> *I raise my head, now thundering against this callous darkness.*
> *All around, the angels gather.*
> *My dread grows as the Dark One's approach falls against my eyes.*
> *It wounds me, and ominously my essence seeps into the fractured ground.*
> *In a strange and terrible pleasure, I call your name while Death's horsemen hover close.*
> *Now on your own, my soul falls upon the blind eyes of the wishing tree.*
> *This is my salvation.*

The dark of early morning began to morph into that of twilight and a calmness moved over everyone, its tranquility almost hypnotic. My finishing the invocation had brought forth the remaining angels, the Archangels, such that they could be seen by all, and they appeared several paces back behind Armaros, alongside Uriel.

Next to Uriel, stood Monica.

Adjacent to them, stood, who I assumed was Michael, as he was with Jeannette.

These women were the last who remained of the mothers. How the two had gotten here I wasn't exactly sure, but like everything else that had happened—was happening, it was all part of this divine mystery, and I was way over questioning any of it now.

Then, as it often does in the presence of angels, time sped changing the charcoal shades of night from a grey washed out colour to that of a vivid new day. My birthmother had written something akin to this understanding on that second page of her letter.

"Happy New Year," I said to all, welcoming in the new day and new year.

In the space that remained between Armaros and my friends, I could see countless forms taking shape across the expansive garden space.

Uriel's long strait auburn hair billowed around him like shiny ribbons as two additional women appeared next to Monica. The first woman, whose likeness I had only ever seen in photographs, was Mac's grandmother, and based on the description from the codex, I knew the second was Uriel's Chosen, *Ashu*.

Mac moved then from standing with my friends, over to stand with Uriel and the other three women. Behind them now the figures of many women began to take shape like the images of a large group photograph.

A few yards away from this collection, stood Michael. His waist-length curly hair too billowed in the early morning breeze. Jeanette's face beamed happier than I'd ever seen her, and she had *both* of her arms up waving to me. The woman adjacent I presumed was *her* mother. Like the images of Mac's grandmother, I'd only ever seen photos of Vicki's, but the theme here was becoming clear. Next to her stood Michael's Chosen, *Pau*.

Vicky then left the group of friends to go stand with Michael and these women. More women appeared behind them in a similar fashion to those of Mac's.

Right of Michael's assembly, stood Raphael. Unlike the others, his hair was short, a fiery red brush-cut in fact, and the only reason I knew it was Raphael, was because of who stood with him, Olivia's mother and Nann. Next to them was Raphael's Chosen, *Ena*.

Olivia too moved then to be next to her mother, creating a new foursome. More women appeared behind them.

Last, and to the far right was Vretil. His wavy caramel coloured hair was neither long nor short, reaching just past his collar. I recognized Alison's mom Claudette, right away. At her side stood her mother. It was the original storyteller, Vretil's Charge, *Nin* who stood next to them. And like the other, Alison followed suit and went to stand with them.

I understood now it was their ancestors who appeared behind each grouping, all the women who had come before them.

Armaros watched as the other leaders fanned out to stand with their brethren, filling in the spaces between each grouping. Then the images of the descendants of these leaders, also appeared.

Dunya and Mitra I noticed had arrived sometime during the commotion, but now they walked forward towards me. Shamsiel, who had remained at my side, moved forward then to meet them. All three of them went now to stand to the right of the last grouping. Then another woman, of similar stature to Dunya's appeared next to Mitra.

I could only assume she was Shamsiel's Chosen, the first *Mitra* in a long line of seers, but it made only *three* women in this grouping. Following the pattern I'd observed, I stepped forward to take my spot with the *Oracles*. All hands, including those of Shamsiel lifted in protest, and I stopped.

Shamsiel shook his head *no*.

Then, from the now all-male group of my remaining friends, came Darius to stand with these women, making up the four. Their ancestors, both male and female appeared behind them, all who possessed the gift of insight.

Luc, Derek and Redmond came forward then to stand to the right of Shamsiel and his assembly.

"Ah yes," I said, recognizing that this was my quartet. It seemed to make, that Luc, Derek, Redmond and myself could be a group of four, and I stepped forward again.

In my way appeared two titans, one with shoulder-length jet-black hair, the other with short waves of deep russet. *Baraqel* and *Azazel,* two of the Four Horsemen. Turning away, they headed over to stand with the others, Baraqel with *Luc,* and Azazel with *Redmond,* leaving only Derek standing alone now.

I moved forward to cross the distance towards Derek, but then a giant with the long white hair appeared next to him. *Kokabiel,* another of The Horsemen. Part of me had anticipated it.

"Star of God, eh?" I said, to Derek, letting out a nervous laugh, recalling the meaning of Kokabiel's name, and acknowledging the three of them as descendants of these horsemen.

"Don't even start," Derek said. "Don't even say it." He laughed then because he knew how much he looked like the guy. I used to tease him about looking like a hippy version of God's famous son, but now we all knew who he actually resembled, *Conquest.*

The last of The Horsemen to move was *Zaqiel.* Then on cue, appearing next to him, stood a woman whose resemblance was so much like my own, *Heather,* my birthmother. Second to her was the joyful smiling face of my dear friend, Louise. Following in unison arriving next to them, in all their health and glory, appeared the figures of both my Aunt Kay… and my Mother.

Although there were already four standing with this Horseman, I figure this had to be my place, and again stepped forward.

But like that of Shamsiel's group, they all held their hands up to halt me. The four women then lowered their hands, shifting to hold the hands of the woman on either side next to them. Their descendants, like all the rest, appeared in the open space behind them.

"Am I not a descendant too?" I question Zaqiel. "My birthmother stands with you—that makes me a descendant as well."

"All this... and still—she does not know who she is—what she is?" Armaros said in challenge, despite his earlier threats being ignored.

I'd almost forgotten about him, but now all eyes were back on him again.

"How could she?" Zaqiel said, responding to his challenge.

"Then why...," Armaros asked, "why did she risk her life, against so much unknown—unseen? Why would she do such a thing?" Armaros stepped up within reach then to face me, but this time without menace.

I stared back at him, searching his face for answers. I'd pondered he might have the answers, that he might know something I didn't. That maybe he knew who I was—who my father was. Of late, he had seemed to be everywhere I was, *and* he'd wanted that letter of my birthmother's so badly.

"For those she loves, Armaros. For those... she loves," Gabriel said, appearing several paces behind the broken Angel. "You have forgotten... *He* loves us all—even you, my lost brother."

Armaros said nothing, only bowed his head. He took in a deep breath, then on the exhale, he whispered, "Forgive me."

I reached out for him, but he disappeared, leaving the new arrival to stand alone.

"Gabriel," I said, in acknowledgement. I had known it, known who and what he was before all this, but I hadn't truly let myself believe it.

He took a step forward. "Yes, Lynn?" His face was calm and beautiful.

"Uhm...." I swallowed hard. I'd kept it together pretty good I thought, but now my head was spinning. All this, and I still had questions where there seemed to be no answers. "... I see there are already four." I pointed to where my Aunt and Mother stood. "But isn't it my turn to stand with *my...*," the word *mother* held to my tongue as I took another look at my mom, and then my birthmother. "... and those who have come before?" My words felt too formal, but how else was I supposed to address an Archangel. I could feel the strength and love emanating from him, from all of them. When he didn't answer, I gazed around at all the faces smiling and glowing in triumph. Even

Redmond, the newest person to all this, had his place. I wanted so much to be happy for all of them, but how could it be that I was once again… *on my own.*

Gabriel shook his head, but still he said nothing.

"So, I stand alone?" I questioned, gazing back at him.

He shook his head again, but then he smiled. "You are the first," he said, taking another step closer. "But you are not alone."

I glanced around at my friends for clarity, only to see those in each line, the descendants of those who had passed, begin to fade away. Zaqiel too began to fade, yet I could still see my mother. She was waving. Something resembling pride mixed with love shown in her expression. "Always with you," I heard her say, as her image faded into the morning light.

I could feel her love, it remained, but why was I alone, *again.*

Collectively, Uriel, Mac, Monica, Raphael, Olivia, Michael, Vicki, Jeannette, Vretil, Alison, Shamsiel, Dunya, and Mitra, all moved closer to stand in an arch at my right. Then, Darius, my Guardian, Derek, my Cipher, Luc, my Theologian, and Redmond….

"Mowmin," Mitra said, in her sweet little voice.

"Believer," Dunya translated, beaming with joy like the others. That was one question answered. … my *Believer,* along with the remaining three horsemen, moved together to stand similarly, at my left.

Gabriel stepped forward again, smiling, this time to greet them all. "With all that has been revealed," he began, "and in the face of all that has been sacrificed, *He* has finally seen the truth. That those who have free will also have faith." He turned panning their faces. "It's not about faith in a deity—it is faith in humanity, in friends, family and in yourselves." His expression became serious then. "He does not promise there will be no more pain, suffering, disease, or death—only that it will never be as a result of anything divine." His smile returned. "Surrounding you, are the friends whom you love. Help each other live a life to the fullest—to excel above expectations. Help each other shine in those dark places which seem impossible to find love. Protect each other—always, lift each other up, when it is needed most. If you walk together, you will always be safe. Remember," he said, taking a moment to look at each of them, "A true friend is someone who knows everything about you... and still loves you." Gabriel turned back to look at me. "Derek," he said, but still looking at me.

I glanced at Derek.

"The letter—the anagrams, Lynn," Derek reminded. "Heart news."

I frowned and shook my head.

"The answer," Derek responded, solving the anagram for me.

I glanced around at my friends and understood, I was *not* alone. But then I recognized that Gabriel... was the lone one now. "Why do you stand alone?" I questioned him, wondering why no souls had appeared behind him.

He smiled again, and said, "I do not stand alone." He took one last step to close the distance between us. "You see... your friends—these decedents." He swept an arm out towards them in an arch. "They, are either a descendant of a Fallen, or that of an Archangel."

I'd known that, we all knew it now. He wasn't telling me anything I hadn't already grasped. My girlfriends were descendants of Archangels, the guys were obviously descendants of these Fallen. I opened my mouth to speak but stopped myself, unsure of what question to ask.

Gabriel continued. "None—not one of them... is *both.*" He took a deep breath. "None—but you... *guard the glean.*"

He paused as if I understood, but I didn't. It only added further to my confusion. "Me?" I questioned, then I looked back over at Derek. *"Faiths fever?"* I directed to my Cipher. We'd never solved the rest of the letter. Well, I hadn't.

"Five fathers," Derek responded, smiling as if loving the riddle game. Then he said, *"Guard the fifth."*

"Guard the fifth?" I shook my head. That hadn't been in the letter, but I remembered that phrase. It was from the second Enochian entry in the codex. "Guard the fifth—what?" I asked, "Father?" I shook my head again. The words *five fathers* repeated in my head, but I was more than confused, I was frustrated now.

"Guard the glean?" I said, giving Derek the last of the anagrams.

"It's not *guard the angel,*" he said, playfully, though I thought we'd already solved that part the other day.

"You are the first…," Gabriel said, cutting into the word play.

"The first what?" I interrupted. "First to guard the angel—the fifth angel?" I asked, mashing up the anagrams.

"*Glean,*" Vicki said, with a nod, prompting me for the translation.

"Angel," I answered. *Duh.*

"*The guard,*" Vicki continued, with a pleased smile.

"Daughter," I answered again, shaking my head at the obvious. "Guard the daughter?" With a gasp, the true answer escaped me on a breath, "*Angel daughter.*"

"You are the first…," Gabriel repeated. "… ever. The first ever of your kind… my first… my daughter."

Epilog 

"I believe in love. I believe in hard times and love winning. I believe marriage is hard. I believe people make mistakes. I believe people can want two things at once. I believe people are selfish and generous at the same time. I believe very few people want to hurt others. I believe that you can be surprised by life. I believe in happy endings."
~ Isabel Gillies, Happens Every Day: An All-Too-True Story

I believe in love, family, and friendship....

Luc and Dunya moved in together. Who didn't see that one coming from a mile away?

Darius, along with Luc, were hired by Derek to do IT support for his company. Both work from home now, just like Derek.

Derek, as we all know, had the answers to the anagrams. He'd figured the rest of them out on the plane ride to Miami, figured out the whole thing, actually. *This gathering will keep the balance, and all shall know the...* bar the fifth = *Birthfather*. Faiths Fever = *Five fathers*, Heart News = *The answer*, and Guard the Glean = *Angel daughter*.

Vicki, she's now travelling the world for work. She'd met a nice guy on one of her trips who owns a private jet company, and I'm sure there will be a lot more travel in her future.

Mac stopped doing her jewelry business to focus on a new business with Olivia. They've opened a doula/holistic health business, where both can spend more time doing what they love, and while having more time with their families.

Alison and Ken had their bouncing baby boy, Kevin, on April 1st. He was originally due to arrive on the 7th, but Alison had had to go in early for an emergency C-section. *"Best April fool's joke ever,"* she'd told me. It was the *denouement* as Alison had put it. That's French, it means they'd all reached *The End...* and they had happily survived.

And Me? Well, I moved on.... but I still believe in coming together at Christmas.

Miami, December 20th, sometime in the near future.

"What, Gabriel? I know you're here," I said, shaking my head.

Redmond was in the yard fetching more wood to place beside the hearth, but I knew I wasn't alone. I snuggled in deeper with my two best buds on the couch, Summer and Snow, the all-white Lab-Shepherd mixes, who each outweighed me now by at least 20 pounds. We'd rescued them from a local shelter last year as pups.

"Do you really think you can sneak in a visit without me knowing?" I laughed out, continuing to warm myself in front of the fireplace. I'd missed cozy nights like these—been forever since it'd been cold enough to use the fireplace and rare to have times like this in Miami.

"Lynn, you can't blame me for trying?" came Gabriel's voice just as he appeared before me. "Aren't you going to tell them what happened to you?"

"Tell who?" I said, moving my hands out towards the fire's warmth. There was something about warming yourself by the fire and sipping hot chocolate that made for a peaceful evening. "I'm excited the others would be here in time for Christmas day," I said. I knew the others were thrilled for what they'd referred to as '*warmer weather*'. But tonight, was just for Redmond and me... and Gabriel, apparently.

"Your believers—the ones who know the story now," Gabriel said.

I smirked and sipped my cocoa.

"This *is* nice," he said, settling into the big oversized armchair next to the fireplace. He extended his hands like I had as if warming them. *Then* he had those blue-grey eyes of his fixed on *my* big mug of cocoa.

"Get yer own." I grinned. "I like you and all, but I'm not sharing my hot chocolate—there's more in the kitchen."

He was gone and back, leaving only the sound of rattling cups in the kitchen upon his return. Comfortably back in the big chair, he happily coveted his own mug of goodness. He grinned back at me and took a sip.

"What would you have me tell them?" I asked, tucking my feet under a Christmas themed blanket, one that had once belonged to my mother.

Taking another loving sip of the hot brew, Gabriel eyeballed the small mound at my stomach, then grinned again. "Due in the spring I'm told," he said proud as a peacock—a *grandfather* peacock.

"Yup," was all I gave him. He'd known before I had, that I was pregnant. I'd had a *feeling*—but he knew. He hadn't said he'd known, only told me, *"You know, Babies smile in their sleep because they are listening to the whispering of angels."* I was sure I'd read that quote somewhere before, but I'd gotten the gist of *his* meaning.

"Twins," he said, his grin widening still. He'd obviously learned more about the birth from the Amulet Angels—checking in with all 70 of them I was sure. He could have simply asked me—his daughter.

"Uhmm yup," was my response. Redmond and I had found out about the duo ourselves only a few days ago.

"Twin girls," Gabriel added. He followed up with a big sip of cocoa, and a wink.

I winked back and grinned.

* * *

THE END... *maybe.*